OASIS JOURNAL

2015

Stories

Poems

Essays

by Writers Over Fifty

Edited by Leila Joiner

IMAGO PRESS

TUCSON ARIZONA

Published in the United States of America by:

Imago Press
3710 East Edison
Tucson AZ 85716

www.oasisjournal.org

Names, characters, places, and incidents, unless otherwise specifically noted, are either the product of the author's imagination or are used fictitiously.

Cover Design and Book Design by Leila Joiner

ISBN 978-1-935437-97-0
ISBN 1-935437-97-6

Printed in the United States of America on Acid-Free Paper

In loving memory of
John Barbee,
whose stories still grace our pages

ACKNOWLEDGMENTS

I want to thank all the writers over fifty who continue to contribute their work to *OASIS Journal* every year.

May we all have many successful years ahead of us.

LIST OF ILLUSTRATIONS

CONTENTS

EDITOR'S PREFACE

This fourteenth annual edition of *OASIS Journal* contains the work of 102 writers over fifty from the U.S., Canada, and Costa Rica.

Instead of contest winners this year, we have an Editor's Choice for each category. I'll do my best to explain my reasons for these choices. It goes without saying that they were all well written.

EDITOR'S CHOICE FOR FICTION:

"Switzerland" by Bill Alewyn

Bill so thoroughly captured the persona of a teenage boy (no small feat when you're over 50) that this piece totally captured me as a reader and audience. I'm sure the rest of you will be equally enthralled and quickly carried back to that devastating time in your life. Thank God we don't have to stay there!

EDITOR'S CHOICE FOR NONFICTION:

"Puzzles with Missing Pieces" by Kathleen Elliott Gilroy

This is a heartrending tale of what can happen when a person is exposed to unnecessary or extreme medical and psychological treatments. One can only hope that such measures are not as common nowadays as they used to be. My reaction to reading this was "There but for the grace of God," etc.

EDITOR'S CHOICE FOR POETRY:

"Avalanche" by Peter Bradley

As I told Peter, I simply fell in love with the last three lines of this poem. In fact, I still carry them around in my head. I'm sure many of my readers will be able to relate, as well.

I do hope you all enjoy reading this year's issue of *OASIS Journal*, and I look forward to continuing for at least one more year, if the fates allow. Thank you so much for your encouraging letters and emails.

L. J.

OASIS JOURNAL

2
0
1
5

Stories

Poems

Essays

Switzerland

Bill Alewyn

Joel opened the kitchen door in a burst of exhilaration commensurate with his thirteen years, two months, and six days. "Come in!" he shouted over his shoulder to his companion lagging somewhere behind. He tossed three textbooks on the counter beside the sink, where they would remain until his mother came home from shopping and forced him to take them to his room.

It was Friday afternoon, finally, and Joel was free again, finally – or at least temporarily. Never mind all the homework. Joel wished now that he had listened more closely to his adolescent priorities and left those books behind in his locker; some dwindling sense of academic obligation had gotten them this far. Of the assignments due on Monday, the chapter on the Spanish exploration of the Southwest stood less than a fifty percent chance of getting read. The science book with all the cool pictures was interesting in itself, if it weren't for all the math questions at the end of each chapter. English, however, that deceptively slender and impenetrable code book on grammar and usage, did not stand a Popsicle's chance in Hell on this or any other weekend. Thankfully, Monday was still too far away to worry about something as painful as eighth grade English, let alone history and science.

Joel's classmate hung back near the entrance to the kitchen. Joel turned with a smile and ushered Linda deeper into the kitchen. Her right arm cradled yellow notebooks.

"Here it is: cellblock sixteen." Joel combed the cowlick from his forehead with his busy fingers. Linda took three measured steps into the kitchen.

She sat in front of Joel in two classes. He could hardly keep his eyes off her silky black hair. Linda wore her hair long across her back with a part down the middle, just like Katherine Ross. Linda's eyes were milk chocolate brown, exactly the color of a Snickers candy bar. They were big and fawn-like, just like Katherine Ross's eyes. Last summer, Joel had seen the dark-haired, doe-eyed actress in a movie where she played John Wayne's daughter, so for three months now he'd had a secret crush on all things Katherine Ross and, by extension, a growing crush on his intriguing new friend, Linda.

"Your parents aren't home?" Linda asked with just a twinge of expectation in her voice. She wore a blue flower-print dress and bright vinyl Go-Go boots that were suddenly very popular.

"My mom's shopping. She always goes shopping on Fridays. Do you want a cookie?" Without waiting for a reply, Joel opened the lid to a large cookie jar shaped like a glossy brown cow. The ceramic cow had an enormous udder, and she was standing on one of her own teats. One of the teats was missing and another had been reattached to her enormous udder with a generous amount of carpenter's glue that now suggested the cow might be leaking.

Linda's big brown eyes took in the cookie cow along with the rest of the kitchen. "So what did you want to show me?" she asked, her schoolbooks pressed tightly to her budding breasts.

Joel handed her an oatmeal-raisin cookie and kept a couple for himself. He stuffed the first one into his mouth. "Wait here," he said through a mouthful of cookie. "It's in my room. Girls aren't allowed, not unless they're invited. Those are the rules."

"What rules?"

"The rules my parents decided on when I turned thirteen."

"I've been thirteen for almost *nine* months." Linda averted her eyes from the ceramic cow. "Nine months is a long time."

Joel noticed that Linda no longer kept her books in front of her chest. She now held them with one hand in front of her blue flower-print dress.

"What's that supposed to mean?" he asked.

"Nothing," she said, nibbling her cookie. "It just means we've got some of the same classes even though I'm older than you by nine months."

"What difference does that make?" Joel asked, feeling vaguely thwarted; he was glad now that he had a legitimate excuse to leave the kitchen.

In Joel's absence Linda nibbled on her cookie and wandered over to three vinyl-covered stools behind the breakfast counter. One of the red stools had a strip of silver duct tape across the seat where the others didn't.

Joel returned to the kitchen with a large framed movie poster in his hands.

Linda picked at her cookie. "What's that?" she asked, politely covering her mouth when she spoke.

Joel turned the poster around and proudly pointed to the big black and white picture of Steve McQueen in a World War II German uniform astride a BMW. "Whatta you think? Neat, huh?"

"I guess," she said. "So how come you didn't want me to see your room? Is it messy?"

"Very funny," he said, holding the poster in front of him. "I bet my room's not as messy as yours."

"You'll never know about that," she said, teasing him.

"What's *that* supposed to mean?"

"It means a girl isn't supposed to invite a boy into her room, *unescorted.*"

"Lisa Thomas showed me her room," he said with a new challenge in his voice. "*Unescorted.*"

"Lisa Thomas has a reputation for showing boys her room. *Unescorted.*"

The electric awkwardness between them was back and bigger than ever.

"Well," Joel said, blushing, and hoping to change the subject. "What do you think of it?"

Linda gave a tentative nod to the movie star in the poster. "Who is it? He's cute."

"That's Steve McQueen," Joel said. "It's from *The Great Escape*, which is just about my favorite all-time movie ever made."

"I never saw it," she said with dismissive hauteur. "My mother and I prefer Cary Grant."

"Not Cary Grant!" Joel was something of an expert when it came to movies, even the ones with Cary Grant. "*Gunga Din* was cool and *Father Goose* was okay, I guess."

Linda seemed to have her own opinions when it came to the movies, and she wasn't shy about expressing them. Relaxing a bit, she set her books down on the counter beside her. "Anyway, did you ever see Cary Grant with Doris Day in *A Touch of Mink*?"

"Doris Day!" the thirteen-year old movie critic gagged. "Don't make me puke. *Touch of Crap!*"

"That's because I bet you've never touched mink before in your whole life. If you had, then you'd understand what the movie's really all about."

"I've touched mink," he said, floundering. "Lots of times."

Bolder now, Linda asked, "Where? In Lisa Thomas's bedroom?"

"My mother's sister, Aunt Thelma, owns a mink coat."

"Mink isn't all that important anyway," Linda said. She suddenly seemed to remember herself and sat up straight. Then, after a minute, she relaxed again and turned her eyes back toward the poster. "So what's *The Great Escape* and what makes it so great?" She patted the vinyl stool beside her, the one with the duct tape patch. "I won't bite."

Joel preferred to hold the poster and stand. "There's this big German prison camp in World War II, see, and Steve McQueen and that actor from *Maverick* play American pilots who get shot down over Germany. They're the good guys, see, and all they want to do is get back to England so they can drop more bombs on the Germans and end the war. And Charles Bronson plays the Tunnel King, only he's afraid of tunnels, see, and that's what you would call a sub-plot."

"A tunnel king who's afraid of tunnels? I don't get it." Linda patted the stool again, harder this time, and Joel set the poster against the wall and finally sat down next to her. "Go on."

"And they all want to get to Switzerland."

"Why? What's so special about Switzerland?"

Joel realized how big and near Linda's milk chocolate brown eyes were, and the fact that she no longer held her books in her lap or in front of her probably meant something. "Well," he said, "there are these big mountains in Switzerland and pine forests where they could hide, and the Nazis aren't allowed to go there because those are the rules of the Geneva Convention, and the Swiss are peaceful and mostly neutral."

"The Swiss sound like hippies to me," she said. "Tell me more about Switzerland."

"So, yeah, anyway, Switzerland's a country somewhere in the middle of Europe, but it's also, you know, something bigger, I guess."

"What do you mean – bigger?" she asked. "You mean like a symbol, or like something that's supposed to stand for something else, like in what Mr. Adams told us in American Lit about *Moby Dick*?" Linda giggled when she spoke the words aloud.

"What kind of symbol?" Joel asked. "I mean sometimes mountains and forests and shit are just, well, you know, mountains and forests and shit, right? What I mean is they don't always have to be symbols for something else, right? What I mean is Switzerland isn't *Moby Dick* and Steve McQueen isn't Cary Grant."

Linda's sudden laughter made Joel blush when he got to the words *Moby Dick*, and now he felt an unexpected pressure inside. "What I mean is – sometimes – can't a country just be a country? I mean, come on, what kind of symbol is that?"

Linda looked at Joel with her big brown Snickers eyes until that inner pressure became too great.

"Okay, maybe for all those guys locked up in a German prison camp, maybe Switzerland becomes a symbol for freedom, maybe?" Joel couldn't help notice how straight Linda kept her back and how distracting her legs below her dress could be pressed together like that, not an inch apart. He figured she must have practiced her posture quite a bit in front of a mirror just to keep her legs and back as straight as she did and still look comfortable. "Do you want another cookie?"

"Tell me more about Switzerland," she said.

"I don't know," he said. "It's just a movie and Switzerland's just a place they want to get to but they've never been. It's kinda sad, really."

Linda reached for his hand. "So does anyone ever really, like, get to Switzerland? Or do they just talk about it a lot?"

"That's the sad part about the movie," Joel said. He held Linda's hand in his now, and he could feel the heat of her thigh beneath her cool summer dress. "Most of them get killed or captured after they escape. One guy goes to Spain, which is almost as good as Switzerland. And Steve McQueen gets real close – I mean he makes it all the way to the border on this stolen German motorcycle where he makes a bitchin-ass leap on his bike, but the Krauts shoot up his bike with machine guns, and he ends up in a bunch of barbed wire instead."

"That's too bad," Linda said. "About Switzerland, I mean. I mean, if he really wanted to get to Switzerland's mountains so bad, he should've tried harder, don't you think?" Without warning, Linda released his hand. It felt strange to see his open palm resting on her thigh, but he kept it there anyway, waiting for Linda to brush it aside, but she kept right on talking like it didn't matter about his stupid looking hand. "Or, I dunno, I mean I didn't see the movie or anything, but if I were Steve McQueen, I'd find a way to get to Switzerland where there wasn't any barbed wire."

Linda's words gave Joel a new confidence as he reached for her hand. "Yeah, well, that's sorta the feeling you get at the end of the movie when Steve McQueen goes back to the prison camp. I mean, you know Steve's all bummed out about being a P.O.W. again, but you also know he's going to keep on trying and trying and trying until he finally gets to Switzerland…or wherever he's trying to get."

He was holding both her hands now, one on the top of each knee as they faced each other intently. Their faces were very close together. He could smell the raisins from her cookie and, behind that, the tart citrus smell from the tangerine they had surreptitiously shared on the bus. Together, with an agonizing but exquisite slowness, they leaned into each other's parted lips as though they both wanted to whisper the same hesitant and well-kept secret. Joel closed his eyes and opened his mouth and saw in his mind that bitchin-ass motorcycle leap all over again.

The kiss itself was awkward and confusing. Imperfect but promising. A stomach-tingling and all too fleeting first kiss filled with the bittersweet aftertaste of tangerines and oatmeal-raisin cookies, and all the coming attractions of a frightening yet irresistible world to come.

"I better go," Linda said, brushing away imaginary wrinkles and crumbs from her dress. She reached for the books beside her and, in a moment, she held them tight against her blouse, shielding her heart. "I like your movie poster," she said, "but I still prefer Cary Grant."

Joel stood up, awkwardly and against his better wishes. "Yeah, well, I guess you got a bunch of homework this weekend. So I guess I'll see you back in the cooler on Monday, huh?"

Joel thought maybe he should say or do something – take her books and walk her home – something! But the more he thought about it the more he realized escorting Linda home would be a little too expected, an obligation he needed to avoid. For now, it would be enough just to kiss her one more time before his heart stopped beating.

So he walked her to the door and kissed her goodbye, cool and unhurried, like Steve McQueen biding his time on his way to Switzerland. *Yeah, that's it: Switzerland. It will take some time, but I'll get there yet.*

A SPECIAL EDUCATION 1951

Marie T. Gass

We were already into giggling,
Holding hands in the cloakroom,
Leaning against the cute boys
During *Birth of a Nation.*

Sr. Marguerite judged it time
To bring in the priest—
For what, we did not know.
He took the boys out first.

How dare they ignore us girls!
We who worked more, tried harder.
Eyes flashed across the room and back.
Sister sat at her desk, hands folded.

Then the priest walked back in alone
Without the boys who had been
Rewarded with an early recess.
He strode to the front,

Cleared his throat and briefly
Looked us over, said solemnly:
It's always the girl's fault—
Remember that. Then he left.

No talking, said the nun.
You may not discuss this.
A few girls pursed their lips and nodded.
None of us guessed what it meant.

Was this another of those miscellaneous things
That always got blamed on girls?
The only thing we were certain of in those days
Was that priests were always right.

ONCE

Judith O'Neill

In a brilliant Kansas meadow,
his blue-green eyes the exact color
of the sparkling creek,
Terry Bilyeu catches my hand,
pulls me close against his chest,
and kisses me.

I am nineteen.
So is he.

The sun scorches
the top of my head.
My heart leaps and thuds,
and pounds like crazy.
His does, too.

Sunday school buddies
since twelve,
we have watched each other
grow up.

After the meadow
he kisses me all the time.
There are dreams and plans,
laughter, fun,
a ring,
in the two summers
and two winters we have
before his life
ends.

A mid-air collision
above a Navy Air training field,
doing what he loves
next best (he always said) to me.

Sixty summers later,
sixty winters lived,
other loves, other joys,
other losses,
an old heart still warms,
remembering once,
in a brilliant Kansas meadow,
his blue-green eyes the exact color
of the sparkling creek,
Terry Bilyeu catches my hand,
pulls me close against his chest,
and kisses me.

OUT OF THE PAST

Bobbie Jean Bishop

I weed in the shadow
of roaming clouds,
         outdoors at last
after years with no yard.
Memories inch uninvited
         like renegade rain
between stone crevices,
little dandelion prayers
         popping up
in a graveled side lot;
         you slip into my mind
as I turn the spigot on,
hose twining around us,
         its spray, a wet drift of love
between the dead and the living.
I recall you kneeling
         beside a flat of pansies
soon to be planted
in your mulched plot,
         that connection between us—
you digging in dirt
         with its mess and heat
as I dig now, down on my knees,
fistful of ferns in a gloved hand,
my breath like a bird
         fluttering all afternoon:
you fluttering with me.

Girl with Carnations

Ruth Moon Kempher

Philadelphia, Pennsylvania
January 11, 1957
7:24 p.m.

Torgus came out of the grime and blackness of the movie without waiting for the story to end. It had centered on a bunch of creepy guys sneaking around dark alleys, with a lot of blood. He'd figured it would be more entertaining than the lusty group-gropes advertised at the other places he'd passed, up and down Market Street. But it hadn't done the trick. A show is just a show.

Cutting across the musty lobby, where smells of popcorn and rancid butter hung in the air, Torgus tried to stuff the flap collar of his blues into his pea coat, hunching his shoulders to try to make it lie flat. The collar bunched at the edge of his shoulder blade no matter how he shrugged and hitched. "Hell," said Torgus peevishly and somehow, in his mind, Hell and Philly were all mixed up.

Pushing on outside, he flinched as bitter air, damp and cold, crossed his face. He stepped sideways to light a match for his last cigarette. A dusky, full-bosomed Italian woman, her dress half torn away, gazed down at him with passion flaring in her eyes. *Thrills Unlimited!* the poster had promised. *Adults Only! Sin! Sin! Sin! Coming next week!*

"Next week," Torgus said with a crooked smile. "Story of my life, next week."

Moving on, he flipped the spent match into the gutter and watched it float aimlessly until it hit against a crumpled candy wrapper, where it stuck, gathering a small oil slick of scum from the water. For the two-dozenth time that day, Torgus wished he could remember Pencil's last name.

A couple of summers back, when the *Sardis* was home from the Med, they'd pulled into Philly at about the same time Pencil's sister had married some guy from the suburbs, a guy who worked at an auto parts store.

The guy she married was called Dominick, and he said he could get you a carburetor for thirty per cent off. If you needed one. But that was all Torgus remembered. Except he wished he'd listened more.

When he'd first checked in at the Base a couple of weeks ago, Torgus had looked through the phone book to find Catholic churches in South Philly. There were six or eight of them that sounded like they might be the place where that wedding had been. He remembered the family. Pencil's fat mother had a little mustache and cooked all day. How they yelled at each other over every little thing. The niece was a junior in high school, dreamed of being a cheerleader, but got so flustered she forgot to give out the little bags of rice. That was in South Philly, too, a nice family kind of place. She would be more grown up by now.

But Pencil had gone from the *Sardis* to some DE, and here was Torgus in Philly, alone. City of Brotherly Love, he thought. You get lonesome enough, any kind of love will do.

Looking up Market Street in the night was like looking up some huge quarry pit lined with slab sheets of glittery rock. Down the street, not far, he saw the City Hall – a clumsy dark hulk of some monument fallen from the stars. People passed him by with empty eyes. Slash red lips on a woman. Kids with woolly ski caps balanced on their heads. A gaunt black woman strolling tight-wrapped in a long leopard coat, a jungle creature, transported. Tip-tapping red boots peeped out from the spotted hem as she walked. Cars driving by made a droning noise. Or was that all the people? All the feet?

Me, Torgus decided. Me, I need a drink.

Somewhere around City Hall, he knew, there was a good bar he'd been in with Pencil. It was a place with a pink neon fish in the front window, or maybe a lobster – he wasn't sure. But it had booths and food and a guy who played soft jazz on the piano. Air-conditioned then, not that it would matter now. Pencil would know. Or his niece would by now, probably, too. Torgus shrugged and looked up at faintly glimmering stars patched above the tops of tall-rising buildings.

"Proceed," he mumbled to himself. "North by…south. By something." The stars looked down impassively. "Or maybe east by west."

You could walk through that City Hall, he remembered. If you were careful to keep out from under the pigeons. Do pigeons sleep at night, maybe? And there was a kind of a park in the middle, where they parked the

Shore Patrol paddy wagon under the archways. If he walked on through, he might accidentally come out by the neon fish. Or lobster. Whatever.

Torgus walked on toward City Hall and its arches, but then slowed down, aware that his cigarette had died. His last, and only one match left in the matchbook. When he stopped to relight the cigarette, the last match flared high and flickered out. Walking onward, he silently searched the pockets of his pea coat. Found a ball of lint. Some flakes of tobacco. He sighed. "Story of my life."

Just inside the high arch leading into City Hall Park, a flower vendor had set up his stall. Rows of pastel blooms in bunches waved from rusty buckets – stalks of white gladioli in stiff splendor, blowsy yellow chrysanthemums, pink and white carnations in rusted cans. Torgus didn't know the names of half of them, but he sensed their loveliness, their freshness, their almost magical aura of spring and hope.

The vendor, standing beside his flowers, looked used-up and ugly, as out of place as if he'd been propped by mistake in front of a board with glowing, soft white gardenias pinned haphazardly to black velvet. A bit of death to advertise, by contrast, the fresh glow of youth and life.

"Buy a boo-kay," yelled the vendor in his hoarse voice. "Boo-kay for a lady."

Torgus stopped and asked if he had a match. The vendor gave him a battered book, half full, to keep. The matchbook cover advertised how to make your fortune selling orthopedic shoes.

"Hey, Swabby," said the vendor. "I give you a light. Now you buy a boo-kay for your girl."

Torgus cackled. "Sure." He relit the cigarette and saw that his fingers were grey and wrinkled. Cupped around the match, warmed by its flame, they turned Satanic red. "You find me a girl, I'll buy the whole damn place." He grinned.

The vendor was not amused. He was a wizened little man, lost in the folds of a dirty flannel jacket that had once been plaid. Now, with age and grime, it seemed more like overlapping squares of differing shades of smudge. The man's hands were raw and scratched, and his nose was running. He snuffled loudly to put Torgus in his place, and then bent to call out to a man with a briefcase who was hurrying by. "Boo-kay for your wife," he yelled. "Make the little lady happy!"

The man and his briefcase disappeared into the night. "Criminighties," said the vendor. "What a lousy night."

A girl came up to them, stepping quietly away from the crowd, out of shadows and movement, at first so intent on something that she didn't see the vendor or his flowers or Torgus standing there. But Torgus saw her, just fine. Her face was sharp-boned, and her light hair under the dark wool scarf had come loose in wisps around her face. Her eyes were even bluer than the blue of her scarf – the blue-grey of sky at dusk, with dark purple tones.

"Buy some pree-tee flowers," the vendor wheezed at her, insistent.

She seemed to see him and the flowers and Torgus all at once, and to be amazed. "How pretty they are," she said. Her voice had an effect on Torgus like a bucketful of warm beer. "I'd almost forgotten flowers, in all this cold."

The vendor wiped his nose with the back of his hand. "They come all the way from Flori-dee, special for you. Glads, you see. And mums. Carnations…"

Torgus liked the way her eyes warmed, the way they seemed greedy to take in the rows of bright flowers. She smiled, and the frigid night turned tropical. "Oh," she whispered. "They do smell so good, like spring, and all good things to come." Her smile was impish. "Of course, my mother would say they remind her of funerals. Or food."

In Torgus's mind, spring had arrived, sunlight and blossoms drifting down from the stars. Daisies, in his mind. He knew daisies, and yellow roses…

"Fiddy cents a bunch," the vendor piped. "Buy a boo-kay," he whined. "Boo-kay for the lady, tree for a buck anna quadder."

Something clicked in Torgus's mind. *Buy a boo-kay for a lady* was followed close on by Aunt Eunice's voice, Christmas leave just past, spiteful, to Cousin Betsy: "Ladies don't talk to sailors, Betsy." And how embarrassed Aunt Eunice had been when she realized what she'd said, fumbling to make it better. "That is, unless they're family. Present company excepted, dear."

"My room is terribly small," the girl's said, her voice sad. "But then again, these bunches are small."

Buy a boo-kay echoed. Torgus pulled hard on the last of his cigarette. "But Real Sailors, Betsy. Ladies don't talk to Real Sailors, not nice girls…" He looked up and watched the faint stars spin.

"I'll buy some." The girl laughed. "I know I shouldn't. My mother fusses about every extra penny." She placed her gloved finger at the side of her nose, perplexed. "But they're all so beautiful." She sighed. "I can't bear to leave them out here in the cold."

Far, far away, a tiny star – that was the Earth, and he was showing it to her. They were so far from here and from everybody else, somewhere near Alpha Centauri. *Wear them*, Torgus suggested, in his dream. *Lay them against your warm neck, near the hollows where the bones meet. Did you ever imagine it could be so warm, out here in the stars? But here, with this daffy-dilly, Lady, I thee…*The stars shook and exploded and fell in streamers like white fireworks, cascading splinters of light. Aunt Eunice had breasts as big as pillows, so big they bulged around the edge of the table, when she leaned forward to eat. The stars splintered and crackled. Bits of them froze to the sky.

"The carnations," the girl decided. "The pink. They smell so spicy clean. Besides, the bunches look a little bigger. There's more to a bunch."

What was left of the cigarette fell, and Torgus stepped on it, grinding it methodically with his toe. Shiny black general issue shoe. Spit shine. All dressed up and no place to go.

The girl took her flowers and paid for them with a crumpled dollar from her purse. Turning to leave, she pushed the soft, pale petals, pink with red fringe, up against her face. She saw Torgus watching her, and smiled, blushing. Then, with a dancer's turn, she moved quickly away.

People moved between them. Torgus stepped forward, hesitant, and collided with a wiry old woman and her shopping bag. "Hey," he called out, calling to the girl with the carnations. "Hey."

"Hey yourself, stupid," snapped the shopping bag woman. "Watch yer step there. Watch you dassn't bust them eggs."

At the corner, the traffic light signal flipped magically to WALK, and the girl moved away faster, hurrying to catch the light. She crossed the street, going up Market, holding the flowers high near her face. Then a bus slid past, blotting her out with its blank, reflective windows, its ads for beer and the Philadelphia Symphony.

Torgus turned away. A blank-eyed dummy in a shop window pointed invitingly at a soft-looking, purple-quilted king-sized bed. He considered the dummy and the bed, and made a small joke. "Sure, doll. Anytime." He could see the shadow of his own face reflected in the window glass. A twisted smile, bitter, like the night. "Story of my life," he said, proceeding on.

January 11, 1957
8:23 p.m.

When the girl reached home, her mother was waiting. A strong smell of cabbage drifted in from the kitchen, along with something faintly like bacon or onions or both.

"You're late," said her mother, stepping out of the kitchen, wiping her hands on her daisy-print apron. "I wished you'd called to say."

The girl shrugged and laid the carnations on the hall table, then turned to hang up her coat on a hook.

Her mother frowned at the flowers. "You spent for those?" She shook her head. "Old Mrs. Monahan had those," she said, more gently. "A whole blanket of them from her kids, pink like those, and white. I didn't much like they way they drooped. But the eats were nice. Those cucumber things, though, the gas they do…"

The girl smiled, as if some secret had pleased her. "What's for dinner?"

The mother turned childlike, smirking. "One of your favorites. Wait and see. Who did you meet today?"

The girl looked surprised. "Who did I meet? Me? No one." She picked up her flowers and again buried her face in their fragrance. "Why?"

"It was in the morning paper," her mother said. "Moon Child. Be alert in p.m. hours. You could meet someone who will change your life in the nicest ways."

Winter in Southern California

Margaret S. McKerrow

Really, it's all about the garden, now in recovery
mode after stress from the hot summer Sun.
I'm re-planting where needed, using drought
tolerants. I give in, I bow to the searing heat
that robbed me of delicate blossoms. No longer
my refreshing English garden, I must embrace our
tried and true desert gems.

I worship the rain after months of drought even
though raindrops bring weeds! My spirit rekindles
as I see the trees draped with twinkling tears. The Sun,
gentle now, sets each sphere on fire as I stay dry inside.
I love misty mornings and conjured dreams, memories
of childhood winters: pea-soupers, Wellington boots, soda
bread and stews, snuggling by the fire with a book.

The garden is full of sweet feathered visitors arriving
from much colder climes. They bring with them a jazz
of new voices and rainbows of colour to add to the
early morn song. A faithful old blue jay caws his
annoyance at having to share his domain, yet secretly
envies their cross country journey while he has no
chance to roam.

The mountains around us are capped with new snow,
giving us choices to stay or to go. Rare winter storms
bring us high tides too, their giant waves pounding the
rocks. Whitecaps ride and the seas toss weed like
confetti over the pier. Each bundled up for our
walk, we observe surfers like pods of sea creatures, black
shiny wetsuits huddled high and dry on the beach.

Sea gulls gather and swarm inland to wait for the storm
to pass. But we are in awe of nature's splendor and enjoy
being swept along. We watch rain heavy clouds pivot into
the ocean, changing the colours to grey, then relish Suns'
lingering last glorious moments as it slowly dips into the
West. We'll be back tomorrow, come rain or come shine;
we haven't yet seen the green flash!

THE SPITE HOUSE

Anita Curran Guenin

In a small New England town, where houses can usually breathe between themselves and keep their laconic Yankee distances, the red spite house crowds its bigger, white, more elegant uphill neighbor. With scarcely an arm's length between them, this creates an unusual pairing.

Legend has it that two brothers inherited land from their father. The elder son, who received the greater part of a legacy, built the fine white house overlooking the cove on a rise above Battle Street. The second son, resentful of his lesser inheritance, built his red house cottage very close to and in front of his brother's house, purposely and spitefully blocking his view.

The second son could have looked from his his parlor window and seen ships being built in the cove, readied for journeys to the West Indies. Hulls were stacked with sawdusted ice from the town's many ice ponds. Granite ballast from the quarry at the top of Battle Street provided stability and heft against storms. After the boats arrived at their destinations and the holds were emptied of precious ice, they were filled with human cargo for the return voyage. Townsmen became rich from trade, invention, and slavery. Their English-sounding names are seen on large gravestones in the hillside cemeteries.

Later, a railroad bridge stopped the river's ebb and flow into the cove, and it silted in. Boatbuilding ceased. The flaccid water became a septic tank for the town. Immigrant Italian stonemasons arrived to build stone walls and houses along the edge of the cove, obscuring it from outlooks high or low. As years went by, the new arrivals' names joined the tax rolls along with the founding Yankee names. The abundance of water power created a center for manufacturing. Once there was even a trolley line that extended all the way to Boston, some 150 miles northeast. Then it all went quiet again.

Nowadays, the vintage houses and commercial buildings have been repurposed into boutiques and restaurants. Sunday visitors stroll the main street, window shop, admire the small scale charm of the village. Not much changes as the small town's footprint is confined by hills and cove.

Still, just above the town square, on what is now called Maple Street, the two old houses sit serenely on their plots, resigned to the scant space between them. Whether the distance was ever narrowed between the brothers, no one knows.

In the evenings

Diana Griggs

my neighbor walks
into her house across the street,
sometimes in a business suit
sometimes in ruby red sweats.
I can see her from my window.
She never pauses to look
in my direction.
The door closes, lights brighten
her kitchen, shine on a maple table
that once held our coffee cups,
laughter and tears.
I watch her lower the window shade.
Between our houses children's voices
scatter like falling leaves,
leaving only silence.

GROUNDED FRIENDSHIP

Barbara Ostrem

Margaret and Madeline had been neighbors on Chester Street for more years than either could say without some mental computation. Long since, they had become Midge and Maddy and were closer than some sisters.

But not so lately. Maddy had voiced her honest opinion about the fit of Midge's new mail-order jeans, and Midge had stomped off in a huff. That was two weeks ago. Not even a friendly wave over the fence broke the impasse.

Shopping at Fred Meyer on Saturday, Maddy stopped to admire the vast array of primroses, always a favorite of Midge's. An idea struck her, and she selected, one by one, the most colorful of the lot, filling a tray. She couldn't stop smiling as she hurried home.

After donning her own faded jeans and garden clogs, she grabbed a shovel and spaded a neat row along the unfenced border between their back yards. A light rain the night before had softened the earth, making the digging quick and easy.

Maddy set the tray of plants on Midge's porch and rapped on the kitchen door. When the door opened, she simply said, "Come on, old woman. We have fresh ground that needs planting!"

A surprised Midge knew she meant the lovely primroses, but she understood that friendships sometimes need replanting too. Besides, she secretly had to admit that the mail-order jeans made her butt look big!

Pushcart

Florence Korzin

At first I heard
Fanueil Hall's history,
a mystery
in Haymarket Square,
where ghosts
still drum
"the spirit of
seventy-six,"
remember
the Revolutionary War
and air political pitfalls
in the townhall.
The basement's
market is more
like a fair.

In this neighborhood
my childhood is
dad's pushcart
lining the street
alongside others,
on market day
heaped
with sweetmeats
and farmer's fare.

In mama's corner
store
a peanut roaster,
steamed,
warmed the way
to coffee,
Moxie
and fruit pyramids.

In the evening
I slept
on burlap sacks,
layered in legends
one by one
like filo dough
in the room
of surplus wares.

Ten o'clock chimed,
the "closed" sign
was turned,
faced the street,
and we left for home.
They bundled,
and laid me
on the pushcart
like a sack
of inert innocence.
Dad pushed hard
energetically over
bumpy
cobble streets
so closely set
like stones
in ancient walls.

Configuring This Arc of Time

Bernadette Blue

Let me linger for a moment in this chair,
bending time across the spaces I recall,
until there is no distance between the yesterdays.
Only Grandma's kitchen, fairy-dusted
by the light sifting through her yellow curtains.
And Grandpa's lap that held the Sunday funnies.
And the white-washed barn where mother found the litter
of half a dozen calicos – teasing out from mounds of hay.

Let me linger for a moment in this chair,
leaping years o'er the roads my father paved—
paying our way, measuring days by hours kept.
Yet I was never bound by time.
Only by walls postered in heartthrob Romeos
did I define my ages, counting blackboard schools
and those gymnasiums where we first danced,
making wishes under streams of crepe paper and disco balls.

Youth speeds the future with its wishes,
rushing days from points of relativity,
while I'd slow the clock by my design.
So let me linger for a moment in this chair,
reconfiguring this arc of time, as I recall
the children running down my hall, and
gliding back in prom regalia as if there were no years,
only smiles and tears escaping me as I watched them grow.

Yes, let me linger in this moment in this chair,
where I rocked a baby, and held her to this heart
that knows no time, but only places
where love's forever housed.

A Perfectly Good Day

Barbara Nuxall Isom

April showers indeed bring May flowers. Our local Fred Meyer store helps the home gardener along this path with its April Fushia planting event. This is how it works: you buy or bring your empty pots (limit of eight) to the store and whatever plants you purchase, they will furnish new planting soil and plant them in your pots. All that remains is to take them home, water them, and watch them grow and bloom. How good is that?

My daughter and I made our usual pilgrimage and loaded her van with our completed pots. We had a half-price coupon for a very large bag of potting soil that we needed in addition. The floor of the van was covered with pots, so I suggested I return later that day for the potting soil.

On my return to the store the first item I tried to procure was the bag of potting soil. It turned out to be a very, very large heavy bag but at half-price it cost less than a smaller bag, so I struggled to load it in my cart. I'm a good-sized woman, accustomed to lifting and toting, but at 75 years of age I am finding some of these tasks more difficult. About that time a large gallant hombre with a deep voice offered his assistance and further inquired if I needed more than one bag, whereupon I assured him with my biggest and most thankful smile that one was enough.

At the check out counter I placed a few items on the moving belt and informed the clerk I was not going to lift the bag of soil, commenting that I would have a difficult enough time getting it in the trunk of my car. She surprisingly replied that she would get me some help for that transfer, and she did.

This was becoming a very good day.

What the hey, I thought I would stop at Cutsforth's Thriftway store and purchase a couple salad kits advertised at 2 for $5. I selected my two salad kits and somehow a $2 bag of sweet potato chips jumped in my cart. Another lady and I were headed for the same cashier. Not being in a hurry, I let her go in front of me and continued to the next cashier. A man and woman were nearly finished checking out a good-sized load of groceries when she questioned why her milk coupon hadn't been accepted, only to discover she hadn't selected the correct brand. So she headed back to replace her selection with the correct one.

As she passed me she commented that I didn't have much in the way of a purchase and apologized for holding me up. I indicated I wasn't in a hurry. Suddenly, the clerk started to ring up my items. I informed her they were my purchases, not theirs. The clerk bagged my items and said the gentleman had offered to pay for my items. I was so surprised I stuttered that he didn't need to pay for my groceries, and he replied it was his pleasure. I assured him I had heard stories of such mindfulness, but didn't expect it to happen to me.

Our lives are a collection of good and bad days, and some days are better than others. Did I say this was a good day?

That evening, I was excitedly sharing my day with a friend. She listened and agreed I had experienced a good day. Then she looked right at me and inquired if I had ever considered having an "eyelid job."

Now was that any way to end a perfectly good day?

Scooby Doo

(the story of an angry cat)

Billie Marie Steele

Quietly,
peacefully,
humming a joyful tune,
I enter my bedroom.
Strange feeling—
Looking up,
across the room,
into the darkest corner
of my bedroom closet;
Bright, yellow eyes
staring at me.
Slowly,
disdainfully,
my orange cat rose,
showed me his rear end,
laid back down.

ALL'S RIGHT WITH THE WORLD

Eleanor Whitney Nelson

Frank stops snoring at 5:04 a.m. I know because I have been tossing and turning all night, waiting for my husband's internal alarm clock to ring him awake. Judging from years of insomnia, I know the time is within a few minutes of five o'clock – before or after – but I look at the clock on the nightstand anyway, its large digital numbers glowing red in the dim light. It clicks forward to 5:05. A smidgen late this morning.

Now that Frank is up, I sprawl across the bed, stretch and relax, my eyelids heavy, while I listen to him splash water across his face and press the Listerine pump, gargle. I hear the scraping sound as he pulls on his jeans and the thunk of his boots as he forces his feet through the narrow opening at the ankle.

Out the window, silhouetted against bands of peach-colored clouds in the eastern sky, a pair of Great Horned owls sit head to tail on the crossbar of the power pole, talking to each other. One bobs forward, hooting a message in owleze, and is answered by a synchronous hoot and bob from its mate.

"Who hoo hoo." Bob. The notes rise, then fall. "Who hoo hoo." Bob.

Again and again, they hoot and bob until color fades from the sky and they fly away for a day's rest in the hollow near the top of the cottonwood tree next to the dry wash. Smaller birds are chittering, a cacophony of sound like the discordant harmony of a symphony orchestra warming up, each species welcoming the day with its own combination of notes. Morning music replaces the chamber music of the night.

The night has been a typical one. Not only does Frank snore, but Pattie, the Siamese cat curled up by my feet, snores. Amber, the golden retriever, upside down on her back, snores while Slim, a big white mutt, yips and scratches the floor with his paws as he flees from some nightmare monster. Only Molly, our little mop-dog, lies quietly, sprawled out on her private armchair.

Just past midnight a coyote pack howls in a communal singsong. The three dogs dash out the dog door – bumpity bump, bumpity bump, bumpity bump – to join in the chorus. The startled cat dashes across the headboard, knocking the telephone on the floor. "If you would like to make a call..." the recorded nasal voice booms through the darkness. The dogs return – bumpity bump – and Amber's snoring recommences. Pattie curls up once more by my feet. Frank's snoring has not missed a beat.

Frank tiptoes from the bathroom past the bed, trying not to wake me, although I suspect he knows I'm playing possum. The two big dogs, Slim and Amber, stretch and yawn while Molly does a dervish dance around Frank's feet as he heads for the kitchen door. I hear Frank twist the deadbolt and, as he pulls open the door, loud whinnies issue forth from the corrals. A scramble of hard toenails scrape across the kitchen floor tiles as the canine mass pushes outside.

Pattie sneaks up next to my chest and snuggles into the hollow below my chin. I feel the gentle buzz of her purring. The two of us doze, waiting for the outside contingent to return with the newspaper, which will be followed by the sound of dog bowls sliding across the floor as the dogs lick them clean.

I hear the sound of coffee being poured and the rustle of the newspaper. The dogs return to the bedroom: Slim and Amber to their mats on the floor, Molly to her armchair. It is then that I know "God's in his heaven—All's right with the world."[1] Everything is as it should be. Our little family is safe and content. Now I can close my eyes and fall into a deep sleep.

An hour later, I find myself dreaming about sewers, the manhole covers in the street rising into the air as fumes blast them from their cradles. A moment later, they crash down on the street. A firetruck's siren sounds. Reluctantly, I open my eyes. Amber is bumping against the side of the bed. She shakes her head to jangle her tags. Slim is staring at my face, emitting dog breath two inches from my nose. Pattie stretches and pats my cheek. All three are letting me know it is time to rouse myself. I dangle my hand over the edge of the bed and stroke the expectant faces. Then with purpose – a job to do – all three dogs trot into the kitchen. They are letting Frank know I am up, and they are ready for their reward. I hear the crunch of dog biscuits.

Moments later, Frank appears with a steaming mug of coffee. His chores for the day are done. It is time for me to assume mine.

---

[1] Robert Browning, "Pippa Passes" [1841], pt. 1

Our routine is as it should be, as it has been for many years. New dogs and cats replace older ones but, with only slight variations, things remains the same.

Only now, the world has turned topsy-turvy. Frank has contracted Parkinson's disease. It comes on slowly and, as it does, he is able to assume fewer and fewer duties. After a while, the chores become mine alone. My alarm-clock dogs wake me early when the horses whinny for breakfast. I pull on my jeans and boots and head for the barn while dawn paints the sky over the mountains.

When all the horses, dogs, cats, and wild birds have been fed, I return to the bedroom to help Frank rise and dress and accompany him to the dining room. He moves with careful steps behind his walker. I bring his coffee to the table and join him with my own. The dogs lie quietly at our feet. On a chair at the end of the table, Pattie licks her paws and washes her face. She yawns, then curls into a ball for her morning nap.

Many days are difficult, but we are thankful for every good one we have. It is hard to say, though, that "...All's right with the world." Nevertheless, we face the challenge of our new reality. Everyone has obstacles; everyone's reality is different, and we must handle, as best we can, what we are given. We must adapt as age and circumstances dictate. Our world changes and, if we are to be content with our journey, we must change with it.

I believe that, at different times in our lives, we do different things. If we are fortunate in having exceptional experiences, as Frank and I have been, we want those good times to continue forever – but this is unrealistic. We have a world of infinite variety to explore, although, more often than not, a world different from the one we thought we would find. Even so, it can be worthwhile and we should embrace it. We *must* embrace it.

The first rays of the morning sun break over the mountains, and I pull the sheet over my face to block the glare. The dogs rub against the bed and bat it with their tails. They jingle their tags. But no pussycat taps my face. Pattie has gone on to another world. Perhaps, after the morning chores are done and two cups of coffee have rendered us wide awake, I'll wheel Frank out to the car in his chair and we'll set out to find another furry feline companion. Maybe today will be one of those days when we start a new chapter in our lives.

TOGETHER

Nancy Sandweiss

I've always walked ahead, my rapid strides as natural as breathing.
Don never minded, kept his pace unruffled. Today it's different.
Our puppy's yanking on the leash, eager to join me. Don yells

Come back! to me and holds his ground till Hugo stops. I balk,
obey; know Hugo will be big one day, we'll need control. Our walk resumes,
but Hugo spots a squirrel, he's off again. Don halts, the leash grows taut;

Hugo struggles, gives up, returns. We move in fits and starts: Hugo lunges,
Don stands firm, Hugo resists, comes back. My muscles scream for release
the simple joy of fluid, forward motion—

A friend says dogs are the glue that's held her marriage together.
The children were our glue. Don wasn't a dog lover, paid scant attention
to pets. But here we are, years after our last dog died, raising a puppy.

Growing old, watching friends fall ill and die, we're buying toys, planning
schedules around crate time. It wasn't my idea, but Don's enthusiasm
pulls me in, I'm washed in waves of love and hopeful energy.

We discuss Hugo's progress, laugh at his antics, bury our fingers
in his cotton candy hair, enjoy quiet time while he settles for the night.
He fills our home with life and joy—

and teaches me to walk in tandem.

The Homeless and Their Dogs

Lee Jones

Years ago I watched a program that said the homeless often collect up to $400 in one day from soft-hearted people like me. After that I stopped donating to them for a while. Then I began to learn about P.T.S.D., alcoholism, and the many types of mental illness that can cause homelessness. Still, I could not understand how one who has nothing would drag a big dog around and, hungry himself, would share his last moldy crust of bread with a dog!

Then one day, when I came home I found, wet and shivering on my front porch, a dog barely more than a puppy. I lifted him and he snuggled right in, getting mud on my new white raincoat. Driving to buy dog food, I told him, "You know I'll have to find you a home. I'm too busy to keep a dog."

He just stared at me with those soulful eyes that seemed to say, "I found your home. Why do I need another?"

After he ate two bowls of dog food and drank a bowl of water, I bathed and brushed him. He was quite beautiful, especially that long, feathery tail that never seemed to stop wagging. I placed an ad and called the Dog Control, but no one claimed him. I was surprised to feel relieved.

Joey is so well-behaved, I let him go everywhere with me now, on foot or in the car. When we pass a homeless person with a dog, I give generously. I understand now.

One Thing We Have to Learn from Dogs

Joan T. Doran

To live truly, you must savor bones—
meaty, rich with marrow
    warm from recent-pulsing blood
    big and thick enough to gnaw on
    just the size to fit between your paws.
Beneath the transient skin, they must be cherished—
Bones of lovers, dinosaurs, of shipwrecks, bones
of fire-ravaged buildings. Wishbones.

Sniff them out, for they are hidden
inside scaffolding, in armatures—
    sun-bleached near dry waterholes—
    cobwebbed under cellar stairs—
    buried with forgotten gods—
They molder in the coffin, tomb, the sepulcher—
They're guarded by a griffin or a snail
or – still glistening – ravened by crows.

Bear bones proudly home between your teeth—
Guard them in the fortress of your paws
    Smell them for their essence
    Lick them, find their flavor
    Bite them, feel them bite you back
    Chomp down until they yield
    Roll on them, feel them in every pore.
Then throw them joyous in the air
and when you've done that, be at rest among them
for all these bones are your bones too.

CHICO

Diana Griggs

"Do you hear that," exclaimed my son.
We'd buried Chico four weeks ago
under the Pepper tree, his place
to wait for the mail carrier's daily treat.
On his last day, waiting for the vet to arrive,
I carried him outside with his beloved
tennis ball while my son and I dug his grave.
Still wanting to play he pushed the ball
with his nose into the deepening hole while we,
silent in grief, returned it within his easy reach.
Later, we laid him in the ground, tucked into
the soft earth with a tennis ball and his collar.
Today we hear dog tags jangle past the door.

Healing a Damaged Heart

Mark S. Fletcher

Last Thursday a close family friend, Amy, adopted a three-year-old who had been rescued and nursed back to health. This poor boy has already had a tragic life, bounced between various foster families before finding a loving home with my friend.

Since Amy will be leaving the country for a couple of months this summer and my wife and I will be babysitting during that time, we all decided it would be a good idea if this youngster got to know us as well. So Thursday and Friday night he stayed with us. Needless to say, we had fallen in love with the little boy by the time we had to send him home with Amy.

Even at this young age, he has an awareness of the outside world. On Saturday morning, as we were preparing to say goodbye and help him into her truck, it was overly apparent he did not want to be put into another vehicle. It broke my wife's heart to see how much he feared the slightest chance of being put into a car or truck. The idea of leaving a loving home only to travel to the unknown terrified him. I had to cradle him in my arms, carry him to the truck, and then spend a long time calming him down before he could travel without being upset.

At that time, he did not even have his final name. Now known as Jet, he is with Amy. My wife, Shelly, and I stopped over at her house on Sunday in late afternoon to see how he was doing. When Amy brought him out to see us, he was excited until he saw Shelly sitting in the van. Panic set in and he started backing up. By this time, you may have deduced that Jet is a rescue dog - specifically, a flat-coated retriever.

It broke Shelly's heart to see him so scared of a person sitting in a car.

What I noticed is the similarity between a human child repeatedly torn away from one home after another and what Jet has experienced. Every time he was put in a vehicle, it meant a new, sometimes less than loving environment. I can't help but ascribe human emotions to the way I view what he must be feeling.

I also have faith that, as time goes on and Jet learns he has at least two loving homes he can safely travel between, he will become less fearful of entering a car or truck. In the meantime, it is my hope and prayer that this traumatized little boy will heal a little bit each and every day.

A long series of tender embraces, with beating hearts near each other, is the best medicine I can prescribe.

Invitation to Tea – No RSVP Required

Bernadette Blue

Dear Friend,
Here I am, with the table set for tea,
leafing through memories of our friendship,
bookmarked for remembrance now,
like the poems of Emily's we read on those summer afternoons
when we quoted ghosts of poets, and
declared our versed ambitions on Lake Erie shore.

Forty years, could it have been so long.
We swore we'd never fall away.
Yet here we are, near as old as pen and paper,
with letters never written, and
but a dalliance with Christmas cards
declaring children, husbands as they came and went,
as if their names were the sole poetry
of our experience. Until there was just us.

And these words I'd post,
with a wish to see you soon.
If I'd not lost the address to your residence,
somehow.

So many days unravel meter,
jumbling all life's rhymes.
Still I remain endeared, my friend,
wondering how we'd fare with
a verse or two recalled from those days
we shared with Dickinson and Frost.

So what is there to do – bottle words,
cast them out on Erie shore that
you should find them on some morrow?
Yes and add P.S.
If fate be a kindly thing,
that you should read my mind,
and arrive today for tea.

THE COLORS OF MY CHILDHOOD, WHEN IT WAS ALL STILL GOOD

Lois Godel

White sheets suspended from laundry lines,
mingled scents of soap, bleach, and sun wafted
into the world. The child ran fast between the sheets
as they slowly dried, released residue of blueing,
horsey smells from the heated straw basket.

Fresh-cut grass, texture of the breeze
delicious on bare arms, legs of the
girl-child as she continued to run,
patting the sheets on her way.
The puppy, Ophie, scampered, tumbled.
The child peeked through gaps between
the sheets, took note of her climbing tree,
saw sky as blue as a colored Easter egg,
wisps of two white clouds
unfurling over fruit tree blossoms.

The child halted in her yard. Knelt
to hold her chick, Cheepee. *Be gentle*,
she remembered, smiled into fluffy down,
marveled at the wonder of the chick, the red wagon,
and the rocking horse that waited for her, every morning.

The whole world was sanctuary, and the universe was kind.

Revisiting New Places

Elisa Drachenberg

The dog looked up at her with those enormous eyes – a Margarete Keane painting turned 3-D – with those grotesquely large, sad eyes that had made her buy him in the first place. She reached down and thumped his forehead until he began nodding, never shifting his gaze off her face.

She'd thought about all this before, about the lightness of being: the ease with which a life was rubbed out. Lately, this thought seemed overwhelming, but she had borne it all her life, exactly eighty-five years today. She did not think of the physical pain – she could live with that, even though it was getting worse every year. What bothered her most was how little everything meant. How senseless it all seemed: the learning of skills and trades, the honing of talents, the little wisdoms acquired along the way; in other words, the growing into a culture, into a role, into a life that was then erased without leaving a trace of you. All the individual effort for naught. What an incredible, unbearable waste. She sighed and realized the dog had stopped nodding.

"You want some water, Oscar?" She got up to refresh the water in the striped bowl next to her lavender bushes. Apparently, the raccoon had been back last night, using Oscar's water bowl to wash whatever food it had encountered. The water was murky with remnants of something resembling breadcrumbs floating on the surface. Early in the morning, she'd watched blue jays splattering around, clearly mistaking the bowl for a birdbath. She'd come to appreciate "the critters," as Johan called them.

Johan wasn't able to be here today. He really could not make it, she knew that for a fact. It was not an excuse to get out of throwing her a party or buying her an expensive gift for this special day. Johan had the best excuse a man could have for not showing up at her birthday. Johan was dead.

She cleaned and filled the bowl, gently balancing it on the flattened rock that Johan had carried to this spot years ago, when he was still strong. He had been a decent man, a reliable man. "A man is only as trustworthy as the promises he keeps," he had insisted, when she would find excuses for people who would say things they may or may not have meant at the moment. "Words have consequences. Don't say something if you don't mean it or, if you mean what you say, actually do what you said you would."

He was old-school with old-world ethics. And so, true to his word, he died, as his father had, of a massive heart attack. "I won't bother you with illnesses or decline," he would say, meaning every word. "You will not have to watch me lose my mind. You won't have to care for me, putting on my diapers or spoon-feeding me." He'd wink at her, knowing how she loathed these meaningless predictions, as if he had the power to make his words become reality. Yet, in the end, he did what he had vowed all along: one night, lying next to her in her sleepless hours before dawn, his snoring stuttered into a drawn-out sigh, a very long exhale that was not followed by another breathtaking.

A man of his word. Johan was a man of his word, of few words, often of clumsy words in his new language, which he insisted on speaking with her most of the time. Most of the time, though not always – not when he made love to her, not when he took her hand into his before they embarked on a trip to the city or the stores or the doctor's or running any other trivial errand for which they got into the car and left the house.

"Vannacht, gezond in ons bedje," he'd murmur, looking at her as if it were a solemn pledge.

"Tonight safe and sound in our bed," she'd answer, less convinced than he that those words would or could actually protect them.

It did not surprise her that Oscar had not followed her into the garden. Over the years, he had always sat next to her chair on the terrace, looking up at her, always looking up with those oversized, goofy eyes. Forever ready to be nudged into a head-bobbing.

Her coffee was cold by now. The golden edge on the cup kept her from placing it in the microwave. She clearly remembered the sparks and the burnt stench from the one time she had tried to reheat coffee in a gold-rimmed cup. Slowly, she added another lump of sugar, just to have a purpose for the tiny silver spoon with its enameled handle. The cup, a delicate, translucent thing from a different era, felt smooth in her hand. It was much too fragile to be put in the dishwasher. It was one of a Spanish set she had bought decades ago in a Dutch antique store, when Johan was still around to try to talk her out of purchasing things she didn't need, but wanted simply because they were "lovely." She kept stirring the coffee long after the sugar had dissolved. The enamel between her fingers was a shiny purple, the cup bright red as the lipstick she had worn as a much younger woman.

"Did I ever tell you about Guus?" The wind had picked up, and Oscar went on nodding. "Silly, of course I haven't, but it's nice of you to cheer me on." She raised her voice a little, just enough for the neighbors to think she had company, not so much for them to actually make out her words. She cared about possible gossip; she did not want anyone to think that she had stopped entertaining altogether.

A few years back, she had decided to begin utilizing all her handsome possessions instead of keeping them in cabinets. About the same time, she had decided to dress up for her meals. Guus had always insisted on appearances; reality never meant as much to him as what others might think of him and her and them.

"I once told a girlfriend that Guus was a charmer who mistook my kindness for weakness. Perhaps I had read those words somewhere. Somehow, though, they felt as if they were coming from a place inside the part of my brain reserved for truth-telling. Without a doubt, I loved Guus more than he was ever capable of loving anyone, before or after me. He was dazzling, smart, funny. His jokes often were at the expense of our friends, but they let him get away with it. Attractive people live a charmed life."

"Why did you stay with him for all those years? He treated you like shit." My girlfriend never could see Guus through my eyes. Not then.

"After I left Guus, no, after he'd left me…let me get this straight…if he kept having affairs with other women while still being with me, doesn't that qualify as *him* leaving *me?* He claimed those women meant nothing to him. Don't you think that's the biggest cliché, Oscar? Of course, they meant something to me. Or didn't my excruciating pain upon discovering his infidelities count? At any rate, once I found out about his brother's wife – by accident, by the way, but I digress – I finally had the courage to leave him. But I still ached for him. I lost weight, I couldn't sleep, my hands trembled as if touched by Parkinson's. I discovered that you don't stop loving someone just because you end the relationship. That's strange, isn't it? The marriage is over, and you still yearn for the man with whom you danced and laughed and cried. I had to dredge up every one of his faults and magnify them in my mind, trying and failing desperately to erase him from my thoughts."

She threw a little piece of her Danish butter cookie in Oscar's direction. He was a fussy eater, initially refusing all the food she presented to him. She would fill his bowl, but could never be sure who had emptied it – he or the birds or the skunks or raccoons. Early on, when she first brought him to the house, she learned to respect his resolve never to eat while she was watching. Eventually, since Oscar did not appear to lose any weight, she stopped fretting. Dogs, like all other creatures, had their idiosyncrasies. As long as she didn't attempt to change him, they both would be just fine. Wasn't that one of the biggest lessons she had to learn? If it is true that you can't ever change anyone – another cliché that everyone knows but hardly anyone respects – then you'd better find someone who didn't need much changing.

Johan had been such a man. He was the proverbial *good man*, and later her sunny, amiable, and utterly decent husband. And even though she had promised herself never to feel anything like love again – not willing to face the inevitable pain that a failed relationship brings – Johan had wormed himself into her life, much like Oscar had. She never realized how easy love could be, if you both cared about each other's well being.

"When I was younger, I would have spurned any kind of union like that. I seemed to seek pain as part of the equation, part of the excitement. Does that make me a masochist? Well, then, I'm a reformed masochist. You know what I once told my girlfriend, when she introduced me to a nice, perfectly pleasant guy from her work? I said, and I'm ashamed to repeat it: 'If I wanted a dog, I would get one.' Can you imagine? No offense, Oscar, but I couldn't bear the thought of someone wagging his tail any time I entered a room. How utterly obtuse of me, how ridiculous. Back then, I really thought that excitement, torment, and anguish were synonyms for love. Why doesn't anyone teach us otherwise?"

Again, she opened the tin of cookies and chose an almond twist with chocolate-dipped ends. "So, now let me tell you what happened about two or three years after Johan and I got married. I received a letter from my first – well, you know, from this man, this former husband. Let's leave him nameless from now on, because he is not worth remembering or being mentioned by name. Funny, that I would say that. After all, I am talking about him." She covered her mouth, as if anyone could observe her, sitting there, laughing out loud, unappealingly openmouthed, as if anyone could detect those unchewed bits and pieces of a Danish chocolate-covered cookie on her tongue, smearing her teeth. She had always been a stickler for etiquette. *Good manners is how you behave when no one is watching,* was one of those phrases she remembered from her youth.

Here, in her secluded garden, she was in no danger of neighbors spying on her. Yet one could never be completely certain. She could sense Oscar's eyes on her, telling her in his own patient way to get on with the story.

"Anyway, in the letter he invited me out for dinner just to catch up..." Without realizing it, she began tapping the spoon on the table in a rhythm to accompany her words. "Oh, I wanted that man to be wretched, I wanted him to have missed me all this time, to have ached for me, to have realized in the meantime that I was certainly irreplaceable and utterly unforgettable. I wanted my image to haunt his days and trouble his dreams. In my mind, I did not even grant him dreams, only nightmares."

Oscar slowly began shaking his head of his own accord, seemingly troubled by her account. The wind was picking up, and the linen tablecloth began to flutter rapidly like an injured hummingbird. She wiped the cookie crumbs off the starched surface as she searched her mind for the most recent image she had created for Oscar's sake.

"Of course, I never contemplated seeing him, not really. I could not bear the thought of putting on fancy clothes to impress him. On the other hand, I realized that, if I went, I needed to look nothing less than absolutely stunning for this man, who had wasted years of my life with his uncaring nonchalance. But if I needed to show him how wonderful I was and had always been, wasn't I then still vying for his approval? Did I really need to look my best to convince him that he had made a mistake? Did I want to look into the mirror to put on lipstick for this nobody? How could I possibly still crave approval or admiration from him? Did I still need or want to see myself through his eyes? And what did that say about my marriage? Ah, Oscar, all these questions I could not answer." She sighed. "Undoubtedly, though, I realized he still mattered. It took me a few days to figure out why I was so upset.

"Johan reacted calmly and left it up to me to accept or reject the invitation from my former husband. 'It's a very elegant restaurant and, let me add, it's also extremely expensive,' he said. Then he winked and went back to reading the paper. It infuriated me that he could be so undaunted about the possible date – even though I refused to consider it to be one – with this man who had once meant so much to me."

The blue jays returned, screeching at her and eyeing Oscar cautiously, but eventually they approached the water-filled bowls without too much trepidation. One jay was waiting in the pine tree, anxiously shrieking and hopping back and forth on his branch. The other, claws firmly holding on to the rim, bent his blue head down low to reach the water.

"Look, Oscar, look, he's drinking your water." Her voice, only slightly louder than before, did not express any other emotion. The incident with the jays seemed to have taken her someplace else in her memory. "They won't be long now," she said, slowly rubbing her neck.

After a while, she began humming a song, then abruptly stopped and said, "Johan loved the wildlife here, especially the birds during the day. He bought book after book about the regional birds. 'Birdbooks for a birdbrain,' he called them. He was so erudite that he never felt he needed to prove anything to anyone. That's probably the reason people underestimated him and his achievements. Did you know, Oscar, that he was a famous professor at the University of Amsterdam? Students voted him the 'most likable prof' and 'the most knowledgeable about foreign relations.' That's how we eventually wound up in this country. He received a visa for *extraordinary ability*. My Johan, my extraordinary husband. I was so proud of him, of his success and, ah yes...also of the way he let me grow old without having to dye my hair or run to gyms. He still loved me with my wrinkles and wilting skin. But then, of course, I loved him, too. It never mattered that he lost his hair or that his hands grew knobby. It was a quiet sort of love, always there, like a down comforter at night to keep us warm. We sheltered each other from the outside world – a world we did not understand, not really. We had no friends; we depended solely on each other. We knew many people, of course. But knowing people does not mean you have friends..."

She got up, suddenly all flustered, again rubbing the muscle on the side of her neck. Again, she removed a few crumbs from the tablecloth. "They'll be here soon," she said. "They promised I could take you with me, but I'll miss the blue jays and the lavender and the rosemary. I'll miss everything that Johan created here. He made this garden for me to sit in quietly and learn to be alone, to forget about feeling sorry for myself. 'As long as you don't feel lonely, you'll be fine,' he'd say. 'You are an amazingly strong woman, a formidable force. Don't let anyone convince you otherwise.'

"We should go for a walk, Oscar, but you look so content just sitting there and, frankly, the way my hip aches, it really takes an effort."

The jays were gone now; only the lizards made rustling sounds in the herb planter.

"Johan asked me specifically for one important thing," she said, turning her head toward the dog. "He said I must not idealize him once he was gone." She cocked her head as if that could increase her ability to invoke his voice again.

"I am not a perfect husband," she heard him say, his accent tying him forever to his home country. "Instead of missing me and feeling unbearable pain, remember the quarrels we had, remember how petty I could be, how utterly annoying in trying to win arguments. Remember, I am far from flawless. Don't let death make me into the perfect man. Don't do that to me, and most of all, don't do that to yourself." Johan's words faded.

"But I can't help it, Oscar, I keep remembering only the good things now, even though I know he was right. Perfect is the enemy of mankind, no one, living or dead, should be idealized into – what do they say here, in this country? – a mister goody two-shoes, whatever that really means. So let me tell you, because I know you won't betray my confidence, Johan was not perfect. Still, he was a good human 'bean' and I was his grand 'garbanzo.' Silly? Yes, silly. The older I get, the sillier. That is, of course, the reason why they are coming. They say the house is too big for me and too much work to maintain. They say I'll love the view in the new place…

"Did I ever tell you about the man before Johan? He wrote me a letter once. Invited me to a fancy restaurant. Wanted to see me for God knows what reason. Today I have…sometimes it appears, like a special gift…clarity, yes, that's what I mean. On some days it comes and visits, sometimes only for a few hours. Sometimes only.…" She let her eyes wander through the garden. "They say it will get worse. They claim I'll need support. Isn't it funny how kids remember that you need help when you get older, but won't give you any of the help that you *want*. They only offer *their* solutions to *my* problems."

She went inside to pour herself another cup of coffee. When she returned to the terrace, she smiled. "It's nice to drink it when it's still steaming hot.

Here in the desert that means you have a window of one minute. Ah, sorry, Oscar, you could use some coffee to make you a bit more energetic, but you never cared for it."

She heard a car coming up the hill, but it did not turn into her driveway. "Right, so, where were we? I thought…about the letter…I've to tell Miriam, she was my best friend in Holland. I'm sure I told you about her, sometimes I can't recall her name…names are fickle, they come and go…anyway, Muriel suggested I should definitely go to the restaurant. 'Slip on your sexiest clothes,' she advised. 'Put on your incredibly high heels, those black nylons he found so irresistible on you. And then stay in your car, in front of the restaurant, and make him wait while you watch how he is getting ever more nervous. When he eventually calls the waiter to pay for whatever he ordered, saunter in. Kiss him lightly on each cheek, hold his face between your hands, look directly into his eyes and, Judas that you are, lean into him. Let him inhale your perfume. Let him feel the warmth of your body. And then, when he is bewildered by all your oozing sexiness, inform him you are on your way to the opera and you only have five minutes, which will upset him, but you'll ignore that and ask him, pointblank, why he wanted to see you. Voila.'"

She smiled, rolling her eyes as if still incredulous. "Miriam always thought her advice was excellent. She was never shy about telling me how amazing she thought herself to be. She habitually had a tendency to dramatize and a theatrical way of interpreting my life. When she described the restaurant scene to me in such a powerful, convincing way, I suddenly knew how to solve my dilemma. Yes, I wanted to find out all there was to know about him: how he lived now, if he was happy with his new wife and daughter – the daughter we should have had together. The daughter, he told me again and again, he was not ready to have, but he apparently changed his mind after I left. No, let me be frank about this, he was not ready for a child with me. He was ready for a child with the other woman. Another cliché, Oscar, I know, I know. We think we are original, but everything has been felt and done before. Love, passion, loss, anger, despair, jealousy, ardor…I can't find any more words right now. D something Lawrence, I can't recall his entire name, anyway, I think it was he who once said or wrote in one of his books: *We like to imagine we are something very new on the face of the earth. But don't we flatter ourselves?*

"Yup, Oscar, we flatter ourselves. Nothing new is felt; it just feels that way because to *us* it's new. But at least I felt big. Nothing of those safe choices for me. I have no regrets, only about Johan. I should have been kinder, more caring – he deserved that." Her eyes blinked wildly. She refused to cry.

"Dilemma, what dilemma? So yes, I was curious. Yet I resisted meeting him. Then, when Marian described how she pictured my dramatic appearance in the restaurant, I simply asked her to go instead of me, to take my place and tell me all about it.

"'Me, why me?' 'Because you can make him suffer more than I ever could, and he deserves a little suffering.' She thought about it, and when she called back the next day, she was all set to meet him.

"Is that a car coming up the driveway? It must be the kids. They said they'd come and pick me up to visit the facility. They said I would feel less alone there. They don't know yet that being alone is better than being with bad friends. Miriam would have staged a fit. She wouldn't have even looked at an old people's home, no matter how plush, no matter how deceiving its name."

She paused for a long time, letting her eyes follow the hummingbirds that buzzed around the feeder. "But then Muriel and I lost touch over the years," she continued in a much harsher voice. "Sometimes, even the best friendship does not survive betrayal. Ah, betrayal, should I ever call it that? I had asked her to meet him, and that is what she did. The dice were cast, and the outcome was surprising to all of us. There was never a confrontation. I guess she just felt strange around me after she decided to marry my ex-husband, or he her.

"First, naturally, I was hurt, then furious, then amused. They deserved each other. They each loved themselves more than anyone else. They had that in common. Still, she lasted longer in that marriage than any of his other wives. Muriel was always living in a world larger than what our little Holland could offer. She craved grand stages for her grandiose performances. She left for the States long before we did, claiming she needed more space. And you know where she's living now? Right here in Scottsdale. Unbelievable, I know. It's a small world, isn't it? Another cliché, I'm afraid. It's a shame, really, that we stopped being friends. She would have liked it here in this house with its breathtaking views. And she most certainly would have loved you,

Oscar. Because you are such a good listener. Theatrical people require good listeners."

Again, she heard a car, this time a sports car, racing up the driveway.

"I just remembered, Oscar, odd how I got that mixed up. I see it clearly now: Miriam got married to what's his name. Shortly after that dinner in the posh restaurant. Why not? He wasn't married then; he didn't have any children, either, not then, not when she went to see him at the restaurant. Why on earth did I recall him having a daughter? My memory frequently guides me through rooms wildly decorated with vivid details. But it's rather skimpy on specific time frames and logical sequences.

"Do you hear that, Oscar? They are finally here."

"Hi," the young couple greeted her, a little out of breath after climbing the steps to enter her garden from the path on the side of the house. They eyed the bright red coffee cup on the table. She stayed seated and waved her hand like an aging queen.

"I always loved that set," Lulu, her daughter said, generating her best social smile.

"You can have it. I no longer have any use for it," the old woman said.

"I thought I heard you talking to someone." Her son approached and kissed her on the cheek. "You smell good," he said. "Chanel number five?"

"Johan bought it, a week before…it was Oscar, I was just talking to Oscar."

Lulu furrowed her brows, but did not say anything. She smiled again and cussed at the gravel. "We rang the doorbell. Didn't you hear us?" She waved her slender hands in the air, the red nail polish as bright as the cup on the table, raised her left foot and examined the scratch on her shoe. "These pebbles are absolutely ruining my heels."

Lulu, all drama, always on stage, never grounded, the old woman thought. We have nothing in common. How on earth did she wind up with a daughter like that? With someone so over-the-top? Neither she nor Johan ever acted like that. How…?

That was not…was that her daughter? Without warning, from one moment to the other, she grew terrified, her words disappeared. She'd never gotten used to that, the sudden loss of meaning, no matter how often it was happening lately.

But now, as never before, now the entire storyline blurred. She stood up and pointed. "Who are you?" she asked with a certain belligerence in her voice to mask the fear.

Lulu smiled, a smile so sweet that she could have punched her.

"I'm Linda," she said. "I'm Marian's daughter, and you know who this is, don't you? This is Gary, my husband. Mom is waiting for us in the car... she couldn't manage the stairs. We've all come to take you to your new apartment at *Years of Wisdom*. Remember we..."

Linda advanced a few steps toward the old woman, whose hands were now trembling uncontrollably. When Linda reached out to smooth a strand of gray hair out of her face, the old women raised her arm.

"Don't," she hissed. She saw the dog's head move violently. That red-nailed intruder had bumped into him. "Careful," she shouted. "Oscar doesn't like to be pushed around."

"Ah, that old thing," Linda said. "It's all rusty from sitting outside. The moment you are settled in, we'll get you a new one, I promise."

Window Gazing

Helen Zenkner

I sit by my window and stare
At the life quickly passing by
Trucks delivering goods
Cars hurrying people to work
Shoppers carrying groceries
A rushing river, never stopping

As I sit by my window I reflect
Back on the days when I was
A bird on the wing, college days.
Marriage, children, teaching, creating
Life was perfect, unspeakable joy
A rushing river never ending

As memories linger, I sit quietly
Gaze out my window, wondering
If my life is over, only memories
Like history books of days past
That sit on the shelf, dusty, unread
The river only a bed of dry rocks

A voice whispers softly in my ear
The world is yours for the taking
You must not look back, only forward
Dream new dreams that bring excitement
They are like the rain bringing new life
To the river bed waiting to be fed

I turn from my window, I look inward
For understanding, that life is a plant
Needing nourishment, needing loving care
Each day a precious gift not to be wasted
Used to bring back joy, love, and peace
Like the river ever changing, ever moving

As I sit by my window, I see a new life
The old one is done, the new life beckoning
No longer blinded by the past, seeing the future
Knowing I am the creator of my destiny
I am no longer dormant and still, I am alive
Like a river ever changing, ever moving

It's Time

Bonnie Papenfuss

This is a new chapter,
and I'm excited to begin.
What I promised myself so long ago
will finally take priority.

I'm scared to start;
afraid I'll not be good enough.
But nothing worthwhile
can be accomplished without failure,
and success means only that I try.

So I'll put my pen to paper
and bare my soul in words of prose or rhyme.
A voice inside me whispers the messages
and whatever they be – it's time.

Thinking Out Loud

Vivian Bullock

I sometimes sit on my front porch, looking for people to go by. Could be, I'm the only one who does this anymore. I've been around a long time, and many things have changed since I was a young woman. Today, when people are at home, they spend their time outside behind a high fence, in their back yard. I'm not complaining, I'm just watching and thinking out loud.

Sometimes people do walk by. If I see a couple, the woman very often is holding a dog on a leash, and the man will be holding a phone to his ear – they don't hold hands or talk to each other. But I'm not complaining. I'm just watching and thinking out loud.

I no longer see or hear children playing. This is true, even outside of Sun City. I hear people say that it's no longer safe for children to run up and down the street playing hide and seek or any other games. Besides, they have better things to do with their time. I'm not complaining, I'm just thinking out loud.

I never see clothes drying on a line in the back yard anymore. I miss the sweet smell of sheets dried in sunshine. Would I give up my washing machine and dryer for this smell? No way, no how, not ever! I'm not complaining, I'm just thinking out loud.

I no longer go to the movies to find a cool place to rest in the summer. Now, with the magic of TV, I can sit in an easy chair and watch a movie inside my nice cool house. You see, I'm not complaining, I'm just thinking out loud.

And I'm counting my blessings.

ONE TIME

Kathleen O'Brien

Ruth was a Rockette—
    for two weeks.
She told me this as
    she lay in
Van Rensselaer Manor,
    a snowman-patterned
fleece tucked to her chin,
    though it was August.

She told me how
    she was the stand-in girlfriend
for two older brothers
    and how they'd take turns
twirling her around the parlor
    to Tommy Dorsey tunes.
She'd accept their challenge,
    "Ruth, show us how
you can kick."
    One time she kicked off her brother's cap.
One time she kicked so high,
    she fell backward
into a heap of laughter.
    "Double-jointed," she said.

On a trip to New York City
    with a friend who knew a friend
    and on a whim,
she auditioned at Radio City Music Hall.
    "You're hired," the manager piped,
"for the two weeks the regular will be laid up."
    And Ruth danced
and her eyes danced now with the telling
    and I wondered how many other
    stories are tucked away
    with residents put to bed
    at 7:00 on a summer evening.

Kid's Day

Anne Whitlock

Below the bridge, on the calm blue-green water, yachts line up like school children, their white masts pointing to the sky. "We're kids today," I tell her. "Remember – we have to buy a toy, ride the merry-go-round, go to an old-fashioned candy store…"

"I got my complexion from my father," she says. "He was Greek."

The grandsons lift the bed and sofa onto the truck. Sonya chooses a few items from her mother's crowded closet.

We cruise the avenue, pass the Bay Books and the Island Surf. The questions begin. "Where are we? What's the name of this street? Where are we going? Today is Monday, isn't it?"

"No, Mary, it's Thursday." The warm spring day has filled the sidewalks with shorts and tee shirts and designer dogs. At the Candy Factory we enter a Willy Wonka world of peppermint sticks, red hots, jelly bellies, jaw breakers, M&M's. "We have to choose one," I remind her.

"I like Junior Mints," she says.

A quick selection of crossword puzzle books, family pictures, socks, shoes, and jewelry joins the furniture.

The well-fed pigeons at the landing drop down from their rock perches to bob for crumbs. We leave the tourist boutiques and head for the carousel by the bay. I help Mary onto a handsome stallion with brightly colored saddle and real straw tail. The music climbs as we spin around faster and faster and the horses bounce up and down, rearing their heads and showing their teeth. "Did you know these horses were carved by a Danish wood carver in 1895?" I ask her.

"I got my complexion from my father," she answers. "He was Greek."

As the sun climbs up over the ocean, the truck merges with morning traffic, carrying its cargo up the coast.

"Where are we going?" she asks, as we disembark.

"We're meeting Sylvia at the Italian restaurant."

"She doesn't have to come every day," Mary complains. "I can take care of myself."

"She's going to eat with us," I tell her. At the restaurant I guide Mary through the menu. Plates of ravioli and spaghetti arrive. I encourage her to order wine. Sylvia sits opposite me, her face as tragic as the heroine of a Verdi opera. She doesn't talk or eat. After the meal, I hand Mary over to Sylvia.

"Where are we going?" she asks.

"To get a prescription," Sylvia lies.

I leave for home.

Tonight the lights are out across the street. My telephone is quiet. I close my eyes – imagine Mary arriving at the Arbors. "Where am I? Who are these people? Aren't you taking me home?"

Reprieve

Judith O'Neill

I am certain my mother will know me – her oldest, the problem daughter of her young days, an only child for fifteen turbulent years when so often there was just her and me against the world.

Flying into a December Missouri out of a still-green Virginia, I find my mother in the therapy room. "She may not recognize you," my brother-in-law warns. "Sometimes she does, sometimes she doesn't." He and my sister have been with her through the stroke, the hospital, the surgery, and now the rehabilitation center. Decisions, decisions, they have had to deliver them all. They are exhausted and scared. I am new on the scene, until now consulted only by phone.

She is sitting in her wheelchair, a tray in front of her cluttered with objects a therapist on either side is trying to get her to hold or identify. She is dressed in slacks and a neat pink cotton shirt. She has a curly perm and a slightly bored look, as though she is determined to remain polite, even though the young ladies are telling her a story in which she has no interest.

Her left arm is in a sling to aid the dislocated shoulder suffered a week prior to the stroke. Her hands lie still on the tray, the left one hampered by the sling, the right one stiffened by the stroke. I pull a stool up to sit at eye level. She turns uninterested brown eyes to me and I say, "Hello, Lady, what are you doing in here?"

Startled recognition flows into her eyes and warmth floods her face. "Well, hello," she, who has not been forming understandable words, says. "When did you get in?"

"That's a reaction, that's a reaction!" the therapists squeal, and confide to us, "That's the first reaction we've seen. It's wonderful!"

My mother smiles at me. I take her hands and squeeze them, and she squeezes back as best she can. I explain to the therapists who I am, and they take their objects and move on. As they go, one says to me, "I needed to see that. It did me a world of good." I think, *me too.*

‿

My sister is just starting her own law practice after many years as a public defender. My brother-in-law has a graphics business. They have children still in school. They can now go back to work and come to visit in the
evenings.

I return every morning, but my mother is busy. I learn there is little rest
at a rehabilitation center. Mom and I settle into our own workable schedule.
I arrive at 10:30 or so to see if Mom is back from therapy or doctor visits.
While we wait for lunch to be ready, I wheel her down to the big glass doors
at the end of the hall to watch giant snowflakes fall, or sleet whip stark trees,
or massive black thunderclouds crowd each other across the sky. She is a
Kansas farm girl, always intent on the weather. Missouri shows off for us
every winter day.

We go out to the dining area, where she sits at a round white-clothed
table with others who need to be fed. These are casually known as the
"Feeders" among the waiters and waitresses. I resent that label, but one day
there is no room with the Feeders, and we sit at a table with three ladies quite
able to take care of themselves. They are friendly and include us in their
conversation as they lift their forks to their mouths, butter their rolls, and
cut their meat perfectly well.

Mom, a very independent woman of ninety-two, has a shoulder-to-
shoulder bib and a plate of soft food because swallowing can be problematic.
She opens her mouth for each bite, but then she looks off into the distance,
or gives her dexterous dining mates a baleful glance, or shoots me a sharp
one. She can't drink with a straw, so I have to toss her liquid into her mouth
and there is spillage.

The ladies are nice, but we can't wait to get back to the Feeders where we
are in familiar, limited-ability company. Our regulars are Sondra, a beautiful woman, not yet fifty, who must be reminded to pick up her fork again
after each bite; Marie, excited to be getting off a liquid diet, but far too shaky
to hold food even with a spoon; and courtly, ancient Mr. Benjamin, telling
us at every meal how lucky he feels to be sitting with so many good-looking
women. White-haired and twinkly-eyed, constantly apologizing for being a
bother, he always wears a suit jacket and cannot remember why he is here.

After lunch I ask Mom if she wants to go to the Ice Cream Parlor. She
nods. I wheel her up the long hall and around a corner. In the sunny room, a

grandmotherly woman in a striped uniform and a perky waitress hat jumps up from behind a gleaming counter to ask for our choice of cones.

Can any kid be luckier than to be born to a woman who can *make* ice cream? My mother could actually create it – either from the ice cream churn (usually reserved for company-coming dinners, but sometimes brought out for private celebrations), the refrigerator (a cooked concoction of milk, sugar, eggs, and salt poured into trays to freeze), or even snow. Yes, she made ice cream from clean, brushed-off snow! That one she had to be quick about, but it was ice cream when she got finished with it.

Mom liked the fancy kinds, like Butterbrickle or Peanut Butter Fudge. We had moved from St. Joseph, Missouri to Brooklyn, New York when I was six, and among many new and exciting places we discovered an ice cream shop only a block from our apartment. We learned quickly that there are more flavors of ice cream than vanilla, chocolate, and strawberry. What a delight that place had been!

And this one rises to the challenge. We take our cones to the center of the room by the atrium, where we can lick and nibble – me holding my pistachio in one hand, the other holding up her mint chocolate chip so she can bend her head for a bite. We watch the lovely birds in their enclosed floor-to-ceiling glass cage and smile at the resident cat's expression as he watches, too. The birds trill and warble for us and fly in fits of color from branch to perch and back again. More sedate than our remembered Brooklyn ice cream shop, this one offers a bright place to visit outside of her shared room.

Sometimes she tries to talk, but when only gibberish comes out she looks at me quizzically and shrugs, then shakes her head and sighs. I tell her, "You're doing good, Mom, every day, you're getting better." She leans forward, listening intently; her eyes fixed on my lips, but seemingly hears no word that makes sense.

Our days are not uneventful. Old, dear friends come to talk and sit, holding her hand. At last, she masters drinking from a straw once again, after days of exaggerated slurping by me, my sister, the therapists, and a little bright-eyed waitress from the main dining room who has taken a liking to my mother. She tells us, "Put the straw in the left side of her mouth, opposite the stroke side. She might be able to feel it better there."

She does.

〜

One day as we head up for ice cream, a group of people turn the far corner and charge down the hall toward us, bringing icy air and electric energy from the outside world with them. They carry huge white plastic bags stuffed full and, as they sweep past, one of the ladies sets a fuzzy tan teddy bear in my mother's lap and says "Merry Christmas, dear."

As startled as I am, my non-speaking mother stares after them, and then cuddles the bear against her with her one good arm and says three times, "How cute, so sweet, how cute, so sweet, how cute, so sweet." I burst into tears. They swoop on down the hall, delivering a teddy bear and greeting to every resident.

Another day, my sister comes to join us for lunch and ice cream. She sits down at the piano in the ice cream room, begins to play, and we sing. An audience starts to gather. She plays old hymns Mom had been raised on and has sung year after year in church choirs. My mother is the happiest I have seen her since the stroke. Her dark eyes shine. She nods her head to the beat and taps her good hand against the bear's tummy, keeping perfect time. The bear, in his little white, high-necked sweater with "I Am Loved" on the front, goes everywhere on her lap now. It is a good day; we are ebullient as we take her down to get ready for her long afternoon nap.

But soon, bad days begin to outnumber the good. She is unhappy with us, all of us. We cannot help her, nor even understand what she wants. She seems better, she can say "No." She can tell her helpers, "I like you," and the opposite. Her shoulder hurts. She doesn't want to be handled anymore. The bear is abandoned on the foot of her bed.

She is most angry with my sister and me. We are not fixing this. She stops smiling.

Our reprieve is over.

An Invitation to Lost Parents

Alison Shaw

Come…. Now…. Walk with me.
Slip each an arm in my arm.
Breathe…. Breathe deep the green heat
Of broom, blackthorn and wild rose.
Wander 'long the seawall path alone…with me.
Listen! Listen! The water laps the granite stones
Shhoowahh…. shhoowahh…. shhoowahhhh

See the sparrow flit, flutter, fthththt!
Amid the long grass,
Grasp the blade and slick the drop of dew,
Cock her head, alight anew.

Stand with me 'neath the sheltering tree.
Breathe the damp, cool musk of soil and leaf.
Feel the cool breath upon your skin.
Breathe…. Deep…. wildrose and musk.

Watch the gilded heron in the setting sun
Lean…. farther…. wait…. wait….
To catch the silvered spray, slick the silvered fin.

Walk with me. Now. For now, just with me.
Arm in my arm, see what I see.
Listen! Shhhhh.
Shhoowahh…. shhoowahh…. shhoowahhhh

Just in Time

Robert Pouriea

What is just in time?
Every thing is just in time.
Was I born too early?
Or was I born too late?
One thing for sure
I was born in time.

I was born just in time
I was born to learn hate
    the pain of the rod
    to work from day to night
    fear of the dark
    the unknown
    love from a dog and horse
    to see the great depression
    service during Korea and Vietman
    In those years was beauty
    comforting, waters saying
    "Go far out, let's see how you
    like the wind and violence."

All this was just in time.
Now I'm old
Just in time
We are given time
Time runs out
I ask
Just for more time.

Left Behind

Mary Margaret Baker

In our town, there are always things to do in your leisure time. You can go to concerts, sport games, movies, ballets, and plays. We have a huge conservatory filled with flowers, trees, and gardens. We have an aviary filled with beautiful birds. The Carnegie Museum was always a fun place to visit early in my childhood. I loved looking at the huge dinosaurs.

Every year the Carnegie Museum gives the Seniors a free day. They honor the Seniors with a fancy buffet. A hall is filled with round tables covered with tableclothes and decorated with pots of African violets. Mini sandwiches of egg salad and chicken salad are piled high on the buffet tables. You can choose from different cheeses and dips, and the museum provides delicious punch and cookies.

We Seniors arrived just as the buffet was being served. While we ate, a man and his two sons provided music with their guitars and a banjo. After the entertainment, we went on a tour of the museum with a guide.

The year before we were so late that there wasn't much food left. We have to rely on a transportation vehicle that picks up the elderly and the handicapped. The vehicles are equipped with a lift for people who can't walk up the van's steps. The van driver in the morning said he didn't know if we were going to be picked up later. Every year we don't know if we are going to be picked up at the front or back of the museum.

The day was over too soon. I made my way to the museum's front entrance. Then a Senior motioned me to go out the back door. I was then directed to go up to the front of the museum. I thought it would be quicker for me to walk up the hill with my Rollater – a walker with wheels and a seat if you need to take a rest. When I reached the front of the museum, to my dismay I had been left behind. I carefully navigated the wide steps in front of the museum and entered the building to call the transportation company. They told me they would be by to pick me up in an hour.

I walked up the steps carefully with my Rollater. Soon after, a transportation car vehicle came by. The driver must have thought the steps in back of me was a road. She drove down the steps while her lady passengers were bouncing up and down in their seats. Halfway down the steps the car stopped, and the lady in the back seat hollered over to me, asking if I was the person they were looking for. But the person they were looking for had a different name. When the driver tried to back up her car, the wheels just spun around. She then drove down the rest of the steps, her passengers bouncing. At the bottom of the steps, the driver turned the car around and was able to drive up the steps, again with bouncing passengers. To be sure, this group of people experiencing this rocky ride will always remember it. I wondered if any damage had been done to the bottom of the car.

I was sitting on my Rollater on a sidewalk and watching all the busy activity around me. A Greek Festival was going on accross the street. Appetizing aromas drifted by me, tempting my taste buds. How I wished to buy a Gyro, but I knew I had to remain where I was if I wanted a ride home.

Another hour went by without a ride home. Down the steps I went with my Rollater and into the building I went to call the transportation company. They told me they could not find me.

The safety inspector came over to me and asked who I was. I told him my name. He said my friend had called the museum, looking for me. A young woman at the museum asked me if I wanted some food or drink. I told her I would like a bottle of water.

The transportation company told me to wait by the main entrance of the museum, and they would be by to pick me up. I asked if this was the main entrance, and they said it was. As I left the building, I thankfully noticed a ramp. I don't know why I missed it the first time. It was a breeze getting back to my station to wait for my trip home.

As time went by, I thought I would have to spend the night in this part of town. I knew I could not ride home on the city bus, and I could not afford to take a taxi. Where could I go for help? Perhaps the church a couple of blocks away could help me. Time ticked by, and a steady traffic of transportation vehicles passed, but none came for me. The Museum head came out to talk to me. He said the museum was closing in five minutes, but said he would wait till the transportation company came to pick me up. He said he was going to walk down the avenue to see if the vehicle was parked there.

The vehicle was parked at another entrance. It's hard to understand why the drivers of the transportation vehicles didn't scout around for me, as I was so close. Finally, I was on my way home. The lady driver of the car was very friendly. She said the driver of the van created my whole problem, as he did not do a good job of looking for me.

I was exhausted from all that happened that day. I don't know if I will ever attend another Senior Day Celebration.

Turning 90

Barbara Scheiber

Another country.
When did
we cross?
No visible border
no visa required
no right of return.

Weather fickle
roads erratic
veering downward
without warning.

Memory tricks us
loses a thought
a key
hides nouns
scrambles for cover—
"whatcha-ma-call-it,"
"what's-his-name."

Time collapses,
now is all—
hand in hand with Death
looming
in fog.

I live in
air of minutes—
cardinal's flash
bud on vine
bite of wind
touch
of your tongue
and mine.

A Fierce Meadowlark

"Ah, grasshoppers
Death is a fierce meadowlark…"
—Robinson Jeffers

Una Nichols Hynum

It's always there, isn't it, this death
who's walked beside us all our lives,
keeping a low profile. Now here it is.
The doctor says inoperable cancer.
You could live a year, maybe five.

We sit, leaning into each other on the front
porch steps under that ancient evergreen
the possum calls home, remembering
how she'd come in the cat door and I'd say,
"But we don't have a white cat."

Your sister says a man has to father
a son and plant a tree before he dies.
You have two sons and the willow
is roof level and growing. It's time to tell
your friends, your family, and your dog.

So here we sit, in a landslide of memories,
the past strewn around us. Suddenly
we don't want to squander a minute
but don't know what to do with the hour.

DISPOSSESSED

Joan T. Doran

It was small miracle the shoot took root at all
so thin the soil, so thick the darkness
underneath the mighty trees whose crowns
ruled over all the world, trading inside tales
among the highest branches, basking in the favor of the sun.
Sometimes the mighty let sunlight fall through
to earth in mottled patches
that the pale shoot clutched and in that faint hope, lived.

It was small miracle the shoot could grow at all
in the shadow of the lichened rock where moss thrived
and insects chewed the toadstools nearabout
with scraps left for sparse sustenance.
And still somehow it grew its spindle stem
and in the spring put out six valiant leaves
that trembled when the rising spikes of morning sun
pierced through the canopy of crowns and stirred a breeze
that moved across the forest floor with gentle hand.

And when the top leaf of the tiny tree touched
the overshadowing rock, it did the only thing it could
and grew sidewise across a path into an airspace of its own
with two new branches, each with a fist of wizened leaves.
It yearned to stretch its limbs to light, to learn the language of the tall.
Instead, it shriveled in the summer heat, and too soon gave up
its withered leaves to earth as if it never lived.
Sometimes, for the dispossessed, in spite of yearning hope
sun's favor is too far away, and miracles too small.

SHERU'S PROGRESS

Tabinda Bashir

After about two years, my daughter Lisa and I came back from the U.S. to Pakistan for holiday. We had been asking about Sheru, whether he was still going to school, but got vague answers. His father, Faryad, was elusive and did not come to see my husband whenever he asked to see him. My husband, Hamid, had come to Pakistan earlier. Now that we were here, I knew Lisa would somehow get ahold of Sheru or Faryad and find out the facts.

Back in the U.S., we had been hearing from friends that Sheru dropped out of school because the teacher beat him.

Two years ago, when Lisa first saw him, Sheru was a filthy boy about six years of age. He was the son of our garbage collectors. When Lisa tried to tell him he should be in school, he got scared and ran away like a wild animal. She approached his parents to tell them the same, but they were quite clueless about what she meant. She visited where they lived and found a large community of garbage collectors living in shacks made out of scrap on a huge dump of rubbish and human and animal excreta. They merely existed, unaware of any finer aspects of life.

Lisa befriended Sheru by giving him a cup of milk daily. She talked extensively with his parents to impress upon them the virtues of education, something they just could not comprehend. They knew nothing about education; their main concern was the loss of an earning member of the family if Sheru went to school. They agreed reluctantly when she offered to pay for his education.

Sheru was admitted to a school near their shanty town. Lisa paid the dues. Sheru got books, a uniform – and shoes, which he had never worn all his life. He also had a difficult job to do. He had to take a bath daily before getting dressed to go to school.

After we left for the U.S. we were skeptical whether Faryad would really spend the money on Sheru's education. Now that we had returned, we were not convinced that Sheru dropped out just because the teacher beat him. Our old fears and doubts came up. We thought his family must have sold the books and the uniform and pocketed the money. Lisa asked his mother, Shireen, to bring Sheru the next day.

Sheru came. Lisa asked him what had happened. He said, "The teacher beat me so much. He nearly broke my bones."

"You must have done something wrong."

"No, I didn't. He beat the whole class. Nearly broke our bones. I did not go after that."

"Did you learn anything? Do you know A,B,C...?"

"Yes, but I will not go to school."

Then he recited the whole alphabet without any mistake. He said *kiaou* instead of Q, a typical Panjabi pronunciation. That was sweet. Teachers beating their students is common in Pakistan. Sometimes they beat the whole class, just because.

Shireen came the next day. She gave another reason for Sheru's absence from school for a whole year. The donkey, their most prized possession, had died. They could not use the cart to come and collect the garbage for many days. They had to take a loan to buy a new donkey and were still paying the interest. They also had another mishap. A wheel of their cart broke. Faryad had to walk to the workshop some fifteen kilometers away and back all in one night so they could go to work the next day.

Shireen had brought a sheaf of dirty papers in a dusty polythene bag. That was Sheru's class work. He had written the alphabet on lines, colored pictures within the outline, written the numbers within the squares, filled in the missing numbers and letters, did addition and subtraction in single digits. He had a star on most pages. He had even written his name – Sher Ali – in a shaky hand. Included was the Principal's report on school letterhead. He had graded him excellent on every subject.

Unbelievable! Sheru? Our garbage boy? It looked like the work of an average class I or II student. I wondered if someone had forged the papers so that Lisa could continue to pay for his school. So Sheru was summoned again. We asked him questions about his work and really grilled him. He came up with the correct answers. He did not seem to understand what all the fuss was about. He knew his work.

Lisa called the Principal and asked about Sher Ali. He said Sher Ali was a good student, but wondered why he stopped coming to school. So she decided to go herself to the school in Hanjerwal, Sheru's suburb, and find out the details. It is a private school that charges fees, not the free government school to which she'd had him admitted. The new school was nearer his house, and he could go there unassisted. For the previous school he had to get up much earlier to take a bath, and then be accompanied by an adult.

The Principal was courteous and remembered Sheru well. His admission fee, fee for Academy, uniform fee, books, and some other expenses were due because he had been absent for one whole year. He would have to be re-admitted if he wanted to continue. He would have to repeat KG I.

Lisa paid the dues, about Rs.4000/- ($40.00) and stressed to Sheru and his Dad that this time there should be no mishap. Faryad agreed and promised to send him to school daily. He also agreed to pay half the school fee, about Rs.400/- ($4.00) every month. Lisa wanted him to take some responsibility too.

So Sheru has started going to school again. Lisa keeps in touch with Faryad and Shireen, when they come on their daily rounds. She gets bits of information about their lives. Sheru is busy in school. He comes every Sunday with his family. They wash his uniform in the canal next to our house. The reason Faryad gave for this was that it was difficult to get water where they live. They buy drinking water in bottles for Rs,1000/- ($10.00) per month from the people who sell it from a tanker. Garbage collectors are kicked and pushed back because they are dirty and smelly. By the time their turn comes, there may not be any water left. The rent for their cottage is Rs.2500/- ($25.00) per month. Sheru's half of the school fee that Faryad has to pay is Rs.400/- ($4.00) per month. Faryad's monthly income, meanwhile, is around Rs.6500/- ($65.00) per month.

A few days ago we had torrential rains with a huge windstorm. Faryad's cottage made of polythene and cardboard was damaged. The land flooded and the garbage on which the cottage stood turned to slush and became impossible to pass through. They had to beg the landowners for a new place and built a new shack. They have to pay Rs3000/- ($30.00) per month for the "plot of land." That place is worse, surrounded by muck, and it smells worse.

Faryad sounded hopeless and made a remarkable comment. He said, "We have nowhere to go, nobody to ask. We thought we were born just to be kicked around, and so we are. There is no way out for us." This from a man who had seemed content and resigned to his existence before Lisa began telling him about the merits of Sheru's education. Had she touched a sensitive nerve that he was unaware of? He had begun to question why some people are better off than others.

A couple of weeks passed, and I asked Sheru to come and bring his work. His workbooks were not very clean, with some pages turned on the corners, but by and large they were in better condition than the papers his mother had brought. His writing was much cleaner with a firm hand. In mathematics he was into tables. He could tell me six times two is twelve. He was doing addition and subtraction in double digits. In English he was doing simple questions and answers and fill in the blanks. His last homework was about vowels, which he had done wrong. That would be taken care of in the Academy after school, where they get help with homework. This was all so good that I wondered again if the teachers were doing the students' work. But he answered all my questions correctly. He really is a brilliant child, a diamond in a heap of rubbish.

Sheru also brought his Urdu books. They started Urdu late in school. He finds it more difficult because in making words, the Urdu alphabet gets shortened and has to be joined together. It is ironic that, in a country with Urdu as its official language, private schools do not give it its due importance. I suspect that help from the International NGOs and our collective westward gaze has something to do with it. Anything white and English is better.

Sheru has broken all the myths. Myths about clean living, healthy and balanced diet, regular hours of sleep and play, discipline by the parents, good, clean neighborhood, etc. Children like him eat just one *roti* (flat bread) with water in a day. After that they eat anything they find in the garbage. I wonder how many more gems there are in that dump where Sheru came from.

The garbage collectors are born free, live free, and die free. They are at the lowest rung of society, so they cannot fall any lower and do not have any standards to rise up to. There are no goals set for them. They have no hangups, no inhibitions, no ambitions, and are as natural and innocent as the day they were born. That probably brings out their hidden talents to good advantage when the conditions are right.

At the end of their workday I have seen Sheru's siblings happily sort out the garbage on their donkey cart. The eldest, usually six or seven years old, takes the lead. She directs the younger ones to put different items in different pouches, and they follow. Toddlers take part in it too and play in the garbage still on the ground. The parents are elsewhere, collecting.

Faryad smiles more often now. He is encouraged by the school report and Lisa's support. He says with wry humor and a bit of pride that Sheru likes to wear clean clothes now, likes to sit in a chair, finds the garbage smelly. Then he adds wistfully, "When I was Sheru's age, I never knew school existed. We did not know there was more to life than our miserable existence. We only knew we were born to be shoved around. We actually believed we were the scum of the earth."

And I wondered again. Are we doing the right thing? Are we driving Sheru away from his own people? Supposing he does continue to study and gets some technical diploma. Will he be able to fit into a society that shuns the likes of him? His past will follow him. On top of that, he will be exposed to the TV and other influences of our society. I pray he does not get into drugs.

One day, as Lisa stood talking to Sheru, she saw Faryad hanging back in the shadows. He looked worried. She called to him and asked if all was well. He said they had had a mishap in the family. Sheru's mother, Shireen, was expecting and the baby died in her abdomen. It was night time, and she was in agony. They did not know what to do. No taxi would go to their area. Ultimately, they put her in the donkey cart and slowly took her to the nearest hospital, which was a private hospital. At first, the staff refused to attend to them because they were dirty. Then, seeing her condition worsen, they agreed to treat her for Rs.25000/- ($250.00). Faryad had to borrow the money from the money lender at a heavy interest rate.

Shireen lost the baby and after a week she was back at work. She is a strong-willed woman. She realizes the good work Lisa is doing. Faryad is a bit slow-witted and laid back.

Lisa called the school Principal the next day and, just as she expected, Faryad had not paid his half of Sheru's fee for that month. Lisa paid her half but made sure that Faryad would pay the rest. She never misses any chance to stress that she is not helping Sheru out of charity. This is a novel approach for us in the East. We usually just help.

Wonderful news. Shan Ali and Waris Ali – Sheru's cousins – have started going to the school. Sheru's aunt wants her children to be educated also. It means that those people understand something is good when they see it. And they can somehow bring up the money for it. They are not just some wretched beggars, as others believe. Up until now they were oblivious of the fact that a vast world lay beyond their hamlet; that they were human.

The latest is that Sheru's brother, Maher Ali, has also started going to school. He cried so much to join the other boys that his family took him there. He is too young to be admitted even in the KG, but the school has allowed him to sit in. But he still has to pay the fees. Faryad worries about the expenses.

The saga continues…let us see what the future holds.

A revelation! Sheru is married!! What can you say? He gives us one surprise after the other.

Lisa and I were hanging around outside the kitchen. It was time for the garbage to be picked up. We saw two young girls about twelve or thirteen turn from the corner of the garage. Like all Pakistani girls, they were whispering and giggling among themselves.

We called them and asked who they were. One of them pointed to the other and said, "She is Sheru's wife, and I am his aunt." And they started giggling again. We were dumbstruck. Then Lisa asked, "Really?" repeatedly. Every time the answer was a yes.

"When was he married?" I asked.

"About two years ago."

"How did it come about?"

The aunt started telling us in broken sentences. She did not know how to put it. From what we understood – after questioning them for about an hour – Faryad's elder brother, Shahzad, has five daughters. Not finding a suitable match, he married his elder daughter to another clan. That raised a lot of objections, especially from Sheru's grandmother, Kalsoom. She wanted to keep her lineage. A fleeting thought crossed my mind: garbage collectors and lineage? Tells you a lot about the human race. Kalsoom's other argument was that when you marry a girl, you give her away, and she becomes the property of her in-laws. If she falls into any trouble or is kicked out, her own clan will not help her, and she will have nowhere to go.

Shahzad wanted to marry his other daughter, Tana, outside the clan too, because there was no one available for her in their family. Others tried to dissuade him from doing so. The arguments grew serious and loud. Some blows were exchanged. Ultimately, Faryad said he was ready to marry Tana with Sheru, if that was acceptable, but the girl should not leave the clan. Everyone agreed, and that is how they got married.

What a disconnect! We are so involved in our own happenings that we know nothing about them. Just as Faryad had said, after seeing Sheru's progress, that he did not know another world existed outside their slums.

I was not certain of the truth of what they said, so I started asking questions. They had never been subjected to such a probing, and did not know how well to describe what happened. It took a lot of back and forth before I could sift the correct information.

I asked if any *Nikah* (religious ceremony) had taken place. They said yes. The way they described it sounded correct. Both the bride and groom dressed in fine clothes. There were sweets and flowers and garlands. The families gathered. The *Imam* (prayer leader) of the mosque performed the *nikah* and had the bride and groom sign the forms. Sheru and Tana and the witnesses put thumb impressions on the *nikah* forms.

Sheru is around ten or twelve years old – we can never be sure of their ages – and Tana is a couple of years older. They are minors and cannot officially be married. People usually get around this problem by putting a note on the *nikah* forms that the girl will go to the groom's house at puberty.

A few days later, Lisa got a phone call from the school Principal. He wanted her to come and collect Sheru and Maher Ali's 1st term results and see where her money was going.

Sheru is in KG II and Maher in the Play Group in Sultan Public School, Hanjerwal, a suburb near where they live. Hanjerwal is about 15km from our house. Lisa, Umar (our cook) and I set off in our car the next day. Sheru and Faryad were to meet us near the school. The roads grew narrower as we proceeded. The traffic changed from semis, trucks, and cars to motor rickshaws, smaller cars, donkey carts, and oxcarts. Crossing each other either way became more and more tricky. Shops became smaller – carrying cheaper versions of things you would find in any mall – with many added shacks occupying portions of the road. Fruit and vegetable carts parked anywhere they fancied. We city people enjoyed it as a one-time adventure because we had an experienced driver. The locals did not seem to mind it either. They were relaxed and hardly cared for any missed time or loss of business. Time itself travelled at their speed. By the time we reached the school (after about an hour), the roads were unpaved. Needless to say, the whole journey was littered with rubbish, which increased as we went.

Sultan Public School is located in the LDA (Lahore Development Authority) housing society for the low income group. The school is probably housed in one of the quarters.

We entered the metal gate and were directed to the principal's office to the side by a smiling girl, who was rushing to her class. Right in front was a large foyer where many students – boys and girls – sat with their heads covered, reciting the Quran.

The principal, Mr. Altaf, bespectacled and with his hair disheveled under his skull cap, looked like the typical dedicated teacher. He sat behind his desk near the opposite wall. A settee was placed on the right, where Lisa and I sat. Umar and Faryad sat on a bench next to the near wall. Sheru stood near the principal's table. A couple of female teachers or helpers sat at two desks. They all received us cordially. Their smiles were infectious.

Mr. Altaf greeted us and looked proud of his students, Sher Ali and Maher Ali. He presented their reports for the 1st term exams of KGII and Pre KG. Sheru stood first with 96% marks and got an excellent report. His writing, numbers, matching of capital and small letters, simple arithmetic, simple sentences were perfect. His Urdu had improved. He could write simple words by joining alphabet. In Islamic studies he did quite well.

We knew that Sheru's report would be good, but still, sensing our surprise, Mr. Altaf asked Sheru to write a couple of sentences, asked him some small prayers and the table of two, which he knew quite well.

Maher Ali was not present, but had done just as well with 86% marks and stood second.

I don't know why, but I found it too good to be true. I didn't know how to pinpoint where the trick was. With the constant political turmoil and the conspiracy theories created after 9/11 – and the public's unrest as a result – we Pakistanis have probably forgotten how to take things at face value.

I asked Mr. Altaf about the Quran recitation going on in the hall. He said a teacher's mother had passed away, and they were praying for her salvation. That was a noble gesture. A good basis for character building.

With the niceties over, the question of payments came up. The fee for the last and the present months was due. Lisa had paid her half already. Faryad said he had also paid his share. He could not produce the fee card because that was with his wife, Shireen, who was not present. This was because Faryad beat her that morning for not getting the boys ready for school in time. She objected, saying she had to go to work with the others too and got no help from him. As a result, she walked off to her mother's house. Faryad was embarrassed by our looks of disapproval. Anyway, he promised to pay his share soon. Lisa paid what was due for her for the next term.

Next, we decided to go to Sheru's house to congratulate the family. We stepped out of the school into the sizzling June heat of about 115F, with not a cloud in the sky. The car could not go any farther. The driver had parked it under a lone tree in front of a house.

We started walking on the narrow road littered with rubbish: plastic bags, bottles, cans, etc. A few papers flew around as if looking for a clean place to rest. As we proceeded, the rubbish increased and took on a blackish slimy look. Pretty soon the heaps closed in and were much higher. A small child could have easily drowned or suffocated there. The smell was putrid, and we covered our noses. We walked in single file on a narrow strip of dirt road still visible in the middle.

On the way we saw some small shops selling cheap sweets, plastic toys, and knick-knacks. The shopkeepers smiled and waved at us as if everything were normal. Small children wearing just a top that had probably never been washed ran around barefoot, completely disregarding shards of glass in the rubbish.

After a few turns, we reached Sheru's place. The distance this time from the parked car was much shorter than what Lisa remembered from her last visit. The settlement had obviously grown. We were greeted with smiles and salaams by some thirty members of the family – adults and minors – who had not gone to work that day.

Their abode was a row of shacks on two adjoining sides of a roughly square area, the roofs supported on rickety wooden poles and without any separating partitions. A fireplace to cook and a few utensils lay in the open space. They had swept the whole area, put clean sheets on the randomly placed *manjis* (cots) – all the furniture they had – and there was no smell! The grownups had clean clothes on. They insisted we sit on a *manji* to rest awhile and asked if we would like to have some Coca Cola or Seven-up. We politely refused. I was touched by their hospitality. They have surely learnt something from Sheru's school's proximity.

We sat on a *manji* and chatted with them. Numerous members of the family were introduced. Sheru's mother was not there. She was at her mother's because of the fight she had with Faryad.

Lisa gave Rs.500/- ($5.00) to Faryad to buy sweets for the family, and there was a loud hurrah! She took a few pictures on her iphone. Then we departed among cheers, salaams, and God bless.

We are still here, in Pakistan. I wait to see what more surprises lurk there...

Author's Note: "Sheru Goes to School" was published in OASIS Journal 2012. *The essay dealt in detail with Lisa's efforts to "tame" Sheru – wild as he was – and to convince his parents to send him to school. "Sheru's Progress" is a casual follow-up.*

Tempus Fugit

June Weible

The young mind blossoms with fresh
Ideas which search for expression

Like a composer who fills a score with music
And will not rest until it's fulfilled.

I have only this tiny sliver of time
To use for recording my memories.

My perception is uniquely mine and
Should be explained as only I can.

Life's minutia gets in the way and slows
The creation of the gift I so want to give.

There is fear of losing my ability to recall
Spectacular moments that should be shared.

Time is ungracious and not on my side.
Still I pursue a goal of leaving my legacy.

Change Your Name and Change Your Fortune

Yasue Aoki Kidd

When I was twelve, my father said to me he was told by three different name analysts that unless we changed my name, I would not live beyond twenty.

My family was living in a small town in the western end of Honshu Island in Japan. My father was a policeman, second in command, in this town known for its natural port and hot springs.

In the late 1950's in a sleepy little fishing town, the police were not particularly busy chasing criminals every day. It was the good-old-days, when people's lives were less hectic and high profile crime ocurred sporadically, if at all. Local folks, or people traveling through town, used to stop by the police station to chat. So it did not seem strange that several men who dabbled in the art of palmistry or the ancient art of name analysis stopped by. They perhaps found an eager listener in my father. He told me they did not come together, but arrived separately. Since all three of them said the same thing about my name at different times, it naturally piqued my father's interest. Maybe it even alarmed him.

Japanese names are comprised of Chinese characters. Each character has a number of strokes. In name analysis, it is believed that the combination of strokes determines whether or not your name is lucky.

My father said, "We picked out a different name for you when you were born, but the old neighborhood intellect, who dabbled in name analysis, told us it was not a good name to go with the last name, and he helped me pick out your name, Yasue. Since you were born in Yasugi, we took the same Yasu for your name. I guess he was not very accurate after all."

My stepmother, Kazuko-san, dismissed the remarks by saying, "Your surname Aoki (Green Tree) and your given name, Yasue (Peaceful Branch), go together perfectly well. I would not bother changing it. It is silly to believe in such a thing. Leave it alone."

What would you do if you were told, when you were only twelve, that unless you changed your name you would not live beyond twenty? What

would Japanese parents do in such a situation? As a child, I never contracted a serious illness, but I tended to catch cold faster than anyone, and the
Perfect Attendance Award remained elusive.

The strange thing was, as a twelve-year-old, I was a bit obsessed with
my longevity, even before the name change issue came up. One day I said,
"I don't want to die young." This surprised my parents. I was already thinking of ways to stay healthy, to beat the odds of dying young. I started to rise
early and went to bed early, and I became more diligent about praying at my
mother's home altar in the morning. I thought maybe my mother would
listen to me and protect me from the spirit world. I don't remember why, all
of a sudden at that age, I started to fear death. I wonder if my mother's death
at a young age and my father's recent hospitalization with a serious illness
prompted me to consider my own mortality.

It was then that my father came to me with the idea of changing my
name, as if someone had stepped in to ease my worries about death. Since I
was already mindful of my mortality, changing my name to extend my life
was a no-brainer for me. I had nothing to lose.

We decided to change the two Chinese characters that spelled my name,
Yasue. With the new ones my name still remained Yasue – the same pronunciation but with different Chinese characters. (My old Yasue had fourteen
strokes, while my new one had twenty-one strokes.)

The moment I saw the two Chinese characters that the three men rec-
ommended to spell Yasue, I liked them. My original Yasue meant *Peaceful
Branch*, but the new Yasue meant *Full of Health*. How exciting, I thought!
I felt healthier already. No way would I die young with this strong name. I
was so excited that I gleefully pasted my new name over the old one on every
notebook.

The most incredible thing was that I felt a surge of power from the core of
my being after my name was changed to the two new characters. I had been
a rather serious child up to that point. I appreciated other children's humorous behavior, but I would not be the one to start it. Now I had this incredible
feeling of happiness that seemed to bubble up from somewhere deep inside
of me. I noticed that my personality became sunnier, and I laughed more
easily. I was able to see more of the positive side of things, rather than the
dark or serious side. There is a saying that "birds of a feather flock together."
Well, it is true. I started to attract people who were equally sunny in their
disposition, and positive things began to happen around me.

Shortly after my name change, my father was transferred to a new town, but I easily made new friends and adjusted to my new school with delight. Teachers told my parents that I was a well-adjusted child with a sunny personality.

My father noticed this change in me, too. He would happily mention, "Yacchan, your cheeks have nice color, and you look very healthy. You smile a lot, too, these days. Maybe the changing of your name was good for you."

We would both laugh, thinking maybe it had something to do with it. Just a power of suggestion? Perhaps so, but every time I write my name with those two new Chinese characters, I think back to when I became more optimistic and good things started to gather around me.

To this day, many Japanese parents pick their child's name after consulting a name specialist, just in case. In Japan, it is not hard to find singers, actors, businessmen, or ordinary folks who claim that their luck changed for the better after they changed their names.

I am definitely glad those three men visited my father at three different times with the same message, and that we took them up on their suggestion. It could all be coincidental, but I can say with gratitude that I have lived a happy life beyond my twenty years many times over. Life takes many mysterious turns when you least expect it. Believe it or not!

MIRACLES

Sherry Stoneback

Miracles: I read the Bible,
Hear the preacher say,
Daniel and the Lions, Part the Red Sea.
Blind who see,
Lame who walk.

What are miracles today?
See 'em every day,
Television and Internet.

Are miracles different for each?
Beliefs, experiences unique,
Could be.

When only faith was left,
What I needed was given to me,
She didn't know my needs.

Someone develops faith
Where there was none,
Life-changing experience.

Stories that gave me faith,
Comments, gifts, filled my heart with love,
Not what I was praying for at all.

Old and sick,
Need to be touched and heard,
Surprised when provided,
Cry when comfort comes.

Does the giver notice,
Recognize the blessing?

Is it a miracle when,
30-year-old prayers come to fruition,
They grew to understand,
Dropped their resistance?

Maybe the miracle comes when we finally take no for an answer.

It may be a miracle that we believe in miracles at all.

Now Is a Good Time To Be Crazy

Una Nichols Hynum

Everyone goes down the street
talking to themselves, waving
their arms, in deep conversation
with a shiny black beetle in their ear.
No one will notice you singing, preaching
to the air, grass, and concrete.
You can recite poetry to store windows.
No one cares. Carry a broken umbrella,
do a dance step or two. You can get away
with anything. Everyone wears
that vacant-lot look, so go ahead,
turn your imaginary apron into a basket
and gather your imaginary pears.

THE FIND

Gered Beeby

"That's a mile away. How can you hear or see anything?"

Sylvia's hushed inquiry lingered in the night air. The Montana desert held any number of secrets. Their objective in the distance promised even more.

"Told you before, lady," Borden began quietly. "Gear like this and my services both come at a price. Let me handle the details."

Sylvia knew there would be issues. Her news agency had assured her of that. She also knew the challenges of dealing with her long-time girlfriend, who waited silently several steps away in the darkness.

"Look, Mr. Borden, you said you could get me and my associate into that place." Sylvia kept her voice low.

"And I also said I would get both you ladies safely back. But whatever your friend's talents may be, rock climbing is not one of them." Borden adjusted his night-vision scope. He peered from their slightly elevated vantage point. "Fairly open country from here. No moon, but we need to watch our cover. Also, you can drop the Mister. Just call me Hal. And by the way, is that your friend's real name? Etheria?"

Sylvia nudged a bit closer. "Originally, she was Brenda. But her parents were, and still are, genuine flower children. They renamed her when she was young. Their early glimpses of her abilities convinced them."

"So she reads palms for a living? She's a psychic?" Borden also spoke in muted tones.

"More specifically, an Empath," Sylvia all but whispered. "She feels. Her powers are strongest with people. But she can function with animals and inanimate objects, as well. And yes, she makes a living at it. Has a large…a very large and loyal following."

"Okay, okay…so far." Borden flicked a bug away from his scope. "But somehow she's not able to work her magic from far away."

"Her skills, not magic, work best at close range. Yes, touching. But she has some capability at a distance. Hence, all the more reason for you to get us there. Soon." Sylvia adjusted her night vision goggles.

Borden checked his new communicator. "My contact assures me this is prime time. He's seen the Feds come and go, always by chopper. Probably from the airbase at Great Falls. All this, and they're still trying to keep a lid on it."

"This is a remote paleontology dig. The point becomes...why so secret?"

"Maybe we'll all find out." Borden rechecked his communicator, then stopped.

Silent as a shadow, Etheria reached his side, then touched his arm. "About eight meters ahead, under that bush, you may notice a sizable rattlesnake, Mr. Borden." Her voice trailed away and dissipated into the darkness.

Borden recalled again that first meeting, when Sylvia had introduced them. Tall, nearly as tall as he was, blond and thin, Etheria presented small, pixie-like features to the world. Her tones matched the image of one who sees much and appreciates even more. He quickly aimed his goggles and exhaled. Coiled and still, the reptile seemed alert, but not yet alarmed. Borden slowly shook his head. "That's one big mother snake."

"You are correct, Mr. Borden." Etheria stepped one pace back. "She is gravid and seeks a safe place to berth her young. She also needs nourishment."

Sylvia joined the brief vigil with her night-vision glasses. "So she's just making a living like the rest of us. I've known you too long, Etheria, to ask how you knew all that."

"Let's move on." Borden kept an eye on the bush and led his small party around the snake at a safe distance.

Lighting at the cordon was widely distributed, but subdued. Camouflage netting draped the entire area, which was about the size of a city block and positioned near a low hill. The woven-wire fencing was mostly clear, but similarly draped in a few places.

Borden exchanged signals with his contact. The trio moved toward an entrance gate with its temporary kiosk. An armed man in military-style overalls approached from inside. "Sam the Man, is this a good time?" Borden greeted his fellow conspirator.

The Man unlocked the gate, rolled it open. "Yeah, but my relief's due in less than an hour. And sometimes he's early."

Quietly, Borden addressed the two women. "If you will stand over by that shed, I need a few words with Sam."

Sylvia took Etheria in tow. For some time her non-flash mini-camera had been collecting images. Neither woman said a word.

"Look, Hal, I gotta stay close to the gate. All us security guys got chip implants done. We get too close to that entrance and some alarm goes off. Only reason I agreed was the pay was so good."

"How safe is it?"

"It's fine. Don't think anybody believes that radon gas story. But look… things may get really unsafe if anybody gets caught." Sam looked around. "Remember, you promised me stuff. And you know the risk I'm taking."

"Once again, you say there are no cameras?"

"Not far as I can tell. My guess is they want no record of those big wigs that come through. Overheard one of them saying, 'Profound implications.' So tell me what's profound about old bones, and we'll both know."

"We'll be fast." Borden turned to join his charges, but was restrained by Sam. "One more thing…who's the tall Tinkerbell?"

Borden delayed a moment, then said, "Someone we need to listen to."

He rejoined the women. When the three reached the enclosed metal building near the hillside, Borden instinctively glanced about before entering. The enclosure was complete with a metal roof big enough to cover a one-story house. Interior curtains formed a light-restricting mouse maze.

They reached the excavation. Well lit, the ancient remains lay partially exposed. Without a word, Sylvia clambered into the shallow pit and began taking photos from multiple angles. Etheria held back. The find lay perfectly straight. Its bones were perfectly intact. Pygmy-sized, its vacant eye sockets stared forever upward. Sharp teeth suggested a carnivorous diet, but the flattened jaw line indicated not a snout, but a face. One upper limb was mostly uncovered. Between the shoulder and elbow, encircling the bone and still lodged in rock, was metal.

"Copper alloy." Borden had joined Sylvia and pointed to the armlet. "And observe, shall I say, the hand. It has three digits, but with a clearly opposable thumb. And check out this." Borden traced his fingers along a straight edge of fossilized wood: primitive milled lumber. At a top corner near the skull, a reinforcing strap and nail-like fasteners were similarly fabricated.

"Like a crib." Sylvia stopped her photography. "With stereoscopic vision and functioning hands, clearly this creature could manipulate its environment. So this lonely little planet of ours supported Bronze Age intelligence tens of millions of years before we came along."

"One smart lizard." Borden cleared his throat. "This equals 'profound implications.' But the obvious question is...how come they aren't still here?"

Sylvia turned to her friend, who had yet to enter the pit. "Etheria, we would welcome your insight. Right now, please."

Throughout their investigation, Etheria had scarcely moved. Her inspection had been intense, yet silent. With measured precision, she descended, then stopped. "I'm frightened." With no further hesitation Etheria approached the remains. Firmly, at first rigid, then trembling, Etheria's fingers enveloped the non-human cranium. Alternately pressing, then releasing, her fingertips worked to absorb unknown truth. Further and further into the ancient aura she probed until, facing the roof, she released her grip. Her body relaxed, then began to slump.

Both Sylvia and Borden stopped her fall.

"We must get her out of here!" Sylvia whispered sharply.

Quickly, Borden gathered Etheria into a fireman's carry, "I'm not waiting."

Eventually, they found a stopping point far enough away. Slumped over Borden's shoulders, Etheria had not stirred. He laid her on soft sand. "Smelling salts are not part of my outfit," he said. He wet a cloth from his canteen, but before he could use it, Etheria stopped his hand.

"You are kind, Mr. Borden...both of you...but my processing is complete." She sat up, helped by Sylvia.

"I see you were overwhelmed, but what happened?" Sylvia found her cassette recorder.

Etheria forced composure. "Fleeting images, so many images and fears. Speculation clouds everything. Of a civilization grown to engulf the entire world. Of advances only now being realized in our own. Of unending conflict. Of devastation so complete that mass extinctions became commonplace." She paused. "But eventually a shimmer of hope. And compassion. A limited few at first, then more, then eventually all perceived the truth. They must leave. And remove all traces of themselves, if possible. Then take their destructive natures with them. All to preserve the Eden they had nearly obliterated."

Sylvia exchanged somber looks with Borden. "Etheria, suppose all this is true, and these creatures had the means of evacuating…to somewhere. What then? Would they someday want their Eden back?"

No one could answer.

One by one, they lifted their eyes to the endless stars.

MUSEUM OF WIND[1]

Neal Wilgus

Welcome to the 599th anniversary
of the Lunar Hall of History,
here in Celestial Dome.
Above us we see the orb
once known as Mommer Arth,
from which we evolved long ago,
before the great winds blew
and forced our kind to move here
where we flourish today.

You may ask: what makes wind go?
There is much speculation on this
and you may go to the records
to explore for yourself.
Most Lunic scientists believe
it is a combination of Arth forces,
including gravity, magnetic fields
and orbital rotation
that causes great air masses
to move in harsh, unpredictable ways.
Be glad we live in a place
that has no such
forces to contend with.

Now we turn to the mystery
of why Arth wind has sound.
Our most recent probes have shown
that there is a correlation
between the force of wind
and the sound levels recorded.
Many theories seek to answer
this intriguing question,
including the idea that
temperature differences
at various levels
generate the vibrations

that produce the humming of the wind.
Another theory is that solar flares
bombard the windy Arth
with particle storms
that are recorded as sound
on our instruments.

There is nothing to support the idea
that wind sounds are
the wailing and cries
of our ancestors' ghosts
who were left behind
when we moved to our new home.
Such primitive superstition
should be avoided at all costs
because it is our duty to
pursue Truth wherever
it may lead.

We hope you've found this
museum visit fun and informative.
And now, may the wind be with you.

---

[1] Credit: Data Dump Awards Winner for SF poems in Britain 2014. Reprinted from DATA DUMP No. 208, June 2015. Steve Sneyd, Publisher, Hilltop Press, 4 Nowell Place, Almondbury, Huddersfield, HD5 8PB, United Kingdom.

A Goodbye Letter

Vivian Bullock

Dear John,
    Do you remember our last walk?
You know, the day we didn't talk,
    The day you failed to see 'old Ben,'
Our pal, our old friend,
    And the red car, missed me just an inch,
You didn't see it, didn't even flinch.

Did I fail to mention
    What had your complete attention?
That little box you held to your ear,
    I know you think it very dear;
Hold it tight, as closely as you can
    And it will, perhaps, replace my hand.

                        Bye,
                        Mandy

FRUSTRATIONS

Mo Weathers

Frustrations come in all sizes and shapes, but there are few things more frustrating than a car with an undiagnosed – or undiagnosable – problem. There's a good reason why Volkswagens are called "Hitler's Revenge." Our Volkswagen Jetta has an electrical problem that keeps running the battery down, and the car won't start. After replacing two alternators, two batteries, and making several trips to a repair shop, the battery still runs down for no apparent reason. It's okay on a long trip – short trips around town seem to cause the problem, especially in the summer with the air conditioner on. It's been going on for a couple of years now, and I'm no closer to a solution than I was when the problem started. Last month I spent six hundred dollars replacing the alternator – again – and yesterday the battery was dead – again. However, there is reason for hope; I think I've finally found a solution to the problem. Next spring we're trading the old car in on a new one.

Not so easy to fix is a frustrating problem – a characteristic, really – with a bright yellow quarter-zip polyester pullover that our daughter got me for Christmas last year. I can eat a meal or wear the pullover, but I can't seem do both at the same time. It's a great pullover and I love it, but every time I wear it to a meal I drop food onto it. Being yellow, it's really easy to see spaghetti sauce spots – or anything else – down the front of it. Spotting with a bit of soap and water only makes it worse. The food will come off but the water spots won't, and into the wash it goes. Again. It's in the wash as I write this.

There was one time between washings that I ate two separate meals while wearing it, without spilling or dropping anything onto it, and that's a record that still stands.

Getting lost is another frustration, especially for a Yank in England. Driving in England is quite different from driving in the United States. The roads are narrow and wind through all manner of small towns with names like Lower Slaughter, Bourton-on-the-Water, Morton-in-the-Marsh,

Shipton-under-Wychwood, Cookham Dean, Cookham Rise, Cookham Station, and just plain Cookham. And there are at least five different ways of getting from one to the other. So, in theory, it should be hard to get lost… in theory. In fact, it's quite easy to get lost. All you have to do is make one wrong turn, and the farther you go the more lost you get. You can't try to find a different route – you're liable to end up in the next county. The only way you can get un-lost is to turn around, go back to where you made the wrong turn, make the correct turn, and carry on from there. That is, if you can still find the place where you made the wrong turn. At least, that's the way it worked for me. And if you miss a turn and have to make a U-turn in the middle of a busy London street to get back on track – like I did – just try not to get caught. Or to get hit by a truck.

Technology can be a major frustration. Sometimes it sucks. Not all the time, but enough to be a headache. And at the most inconvenient times. Take the following hypothetical story (which is an amalgam of several true incidents):

We're driving through Lassen Volcanic National Park when we come upon a doe and her fawn grazing beside the road. I stop the car, grab my camera, ease out of the car and creep up a little closer. I frame the picture and get ready to shoot…and the camera battery is dead. As I head back to the car to change the batteries, mumbling mild obscenities with every step, both deer suddenly turn around and bound off into the trees. Rats! Back in the car I grumble as I change the camera's batteries. Then I try to start the car to resume our sightseeing trip…try to start the car…try to start… It won't start. I haul out my cell phone and try to call AAA…and try again. There's no signal. So I walk up and down the road looking for a signal. I finally find a weak one and I'm barely able to call AAA – just barely. About an hour later, the AAA truck is leaving and the car is running again. We're off.

That evening in our motel room I set up our laptop to send an e-mail to tell our kids about our day. The motel's Wi-Fi network is down. So we pack up the laptop and head to the nearest Starbucks. Feeling guilty about using their free Wi-Fi – for free – we buy a couple of drinks, then a couple of pastries and a gift card. Thirty-eight dollars for free Wi-Fi. As I'm in the middle of composing my e-mail, the computer crashes. I start over again, trying to remember what I said the first time. I finally manage to send the e-mail, then I decide to check my alternate e-mail address for any new messages. I've forgotten the password. And so ends another day of enriched living through the miracle of modern technology.

The next morning the alarm on our fancy electronic clock radio fails to go off. It was set for 7:00 p.m. instead of 7:00 a.m.

I've enjoyed just about as much technology as I can stand. Just stop the world and let me off.

Never Enough

Nancy Sandweiss

It's futile to bemoan time's passage. Rushing forward, it shrinks
all possibility heedless of our wishes; leaves us grasping at air.
There's always more to read, to see, to learn – never time for enough.

My grandson hasn't learned yet. On the carousel he pleads *again, again*
before his stallion even stops; cries for more no matter how many times
he sweeps the dizzying circle.

I could devour experience and never be sated, each moment another prologue,
new questions. Will my children stay happy, my grandsons love wisely?
Will peace ever come? Is there life beyond the stars?

Enough would be to know what happens next.

ENOUGH

Celia Glasgow

She could never do enough,
Be enough,
Have enough.
But then over time she learned:
That "now" is enough—
That "here" is enough—
That she is enough!

An Elephant Advocacy

Linda Klein

Elias appeared before a panel of five human judges
appointed to decide whether or not to take action.
As he entered the chamber, they endeavored to suppress elbowing nudges.
There were four men and one woman, each from various factions.

The chairman motioned Elias forward. Huge and ungainly his body seemed,
and yet he had a gentle kind of elegance.
The proud pachyderm, it had been deemed,
would represent all of nature's elephants.

Elias moved closer, humbly bowed his enormous head
and twirled his agile trunk,
eliciting a chorus of gasps, which finally led
the chairman to put down his gavel with a clunk.

The elephant began, "Sirs and Madam, I speak on behalf of all elephants,
both African and Asian alike.
I plead for your consideration of our relevance
in the ongoing cycle of mutual life.

"Not withstanding the danger from fierce carnivores,
we face a greater threat
from the avarice of ivory poachers, more
murderous than any animal yet.

"We need land on which our herds may roam safe and free,
to live and breed in harmony
with both man and beast,
while using our tusks and heft for self-defense and clearing dead trees.

"We consume shrubs and plants, thus preventing fires.
The steps of our heavy feet till the soil topping,
creating space in the muddy mire
for new seeds carried and deposited with our droppings."

The judges listened to Elias with care
as the elephant explained, and were aghast
at how this simple creature could lay facts bare,
then remembered his descent from a mighty mammoth and mastodon past.

Elias waited while they conferred together.
He felt their compassion and understanding,
and was confident it would no longer be a question of whether.
For survival of the elephant is, as their own, immediate and demanding.

Yes, they would set aside some land where elephants could live and breed.
For poachers, there must be stricter prohibitions and punishment.
All five of them would work for what they now agreed
is an absolutely necessary accomplishment.

They saw how all existence intertwines,
the give and take of every living thing.
To lose another species could undermine
whatever master scheme our world is following.

The Gatherer

Maurice Hirsch

Possibly nearby, perhaps
renovating his den, hoarding
his accumulation in a shed, or
constructing something
out of Poe as in "The Cask of Amontillado,"
the old man with close-set eyes, pointed nose,
on tiptoes at construction dumpsters,
extracts scrap plywood and 2x4s, broken and whole
bricks, shards of ceramic tile, dollies them
back to his lair, glares if you
look his way. In this clean-cut
neighborhood with shouting
young children, their barking dogs,
he seems an anomaly, a creature out
of a dark comic book, lacking only
the garb and makeup of The Joker,
but perhaps the aura of Professor Moriarty,
a hint of sulfur as he passes our front door.

THE DUST BUNNY REBELLION

Jack Campbell

As I begin this little foray into Spookville, I must tell you that it's kind of embarrassing putting the whole thing up for world debate. To tell you the truth, I'm not sure it even happened. So bear with me while I lay it out the way I remember it, and see if you can either vindicate me or agree with my wife that I've crossed the line and could use some help. Just read on with the proverbial jaundiced eye, my friends, and decide for yourselves: am I playing with a full deck or should the boys in the white coats be giving me a free ride downtown?

The particular Saturday morning in question beamed up bright and clear, much to my dismay. Bright light is a hangover's worst enemy, followed closely by crying babies and a vengeful mother-in law, not necessarily in that order. Leprechauns were playing soccer with my left eyeball as I crashed on the couch for some temporary relief. Earlier in the morning, the wife had withheld my hangover coffee until I agreed to retrieve all of her record albums from under our bed and ready them for a church benefit. I'd thrown her a couple of "Yes, dears" for a stall, but here she was, prying me off the couch and pushing me toward the bedroom.

Why does my hair hurt? With her final instructions ringing in my ears, I slumped down to the rug, lifted the bed skirt and peered down at a dust-covered maze, which prompted an immediate flashback. Had it really been ten years since we moved into this place and stacked all of these albums here? Our belongings had quickly gobbled up all available space in the house, so with a few scratches of her head, we were both on our knees piling those damn albums up as high as we could, using all of the space underneath the bed to accommodate the lot. I remembered looking down at all of those recording artists as I started to lower the box spring, watching Como, Sinatra, and all those Village People frown in disbelief as shadows, then darkness, began to engulf them. Was it indeed their final curtain?

Those Leprechauns switched to my right eyeball, and I flipped up the bed skirt and leaned in to get a closer look at what ten years of complete neglect looks like. Not wishing to take the bed apart, I proceeded to retrieve whole stacks of albums, each covered with an inch of crud and assorted debris. As I dusted the top of each stack, the resident artist seemed to blink at their sudden resurrection. "Curtain up, folks."

When arm's length could no longer reach the stacked albums, I knew the tough part of this job was coming up. Armed with my flashlight, I scooted under the foot of the bed and started working my way toward the headboard, pushing stacks of albums to each side where I could retrieve them later. Each time I would belly-scoot forward, I would bang my head on the box springs and get a shower of thick dust. As I pushed the flashlight ahead of me, getting deeper into the abyss, long dead spiders clinging to aged webs did a puppet dance every time my head hit the box springs.

Nearing the headboard, I ran into something that made my hangover the least of my problems. I reared back, banging my head on the box springs again, causing another puppet dance in a rain of dust. Focusing my flashlight straight ahead, I illuminated in more detail a fantasy world come to life. Oh yes, *I will definitely give up drinking!*

I went from passive to highly concerned in a hurry, as my flashlight scanned row after row of dust bunnies lined up infantry style. I leaned in slightly to assess the situation and got attitude, lots of it. They were really ticked! Apparently, they weren't going to take my invasion lightly. I suddenly realized I was about to get my butt kicked by an army of dust bunnies, and I had no plan.

It dawned on me that these bunnies had had ten years under my bed to grow this huge Army, and I knew I was going to have to come up with some cool moves to get out of here in one piece. Recalling some tactics from my Army days and a few things from the History channel, I remembered that a surprise strike will usually buy some time to set up an organized retreat. Relying on my flare for nonchalance, and with complete indifference to the chaos around me, I think I even whistled nervously. I flattened my free hand against the carpet and whipped through their ranks, slamming bunnies in all directions. I soon regretted that stupid move when dead bunnies started clogging my nose and throat. I was coughing and spitting, while trying to focus the flashlight for a look at the damage I'd surely done.

When the dust settled, I got a sobering reality check – I was far from out of the woods here. Those banzai little bastards were back in formation and leaning in for a full-out charge. *So much for Army tactics.* This time they didn't wait for my reaction – they charged!

Their attack was fierce and absolute. Make no mistake, they wanted me dead. My mouth and nose were filling up with suicidal bunnies, and if I hadn't been so damn close to suffocating, I'd have saluted those brave little guys. Most people have their lives pass before them about now. All I got was a headline: DUST BUNNIES KILL DRUNKEN INTRUDER.

Panic was now the plan of the day, and I rebuked myself for not having made out a will. I was being slowly dragged from under the bed, "Oh God, to my grave?" I gave it one last kick and a scream before reality and sobriety found me staring up at a perplexed wife holding one of my legs under each arm and pulling me out of the darkness. "What the hell were you doing under there?" she ranted. "You gave me the last of the albums an hour ago! I could hear you banging and yelling all the way in the living room."

As I lay there, still spitting up invisible dust bunnies and really feeling stupid, she shook her head, dropped my legs and, with a half-smothered, "Idiot," ambled off to another room. I sat at the foot of the bed, trying to wring some kind of sense out of the whole thing. All I could come up with was soft carpet, dim light, and a nagging hangover that had taken me a lot farther down the bunny trail than I would have preferred. No wonder some guys swear off booze!

The wife requested I vacuum under the bed, so I proceeded to pull off the mattress and box spring and lean them against the wall. Apprehension gnawed at me as I slowly turned to view the battlefield that only moments ago had two factions fighting to the death. But alas, all I could find were some dead spiders, old cobwebs, some assorted cough drop wrappers, and yes, millions of dead dust bunnies that had given their lives for the only home they ever knew. Or maybe they just hated drunks.

My Oreck vacuum cleaner soon had the former battlefield free of any evidence to lend credence to a "dust bunny rebellion." Mattress and box spring back in place, I sat on the foot of the bed to contemplate the entire matter. Was it indeed a dream wrung out of an early morning hangover? Or did a combination of strong light and bad breath enrage a normally tranquil village into fighting to the last bunny?

I did come away from the whole experience with a few new resolves. Primary among them: I will definitely go to church tomorrow morning, and I will forever do the vacuuming in this house. Let's face it, it took those damn dust bunnies ten years to build up that huge army. This time I'm cutting them off at the pass.

A few months after my dust bunny encounter, I was preparing for a day in San Diego aboard the carrier Midway. With camera hanging from my neck, I entered the bedroom to retrieve a favorite hat to shade me on this bright sunny day. God help me, if I didn't catch a surviving dust bunny out in the open, ready to scamper under my bed. I had that camera up and clicking in an instant, catching him by complete surprise.

My wife passed the picture around to her friends, who got a big laugh out of it. Somehow, our Oreck salesman got wind of it too, and now they're adding steel thread to their dust bags.

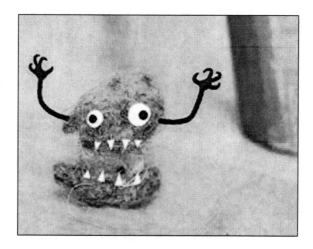

CONSTRAINT

Nancy Sandweiss

We worship bounty, chase the open road—
a plethora of options is the goal,
our every whim legitimate, we're told—
deserving to be satisfied by those
who fuel our endless grasping for the stuff
that fills our closets, drains our pocketbooks
creates anxieties around *enough*
and blinds us to the way we're being duped.

We squander finite hours in pursuit
of perfect products – cruises, laundry soap—
exhaust discernment, misperceive the truth.
Unbounded choice is not real liberty
but leads us down exhausting, fallow roads.
Constraint can ease our minds and set us free.

Rebound

Maurice Hirsch

Wadding up some old office papers,
we filled the kindlng teepee,
lit it all with a wooden
match. Then dry cedar,
small branches, to foster the fire.
When all was ablaze, we added oak
all night feeding the flames
through an era, however you
measure time passing, not seeing
we were like a lumber company
clear-cutting, laying all bare
where the rain eroded top soil.
At a new genesis, grasses now coat
the hillsides. Wildflowers abound,
like the aftermath of lightning
striking a prairie, nourished
by the ashes – milkweed,
red clover, chicory, goldenrod.
We stay, camping by a stream.

OLD WOOD TO BURN

Bill Alewyn

My wife and I have a plaque, weathered by the Arizona sun these many years, which hangs outside our front door. The plaque reads: "Old wood to burn, old wine to drink, old friends to trust, old books to read." Old books, old wine, old friends – that's our philosophical motto in a walnut shell. I especially like the part about old wood. My wife and I are staunch proponents, if not unrepentant zealots, when it comes to the burning of old wood. Who can deny that something primordially deep-in-the gut pleasing comes from this momentary combustion of organic energy into a burst of warmth and light? Or, as Goethe once so aptly put it, "Wood burns because it has the proper stuff in it."

Here in southern Arizona we live in the desert where natural firewood is scarce and winter evenings often chilly. We don't require eight or nine cords of mixed hardwood to see us through to April. Nor are we choosy. Scrap wood is fine by us, preferable actually – an abandoned mesquite fence post that has seen its day, Grandma's sun-splintered glider, or those old John Kerry signboards sequestered behind the garage – old and otherwise useless chunks of wood work best for our purpose.

We burn on an average thirty to forty fires in our fireplace each year, nothing compared to the long winters of Montana, but for me it's turned into no small matter of pride (not to mention frugality) that the firewood we burn be scavenged, not purchased, hence we gather old wood. Trust me, that twice recycled kitchen table turned potting shed workbench on its last wobbly legs still makes for a couple of warm and cozy winter's eves. And, for us, these votive winter evening offerings are as traditional as any New Year's Eve celebration.

Since time immemorial our ancestors huddled about stony hearths to warm themselves over reassuring fires – be those fires made of heartwood or peat or the letters of long departed loves. I'm willing to bet the preservation of mankind's histories and mankind's myths first began centered around a communal fireside. We know that, as a boy, Abraham Lincoln (if we are to take any stock at all in our country's folksy fables) read by the flickering light of his family's fireplace. In any case, you can bet those thrifty Kentuckians burned a Lincoln log or two in their fieldstone inglenook.

Forget if you can for a moment global deforestation and the billion folks in this world who can't afford firewood. Over the years my wife and I have learned to live on a small and (as much as possible) sustainable scale. As stewards of the earth beneath our feet, we are blessed. This stewardship and its blessing comes with responsibility, and so our arid little acre in the desert has been planted with its sustainable share of drought-resistant trees: mesquite, foothill Palo Verde, China berry, eucalyptus, and saguaro. True, our little fireplace in southern Arizona isn't the most fuel efficient method of heating and lighting a home, nor am I advocating the wholesale return of surplus carbon and fossil fuels, though in this case you have to admit a wood fire is more companionable than coal, more romantic than a gas or electric furnace, and certainly more pleasing to the eye than all those solar panels currently stacked like so many fallen dominos on everyone's rooftops. And remember, too, when you collect the firewood for free off the side of the road, as we often do, that's as cost-efficient as it gets. Broken two-by-fours, abandoned rowboats, stray chunks of cordwood that bounced off the back of a pickup truck – it's all recycled fuel for the fireplace.

What might be regarded as unsightly litter to others becomes, for us, a bit of fleeting light and warmth. Once we made a three-night fire out of a broken skid we collected off I-10. Believe me, if I had my way, no piece of abandoned firewood would ever go to waste. I even save those disposable wooden chopsticks from Panda Express to take home for kindling.

As a kind of bonus in our hunts, we've often scavenged perfectly good two-by-fours for other projects. My wife also finds – in her more artistic estimations – an occasional wind-sculpted stump that borders on the expressionistic. "Something ornamental for the garden," she tells me. And so these expressionistic stumps we do not burn – leastways, not yet. There is, she reminds me, something pleasing to the eye and sensuous to the touch about old wood. If you've ever seen or touched the aged trunk of a two-thousand-year-old Bristlecone Pine, then you know of what she speaks.

Conversely, there are moldy specimens too old to burn – too soft and punky – and too far down the decomposition chain to be of much good.

These moldy pieces we leave to the insects and the soil, as well we should. Ideally, this leaves us with old but not *ancient* wood, weathered and discarded pieces that have already served their time in some previous incarnation. Wood, when you pick it up, speaks directly to you: "My time of splendor hath passed. I am no longer a stout apple branch that sways in the wind or that walnut leg that supports a hundred-year-old roll-top desk. Now, take me home, please, back to your chimney and enjoy my fleeting warmth." Which we do. In gratitude and in great respect for the ongoing cycle of once living things.

Buddhists say, "Ashes do not return to wood." Maybe that's why here in the pragmatic West we are constantly warned not to "burn our bridges." Whatever the case, in the final analysis all is heartily consumed. One day, many years hence, when the letters on that weathered old plaque hanging outside our door that now read, "Old wood to burn, old wine to drink, old friends to trust, old books to read," fades away into illegibility and the wood itself begins to split, then with a solemn pinch of acquired affection I will ceremoniously burn, wood to ashes, that last scrap of bridge.

As for myself, I have no qualms about my own wood into ashes never to return once the mortal spirit moves on. So when my time of useful purpose on this whirling sphere has passed, it's the crematorium for these old bones, though the funeral pyre in and of itself has always struck me as a self-indulgent waste of accelerated atoms. In death what are we, after all, if not untapped repositories of latent energy and light? So it seems only fair, ecologically speaking, that this final furnace be connected to some universal power grid engineered for the greater good, in partial payment for our many earthly sins perhaps. Or, who knows, maybe by then mortuary science will have perfected a process to freeze-dry all the messy moisture from this old stump and shrink me down to the size of a Presto Log. I wouldn't mind. Really. This energy efficient mode of transformation would be my preference. My wife could take me home and I, in my turn, could give her one last fleeting night of warmth and flickering light where she could stretch out in front of the fireplace like a young Abe Lincoln and read a book.

Or, knowing my wife's preference, I might just end up as "something ornamental for the garden."

Maple Syrup

Peter Bradley

Our first Christmas together was bitter cold,
with no money for oil,
and scant wood to burn.
We awoke to a cold stove and little cheer.
Still, we laughed at the frozen water in the dog's bowl,
and then set about building a small fire.
We placed the card table close by
to eke out what little heat there was,
and prepared a special breakfast
of pancakes, with real maple syrup,
strawberries and whipped cream,
and a bottle of cheap champagne.
There were no presents to give,
only the promise of the future,
to which we toasted as only the young can,
with absolute belief and certainty.

In retrospect, I can say that my life
has had its fill of triumphs and tragedies.
Through it all the tradition continues.
The hearth and home are warmer,
the champagne more expensive,
and the meals richer.
But looking back to that first cold Christmas morn,
none have ever been sweeter.

SILK POINSETTIAS

M. C. Little

A December stop at the market,
       to purchase some last-minute things.

Scotch tape and red ribbon and tinsel,
       a little plush snowman that sings.

Close by stood a low, festive table
       of dazzling, white Poinsettias.

A silk plant soon sat in my full cart—
       oh my, how enchanting it was.

While standing in line at the check out,
       my feet seemed to feel somewhat wet.

Could this plant be (possibly) leaking?
       I pressed 'round the soil to rid doubt.

Then cart, about faced, followed droplets;
       now, how could this be? It just can't!

Thus, perfect white blossoms were returned
       to some 60 silk, well-watered plants.

Discovery

Kathleen O'Brien

Curly-headed four-year-old,
skinny in red pajamas
stamped with trains and fire engines,
exclaims to family seated
in canvas chairs around the campfire:

"Look at my shadow!"

Behind him a floodlight
cuts his shape from the cloth of night,
casting silhouettes on a path
strewn with pebbles and pine needles.

LED'S on his sneakers flash
like fireflies; Peter Pan, he's prancing
in circles, running back and forth,
dancing in surprise at
how his body stretches,
how he becomes a giant.
I join him to check my own image,
to see how grown up I've become.

Exercise Time

Terrie Jacks

Bend and stretch
touch your toes
stand up tall
wiggle your nose

Flex your arms
count to four
take a walk
flex some more

Sit right down
march in place
marching low
is no disgrace

Tap your toes
then your heels
clap your hands
give a little squeal

Stand back up
behind your chair
dance a bit
waltz a square

Now it's time
stand tippy-toes
hold the chair
don't fall on your nose

Okay now
let's sit back down
stretch a bit
smile don't frown

Clap and shout
Hip-hip-hooray
we're all done
for today

COLD

Robert Pouriea

–

The only time I can say that I was really cold was the time my friend, Howard, and I went hunting in the Black Hills of South Dakota. I turned and went up to the ridge, figuring we would join back up together just a little farther on. But when I got to where we were supposed to meet, he wasn't there. Then we were hunting for one another as much as for game.

The hills we were hunting in were about one mile high, so the air was thin, but by then we were pretty much accustomed to the thin air. It was winter or late fall, and we had been walking all day in the snow. Most of the time the snow was up to our knees, so walking was difficult. The temperature was below freezing.

I became so tired that I sat down in the snow to rest.

I was relaxed and what I was starting to do was fall asleep. In that state of mind, I don't think I realized what was happening to my body. I felt comfort and was not cold. What I was really doing was freezing to death.

I can only thank Howard for finding me and making me get up, as we still had a couple miles to go to get home. Once I got walking again, I realized what had been happening to me.

I owe my life to Howard, and we were the best of friends all his life. To me, he is my blood brother for ever and ever.

LIVING WITH DROUGHT

Kathleen Elliott Gilroy

And now, hoped for rain is granted:
splits and splats ping pavement,
wake the scent of earth, resuscitate it.

But close the lid of that rain barrel;
it's now against the law to save it
for watering plants and flowers...

Let it puddle on the dirt,
let it roll across pavement,
let it spin along the gutter

let sun eventually evaporate
whatever's left of that rainwater.
Or let it mingle with roadside clutter.

If your deed doesn't have Mineral *Rights*,
even environmentalists violate
government claims to what's underground.

Rainwater saved violates those Rights;
Big Brother can give you time in jail
for using what they deem as theirs!

Save! Save what you can, alter your lifestyle,
but forego rain barrels, watering cans at eaves,
watering bowls filled to full, even for outdoor animals.

Water well and water deep before sunup,
or when neighbors sleep, but forego grass,
long showers and luxuries... or be prepared to go to jail.

Juvenile Hall 2008

Maggi Roark

We're choralers on a December night in our Santa sweaters and tinsel ties welcomed with metal detectors and rules. A guard gives us the serious eye and thin-lipped warning: no touching, no hugs. Groups of children overflow the sprung sofas and hard-angle seats. There are no windows to the outside; clanking locks remind us these are not living rooms. Teens drape across folding chairs like forgotten coats – one hides his moving lips behind a tattooed hand. Little ones with thousand-watt smiles sprawl on the scarred linoleum. Beside them a guard's runaway foot taps along with our Jingle Bells. We rush through our first song then let the music carry us beyond our nerves, to a final Silent Night. A pre-teen with lips pierced and hair striped red and green calls out, *Please come back next year. I'll be here.*

Moccasins

Antoinette V. Franklin

Ancestor's shoes
worn, tired
soft covering
traveling
to a
new destiny.

Massacre at High Noon

Aleane Fitz-Carter

Back in olden times the western frontier rang out with the sounds of horseback riders galloping down dusty roads at breakneck speed, stage coaches rumbling down rough rocky hillsides, the haunting whistle of trains rolling into the station, and tinkling piano music coming from the town's saloon. The saloon with its gambling tables and dance hall girls attracted cowboys who came to town to relax after a long, hard cattle drive. It beckoned to wayfaring strangers passing through, local citizens, lawmen, and those who operated outside the law. Barroom brawls and shootouts were common occurences and kept the town marshal busy trying to keep peace and order.

The saloon furnished living quarters for the girls who worked there. These girls led a fast life, made fast money, suffered from disease, and died young. Some even committed suicide. Society did not permit these lively ladies to ever be in the same company with the respectable women of the town. However, whether respectable or of ill repute, all women were regarded as delicate flowers to be protected and cherished – even the likes of Calamity Jane and Belle Starr were treated with royal reverence. Belle Starr had a price of $10,000 on her head, wanted dead or alive for murder and armed robbery. When a man ambushed her and killed her, revenge was swiftly and fatally wreaked on him for breaking the Ninth Commandment in the Code of the West:

"Thou shalt honor and revere all womankind: aye, shalt thou never think of harming one hair of a woman!"

The First Commandment said: "Thou shalt not appear too inquisitive about one's past." (In other words, don't ask too many questions!)

Second Commandment: "Thou shalt be hospitable to strangers" (Howdy, stranger. Come on in. Stay awhile.)

Third Commandment: "Thou shalt give thine enemy a fighting chance."

Fourth Commandment: "Thou shalt not shoot an unarmed man."

Fifth Commandment: "Thou shalt not make a threat without expecting dire consequences."

Sixth Commandment: "Thou shalt not practice ingratitude." (Much obliged, ma'am. Much obliged, stranger.)

Seventh Commandment: "Thou shalt defend thyself whenever self-defense is neccessary."

Eighth Commandment: "Thou shalt not rob."

Ninth Commandment: "Thou shalt honor and revere all womankind."

Tenth Commandment: "Thou shalt look out for thine own."

This was the unwritten law of the western frontier, and it was understood, appreciated, and enforced.

The eighth commandment, "Thou shalt not rob," kept lawmen such as Wyatt Earp, Bat Masterson, Doc Holiday, and Wild Bill Hickock busy enforcing it. The Pinkerton Dectective Agency, Wells Fargo, and Union Pacific undercover agents were champions of justice to be reckoned with. But notorious criminals like Jesse James, Billy the Kid, Butch Cassidy, the Apache Kid, and the Dalton Brothers ignored the eighth commandment.

The Dalton Brothers – Bob, Bill, Grat, and Emmett – were blond, blue-eyed bandits who robbed banks and trains. The very mention of their name struck fear in the hearts of law-abiding citizens. My grandparents, parents, uncles, and aunts all lived during the time of the Daltons in the small town of Coffeyville, Kansas. The Daltons lived there too...on the outskirts of town. Mr. and Mrs. Dalton (Lewis and Adeline) had fifteen children. They'd drive into town in their horse-drawn wagon to get groceries at the General Store. Mrs. Dalton would purchase muslin and thread for her sewing, and Mr. Dalton would pick up some hay at the Feed Store for his horses. The townspeople shied away from them and were always glad to see them leave.

On Wednesday, October 5, 1892, the Dalton Gang rode into Coffeyville to rob the First National Bank and the Condon Bank. My eighty-five year old Aunt Rella tells the story, reaching back to share thoughts, emotions, and perceptions as seen through the eyes of a little eight-year-old girl attending Cleaveland Elementary school in Coffeyville.

"I was there. I was in the third grade when it happened."

I stare at my elderly aunt. I'm excited and awed at the same time. "Aunt Rella, take me back to that day."

Aunt Rella smiles and settles back in her chair, pleased to have an audience with which to share this incredible excerpt from her life. She begins.

It was high noon. We were just opening up our sack lunches when somebody on horseback rode over to the school and left word that the Dalton boys had just robbed the bank, and that there had been some killing and shooting. Our teacher marched us down there to see it. We took our lunches with us and ate on the way, juggling biscuits, sausages, baloney sandwiches, pickles, muffins, cinnamon rolls, tea cakes, and licorice sticks. It was three miles to downtown. We were talking all loud and excited.

"Wonder who got shot?"

"Wonder who got killed?"

"Wonder if they still shooting?"

"Robbery still going on, I wonder?"

"I can hardly wait to get there!"

"We'll get to see a real robbery!"

"Did they catch them, or did they get away, I wonder?"

I then begin to think about my money I have in my savings account at the First National. I have $1.03 and those robbers took my money! I was saving that money to buy Mama a birthday present. Papa has money in the First National too. He's saving up to buy a new horse, 'cause the one he's got can't stand up by himself. He's hide-bound. Papa's got to get two or three men to help him put a board under his butt and raise him up to his feet. Papa needs another horse so he can do his hauling. We need that money, and now they took it. It's gone.

I start to cry softly.

When we get downtown, there's a crowd of people milling around. There are kids from other schools there with their teachers. Folks are talking loud, people crying, some talking in hushed tones. Gunsmoke clouds the air and the smell of it is enough to choke you. There's blood everywhere. Our teacher carves out a path through the crowd for us to go through so we can stand right up front and look. There they are – one two three four – all dead, lying in the street. Then some men lift up two of the Daltons and prop them up next to the sheriff, so he could have his picture taken with the dead men. One of them has his eye half shut, and it looks like he's looking straight at me.

I get a little scared. I want to go back to school. I look at the teacher, but she's talking to a man in the crowd. He says, "Oh, the Dalton boys...they come riding into town 'bout twelve noon...thought they was goin' to rob both banks. They didn't know the street between the two banks was torn up for repairs, so they had to leave their horses one-half block down the street and walk up to the banks. They were all dressed up in business suits, wearing hats and fake moustaches and false beards. But when Emmett and Bob went in the First National, a passerby recognized them as they were helping themselves to twenty-some thousand dollars. He ran out into the town square yelling, 'The Daltons! The Daltons!'

"Well, we all drew our guns, and men who didn't have a gun hastily borrowed some from nearby stores. Meanwhile, across the street at the Condon Bank, Grat Dalton and the rest of the boys were having some trouble trying to get the clerk to open up the vault. They put a gun to his head and barked, 'Open up the vault!'

"'Open it up! I can't open it up. It's got one of them new-fangled time locks on it. It can't open up before time. It's got 'bout five more minutes to go. Please, there's nothing I can do. Please!'

"This slowed things down a bit, giving the townsmen on the outside more time to get ready for the action. Grat and the boys got nervous waiting around, so they decided to make a break for their horses. That's when the fireworks started! When it was all over, four of our good citizens were dead! And the Daltons? All killed 'cept Emmett. He tried to make a getaway on his horse, but they caught him and took him to jail."

After listening to that man and seeing all the gory mess and all the smells, I begin to feel sick to my stomach. I run over to the teacher. "Miss Hall, I feel like I'm gonna throw."

"Come on, child," she says, putting her arms around me. She ushers us out of the crowd and lines us up to go back to school.

On the way back, we walk slow and nobody hardly talks. We're too busy thinking. Why did the Dalton boys have to do that? Didn't they know it's wrong to steal?

So I ask Miss Hall, "Miss Hall, did the Dalton Gang get the money? I had $1.03 in the bank."

"No, Rella. They didn't get any money. The $20,000 they took, they had to give back to the bank, so your money is safe."

"Oh goody! Papa's money is safe too. Now I can buy that birthday present for Mama…and Papa can get that new horse! And when he gets that horse, I'm going to go horseback riding on its back, and I'm going to name it High Noon!"

EPILOGUE

Emmett Dalton was given life imprisonment at Lansing Penitentiary. After serving fourteen years, he was pardoned, and he went to Los Angeles, California, where he worked in real estate, led a straight life, and was a consultant on westerns for Hollywood movie companies. He died of natural causes in 1937. My Aunt Rella was 91 when she died of natural causes in 1975.

In Coffeyville, Kansas the Dalton Museum is located at 113 E. 8th St. The zip code is 67337. I have visited the museum many times while visiting my relatives in Coffeyville. The museum houses the Daltons' guns, the hearse that took them to their gravesites, their saddles, newspaper accounts of the robbery, pictures, and many other items. There is also a museum for the defenders who lost their lives in the shootout.

MY AUNT RELLA AND MY GRANDMOTHER

Missouri State Penitentiary

Maurice Hirsch

Retired prison guard Howard, white
coiffed hair, showing Cell #40, Unit 4, said,
"They ripped an inmate's eye out

over a pack of cigarettes." More grisly
tales, four floors of tiny cells
with tiny windows, in one

a life-sized cutout of Sonny Liston,
once an occupant. Rusted bed frames,
some twin, some bunk, small tables, toilets

now covered with plastic wrap.
A 1920s movie projector sat
on the ground floor, old reels of film

stored there, screened on sheets strung
from the third balcony; convicts
on metal folding chairs

knew every scene, every line, as
I do now with HBO and Showtime.
In the basement, the dungeon, original

limestone from the 1800s, primitive,
windowless, low doorways, became
a shower room. But most terrifying,

in the women's Housing Unit 1,
an all-brick cell, only a toilet, no
windows, no light, solid door with slot

for food. Howard said, "Some of the women
were mean and vindictive, most pretty nice."
Metal mirrors reflect wavy images. Then

to the gas chamber building,
on its stone wall
photos of the 40 men and women

executed there, each having walked
on bricks stamped "A. P. Greenab Co."
The room on the left was for viewing

by victims' families, on the right
a holding cell and the chamber itself,
its two chairs, one with a head rest,

bleacher seats outside its windows;
next to the red lever on the other,
a chair where the warden waited.

Foiled Plans

Gilda A. Herrera

I'd finally had enough
Of his snarls, abuse and stuff.
Forever the nasty grump,
Calling our sweet home a dump,
Filled to the brim with his junk.
Not to mention how he stunk!

Easy to plot his demise
For a wife cunning and wise.
He swallowed so many pills
All for imaginary ills.
I slipped him a deadly one
Grinning at what I had done.
With a mean gleam in my eye
I waved a taunting goodbye.

He shot me a frantic look,
His eyes wide; his body shook.
Soon it became his turn to gloat.
He stuck a finger down his throat
Drenching me with pills and spit.
Foiled! I planned another hit.

His wooden cane had a crack
Enlarged by me with a smack.
I waited for him to fall
Down the stairs or into a wall.
The cane split, he took a spill
I smothered my happy thrill.

Foiled, twice! That blonde volunteer
From Kind Meals destroyed my cheer.
She caught him, saved him, then pressed
Him to her well-endowed chest.
Soon I was rid of him, free.
And he got rid, was free of me.

I heard Blondie cried and cried.
When he shortly up and died
Choking on a chicken bone
Stuck into an ice cream cone.

She'd been a killing machine
My dead Ex, victim fifteen.
So I got all his money
But life is less than sunny,
I miss that cantankerous mule
Old women need an old fool.

NIGHT BY THE BAY

Anne Whitlock

Near the water's edge
where yachts are shrouded
by a cold October moon
the Inn of Seven Sirens
beckons in the night.

In the crowded club
bodies rock, waves of music
drown the conversation
and I cling,
fingers moored to you.

Faces float like fish
and in the corners of the room
women sip their loneliness
like ships immersed
in anesthetic fog.

Beside the jetty of the bar
a man stands,
eyes like beacons,
searching.

I'M NOT ROGER BLAIME

Lawrence Carleton

I was tired and hungry and disoriented, not sure where I was nor where I'd been. I'd ripped my pants coming down over the wall, having panicked a little at the nearness of barking dogs, which is why I'd climbed over. I was alone in the delivery space behind a strip mall, except for a dumpster sitting at the other end of the alley. Maybe, I thought, it would hold some discarded food or clothes for me to rescue.

On closer inspection, I found no discarded food. Only a shirt and, yes, pants with a belt still in them. My new outfit kind of hung on me, but at least it wasn't torn and, so far as I could tell, it didn't smell too bad. To my surprise, the pockets contained a wallet and a set of keys. The wallet held cards and a license and, best of all, nearly forty dollars in cash.

I walked casually down the street that passed in front of the mall toward some lights in the distance, which I took correctly to betoken another mall. I was hungry, but I didn't want to be seen hurrying from the scene of my discovery. When I arrived at the larger mall I paid about eight dollars cash for my first sit-down meal in I don't know long. I chose a seat in a corner not far from the door and tried not to look like I was watching everyone else. I carefully took my time eating, as though I belonged there. Best of all, after I finished eating, I got really clean in the men's room. That night, as I curled up with my trove under some bushes near the freeway, I reflected on my good luck and dreamed about what I should do next.

I made the cash last a few days, and then tried the bank card. I found a scrap of paper tucked among the business cards and guessed the numbers and otherwise meaningless phrases on it were pin numbers and passwords. It didn't take long to figure which was for the bank card. Whoever he was, he had a nice bank balance, so I hoped he wouldn't mind my using some of it.

Eventually, I started to get curious about my benefactor. I took the trolley downtown and walked from the station to the San Diego Main

Library. According to the driver's license, Mr. Roger Blaime was physically a lot like me – an old guy, five-ten with blue eyes and brown hair – but he had a slightly pudgy clean-shaven face. At the library I found out that Roger Padraig Blaime was an author who'd written a couple of books – the "Bridge" stories – about a guy named Paddy who prefers living in anonymity.

Unfortunately, Paddy cannot avoid the mounting evidence that he's working for a company that operates a real estate scam. At first, he tries not to get involved, and when he does get involved he attempts to cover his tracks: "Rule One: Keep Your Nose Clean." Despite his best efforts, notoriety finds him. Eventually, he finds the obscurity he seeks by becoming a bum and living under bridges.

In recent years Blaime had become a recluse himself, and not long ago disappeared entirely. That got me thinking. In the men's room I compared my face in the mirror with the driver's license photo. My face was thinner and, of course, hirsute but enough resemblance was apparent. I decided to try out the obvious next step. I walked over to Horton Plaza and bought myself a new belt for my loose pants. I chose a checkout counter near an exit, produced a credit card for payment and, on request, the driver's license.

The clerk looked back and forth between the license and my face for what seemed forever. I felt my pulse pounding in my ears until at last he remarked, "Change of lifestyle, Mr. Blaime?"

"Something like that," I answered. On collecting the goods I turned and left the store at what I hoped was a relaxed pace.

A few trolley and bus rides and a short walk later, I was at the address on the driver's license. I went in the main entrance, found the elevator and pressed "4". As I stepped out of the elevator someone said, "Welcome back, Paddy" and disappeared through a doorway. Blaime's door, #423, was just a few steps from the elevator. I listened but could hear no sounds within. I decided not to knock.

The first key I tried worked.

The apartment was small but nice, obviously unattended for a long time. In the main room a table next to a computer nook faced out the main window and away from the door. To the left was a small kitchen, to the right a bathroom and bedroom. The refrigerator's contents were all past their sell-by date, but the cooking utensils and tableware were clean. The bedroom closet was neatly arranged, with no dirty laundry in the clothesbasket. I decided I would leave before dark. Meanwhile, I rummaged through the computer nook and found more addresses and passwords, then amused myself fooling around with the computer.

The place seemed set up to run on autopilot: all the bills were paid automatically from a fat checking account, all receipts forwarded to an accountant. No emails from relatives – did he have any? – though some woman, apparently his agent, had been sending reminders once a week concerning one more book he owed her.

Did I say no relatives? Wikipedia listed a wife and a kid. Google turned them up. They didn't like to talk about him.

"Disappeared?" announced the kid, Pat, in one recent interview. "How can you tell? He was never really there anyway. Can *he* even tell he's gone?" In another interview Pat recalled a childhood in which her father was so aloof and strange that she concluded he was a space alien, and she spent years with a doctor dealing with her fear that she was therefore part alien too. That was long ago, and apparently wife and child were getting along now as well as ever.

Back to the agent: "This is like waiting for Godot, except I'm not even getting a boy to announce you'll appear tomorrow without fail. You said you were finishing one more novel before you dove into the dumpster of oblivion. Before, not after, right? Materialize in some form, Paddy Ghost, if only in email!"

I called it a night.

The next morning I ate some stale toast and read through the originals of the two Bridges books on the computer. There were three folders: Off the Freeway, Burned Bridges, and Paddy Wasn't Here. The first two folders had the complete texts of the published books; the third had some notes.

The gist of the connected storyline concerned a dishonest real estate investment meant to fail, but which turned successful against its perpetrators' wishes. Potemkin Villas was launched in an isolated inholding embedded in a nature preserve far inland from San Diego, connected to civilization only by back roads. The idea was to set up some cheap models, sucker in investors and buyers, and then, when the deal collapsed, abscond to Belize with the proceeds. Unfortunately for the schemers, there was too much monied interest for any real estate project, however hare-brained, to fail in the local environment of the time. Permits? Granted against all reason. Roads? Government money materialized for highway construction. Environmental destruction? Not a crucial concern in the face of promises of jobs jobs jobs.

In "Off the Freeway" one Patrick Freeman, an accountant for the Potemkin Villas project, is delighted to be an inconspicuous cog in the corporate wheel. He trusts his bosses at first but, detail by detail, cannot avoid seeing the scam for what it is. He wants to hide. In time he soothes his conscience by posting anonymous tips to the authorities, unaware that they in turn inform his bosses. The bosses figure out that he's the whistle blower and alter records to make it appear that he forged documents to siphon off funds to a secret account – in Belize, of course. Overwhelmed and powerless in the face of the doctored evidence, our protagonist regains his anonymity by living as a bum under one of the new freeway bridges. He spends the rest of the book scurrying from one hiding place to another, keeping his nose clean and vanishing when further incidents occur.

In "Burned Bridges" our fugitive, now calling himself Paddy Bridges, learns the art of burglary from fellow transients, then narrowly escapes one night when their encampment gets raided. He uses his newfound skills at first to forage for the necessities of life as he wanders up and down the freeway. Then one night he finds himself at the Potemkin Villa company field office and breaks in to search for snacks. Once in, having raided the vending machines, he becomes curious and finds he can still access the company records. He seizes the occasion to re-cook the books and send spurious emails to the local newspaper; then he changes the passwords to key accounts before disappearing again into the hills. That escapade has no effect: the newspaper publisher is a major Potemkin investor and urban sprawl advocate. But eventually there are heavy rains, landslides occur, and the Potemkin models collapse into an inglorious heap at the bottom of the hill. Paddy appears out of nowhere and accosts a TV reporter on the scene and on camera. The cameraman disobeys the reporter's "cut" signal and keeps filming as Paddy spills his guts to the embarrassed reporter and to the world. He vanishes without identifying himself, but the news clip goes viral, and eventually the scandal is exposed.

It occurred to me I could write the third book if I wanted to. I snuck out when no one was looking and returned with some groceries. After supper, including cleaning everything and putting stuff away, I turned in. I kind of daydreamed how the third story would go. Yes, it practically wrote itself. It was as though I were reading it, not making it up as I went. But then things happen that way in dreams. Basically, Paddy becomes famous but nothing else changes much. He lives the life of a celebrity with a tell-all book and TV interviews, but the story is him, not the way business is done. Eventually, he understands how things really work and decides to return to his life as a bum.

I woke to the sound of tapping from some distance. As I regained consciousness I realized that someone was knocking on the apartment door. What should I do? I'd gone to sleep with a light on. Could someone tell from outside that the apartment was occupied? I slowly made my way across the room and looked through the peephole. I saw a young woman, tall, with blue eyes, brown hair, round face.

"Come on, it's all right. You can open. I'm alone," she said quietly, her face pressed against the door. "It's me. Pat. I need to see you, Daddy."

"I'm not Roger Blaime."

"Really? What time is it?"

I looked at my watch. "2:14 a.m."

She smiled. "Not 'quarter past two' but 2:14 a.m.," she observed. "That watch is a beat up Timex Expedition with a ratty black Velcro band, isn't it? You've had it for years. You never take it off, even in the shower. 'Water resistant to 100 meters,' you used to say. Mom gave it to you. You don't wear your ring, but you wear that watch. If something bad ever did happen to you, we wouldn't need dental records to identity you. We'd just see the watch and know it was you." After a pause, "Who did you think you were?"

To tell the truth, that question had not occurred to me. "Paddy Bridges?" I guessed.

"That's you, all right, switching yourself with one of your characters."

I let her in, after checking that the hall was otherwise empty. We looked each other over, crossed to the computer nook, and sat down.

"Do you realize," she remarked, settling in, "that you have stolen your own identity?" I had to admit it did appear that way. Then she got to the point of the visit. "I know you don't like being found when you're writing, so we go along with your disappearances. No one really disappears these days, but we leave you alone. This is a special case, though," she announced. "A bum has been arrested on suspicion of killing you."

"What the—?"

"He was wearing torn clothes with bloodstains on them. The blood was identified as yours. He claims he just fished them out of a dumpster." She paused. "He also claims to be the real Paddy Bridges." She studied my face a while, then announced, "Anyway, he's in the jail downtown, You need to go there to straighten things out."

A few minutes later we were in Pat's beat-up Honda Civic, handed down to her from me when I stopped driving and she left for college. Things started to come back to me as I sat in the passenger seat and watched her drive. I taught her to drive in that car. Polly wanted to teach her in her newer car with airbags and automatic drive, but Pat insisted on my old stick-shift beater, even though that meant her father had to do the teaching.

I hazarded a conversation. "Am I still a space alien?"

She laughed. "That notorious interview! It took me years, but now I know we're both aliens, living in our own space. Remember me learning to drive? Mom is so fussy about things that don't even matter, I knew she'd drive me up the wall, so I insisted on you teaching me 'cause I knew you'd mostly let me figure things out on my own and only say something if you had to." She shot me a knowing smile. "We're loners. We're at home in our own space and deal as outsiders with the inhabitants of the common space most people know and love. You deal with the common space by avoiding it when you can. You like to write, but you don't like to talk about writing. You read ferociously, but don't like to discuss what you've read – except, now and then, with me when you're not disappearing."

I had to agree.

"I've learned to live as an amused stranger blending in with the unsuspecting crowd. That's why I went to San Diego State, even though Mom wanted me to get the personal attention and connections of her small Catholic college alma mater. That's exactly what I *didn't* want. I wanted the option of disappearing into my private space and being an anonymous fish in the vast sea of humanity inhabiting a large university."

"How is Polly?"

"Getting along. She has lots of friends she sees every day at work and still hangs with her old friends from when we kids all went to that expensive private school together. Always doing something with someone, everyone giving everyone else advice about everything. I don't phone her any more. You can have better control if you text."

"Even when I had a phone, I didn't text."

"No paradox there. You write. You don't text. I text and have to keep texting some, but I do it less now that I've started to write." She stopped talking, and concentrated on turning off on the correct street to get to the jail.

I wanted to ask her what she'd started writing about, but that would have to wait.

In the station we met with some of America's Finest and with just a little patience satisfied them that I am indeed Roger Blaime. The lead investigator, Detective Charles Snyder, then queried whether we'd like to meet the suspect – no longer a murder suspect, but still charged with attempted robbery and aggravated assault.

Officer Snyder introduced me to the surly individual slumped on the other side of the table in the interview room. "He first said he was Roger Blaime. Look up and meet the real Roger Blaime."

The prisoner shot me a fierce glance and grunted.

"Now he says he's Paddy Bridges. Is this Paddy Bridges, Mr. Blaime?"

"The Paddy Bridges I created would have a more prominent nose and be older. What are you, son – thirty?"

The ersatz Paddy stared at me and mumbled, "Lost count." After staring past me at the doorway for several minutes, he added, "Lost a lot of things." He watched as I heard the door open and someone enter and step up just next to me.

"He's Lester Hope," I heard Pat announce. "I was in his 'modern nihilist lit' class at State. Becket, Pinter, and you, Daddy, were the focus of the course. I remember 'specially his obsession with the Potemkin Villa story line in 'Off the Freeway.' I also remember he tried to pick me up at a Barking Dog Howland concert while I was still in his class."

"Thank you for blowing my cover. I had seized the unexpected opportunity to do some personal research from a vagrant's point of view." Hope shook his head. "Oh well. Anyway, I apologize yet again. I didn't know who you were, nor that you were my student then," he recited wearily. "I was drunk, and you were in the crowd and yet alone, and hot. I was, on that occasion, just a single guy on the prowl." Then, "To be honest, you didn't exactly stand out in my class, even when we discussed the work of an author who turned out to be your father."

"I didn't think anyone would understand. 'Off the Freeway' isn't about a real estate scandal nor the pervasive anomy of our current culture."

"What is it about then?"

"If he could say it in a sentence or two, he wouldn't have had to write whole books."

"Copout!" the professor replied. "Still, there is also the realization that Paddy's efforts have not led to redress for the scandal nor changes that would prevent more of the same. All he's gained is a loss of personal privacy. That's why the trilogy ends with his erasing all traces of his existence."

"How do you know that?" Pat and I remarked in unison.

"It's on the flash drive."

"What flash drive?"

"The one lying on the ground next to the dumpster where I found the ratty shirt and torn pants."

Lester Hope, consumed with the nihilism he perceived in the "Bridges" novels, had taken to roaming this neighborhood randomly, taking in what he saw from the perspective of a bum. Late one night in his wanderings he came upon the trash bin after I'd made my exchange, and he seized the opportunity to dress the part. The flash drive was simply there, a thing of value a bum might pick up. One afternoon before going out on his wanderings, he plugged in the drive on a whim and was surprised to see it contained the finished text to "Paddy Wasn't Here."

I *did* know how it ended, after all. It's all a bad dream for Paddy. To him, he *isn't* really there; he's an outsider trapped in a kind of ongoing party where someone with the same name as his is the honored guest. Everyone thinks he's the honoree when only he knows he isn't. One night, Paddy wakes up to an epiphany. He fishes out the last of his bum clothes, leaves all of his belongings in the apartment rented in Paddy Bridges' name, slips his key under the locked door, and wanders off into the foggy night. Paddy wasn't here, and now he's gone.

I now remembered finishing the book. From habit, I had backed it up to a flash drive. Then impulse overtook me. I deleted the story from the computer and took off for a nighttime stroll. Just as in the novel, it was foggy, dark even near streetlights. I wandered aimlessly and inattentively for some time. I came upon a strip mall with a used clothing store. In I went, to emerge a short time later attired in my own idea of bumwear. In the back of the mall I found a convenient dumpster, where I jettisoned the clothes I'd worn that night, together with all their contents. I was no longer Roger Blaime.

"Wake up, Daddy. Time to go."

It was Pat. She passed me the flash drive with "Paddy Wasn't Here" on it, and I slipped it into my pocket as I got up. We left Lester Hope to face charges of attempting to break into his own apartment – he'd lost his keys somewhere during his nocturnal prowl – and tussling with the night manager, who had not recognized him on the occasion of his return.

"I'll take you home," Pat announced. "Wait. I need to go to my place for something first. Then I'll take you."

It was just beginning to get light when we got to Pat's apartment building. It was in one apartment tower looking pretty much like the others, across the street from campus. We took the stairs to the second floor and started down the hall. "There it is— what the? Wait here, Daddy."

I waited. She stole up to the young man sprawled asleep in front of her door, leaned over him to quietly unlock and open her door, stepped gingerly over him, and just as silently shut the door behind her. A few minutes later she emerged neater and fresher and reversed the procedure. As she approached me she paused, smiled, and returned to the dormant visitor. She kicked him gently, then more forcefully, until he stirred. As he sat, she crouched, held his face in both hands, and mumbled something about "Is this your idea of not smothering me?" Then she kissed his forehead and told him, "Go home and clean up. I should be back in two hours. We'll talk then." She patted his butt as he turned to scramble to his feet. She followed him with an amused smile as he trudged down the hall and turned out of sight.

In the car, Pat brought me up to speed. "The sex was good, and at first that was enough. Actually, he gave the impression of being very accomplished, and I thought he would just count me as one more conquest and move on, so I could have my first experience with no consequences. On the big night I was surprised to discover he was as much a virgin as I. Worse, some kind of imprinting occurred, so now he cannot imagine sex without me. Cool, you might think, if you weren't me. As I got to know him better, our relationship reminded me more and more of you and Mom. He's always fussing about details I don't want to care about, always making plans far too detailed to be practical. And the parties! I'm like you: I can be in a crowd, but I don't want to be part of it. When I'm in a gathering of his friends or relatives, they expect me to be an active participant. I just want to stand apart and be an observer or maybe tune them out and be alone with my thoughts. Still, he is learning to adjust. He sees a future for us. In time I think I might see one too. But also I think about you and Mom."

"I'm afraid from time to time that Polly misses me." I didn't add, "But does she miss *me*?"

"She misses your presence more than she admits. Still, she wants you to live the way you want, even though she doesn't really understand it. Tell me. Do you ever think about what you truly want? You were Roger Blaime and got famous by inventing Paddy Bridges, who escaped from society the way you thought you would have liked. Then you *became* Paddy Bridges, and you discovered Roger Blaime, who seemed to have it made. So Paddy became the Roger you imagined. But you really didn't like being either one, did you? Maybe escaping isn't what you really wanted all along."

I guess I passed out in the car. Next thing I noticed was that we weren't moving.

"You're home now, Daddy. Get out."

I got out, but it wasn't at the apartment. It was the old house, where Polly still lived. I turned just in time to see Pat drive off. *Home*, I thought. I fingered the flash drive in my pocket. *Have I come home?*

I stopped at the entrance and waited, sorting out my thoughts. At last I knew what I had to do. I fished the flash drive from my pocket. I unstrapped my watch. I studied both in my hands for a few minutes. I crouched to lay the items at the door. I straightened, turned, and started to walk away.

I heard the door open. It was probably Polly. I don't know. I didn't look back.

Hats

Roy B. Laos

Give me a new hat any day.
So I can top off life's play.

Adorned aloft hats reflect our personas, they're flags we proudly wave.
Hats alter behavior…introverts become extroverts and the meek become brave.

They're simply head covers! Not so, sporting one proudly or left aside and
    forsaken.
With my hat in hand…Suddenly, things can begin shakin'.

How lite-headed I become with my favorite hat on.
Strutting my accessorized head around, even if frowned upon.

Hats enhance the moment, conjuring improvement.
Choosing one from another empowers movement.

Hats are expressive and bold.
Made to shade the sun or shed the cold.

Hats signify authority, style, typifying cultural diversity rather resoundingly.
Hats may be any size, shape, color, soft or hard, varieties flow abundantly.

My hats blend with me, becoming an extension of my soulful grit—
Kinda like the cherry that sits atop the banana split.

Whipping winds send my hat rolling down the street, spinning on its rim.
Catching it under my shoe, it's saved again with only a smudged and dented
    brim.

Weathered hats become grungy cripples crying out for care.
But alas our abuse persists…"Wow, that's one ugly hat"…while others just
    stand and stare.

Crisscrossed and matched, I guess we're soundly attached at that.
At my beckon, always within reach, my trusted and beloved hat.

1931 Recipe for Learning to Smoke

Irene Thomas

Ingredients:

Two eight-year-old girls with desire to look like smoking movie stars

Fifteen cents to purchase Lucky Strikes

Gullible clerk to believe cigarettes were being purchased for father

Yesterday's copies of *The Post Dispatch*

Additional copies of *Globe Democrat*

Small box of "strike anywhere" matches

Available auto to practice in (Dad's car will do)

Instructions:

1. Early evening best time to place papers in car, covering all the windows and wherever needed to keep smoke from escaping car.

2. Carefully take one cigarette each, and light each other's cigarette.

3. Strike pose that movie star would be likely to do, keeping check all the time to see that no smoke is escaping the car.

4. It's more fun lighting a new one, so don't bother smoking one all the way to burning lips.

5. One at a time…and it isn't long until the package is emptied.

6. Speaking of burning, when your stomach begins to burn and your eyes begin to tear, it's time to get out of the smoke-filled car and run to the nearest place where cold water would be found.

Bon Appetit!

DRUNKENNESS

William Killian

he made the last one a fast one
not a closing-time kind of thing
it was a midsummer afternoon
lazy and hot
nothing scheduled

there was no thinking
in his drinking
he would just show up
and pour them down
it was his way of life

the gulping had no meaning
to this pitiful frame of a man
who used alcohol
to separate feeling from fact
and then to bury both

this would be the last time
that booze would wash his throat

he made the last one a fast one
not a closing-time kind of thing
it was a midsummer afternoon
lazy and hot
nothing to do but dive into oblivion

it wasn't long until the family called
enlisting pallbearers from the bar
would one of you like to speak
at the service
say a few words on his behalf
none of us will be able to speak
we miss him so much
thanks for being his friend

Museum of Mistakes

Kathleen O'Brien

In the first room we see
a sculpture of a high school student
dressed in plaid uniform
seated at a desk
staring at returned math exam.
Notice the stunned expression,
a mixture of shock and fear.
The brass plaque simply says, "F."

In the Father-Daughter Gallery,
your attention, please,
to the featured diorama:
Daughter, dressed in Easter finery,
a pink suit with matching gloves and hat;
Father, ushering the family to the car.
The daughter stands alone
like a stricken deer,
hoping to hear the words, "You look pretty."
The title: "Please Notice Me."

Moving right along…
in this black and white photo,
a woman reads a book in bed,
her husband asleep beside her.
The inscription, "Missed Opportunity."

In this last exhibit
painted in oil,
a man in a hospital emergency room
has died.
The wife talks to him anyway.
Beaded tears fall down her face.
The painting titled:
"If Only."

Exiting the museum,
please watch for construction debris.
The "Hall of Forgiveness" will open soon.

My Father and Fred Astaire

Lollie Butler

The way my father walked, you would have thought
he was a close friend of Fred Astaire. He was busy
in the way fathers make money for their hungry:

the wife wanting new things, children needing
certain books and boots and how we outgrew everything
with numbers on them. In the early evenings of winter,

when darkness fell like a snow-laden branch,
my father turned on the Philco radio. So many colors
bounced out that I could scarcely gather them
to fill my crayon box. The music flared

like a circle skirt and the words said,
"…It brings back a night of tropical splendor…"
My father's feet tapped until they led him back
to some polished floor, confetti lights sticking
to black ties and feather boas. He glided

across the living room floor—my mother did not
look up; bending over her glasses, she mended socks,
a wooden fist in the heel. He softly sang

words he must have sung to her
when they dreamed me. He danced in his pajamas
and flannel robe as though floating under a top hat
with a glittering girl in his arms, as though Fred Astaire
taught him every step and they practiced

while I slept under the patchwork. My father sang
as he climbed the stairs,
"…And we suddenly know what heaven we're in…"
and the radio swallowed the tune.

I dreamed of glistening taps
and I can still hear my mother's voice
out of the darkness,

"Go back to sleep, dear. It's only the rain."

Yellow

Shirley Shatsky

Yellow is not my color.

It makes my skin appear
    medically challenged,
    sunflowers are too big
    for any of my vases

however

Post-it notes are handy
    for memory cues,
    bananas go well with
    morning cereal or yogurt,
    lemons add zest to
    a favorite fish

however

yellow brick roads
    are good only for cowardly lions
    straw men and other seekers
    of wizardly truths

and

yellow submarines
    are not needed by travelers
    of rutted and winding roads
    who made U-turns whenever
    life was nearing a cliff;
    they color their experiences in
    blood, fire and love.

Around the Proverbial Bend?

Phyllis J. Seltzer

A s I absentmindedly picked up the phone, I heard a Liberace voice sing, "Smile when your heart is breaking, smile even though it's aching, when there's a cloud, you can smile, you'll get by..." It continued singing till the very end of the lyrics, the voice reaching a crescendo that by now jarred me back to reality.

It was my friend, Kick, calling from across the country where he now lives. He wanted to talk about betrayal and black diamond fur. Perfectly normal for the kinds of conversations Kick and I have had over the many years we have known each other. Kick was a colorful character. He had once possessed how much money no one knows, but after being the victim of a Madoff-style financial scheme, he now had none! He had lived with eight dogs for most of his life and talked with a dog psychic by phone regularly, holding the receiver to the dogs' ears, as well, so she could communicate with them.

Now, though his situation has dramatically changed, he carries on with the same wildly eccentric take on life he always had. I think it's that vibrancy that attracts me to him and his devoted friendship. Only now am I questioning how to tell if I'm actually going around the bend into "La La Land" or if it makes sense to have these kinds of exchanges that seem perfectly normal to me.

I'd love to give you a synopsis of this morning's call, and maybe in the telling I might get a better insight into what I want to know. Please indulge me as I do this. After his song ended on an emotionally charged high note, Kick, without taking a breath, described an event to me in this way:

"Sir Fredrick's daughter called to say she was in town staying at the W and would I meet her for lunch, as she had something from her father to give me. I had not heard from her since Sir Fredrick was killed in that car accident three years ago. It happened, as you know (I didn't recall), just a short time before we were going to Dubai and around the world. When I was his escort on an earlier trip to New Orleans, we ran into Christopher Plummer, you remember (I did). Well, Sir Fredrick left his mansion to the two boys who lived with him as caretakers for years. It had to be sold for three million dollars because they could not afford the maintenance. But the condominium, which contained so many of his treasures, now needed to be dealt with, so she had come down from Canada to begin the process. His son, the Ahole, of course couldn't be bothered. The gentleman farmer, who never worked a day in his life and was supported by Sir Fredrick, was always worried about the money his father spent, greedy thing. The daughter, although a spoiled very rich heiress who has been married four or five times, has always been sweet to me."

This was all said with barely an audible breath between words on Kick's end of the phone. I attempted a few appropriate shrieks of response, but they were cut off in mid-shriek as he continued.

"Well, at any rate I met her for lunch at the hotel, after which she asked me to come up to her suite so she could give me something. Once there, she presented me with a full length, black diamond mink coat, notched collars with epaulets on each shoulder, and a half belt in the back. Inside, the blue brocade lining had my name embroidered on it. She found it in the closet with a note that said "for Kick Howell." It had been hanging there for the last three years. I know Sir Fredrick liked me because I never asked for or expected anything from him. I thought about selling the coat, but found out I could only get *bubkus* for it, so it's now in Macy's storage."

When he did come up for air, we discussed how he was treated differently as Sir Fredrick's companion compared to the horrific treatment he received from the niece and nephew of his wife, Karen, after she died. This information came as a result of me attempting to tell him about my writing assignment in Tuesday's class about young love, mature love, and betrayal.

Kick seized happily on the betrayal theme and outlined a hurtful depiction of his unappreciative relatives-in-law after all he and his wife had done for them. He was right about how generous and caring he and Karen had always been to these people and about how really callous and unfeeling they turned out to be. I would like to have had more time to respond more fully, but aside from getting out a few moans and groans of sympathy, it was difficult to have a two-sided conversation.

So what I'm trying now to sort out is whether or not my response to these calls seem fine, or if simply squealing whenever Kick takes a rare breath is nuts. Would a normal person say to Kick, "WHAT ARE YOU TALKING ABOUT?" I have never found the need to ask him that question. I've always just listened and accepted that this is his reality, and it doesn't have to co-incide with mine. I never wanted to grill him on the details of his unusual life because I feel he would tell me more if he wanted to. Kick is my friend. I accept him as someone who is, to say the very least, eccentric. His eccen-tricity seems normal to me, though not to other people who know him. My question is: Does this mean I'm also eccentric? Or does it mean I am, finally, rounding the proverbial bend?

I remember how Kick and Karen stood out in the crowd – oversized, loud, looking like cartoons. Karen, red-haired and smiling. Kick, dark strands of wig not quite managing to sit correctly upon his huge head, car-rying a man purse years before anyone ever heard of one. They lived their life together with eight poodles and Kick's mother, Clara.

At one dinner party we attended in their elegant home, we were sur-rounded by enormous framed portraits of the dogs. The table was laid with the finest china, silver, crystal, and linen. Smells from the kitchen wafted into the dining room. The current eight poodles were being offhandedly treated to dog food from a cut crystal bowl on Kick's right.

Clara sat across from me. Over her head hung a picture of "Spiro," a long dead but still grieved for white poodle. I turned to Mandy, my friend sitting beside me, and whispered, "Am I losing my mind, or do Clara and Spiro have the same face?"

Mandy looked at the portrait above Clara's head and saw the same white hair, same pointy nose, same color eyes. She gasped and tried to control the deep laughter rising up in her chest.

I grabbed her and said, "The poor thing is choking on a cashew! She'll be okay in a moment."

A night to remember, one of many we spent with our friends, the Howells.

Umbrella Attack Recipe

Ila Winslow

Ingredients:

Take one green patio umbrella
A board fence
Mix with North to South breeze
Add one medium-tall female

Directions:

1. Combine female head under umbrella with hand on winding handle to lower. Mix with eighty degrees or more temperature.

2. Keep winding and start to step out from under umbrella. After adding a whoosh of wind, discover can't get feet flat on concrete. Keep trying to put feet down flat. Hold metal shaft of umbrella stand to keep upright. Let body fall back against board fence to avoid hitting concrete.

3. Look up, see umbrella stand leaning forward. Don't let it topple. Grasp patio gate handle with left hand and release umbrella stand. Sway until gravity returns. Pause to enjoy better hearing.

Time:

Sit for ten minutes. Do not lower umbrella.
Do not rise again until heat wave lifts.

To avoid repeating umbrella attack, let stand indefinitely.

Ruth

Robert Pouriea

A funny thing happened on our honeymoon.

That was a trip to remember. We got onto a hill in Montana at night. The fuse for the headlights blew out; that wasn't bad, I just put in a new one. We started down the steep hill and winding road when the last fuse blew out. I pulled off the road and when a truck came by, I got close behind him and followed his taillights into the next town, where we got a motel. From then on we traveled only in daylight hours.

We stopped in Livingston to see Ruth's aunt, but just for a few hours, then we were on the road going through Yellowstone Park. The bears were everywhere. I think Ruth took a picture of every one of them. Finally, she said, "I think we have enough pictures of bears."

"I agree," I replied. "Let's get out of the park. We still got two days before we get to Deadwood." We were just about out of film anyway.

Just a little way down the road, Ruth yelled, "Stop the car! I want to get a close-up of this bear."

It looked like a young bear just sitting all alone on the side of the road, waiting for a handout. With the window rolled down, Ruth pointed the camera out the window while looking through the view finder. The bear thought he was going to get something to eat and started walking toward the car.

Ruth, still looking through the the view finder, lost sight of the bear, so she moved the camera down and found she was nose to nose with the bear! She screamed, "MOVE THE CAR, MOVE THE CAR!!"

The bear. seeing that he wasn't going to get any food, turned and started walking back to the side of the road. At that point Ruth raised the camera and took his picture, but all she got was his rear end. So I always said, "That is a picture of my wife's bear ass."

Fewer Or Less

Jean Marie Purcell

Someone decided it's okay
to throw out Fewer. Just use Less.
That's a game I refuse to play.

Less describes quantity or things
in bulk: rice, beans, cheese, or respect…
not cattails or butterfly wings.

Fewer refers to things you can count:
toes, nozzles for the garden hose,
reasons, dogs – *not an amount.*

Another fool decided we—
I wish I knew where he's hiding—
should use them interchangeably!

Is this a sentence you'd compose?
"I have fewer respect for you
since I saw you picking your nose."

Some Assembly Required

Buck Dopp

My attempts to build, repair, or assemble anything in our home usually ended up costing money. My installation of the easy-to-operate garage door opener started the house on fire. A plumber was needed to renovate our bathroom pipes after I tried to save money by unclogging the drain myself. The plumber told my wife, "Your hubby should have used the plunger instead of taking the pipes apart with a wrench."

How unprofessional of him!

Some assembly required. Those three words, which can be spoken in less than two seconds, hide the reality that a lot of work on your part will be required before the purchase will function the way the advertisement said it would. Those simple words hijack common sense and launch the unsuspecting victim into a fantasy world where truth has vanished and unicorns rule. Those words delude the buyer into thinking that what is required is no big deal.

"Some assembly" sounds so minor. The color picture on the front of the box adds to the deception. You start out thinking it's going to be easy, *but there probably aren't even any written directions.*

Before long the consumer will be spending hours cross-legged on the living room floor, legs numb, screaming at no one in particular, in the midst of a roomful of scattered parts that have yet to find a home.

A case in point is the time I put together the new vacuum cleaner. I was having a little difficulty.

"Why don't you ask one of your friends to come over and help you out," my wife suggested. I was sure I detected a slight smirk, which she quickly covered up.

Looking up with my fists full of parts, I replied, "Because I don't need any help. That's why."

Then she handed me the manual that came with the vacuum. "Why don't you just read this?"

"That's not the way I roll," I said. "Those directions are written by engineers, and everyone knows they can't write. Besides, I'm an intuitive person and learn better by visualization."

Standing with her arms folded, she stared at me with a glare that would have burned a hole in a piece of steel. However, I stared right back at her and said, "And, by the way, if you'd quit interrupting me, I'd have that darn thing put together by now."

"Fine. Whatever. I'm rounding up the kids, and we're going to visit my mother for the weekend. Call if you need anything." She stomped out of the room.

I didn't mind her leaving one bit. I work better alone anyway. When she's gone, I enjoy being by myself. Of course, I never tell her that because I don't want to hurt her feelings. I may not be mechanically inclined, but I am very kind, and she knows that. I'm sure that's why she married me: my kindness.

After she and the kids drove away, I went to the kitchen and made myself a cup of coffee and opened a package of chocolate chip cookies. It's important to get your blood sugar to the proper level when you're assembling stuff.

While I munched on those cookies, I imagined what would happen at my mother-in-law's house. Her name is Florence, but I've nicknamed her Daughter of Satan. I could imagine her bad-mouthing me behind my back. She'll remind my wife that she used to date an engineer named Bob. The old bag will sneer, "Remember Bob? You should have married him. Bob would have been real good at putting your vacuum cleaner together."

Yeah, maybe so. But would Bob be kind?

It took all weekend, but I got the vacuum put together. When my wife showed up Sunday night, I showed her the finished product. I expected her to say thanks and give me a hug. Instead, she pointed to a box of parts. "What's that? Aren't those supposed to be attached to the vacuum cleaner?"

She's always finding faults and imperfections with everything I do, but I know she means well. "Those are spare parts," I said.

When I fired up the vacuum cleaner, it sounded louder than the lawn mower. She noticed how loud it was and yelled so I could hear her over the vacuum: "Howard, if I use that thing, it will make me deaf."

I had anticipated her concern about the volume and had bought a bag of disposable earplugs. "Here you go," I said and handed her the bag.

"What am I supposed to do with these?"

That was the day vacuuming became *my job*.

By the time our grandchildren came along, it had been years since I had tried to assemble anything. The passage of time had erased any recollection of the kind of damage I was capable of inflicting. When I ran across a little toy train set called the "Polar Express," I thought it would be the perfect Christmas gift for my grandson. I paid no attention to the wording on the box: "some assembly required." I hadn't read those words in a long time, and now they meant nothing to me – though they should have.

Actually, I thought I did a decent job assembling the "Polar Express." It only took about twenty minutes to set up the track. As I gathered my wife and grandchildren into the living room to watch the maiden voyage of the "Polar Express," I told my grandson to turn off the lights because the picture on the box showed a light on the engine.

Feeling so proud of myself, I made an announcement. "Everyone find a comfortable place to sit so you can watch the train." I pushed the "on" switch, but the "Polar Express" didn't move. "Someone please turn on the lights," I said.

Reaching for the box to take another look, I noticed three little words on the cover I hadn't read before…

"Batteries not included."

Patience? Yeah, Right!

Jack Campbell

The dictionary defines the word *patience* as not being able to bear pain, trials, endure delay or annoyance *without complaint*. The joke about the old vulture and the young vulture sitting high up on a tree limb should serve as an adequate segue and make my point, if indeed I have one!

The old vulture perches for hours looking out over the African savannah for any sign of a carcass. The young vulture paces back and forth on the limb, at times viewing the savannah himself. He finally exclaims to the old vulture, "I'm hungry."

The old vulture, without interrupting his stare, says, "Patience, my son, patience!" The young vulture takes another long look out over the savannah, turns to the old vulture and says, "Patience, my ass. Let's go kill something!"

Like the young vulture, patience has never been my strong suit. That's why I truly admire my dear wife and others like her, who never seem to buckle under pressure. At one time or another, she has either stared me down from making a faux pas or saved me from a mob after I made one. On reflection, that's probably why the Army put me in the infantry. I guess they figured a guy with a short fuse like me ought to be right up there on the front line, where I could do the most damage.

Here are some of the things that test my mettle on a daily basis:

1. The long wait at a doctor's office (the big room and the little room)
2. A long line at the checkout stand or standing behind the little old lady who waits until the clerk has checked through all of her groceries before she starts fumbling unsuccessfully for her checkbook and pen
3. The guy ahead of you at a red light, texting or contemplating his navel when the light turns green

To start with, I have an unusually loud voice; even when I talk normally, it carries more than most. So this particular day my wife and I are in the checkout line at our local market, and we're one or two or customers from checking out. At the register, two portly, middle-aged ladies are venting their woes to the clerk on their efforts to lose weight and present themselves (physically) in a better way. The clerk has indulged their banter much longer than I thought she should, thus adding to my rising blood pressure. At one point I hear one of the ladies exclaim, "I just want to change my look entirely."

Well, I lean in close to my wife and say, "Some aluminum siding would be nice!"

Needless to say, everybody in that line and the adjoining line heard me. My wife was trying to hide her extreme embarrassment, while the guy in front of us just plain lost it. The two portly women were "mouth-open" shocked and, in unison, they gave me a "Well, I never," as they turned and quickly departed with their cart.

Now, I hadn't intended for anyone but my wife to hear me, but my impatience with their jawing got to me, even as all around me kept their cool. I was truly not proud of that particular incident.

The doctor's office has, of course, proven to be another chink in my armor. Just last week my wife had an appointment with her cardiologist to wear a 24-hour monitoring device. I volunteered to go with her but she waved me off with, "They're just going to hook me up with the thing. Don't worry about it. I'll be fine."

Later, she came home complaining about waiting almost two hours beyond her appointment time before the doctor finally saw her. The hair on my neck always comes to attention just listening to this kind of crap. So I volunteered to go back with her the next day and vent as only I know how. She pulled a gun on me and threatened to shoot me if I go anywhere near her doctor.

I think you can see my dilemma. Having a short fuse is one thing, but having a big mouth to go with it is just wrong. You usually run into one or the other, but not in tandem. My latest annoyance is the jerk that walks around the pool table for two or three minutes on each shot, looking at every combination on the table before he finally shoots. At my age, he's tampering with my life expectancy! Hell, I can't even get a three-minute egg in Sun City without paying up front.

Oh, it's a curse all right, and I'll probably need a priest to end it!

MESSAGES IN THE SAND

Dorothy Parcel

HUMBUG

Growing old is interesting since we gradually, or sometimes abruptly, need all kinds of artificial parts and props. Personally, I feel my hearing has gone south. I haven't been fitted for hearing aids yet, but it's only a matter of time. I blame television.

The speakers on commercials talk so plainly, I can hear every nuance, even if I don't want to. The actors on actual programs talk as though they're learning ventriloquism. Their lips hardly move; it seems to be a matter of pride. If the programs weren't made for twelve-year-olds, I wouldn't be able to follow them at all.

The other night on an episode, one character pulled his gun, and said, "Butter the dog, silly hot!"

The other guy answered, "A slumber brisket bluet!"

Then they began shooting. Maybe the problem is, I watch too much television.

MY ATHLETIC CAREER

We didn't have gym classes in the tiny schools I went to until ninth grade. No. The teacher opened the door for recess, and we were on our own. The only thing she told us was for the boys to stay away from the girls' restroom, and for the girls to keep their dress down while on the swings.

My dad listened to ball games on radio, but I didn't pay much attention to that until suddenly, in fifth grade, I was handed a bat and told it was my turn. That surprised me. I hadn't done that before.

I stood on home plate and waited for the teacher to tell me what to do next. Then the pitcher, a girl who was in fifth grade for the second time, hurled the ball at me. She missed. But I took after her. It was a foolish thing to do. She could, and did, beat up boys in the seventh grade. But I had a bat.

She ran. The teacher grabbed me and sent me to my room. That was the end of my athletic career, which was okay with me. I wasn't built for it, anyway.

VIEWPOINTS

When I was young, I learned the hard way that there were other viewpoints than mine. I found out that, because of my size and age, my opinions about practically everything were as important to other people as those of my dog, Buddy.

One of Buddy's opinions was that anyone in a uniform is the enemy, and he hated them.

I don't hate people in uniform, but they scare me. I think that opinion goes back to the Principal of the schools I went to. Their uniform was a suit and, where I lived, men only wore a suit if they were going to a funeral.

I guess that's why, when a cop in uniform passed me in the doorway of the market the other day and said, "Hello, young lady," I almost fainted.

Into the Tuscan Sunrise

Susan Thompson

The trip by plane and car to our Italian vacation apartment was a long one – nearly 24 hours – so I slept long and well that night. To start the first day in my new Tuscan setting, I set out on a brisk walk upon arising in the morning.

Driveway stones crunch beneath my feet as I leave our apartment. It's all downhill from here, as we are set atop a good-sized hill surrounded by verdant valleys and undulating hills in all directions. Leaving the driveway with its sheltering grove of plane trees and making my way down the dirt road, I am soon greeted with the full expanse of the vista from atop our hill.

Before me spreads a patchwork of silvery green olive groves, recently harvested vineyards, lush family farms, and tiny villages. The valleys are replete with newly plowed fields, and the hillsides are fringed by stately cypress trees. Not far off on a nearby hill sits an old church, its rugged bell tower now used only monthly for services. It has its own row of cypress trees marching up the drive to the little cemetery near the entrance.

One of the special aspects of an early morning walk is the play of light on the landscape. As I start out, the sun has yet to appear above the horizon, but is already lending a gentle silvery glow to the darkness of the early morning skies. A heavy layer of mist lies sleeping in the valleys and provides an ethereal quality to the perspective. As the sunlight begins to pierce the low-hung clouds, the lower portion of the sky grows rosy in color. Close to the road the abundant Queen Anne's lace flowers, now shriveled and brown, are a favorite of spiders for web creation. The increasing light plays upon the dew that decorates the myriad spider webs. In the early glow of sunrise, the dewdrops sparkle like gems adorning the intricate webbed designs. Such a lovely sight – I wish I had brought my camera.

As I make my way past a faded cornfield, I am startled by the sudden flutter of wings and the raspy clucking of several pheasants, whose morning meal I have apparently disturbed. Farther on I am treated to another bird song – a chorus of unidentified origin, but clearly emanating from a large grove of plane trees. The only other sounds to greet me are those of the sheep in a barn not far from our apartment. The gentle sound of their bleating blends with the tinkle of the tiny bells they wear around their necks. The morning serenade invigorates my walk.

After walking the two miles down to the main road, I turn and head back up, still enjoying the loveliness of my countryside surroundings. When I am nearing the top of the hill, just below the little church, I spy a rainbow. It appears to be arching right out of the church and into the now blue expanse of sky. The visible clouds are puffy and white, so I take the rainbow as a sign of a great day ahead of me for the start of my vacation in Southern Tuscany.

A Visit to Sunny Arizona

Bonita Papenfuss

I recall my mother's indignant words to our grown children the first Christmas after my husband and I had retired, sold our home, and moved from Minnesota to Green Valley, Arizona. "It's so hot there," she told them. "You wait and see; they'll be home in six months!" So three years later I was surprised when my mother announced she and my sister were planning to visit us. They were looking forward to leaving the cold and snow of February in Minnesota to spend a week in warm and sunny Arizona.

After much anticipation, the day of their arrival was upon us. As Larry and I drove to the airport that chilly evening, I thought about our departure from Minnesota and the hurt and disappointment on my mother's face. I wondered what she would think of our modest home in the beautiful Sonoran Desert, and I hoped this visit might help her understand why we loved it here so much. My thoughts were interrupted as Mom and Cathy emerged from the escalator, and we were greeted with hugs and tales of their bumpy descent through the clouds into the Tucson airport. There was much chatter on the short drive home to Green Valley, but since it was late, they decided to turn in as soon as they were unpacked and settled in the guest room.

We spent the early part of the week introducing them to our favorite tourist attractions, including a day at the Arizona Sonora Desert Museum, a morning tour of Kartchner Caverns, and a dusty afternoon ride (in the back of a friend's open Jeep) over the Santa Rita mountains by way of Box Canyon Road. Toward the end of their visit, Mom, Cathy, and I prepared to set out on a girls-only adventure to Tombstone, Arizona with overnight reservations at The School House Inn, an historic bed & breakfast in Bisbee.

We were loaded and on the road early that crisp February morning. The sun attempted to peek through the unusual cloud cover as we drove through rolling hills covered with fuzzy-looking cholla cactus and spindly ocotillo on our scenic route to Tombstone. Strong winds buffeted the car and outside temperatures dipped so low we found it necessary to ride with the heat on. However, we let none of it put a chill on our spirits. We were just happy to be sharing this time together. After reaching Tombstone, we settled Mom into the wheelchair I had borrowed from a friend, wrapped a blanket around her, slipped on our hats and gloves, and braved wind and near-freezing temperatures.

Our first and most important stop was at one of the many photo studios to have an old-time, Victorian-era group picture taken. This was something my mother had talked about for a long time, and she was giddy with anticipation. The shopkeeper was patient and lighthearted as Mom's arthritis-ridden knees made the process of getting into her costume an arduous, time-consuming affair.

Once we had donned our lace-adorned, high-necked, floor-length dresses, the photographer began to accessorize each of us with cameo-studded chokers, fingerless mid-length gloves, and multicolored felt hats. Then she staged us for this very serious (they didn't smile for pictures back then) black-and-white photo. Mother was seated in front with her flowing dress covering the small chair; my sister and I were situated behind her on either side. Cathy was positioned with her palm resting on the handle of a small parasol, and I was handed a lace fan to be held daintily near my cheek. Lastly, off came our glasses (too modern-looking), and the camera started clicking. It was a thoroughly enjoyable experience and Mom had a lot of fun with it, even to the point of announcing to the photographer that this was to be the cornerstone picture of her funeral collage!

Warmly dressed again with photos in hand, we struggled to push open the heavy, weathered shop door only to be assaulted by whirling, sleet-filled, frigid winds. With hats on and heads down, we bumped the wheelchair along the uneven wooden walkways, fighting our way through the elements. After only one chilly stop at an open-air merchant, we decided to take refuge in a nearby cafe. It was the place Mother had hinted at earlier in the day: The OK Cafe, Home of the Buffalo Burger. The restaurant had a dusty, Western decor, but it appeared to be a favorite dining and gathering spot for the locals, so our expectations were high.

We were seated in a small booth by the window. While Cathy and I enjoyed steaming, delicious bowls of soup, Mom savored every morsel of

her buffalo burger. We chatted and lingered and took pleasure in this re-
spite from the weather. When Mom thought we'd loitered long enough, she
hailed the waitress and generously paid for our meals. Before leaving, we
glanced out for a visual weather check and were awestruck to watch as the
sleet turned to the biggest, fluffiest snowflakes imaginable. A winter won-
derland in Arizona! Then, just moments later, it stopped as quickly as it had
started.

We'd had little opportunity to shop but we had accomplished our most
important task, and this break in the weather was our chance to hit the
road. So I quickly ran down the dirt alleyway, retrieved the car, and swung
by the café to pick up Mom and Cathy. After stowing the wheelchair and
peeling off a couple layers of clothing, we snuggled back into the warm car
and began rounding the curves up into the mountains toward Bisbee. We
hadn't gone far before my sister and I exchanged concerned glances when we
spotted dark, ominous-looking clouds up ahead. Sure enough, we round-
ed the next turn into a winter storm comparable to blizzard conditions in
Minnesota! My rusty winter-driving skills were sorely tested as the blowing
snow created a thick layer over the asphalt, making it very slippery and demanding all my focus while we climbed in elevation, winding our way over
treacherous bridges and through the mountain passes.

After what felt like hours, the snow stopped, and we spotted the exit sign
for Bisbee. Finally, we were off the highway and on our way down the main
street toward our overnight B & B. As we got close enough, however, to get
a glimpse of the long, glistening uphill driveway, we could tell yet another
challenge was upon us. But I was determined. I'd gotten us this far, and no
snow-slicked driveway was going to stand between me and a warm bed! So
up we went, slow and steady. Fortunately, only one other car was in the small
parking area, and I was able to maneuver us into a spot near the door. We
had arrived safe, though weather-weary, at our evening's destination.

We rang the buzzer at the front door, and our bed and breakfast propri-
etors greeted us with warmth and smiles. After Mom's slow journey up the
steps, we were shown to our lovely two-bedroom suite decorated with an-
tiques of all types – from an old steamer chest full of vintage dolls to a delicate, wood-trimmed settee covered in gold brocade upholstery. Mother was
exhausted and made only a few unpleasant grumblings about the weather
before plopping down on her bed and nodding off. My sister and I escaped

to our own area of the suite and settled in to chat and laugh about the day's events.

An hour later the three of us were enjoying a snack of cheese and crackers as we relaxed in the warm and homey refuge of the downstairs dining and living area. With our hands wrapped around soothing cups of hot chocolate, we peered out through ice crystals on the window at the serene, snow-covered patio where we had anticipated spending a sun-drenched afternoon sipping iced tea, listening to the birds, and enjoying the beautiful greenery.

The night in our charming room was restful, and in the morning we were pleased to join the other two guests for a tasty, home-cooked breakfast of eggs, bacon, toast, and crispy hash brown potatoes. After thanking our host and hostess, it was time to load up and head back to the lower elevations of Green Valley – but not before Mother Nature had one more giggle at our expense. There had been freezing rain overnight, and every entrance to the car, including the trunk, was frozen shut! Some muscle (and a few choice words) later I was able to crack open a back door, crawl to the front seat and start the engine. Soon we were packed up and settled in our cozy vehicle, ready for the journey home. Later that afternoon, while driving down our street with our house in sight, we gave a collective sigh of relief. We were happy to be home with a bit warmer temperatures, and – except on the mountain tops – the absence of snow.

Mom is back in Minnesota now, but it was wonderful having her here for a few days. I think she really enjoyed her stay. She was able to relax and spend quality time with us at our home, enjoy a few desert tourist attractions, and go on our unique and exciting girls' adventure. But I have to wonder: what is she telling people now? *"I went to sunny Arizona in February to visit my daughter, and it was as cold and snowy there as it is here! Give 'em a few more months – they'll be home by Christmas!"*

Sit A Lot

Louise Larsen

I sit a lot
Sometimes I sit and think
Sometimes I think of
Birds and flowers and mighty oaks
Sometimes I just sit.

I read a lot
Sometimes I read and think
Of Shakespeare and Alcott and
Robert Frost
Sometimes I just read.

I dream a lot
Sometimes I dream
Of the snowy Alps,
Mt. Olympus and dead Chinese
Warriors
Defending emperors
Of long ago
Sometimes I just dream.

I imagine a lot
Sometimes I imagine and think
Of David Copperfield,
Miss Haversham
And Davy Crockett
Sometimes I just imagine.

Remembering Marcel Marceau

Muriel R. Sandy

May 31, 1988: My husband, Bob, and I stared at each other and shook our heads in disbelief at our first view of Jakarta, Indonesia. Everywhere we looked, we saw black three-wheeled bicycles, loud two-stroke-engine taxis, small green busses and large orange ones, each spewing exhaust into the air as they weaved in and out through streets jammed with pedestrians.

Overcome by smog, humidity, and crowds, unsure of what to do next, we slipped into the nearby Sari Pacific Hotel. The spacious lobby looked like a gathering place for businessmen in western suits who chatted with others in like attire. Hotel staff in traditional long, wraparound sarongs and batik shirts walked about silently, delivering iced drinks. We eyed an empty sofa and headed towards it, took a seat, stretched out our legs, and placed our backpacks underneath, hoping to give the impression we were not there to take advantage of the air conditioning – which, of course, we were.

Next to the reception desk, I saw a stand with a gold picture frame. Wondering if it held a menu for the hotel dining room, I got up to have a look. It held today's schedule and stated in French, "Press Conference for Marcel Marceau, 4 p.m., fourth floor." I read it twice, then checked my watch: 3:06.

Do they mean the world renowned French master of mime? I wondered. Years ago, while living in Los Angeles, Bob and I had seen Monsieur Marceau perform on stage at the Biltmore Theatre. The house was packed. He portrayed, in mime, the following:

- a man's reaction to a patriotic parade

- walking against the wind

- climbing a staircase

- a peevish waiter

- a tug of war

- an old woman

- a lion tamer

and many other universal images of everyday life. We were spellbound.

Now, if I was right that he was in the hotel, this was either serendipity or a gift from the gods. In either case, it was not to be ignored. Excited, I went back to Bob and told him what I'd just discovered. His eyes lit up like a child who just heard Santa was on his way.

"Do you think we could get in to see him?" I said.

"You never know until you ask. Check with the desk clerk."

The young fellow couldn't help. However, he gave me a phone number. After fruitless attempts to find a functioning and unoccupied public phone in the hotel that didn't have a line of twelve people waiting to use it, I gave up in frustration. By now it was 3:45.

On my way back to the sofa, I caught sight of a tall, thin man with unkempt blondish-grey hair wearing a white shirt and trousers. *Oh, my goodness. That's him,* I said to myself. When I got back, I said to Bob, "He's here!" I tilted my head in the man's direction.

"How do you know that's him? You've never seen him out of costume and white face."

"That's true. Look, his press conference is in a few minutes. Why don't we go upstairs and see what happens?"

We checked our backpacks at the front desk and headed to the elevator. When we stepped out at the fourth floor, we found ourselves facing a reception table. A young Indonesian woman was talking in French to two men. When they finished, I stepped forward and whispered in English, hoping she understood, "Is this conference open to the public?"

"I don't know. One moment, please."

I stepped back. She spoke to her colleague, then turned. "Yes. You may go in."

Bob and I looked at each other and grinned like a couple of Cheshire cats.

Inside the room, rows of chairs lined either side of a center aisle. In front sat a table covered in a green cloth. A bouquet of red roses softened the austere arrangement of microphones. We took seats at the back, behind the reporters and photographers. I looked about to see if I recognized anyone.

I haven't a clue what made me think there might be a familiar VIP in the crowd. In any case, I saw no one familiar.

At 4:15 Monsieur Marceau walked in.

I turned to Bob. "Isn't that the man I pointed out to you in the lobby?"

"You're absolutely right."

Marceau was accompanied by his assistant, a young fellow about thirty years old, sporting casual clothes, earrings, and a ponytail. Another man, who turned out to be the translator, joined them, and they all took seats at the table.

For the next two hours we experienced a multilingual press interview. Monsieur Marceau was gracious, attentive, and seemed impressed with the questions the reporters asked. Question were asked in Bahasa, the Indonesian language, then translated into French. Marceau would reply in French, and the answers were translated back into Bahasa. I was kicking myself for not having worked harder on my French lessons years ago, but Bob helped fill in the missing words.

When the interview was over, Monsieur Marceau invited everyone to join him for coffee, sweets, and informal chat in an adjoining room. He stopped by the table where we sat with four others. My mind went blank. I was overwhelmed that someone so important in the world of entertainment had come by to talk to us. Bob asked if he would sign a handout I had picked up earlier from the hotel reception desk. I handed him my pen. He asked our names and began to sign.

"Monsieur Marceau," Bob said. "We saw you perform in Los Angeles."

"My God, that was a long time ago. I'm better now."

The next morning we took a couple of busses to the agency office to buy tickets for that evening's performance. The wife of the French Cultural Attaché was there. We were introduced to her. When Bob mentioned how excited we were to have tickets for the performance that night, she invited us to the post-performance private buffet dinner party in Marceau's honor.

I could hardly believe my ears. My eyes filled with tears as Bob accepted her invitation, and she added our names to her guest list. That evening, Maestro, without uttering one word, kept us enthralled with his vignettes depicting incidents from life we all recognized.

Afterwards, Bob said, "*Vous etes magnifique, Monsieur Marceau.*"

"*Merci beaucoup,*" he said with a smile.

"*C'est une grande nuit de se souvenir.* It is a grand night to remember," Bob said.

But the story doesn't end there. Eleven years later, at the Performing Arts Center in Escondido, California, we were chosen to work as volunteer ushers the night Monsieur Marceau performed. When the lights dimmed, I sat once again mesmerized as he portrayed the following classics:

- the pickpocket's nightmare

- the seven deadly sins

- youth, maturity, and old age

After the performance, we stood in the reception line to meet him. Bob turned to me. "Do you realize this is the third time we've met Marcel Marceau?"

"I know. I can hardly believe it myself."

When our time came, I carefully pulled out from its original shipping tube the one-and-a-half-foot-wide by two-foot-high publicity poster we had purchased in Jakarta. On it Marcel Marceau is pictured from the waist up, wearing a black wig, a deep blue-grey shirt, his face in white grease paint, his eyes almost closed, with mascara eyelashes and red lips outlined in black, his head slightly tilted upward against a dark background. I spread *l'affiche* in front of Maestro, who was seated at the table He stared at it for the longest time, then pointed to the lower left hand corner which read: Graha Bhakti Budaya, 73, Jl. Cikini Raya, 1er et 2 juin 1988 a l9h30.

He looked up at us. "*Mon Dieu,*" he exclaimed. "*Il y a longtemps, n'est-ce pas?*" He picked up a black magic marker pen from the table and said, "*Comment vous appelez-vous?*"

Bob gave him our names, and he wrote on the righthand side of *l'affiche,* "*A Muriel et Bob, Retounee a votre coeur.*" *To Muriel and Bob, returned to your heart.* Below, he put his signature, Marcel Marceau, and drew a sketch of his mime character, Bip, the white-faced clown with a tall battered hat and flower, often referred to as a modern day Don Quixote.

Today, that poster hangs on the wall in my home, a silent reminder of those magical moments from the past with the silent storyteller.

MEMORIES

Erin Gilroy Thomas

So many memories
In an antique store
Of dreams and hopes
That are no more—
Now merely a remembrance
Of times gone by
The echo of laughter
Somewhere lies.
The events of yesterday
Once reflected
In the dust-layered mirrors
Time has not affected.
The stains on the post
Of an old oak bed
Left by teardrops
With no words said.
The memories of yesterday
In an antique store
Tell the story of
A love longed for.

Cloud Pocket

Una Nichols Hynum

The sky is birthday-party-blue,
small, playful clouds chase
each other like white train cars.
They never catch up.
One cloud wears a larger cloud
like a deep gray pocket.
What would I put in a cloud
pocket knowing how soon it will melt
into nothingness like spun sugar?
I'd fold myself into the lint
at the bottom like a cat, eyes closed
paws tucked, ready to purr.
Maybe I'd bring an armchair
to curl up with the ever-present
book that falls when I doze, surprising me.
Probably this is how I'll die
under the weight of *Moby Dick*
or Rilke's *Sonnets to Orpheus.*

The Perfect Present

Nancy J. Alauzen

Dad was hard to shop for. Finding the perfect present was always a challenge. It wasn't that he was particular in his tastes, but rather that material things didn't matter at all to him. If he had a clean pair of trousers and shirt he was content. If we wrapped clothing for his birthday, Father's Day, or Christmas, Dad politely smiled and said thank you, but he closed the box. Our more creative ideas were more welcome. Coffee mugs with funny sayings, a plastic can that made obnoxious sounds generated several laughs.

Dad was a steelworker, but enjoyed reading and watching programs about finance, investing, and real estate. One of his favorite gifts was a subscription to the *Wall Street Journal*. He enjoyed reading the paper cover to cover and in retirement spent plenty of time watching programs on finance and investing.

Our present for Father's Day 1996 needed to be special. Dad had just been diagnosed with pancreatic cancer, and it appeared this would be the last Father's Day we would spend with him. I had an idea! I talked with my sister and four brothers to run it by them. Since Dad thoroughly enjoyed watching Bill Wolman on CNBC, I would send a letter to Bill Wolman, the Chief Economist at the time for CNBC to see if my dad could take Bill Wolman to lunch in New York City.

Several weeks later, I received a call from the staff at Mr. Wolman's office. They agreed that Bill Wolman would meet my dad. My siblings and I all chipped in, and my dad and two brothers were off to New York City. What an adventure they had! They toured the CNBC offices, the CNBC studio, watched Bill Wolman record his program live, toured *Business Week* magazine and lunched with Bill Wolman via Bill Wolman's own limousine. That night my dad told me, "I had the time of my life!"

Several weeks later, I suggested Dad write a thank you note. My dad dictated and I transcribed. He thanked Bill Wolman for the wonderful day, the tours, and the opportunity to watch him record his program. Dad told Bill Wolman that "all of my friends at the coffee shop enjoyed hearing the story of meeting Bill Wolman and Neil Cavuto." He closed the letter by thanking Bill Wolman again for making his Father's Day present one he wouldn't forget!

That was our last Father's Day with my dad, and I am glad a celebrity made the time to help give my dad the perfect present.

Quilts I Have Known

Mary L. Kulm

1. The War Effort Quilts

I remember they all wore housedresses – these women who gathered around a quilt. A frame kept the quilt very tight as they surrounded it with busy fingers. The talk was of families, sons who were overseas, daughters maturing and confusing their mothers, stretching rations and saving gasoline, how the "victory garden" was doing well – ordinary things.

Some cut fabric at the dining room table. Others threaded needles to keep the rhythm going so quilts would be mass-produced as fast as the Ladies Aid Society of the Baptist Church could make them. The treadle machine made its even noise as one of the ladies pumped it, joining squares. The feeling was patriotic. The product was intended for "our boys" – maybe the wounded ones.

It was a beautiful scene in Grandma's house.

I do not remember if the quilts were lovely, but we all knew they were going overseas for the war effort, and the quilters were dedicated to their task. They would have tea before they went home – on foot.

2. My Brother's Quilt

In my childhood home, the backdrop for every evening's good night ritual was the quilt on my brother's bed. It had 48 squares, one for every state. Each state's name was embroidered on a square with a depiction of the flower for that state. The predominant colors in the strips surrounding the blocks were red, white, and blue, and each square set at the corners of the blocks was embroidered with a star. This quilt had been lovingly made by our father's aunt.

Our mother sang to us there or read. She encouraged us to pray, quizzed us about the states and helped us delay bedtime. It was our routine and the quilt was an integral part of the scene.

When my brother left our home for his independence, he took the quilt. It was his. It was always kept on a bed in his dorm room or home. He died of a near drowning/heart attack in 2005. His wife lived a few years longer, and when she passed away her sister sent us the quilt. It is very worn. Some squares are barely readable. I really feel a strong attachment to it. Memories flood over me. We lost our mother when we were quite young, but some of her spirit is still there.

3. Grandma's Flower Garden

My mother hand-pieced the blocks for a Grandma's Flower Garden quilt for me before she passed away in 1945. They were held onto for some time, then were sent off to Goodwill or some such organization, since no one quilted in the immediate family. I used to play with them. They were quite lovely – yellow in every center, a solid color in the next ring of pieces, then a print of the same color in the outside ring. Remembering them was a part of my grief process.

When my husband's parents moved from their final home together, we sorted through much accumulation of household treasures. Among these was a Grandma's Flower Garden quilt, obviously made during World War II because some of the fabrics, particularly the back of the piece, were flour sacks from the WWII era. This quilt is now in our beach home. I'm happy to have a Grandma's Flower Garden quilt, even though it was not the one intended for me.

4. Friendship Quilt

The school staff, certified and classified, all made one quilt block, and the secretary, whose idea it was to make a friendship quilt, made a center square outlining my husband's work history for a grand gift when he retired as former principal Harold. It is one of our treasures.

5. My Efforts

Over the years I have made several quilts. Because I had three daughters for whom I sewed, I always had lots of scraps. It was fun to incorporate these into someone's comforter. These were for family warmth or gifts for special occasions. This kept me up at night after the children were in bed.

It's a practice that connects me to the generations of women who have cut up perfectly good fabric and sewn it back together artistically for practical purposes and sheer pleasure.

Our oldest granddaughter swam from the time she was eight through her college years. Her quilt blocks had photos that chronicled her career, and even a newspaper article.

Three times I made quilts to auction at fundraising events. It's amazing that people will pay to sit at a table where they know they will be given enough wine to entice them to support a good cause. Thinly disguised as a party, these occasions do bring in a healthy contribution to whatever cause is being promoted.

I sew very little now. I tried to get some young women I know to come look at some of my fabrics, which I would gladly give them. They declined, saying they would prefer making their own mistakes. Nevertheless, I'm glad the practice is alive and well.

What an Eyeful!

Joan E. Zekas

He opened the Christmas gift very carefully. Then, with a flourish, Dad pulled out the scarf and swirled it around his neck. "Just what I needed," he said. Truth to tell, the scarf I made was no great shakes, but Dad was always a cheerleader for his kids. The handmade scarf was my first attempt at knitting...a little waffle-weave pattern in a dusky burgundy color.

I thought of that long-ago, modest effort of mine as I strolled across Pittsburgh's Warhol bridge in September of 2013. The city's decision to clothe the whole bridge with knitted and crocheted works of art struck me as an impossible – maybe insane – effort!

The Warhol is one long bridge – 1,061 feet! Two huge upright towers anchor the bridge. The ambitious plan was to cover the towers, cover the bridge railings and, most extensive of all, to cover all four sides of the bridge with 580 knitted and crocheted panels.

And they did it! The knitting and crocheting were done by a varied group of 3,000 enthusiasts from teenage boys to clusters of neighbors who did "knit-ins" to out-of-town folks who wanted to contribute.

Opening day was a bonanza of sights and sounds. The whole bridge was shut down to traffic. Six musical groups performed, 780 yoga practitioners strutted and posed, hula hoopers twirled and rolled along, while arts and crafts people carried their creations.

Did somebody say sensory overload?

I went down to see the bridge display twice, each time on a brilliant, sunny day, my camera at the ready. As I walked along by the water, I could see one of our party boats gliding toward the Warhol Bridge. The passengers were able to get a good view of the ribbon of colors as they slid beneath the bridge. The knitted panels were on all four sides of the bridge, so river traffic below, as well as automobile traffic above, could see the display.

On one of my walks across the bridge, I could see more detail: squares inside squares, with vividly colored flower shapes (the kind of crochet work you would find on sofa cushions in your Grammie's parlor). Feeling the patterns under my fingers, I was suddenly back home.

I had been a real skeptic about this project. Where would the money come from (especially in our worrisome economy)? And what would happen to all that handwork in the wind and rain during the two weeks it was on display? Would the pieces sag and distort? Not to worry. No tax funds were used, and the knitted and crocheted work held up just fine.

At the end, all of the pieces were removed, divided into segments and laundered. The items were given to the homeless and to shelters. (Even in the animal shelters, the kittens and dogs enjoyed their cozy comforters.)

Tucked away in a drawer somewhere, I still have that dusky burgundy scarf I knitted for Dad so long ago. Maybe one cold winter day I'll get it out...drape it around my shoulders and revel in the warm memories.

Down the San Juan River

Claudia Foster

I have run rapids before, but never ones like these. I have breast cancer. Two months ago, a phone call changed the course of my river. "Your biopsy was positive," the detached distant voice on the other end was saying…and my kayak suddenly veered down an unknown tributary.

The red walls of the canyon loomed on either side of me. Shut from the sun, the sky darkened, and I steeled myself for an uncertain ride. I felt fine, and yet I could hear the terrible rumble of the rapids distantly up ahead, so I stiffened my body and set my oars. The canyon walls were steep, and I knew that these rapids I could not portage. "I can't go around them; I have to go through them," I instinctively knew, and I knew there was no returning upriver…going back was not an option. Even with the roar in my ears, I couldn't yet know if the rapids were going to be a Class 1 or a Class 5, a Stage Four.

But I had River Guides. They knew the river. I banked my kayak on a sandbar and climbed a cliff to confer with them. Surgeon, plastic surgeon, oncologist and radiology-oncologist… These were new words, and at first I didn't even understand each specialty. So much to know and so little time to chart my course, yet my river guides know the river and I'm not the first, or the last, to gain from their experience. We stood on a ledge of red rock, reading the river below, studying the rapids. I felt slightly lightheaded at this height, focused on the rush of water that coursed over and through the massive boulders…the boulders I needed to clear. "Depending on the water level and the subtle relocation of rock, the rapids change with each person that runs them," I was told. I listened. Intently. "Keep your eyes just three feet ahead of your boat," they continued. "Imagine the smooth water ahead, but don't get too far ahead of yourself. Know that there are friends downriver below the rapids watching for you, ready to celebrate with you, but keep your eyes focused on the water and not the rocks. The boat goes where your eyes go."

In the month before the surgery, as tests were run and the massive rocks studied, some of the decisions were mine to make. Their sage advice was tantamount, but I still held the oars. No one could run the river for me. As I continued to plot my course – (Mastectomy, lumpectomy? Unilateral, bilateral? Silicone, saline? Tram-flap, lat-flap?) – I kept taking the boat out of the water, re-studying the river, conferring again with my guides, confirming again our decisions…and each time I would put the boat back in, reassured. It's both blessing and burden that there are so many options, especially with breast cancer, which can include reconstruction. There are many different possible channels one can choose to run between boulders.

For me, the worst was the month of decisions. My kayak and I would sometimes get caught up in eddies. I was "supposed to" be strong, to fight, to not give up, but there were nights when I just wanted to let go of the oars, to let the kayak crash at will on the rocks, to let the river have its way with me. But for all the angst of anticipation, once the decisions were made and my course determined, the surgery and recovery proceeded with relative calm and grace. I straightened my boat, I set my oars, and I kept my eyes three feet ahead of me in line with the head of the rapids.

The undercurrent pulled me downriver towards surgery, steadily at first, then increasingly more intensely. There was no turning back. I was ready. I gripped my oars and with a steady firm pull I became one with the river. I was excited now. There was no fear in it. My heart beat instead with excited anticipation and I was glad to go through them.

And then I was. It was just a blip on the river, a fraction of a moment of time. I had skated through the boulders, just as we charted it. In the blink of an eye, I had cleared them.

And sure enough, my friends and family stood on the sandbar below, just as I hit flat, still water. What had been the water's roar became the roar of them cheering. My Rite of Passage. "All Grace and Glory," one good friend said. "A Trooper," according to my mom, who should know, since she's one herself – a River Runner. "A Woman Warrior." "Amazonian Women Warriors had cut off their breasts to be better archers," one friend said. And I can now count myself as one in a company of brave women who have faced the white churning water. I hadn't chosen this river course, but a soldier is no less a soldier for having been drafted.

There are more rapids, I know. Some might be quite large. Who knows what bumps and rapids lay ahead downriver, beyond the bend? But my boat is strong and so am I. I have more support from more friends than I ever knew I had. And I have the compassion and wisdom of my river guides. They'll be there watching, and there when I need them. My oncology team. My river guides.

Editor's Choice for Poetry

Avalanche

Peter Bradley

The early October snow storm buried our raised bed garden,
covering the strawberry plants, winter greens, and parsley.
It seemed like only yesterday that I filled those frames with good soil
and you planted our garden with diligence and hope.
It's small wonder that I see life measured in days and weeks now.
The years that rolled like clouds passing are barely an echo in my memory.
At season's end I try to recall the tender young plants,
the battles with weeds and insects, the hope born of a ripe tomato.
But this garden in winter, so beautiful in summer's bloom,
looks like a graveyard this dark cold morning.
The snow covered frames remind me of freshly dug graves,
Ghostly visages of better days gone by.
When old age comes,
it comes hard like an avalanche,
erasing all that came before it.

THE ATTIC

Lee Jones

My mother died of cancer when I was just three years old. My wonderful grandmother raised me. My father had made it clear he did not want to have children, so when my mother got pregnant, he just disappeared from our lives. I've never had any desire to find him.

Gramma has been a super parent for me – with just one problem. Losing her daughter (my mother) was so painful for her that she has been reluctant to speak of her. She had my Uncle Edward pack up all my mom's belongings and take them to the attic. My uncle later explained to me that Gramma could not speak of my mother without crying, and she did not want to do that in front of a little child. She believed that, as young as I was, I would soon forget my mom.

I didn't want to forget, so I played the few memories I had over and over in my mind. She loved to sing and taught me some songs we could sing together. Sometimes I helped her make cookies and we sang while we were doing that. She bought color books, and we would color together. She would read stories to me. Sometimes she'd tell me true stories about things that happened when she was a little girl. She taught me to print my name and to say the alphabet. I always had a special dress to wear to church on Easter. We colored eggs together, and she would hide them around the house so I could hunt for them when I woke up on Easter morning. Gramma continued many of those traditions.

Mama would also take me to the park and push me in the swings. I loved to swing high, and when I was high enough, she'd jump on the next swing and we'd swing together. Gramma said she could hear us laughing and squealing all the way down the block!

After she got sick, they didn't think I should be in her room, but she insisted I could be there as much as I wanted to be. As she lay dying, she told me things she wanted me to remember. "You are very smart. I think you'll be a good student, and I hope you'll always try your best at whatever you do.

You are very beautiful! I will always love you. You can talk to me any time. Even though you can't see me, I'll be with you, loving you, proud of you. Things may not always work out as you hope they will. That's because sometimes we don't know what's best for us. We have to trust that God knows what we need better than we do. Your grandma will not do everything exactly like I do, but remember that she loves you very, very much. She will be sad that I have to leave, but you can help by being a very good girl, just as you've always been, my sweet girl."

When Gramma decided to visit her sister one weekend, I decided to visit the attic. Gramma had never forbidden me to go there, but I believed she would not really approve. With heart pounding I crept up the attic stairs. Although I knew no one was home, I felt like I had to be secretive. Mama's things didn't occupy a whole lot of space. There were some books, school records, three well-cared-for baby dolls and doll furniture, a box marked "shoes and underwear" and a couple boxes marked "photo albums." There was a plastic-covered hanging clothes rack. I unzipped the plastic cover, and as the sweet smell of her filled my nostrils, I burst into tears and buried my face in her dresses. "Oh, Mommy! How could I miss you so much when I had you for such a short time?"

I was suddenly aware that I was not alone. I looked up and my gramma was standing there brushing tears from her eyes.

"Gram! I thought you'd gone!"

"Before I got to the edge of town, I remembered I hadn't turned off the coffeepot. I tried calling, but when you didn't answer, I decided I should come back. I think I'll call my sister and tell her I'll drive over in the morning. Meanwhile, let's go down to that ice cream place where we used to go with your mom. We have a lot to talk about, and it's easier over ice cream, don't you think?" She gave me a quick hug and looked at the stack of boxes. "I'll have Edward bring all this stuff downstairs, and we can go through it together. There are a couple boxes of pictures of your mom from the time she was born, and lots of pictures of her with you, too."

I felt my heart brimming over with happiness, and I swear for a minute I saw my mamma standing there smiling.

Sometimes I Wish...

Terrie Jacks

Into myself and turned away
nothing I do is important today
except for the dog
no one cares, no way.
No one asks
or wants to know
am I alive, how does it go?
They all have their lives,
which is how it should be,
but sometimes, I wish
they'd think of me.

I often phone, say "Hello."
They tell me, "Busy, we've got to go."
When I visit I sit alone
making me feel I should have stayed home.
People tell me *their* children care
phoning, visiting, always aware,
sharing a meal or taking a trip.
Sounds like fun, where did I slip?
Then I remember that old proverb
about a son and his wife—
how Mom becomes unimportant in his life.

Was I that way to the Moms in my life,
when they were alone and I was a wife?
But I'm a daughter and not a son
and now I'm alone, a party of one.
So into myself and turned away
nothing I do is important today,
except for the dog
no one cares, no way.
They all have their lives,
which is how it should be,
but sometimes, I wish they'd think of me.

Limes in Time

M. C. Little

Bones pop behind my neck,
as I lean far back
into a plastic patio chair;
eyes closed, a weary face
toward the ceiling.

My solitary spirit
savors a soothing, random aroma of fresh, yellow limes
nestled in a white, two-handled bowl
on the bookshelf
close by.

Train noises become everywhere,
filling the dimly-lit room,
along the back
of the well-aged frame house.

Loud layers of train signals
pulse and echo, through; pulse and echo,
flowing, left to right,
west to east…
in the early hours.

Ribbons of sound begin to fade… into the right side of
a new morning; faintly… fainter…
soon followed by a familiar, rhythmic rattle of
wheels-and-metal… wheels-and-metal…
on the 3 a.m. tracks…

Eventually, there is silence, stillness, and limes.

HOME

Janet Kreitz

It's been twenty years of yesterdays since she left home after high school graduation. Faster than a barefoot kid navigating an asphalt street on an August afternoon.

She waitressed at a chain restaurant, bartended at a dive, clerked at a convenience store while taking creative writing classes at the community college.

A story was sold to an online magazine. Success began when an agent noted her novel about a young woman grinding through poverty for a better life.

Today, home is an apartment that overlooks the New York City skyline. She vacations in Aspen, spends summers in France, married in Rome and honeymooned on the Isle of Capri. The marriage endured for only a year, as both were committed to their careers, not each other.

She only went back home for Mother's Day, a long weekend in September, and her sister's wedding three years ago. Then Mom called last month and said Dad was in hospice.

She came home, sat by his bedside, remembered him wearing bib overalls and white tee shirts. He would be up at five, on the tractor by seven, and supper was taken when it was dark outside. He never complained.

The funeral was two weeks ago.

From her bedroom window she watches falling stars plummet to earth while an owl lullabies her to sleep. She is mesmerized by a bevy of quail that marches across the back yard, and the splash of bluebirds that have built a nest in the hickory tree outside the kitchen window. Mornings she savors the aroma that slides under her bedroom door of bacon frying in the cast-iron skillet. Some mornings her mother dons an apron and makes biscuits slathered with sausage bits and gravy. The radio announcer speaks of upcoming weddings, babies born, neighbors in the hospital, and those who have passed on to their maker.

A funny thing. She doesn't miss her apartment, Friday evenings with friends at the sushi bar, shopping at upscale boutiques, or the noise of screeching tires, blaring horns, and squawking sirens.

Maybe she will stay a few more days.

THE APARTMENT

Rita Ries

When I was 5, my mother, my 14-year-old sister and I
lived in a tiny studio apartment about 30' x 18'.
A double bed swung out of a closet into the main room.
I slept on the sofa.
There was 1 window opposite the door,
by the door a dressing room closet, an 18" x 18" mirror,
4 or 5 stacked drawers, a high dinky cupboard
and a few hanging clothes all in a 5' x 4' space.
Collapsible doors hid the narrow rectangle kitchen,
bathroom was minimal, and of course, no shower.
A church with chimes lived next door to us.
One time I put 3 eggs under 1 of their bushes.
I really expected them to hatch. A kind neighbor gently
reduced my young naiveté and I threw the eggs away.
Once when daddy came to visit, he brought me
a 3' stuffed penguin. Mother was angry with him, said
"It has to go in storage, it's too big for here!"
To be caught between them wasn't unusual.
I did get to keep the penguin, much to my delight!
I had a cowboy costume complete with real boots.
One day in those boots, I was going down the back 10 stairs,
slipped, fell through railing's bars onto cement steps,
ricocheted through the next bars and bounced down a few more.
Hard to believe but it only caused bruises.
Mother couldn't handle my sister, so Keyo went to daddy.
She teased me unmercifully so I didn't care she left
and I could sleep in the bed with Mother, just the 2 of us.

Sorry Don't Mean a Hill of Beans

Maurice Hirsch

I put ice in your water glass although you asked for it without.
Yes, I was slow to come to the table for your order,
fumbled through the specials of the day. Ever work
a twelve-hour shift on a Saturday? The food wasn't hot?
Not my fault. $25 for corkage? Bring
your own wine and you take that chance.
Oh, I always disappear when someone wants the check.
It's in my waiter's manual. Sure, I'm sorry
you ended up surly and dissatisfied. But mainly
sorry you didn't leave a bigger tip.

The House on Fresh Pond Road

Teresa Civello

The three-story brick Romanesque-style houses along tree-lined Fresh Pond Road are more than one hundred years old, well-tended building facades with clean sidewalks. Inside every home, behind every door, and beyond every window reside the stories of those who live within.

The outside of Number 48 Fresh Pond Road is so tidy. Several times a week, the sidewalk and curb are swept clear of leaves, scraps of paper, candy wrappers, and cigarette butts – the general litter one finds even in the most pristine neighborhoods. Maple trees bud in the spring and drop their seeds, blanketing the streets with the wing-like samara the kids call *polynoses*. They pick up the freshest ones, splitting the thin tissue-like wings just enough to press the sticky flat ends onto the sides of their noses. The youngsters pretend to be green monsters, waving their arms and making scary noises as they walk down the block to school.

During the spring polynose invasion, the eye-catching, shapely woman in her late thirties is outside every morning, ready to do battle with the seedpods. She doesn't look like a warrior outfitted in her freshly-ironed floral cotton dress, her russet hair held off her face by tortoiseshell combs. She angles her broom, dragging the accumulated debris into a long-handled shovel. She makes several trips from the sidewalk to inside the wrought-iron gate to dump the rubbish into plastic-lined brown garbage pails. Both had been stolen this past New Year's Eve. The police suspected partygoers looking for clean barrels to hold their booze on ice. Now she keeps her pails chained to the iron fence.

Every Saturday she hoses down the sidewalk and cement stoop. Passersby praise her for maintaining a tidy front.

Then she begins inside the building, vacuuming hallway carpets and dusting the maple staircase risers and banisters. The linoleum is damp-mopped. A scent of Pine-Sol lingers. All who enter mention the cleanliness. She repeats her routine every weekend. But the dirt keeps coming back.

She lives with her husband and their two daughters, ages nine and five. The street-level apartment is in spotless order. The parlor furniture is Italian Provincial. The sofa and club chair are protected by plastic slipcovers. Knickknacks, displayed in the corner hutch, are sheltered from dust by a glass door. An array of black-and-white photographs the husband has taken of their daughters from infancy to their recent birthdays hangs horizontally in two straight lines across the entry wall.

Every weekday morning, before the wife leaves for her factory job, she makes all three beds, although she skips hers when the husband refuses to work. It's been his pattern since they moved to Fresh Pond Road. His parents live upstairs. He's a teamster and earns good money, but he hates driving a tractor trailer. Last year, he stopped paying the bills, so she sued him for support in family court. His garnisheed paycheck covers household upkeep and his daughters' expenses. She allowed him to stay. They are cordial for the sake of their children.

Each school day, she prepares breakfast and packs the girls' lunches. They walk to school hand in hand, immaculate in their pressed blue jumpers, white blouses, and polished oxfords. Their dark hair is curled and ribboned.

In the late afternoon she comes home and begins to cook supper. If he hasn't worked that day, she empties the ashtrays crammed with his unflltered Camel cigarette butts. While she cooks, he sits in the living room listening to Sinatra love songs. The girls do their homework, and he reviews their arithmetic. They think their father is a genius because he solves complex mathematics in his head.

The wife knows her husband dreamed of a career. He is bitter, knowing he could have become so much more if his mother hadn't pulled him out of school when he was fourteen. But she wanted money and plenty of it. He's been driving trucks all his life. His mother owns the house.

The older daughter sets the table with placemats and cloth napkins. The family takes their assigned places, waiting for the mother to bring in a platter of steaming food. He compliments her cooking. The girls chat about school. It's a perfect Norman Rockwell tableau.

After dinner, the dishes are washed and put away. He sips from a snifter of Hennessy cognac and watches television. She sets out the family clothing for the next day, even for him.

It is late evening. The kitchen is spick and span. The house is quiet except for his snoring. She retreats into the silence and prepares for bed. She passes through the girls' room. The older child blows her mother a kiss and whispers, "Mommy, I love you." The mother kisses her daughter's cheek. The girl goes to sleep.

She enters her own bedroom. A lamp on her bedstand spreads a glow over their wedding photograph. The bride and groom gaze into each other's eyes. A beautiful Scarlett O'Hara. A handsome Rhett Butler.

He is asleep, sprawled across the mattress. She slips into bed and curls to the edge. He stirs. Out of habit, his arm covers her shoulder. Her body stiffens. She is tired. In spite of her hard work, the dirt keeps coming back.

His snore softens to rhythmic breathing and lulls her into slumber, dreaming of her girls.

It's so tidy, Number 48 Fresh Pond Road. The facade of their life together.

BLUE PONTIAC

David Ray

"Come on and get in."
He showed up with Goldie,
the blonde he had run off with,

had driven miles out of his way
just to get me. How my heart
thumped as I longed to climb in,

sit between them. She stepped out,
held the blue door open for me.
I stood on the cobbled red bricks.

"Come on, Son," he said
from the driver's seat. "Get in!"
That chrome Indian chief

hood ornament would be slicing
the air like the prow of a ship
all the way to Los Angeles.

I would sit between them—
the man my mother cursed daily
and the woman she spit out.

But how I longed to be the disloyal
son, sitting between my dad
and his blowsy blonde.

He, my father, had come back for me,
parked the blue Pontiac, angled
in front of the post office.

But I sent him on his way
and shuffled, head down,
back to that shroud of bitterness,

bragging to her: "I saw him,
I didn't say a word to him."
She could have pinned a medal on me.

SISTERS OF THE LAKES

Claudia Poquoc

Because our native roots run as deep as willow's
along Lake Erie's edge where you and I grew
from so much green—

lights and darks, avocado and mints, flashing and flickering
orchestrated to the music of rustling leaves and cottonwood
trees that wait for the right moment to release seedy down

and because the shores of Lake Michigami bathe in turquoise
waves that curl like billowing silk scarves around its sandy banks,
then echo to a full moon throwing out its fiery-orange carpet
on the hidden channel of Squaw Lagoon,

where your home offers us a grassy bank to feed a mother swan
while her two signets duck and plunge close by and a chipmunk
scuttles to our side stuffing the pockets of his cheeks

is why two sisters, so close they could be twins—
open their gathering baskets on memory's shores,
share their love for branch and feather, critter and call,

two sisters—
clearing away any debris with multiple waves of gratitude.

Adventures with a Used Car Salesman, Or He Who Hesitates...(Probably Needs a New Carburetor)

Aris DeNigris

The personal vision I have always held of myself as a reasonably stable, sound-of-mind woman has been thoroughly damaged by the events reviewed on the following pages. And while I must admit weathering many trials and tribulations in my thirty-odd years of marriage, nothing has ever prepared me for having to deal with the "used car salesman" and his contemporaries in their related world of nuts, bolts, exhaust fumes, and gas guzzling engines.

As I recall the situation leading up to my "ordeal," it began with a long distance call from our musician son, the joy of which rapidly changed to urgency expressed in terms that went something like this: "I've been offered a job as a writer and arranger with a new group twenty miles from here, and my car just died! I had just paid $350 to have it repaired. Mom, you and Dad have already helped me so much, but I'm sleeping on a sofa at a friend's house until I can get new wheels. Can you help me?"

In the past, I have always been pleased that our children turned to their father and me in time of trouble, but somehow this particularly beautiful day did not lend itself to a crisis...certainly not one involving the price of another automobile! But then I thought: what's a mother to do? He was sleeping on a sofa at a friend's house.

Gingerly exploring several alternative possibilities with my husband (who was only partially recovered from the $1200 amplifier order a few months ago) we agreed that a good used car was all we could afford. With that decision made, and the urgency of the prevailing situation, I began an attack on the automobile classifieds. Cautiously, I began making telephone inquiries leading into more specific reasons for the sale: age, condition, original owner (?), gas mileage, etc.

My husband breakfasted like a king in the days thereafter, but I noticed I could not entice him into any conversation regarding the suddenly fascinating world of used cars. That was where I lived, the air I breathed, and the nourishment I took. Friends were amazed at my suddenly acquired knowledge of automobiles, even though I was not really all that expert. I have been languorous much too long in the knowledge that my dear husband will buy me a new car every two years, whether I need it or not. After years of rambling around in older cars, we vowed to give ourselves a new car the first time we could afford it. So for many years I've heard nothing but a soft purring motor and a quick engine pick-up. No blow-outs for me, no trips to the body shop, no towing charges. My car gets a "grease job" and an oil and filter change every two thousand miles. A grease job, I have found, is what I call a quick repartee of mechanical jargon that I'm told is necessary in order to keep all the engine parts running efficiently – evidently true, because we've had no auto troubles.

So it could only have been that ever prevailing, invisible band of steel known as "mother love" that sent me, blind and senseless, into the ogling and intimidating six- and eight-cylinder world of rack and pinion bearings. The real issue here was mother love versus the "rip-off" artist. No hour was too early for me to begin my telephone search. I reasoned that if people had not wanted to be called at an early hour, they most surely would have mentioned it in their ads. After all, selling their car was the name of the game. Was it not?

I missed out on one gem the very first day I began my search simply because, on some unknown whim, my husband had taken my car that day and hadn't returned it until afternoon. The car in question was an earlier model Chevy Nova, six-cylinder automatic owned by the advertiser's elderly aunt, and until last year only had 12,000 miles on it. Her niece had inherited the car and put another 10,000 miles on it. Now, 22,000 miles later, she was willing to sell it for $2,000.00. By the time I got to her house, after my husband finally returned my car, someone had driven up and taken the car away in a big truck – only two hours after the ad first appeared in the paper. I became so paranoid over that situation that I repeated it to everyone who laughed whenever I mentioned buying a good used car for about $2,000. That's when I began to go into my on-cue spiel about good cars being around and..."why, just the other day, etc...." All the while, I was in a frenzy over the thought of my young son huddled in a sleeping bag on a friend's couch somewhere in Pittsburgh. I was fair game for any deal, becoming more exhausted by the minute as I chased down every appealing ad for used cars that popped up in the morning newspaper.

Now Enter: The Automobile Auction!

There just happened to be a big one not too far from my home. At an automobile auction, pre-listed cars are on display, just as at any auction where people can carefully scrutinize items they are interested in. I didn't see anyone kick the tires, so I decided it must be a rather gauche thing to do, and probably passé. My memory seized upon something vaguely reminiscent of that action but when or how long ago that had been, I couldn't be certain. However, I did manage to peer inside the cars to check the mileage. At that point, after watching other potential car buyers knowingly look at the tires, I began to give them the "once-over" also, but didn't really know what I was looking for. Somehow, I couldn't bring myself to open the hood. I was afraid I couldn't raise it with the same flourish I had seen others assume. So I would follow someone who did and peer over his shoulder (since I was the only "her" around).

Later, intent upon trying to establish myself as a serious buyer, I approached the auctioneer to inquire whether he would accept personal checks. "Well, of course," he said, "with proper identification." After that chat, I received quite a bit of attention, and in fact attracted the very special attention of an honest-to-goodness humanitarian.

Enter: A Used Car Salesman!

Such a nice man! He told me he liked to help people and smiled all the while he spoke, with a slight big city accent, about his wife and family. It was indeed my lucky day. This man was the answer to a prayer, which feeling was more than fortified when he presented me with a beautifully printed card that stated simply, "HONEST PRICES FROM A WORKING MAN'S DEALER." Now I ask you...given all of these circumstances...wouldn't you have been impressed? I began to explain my problem to him.

He then told me about an auction for "dealers only," where he would be willing to take me. Of course, taking advantage of his expertise and knowledge, I would be certain to find a "gooda" used car for my son at dealer prices. Naturally, I would be expected to pay the entrance fee of $15.00, plus an ordinary salesman's commission of $75.00 for his services. After all, he said, he didn't expect to make a lot of money, but he felt sorry for me and my predicament. He only wanted to help. To further show his good intentions, there would be no charge at all if we could not find a car I liked. So I took his card with his business number and proceeded home to relate all to my ever dubious husband.

At this point, I should mention to those of you who are wondering just why my husband hadn't become more involved in the heretofore unfolding of events, his reasons. It was because he'd been through all of this with me and our son many times before: college entrance days; publicity for music concerts; rock groups; musical and special effects equipment (sometimes multiplied by three in various forms); and the most recent problem, an expensive amplifier that had to be returned, twice, from Pittsburgh, by bus. Try dealing with all the people involved: from the salesman who would only give me another amp to replace the defective one at a price increase of "only $100.00," to the manufacturer of said defective amp who disclaimed all responsibility for such defect, to the employees who work in the baggage section of the bus terminal, here at home and in Pittsburgh…and it's nervous breakdown time!

So with all of this past experience my husband decided to patiently sit back, listen, watch, and manage to be around to pick up the pieces whenever I began to have problems. Although, I must say, it's only occasionally that I do have problems and never, never, never like this. Besides, my husband's job is a very demanding and time-consuming one in which he matches wits with some sixty-odd attorneys (sometimes all in one day) who are always trying to out-maneuver, out-finagle, outwit, and out-talk everyone else. It's no wonder I try to do my bit to spare him the smaller details of these aggravating situations.

The day of the auction was rapidly approaching. On that particular day, with my husband's suggestions and warnings in mind, a positive mental approach, and my $3,000 tucked firmly in the deep recesses of my purse, I drove to the auction grounds. My elder son had to cancel at the last minute because he had an emergency at his business.

The day was a rainy one. With the combination of my son's sudden cancellation and the bad weather, I should have been sufficiently superstitious to grasp the ominous portent in the situation. Nevertheless, I drove twenty miles to meet with Swindalapera, parked my car, and then drove with him two short blocks to the gate where dealer identification had to be furnished. As I review these events, I am absolutely amazed at the naiveté of the seemingly intelligent woman I had always thought myself to be. But those were the days before serial killers enjoyed such notoriety. Even so, I probably would have taken the same chances because my son was still "huddled"… (you know the rest).

Looking out at row-upon-row of automobiles of every shape and kind, as far as the eye could see, was an amazing sight. And my heightened anticipation was such that I joyously envisioned myself driving off into the sunset that very day in a slightly used Thunderbird for only $2,000.00. Such had been my build-up. Also, if you have found yourself impressed by my mere novice's knowledge, you should have seen my friend, Swindalapera. He agilely lifted car hoods, opened trunks, switched on the motors (whispering to me that the keys were always left in the ignition), checked the color of the exhaust fumes, listened to the sounds of the engine, checked under the mat in the trunk for rust, looked at the tail pipe, all the while explaining to me just why he was doing these things. Ecstatically, I began making mental notes so I might remember to tell my husband just how thorough Swindalapera was and how very much I was learning from him. Never again would I feel helpless when looking for a used car. I could now look and judge with the best of them. There was absolutely nothing to it!

The auction began promptly at 11 a.m., at which point the day became a long and exhausting one where bidding prices on one car after another (that Swindalapera had previously chosen as being a "gooda' cah for you son") rose to much higher prices than I could afford. Also, since I was standing all the while, the exhaust fumes began to get to me as the parade of cars were driven through the line, accelerated, auctioned, and then driven off into the wild blue yonder. It was about that time I began to notice Swindalapera bidding without first checking with me as to whether or not I would be interested. Once, I became really upset when he bid on a car for $2,500, since I had previously explained to him in great detail that I only had $3,000 to spend, and out of that would have to come his commission, expenses, and the state tax. Luckily, he was overbid.

On and on it went until about 5:00 PM. I would gladly have traded my charge card for a chair, a drink, and a hot dog. While reviewing these events in a much calmer state, it is now obvious to me that Swindalapera was growing agitated and was beginning to perspire profusely. At the time, I attributed it to a long and unprofitable day. And as I bent to brush something off my coat, out of the corner of my eye a white car came roaring through the line. I heard the auctioneer shout SOLD!!...then Swindalapera's gleeful shout over the reved-up roar of the engines: "YOU BOUGHTA YOUSELF A CAH!"

I'll never forget the flood of emotion that came over me. My long ordeal for a good used car for our son had ended, and I had saved my husband almost $1,000.00. I was so happy! "What's the car like," I asked, since it had gone through the line so quickly I had only caught a sudden blurred image of it.

"It'sa '92 Chevy," came the reply, "an eight-cylinder, automatic." Up until that time I had specifically been searching for a six-cylinder car. "And it only has 89,000 miles on it," he continued. "But," Swindalapera assured me, as he noticed the uneasiness in my voice and demeanor, "that'sa okay. Those are probably true miles. Everybody knows the odometer is always turned back, so with such a high mileage you can be sure it'sa true. Probably all highway miles too!"

I was the luckiest girl in the world a few minutes ago. Why then did something in my brain keep nagging me, and why did I no longer feel lucky? I think it was right then and there that my brain stopped functioning. It must have been so overcome with grief at not having its frantic signals answered that it just plain got tired of sending them out. Brains get tired too and mine took a leave of absence at that point! Not only was I fortunate to get such a wonderful buy...only $2,000, including Swindalapera's commission, but the "cah" had a new transmission. In other words, if a car had a defective transmission, it could not be returned. Soon after that I learned about HESITATION. Before this time, I would not have thought to associate that word with automobiles. But before too long I was to find out that hesitation meant the following: stalling when deciding to accelerate into the street from your driveway into oncoming traffic; also, when trying to change lanes in traffic of any kind. When this occurs, a new carburetor is needed. All I can say is that someone upstairs must really and truly love me. Test driving that car could have been a real "happening" for me, to use modern-day vernacular.

Nevertheless, Swindalapera assured me that only a minimum amount of work would be required to put this particular car in tip-top shape. He would have to drive it to his home to check it out and have his wife fill out the necessary papers of ownership and transfer, and then return the car to me in two days…it being the weekend. That certainly fit in with my plans because by then, according to Swindalapera, after a few minor adjustments, the "cah" would be ready to be driven to Pittsburgh so our son could get on with his life and career. After all, he was "sleeping on a couch, etc."

So when Swindalapera returned the "cah" to our home two days later with the signed papers, we thought all we had to do was have the oil and filter changed and a general check-up for things Swindalapera might have overlooked. Exit Swindalapera.

ENTER: GARAGE MECHANIC!

On occasion, my husband had used the services of a neighborhood garage nearby and had some confidence in their work. We told them we wanted the brakes checked, oil and filter changed, and a general checkup, as the car was to be driven to Pittsburgh.

The fatal call came an hour later. After the first shock of learning that the car needed all new brakes (over $300), I calmly reasoned that we would still be ahead of the game, since we originally intended to spend $3000 for a car. After talking it over with my very busy husband, I advised the garage mechanic to go ahead and put the car in good condition. Then it was one thing after another. First, the battery, then the hand brake, then a piece under the car holding the hand brake was falling apart and needed welding. Soon, very soon, the car would need a new carburetor. Next, a new exhaust system. A loud knocking in the rear might mean an additional $300, and on and on it went, ad nauseam. And so it would always be, the mechanic told us, because, in words so indelibly etched in my memory, he said, "This car has been through the mill!"

This whole experience has been an in-depth study in human nature. For instance, I now wonder why our "friendly" garage mechanic didn't mention additional defects sooner. Why did he wait until after I had paid him $300 for new brakes before he gave me the final and seemingly endless bad news? Lately, I have come to believe that some personalities cannot overcome basic primal instincts to attack once they get the scent of fresh blood. In my case, the garage mechanic was simply "getting in on the action," as our sons would say.

Ah well, as the story goes, what I have neglected to mention is that Swindalapera had the "cah" inspected before he turned it over to me. A "friend" of his did him a favor, he said, but our "friend," the mechanic, couldn't understand just how it ever passed inspection.

ENTER: THE DEPARTMENT OF MOTOR VEHICLES!

For those of you who have never found yourselves in this sort of a situation, you may be indifferently following the procedures I am going to mention. For those of you who have had similar problems, I weep for you. Just remember me in your prayers when I tell you there is justice...no matter how slow moving.

First of all, we contacted Swindalapera and told him about the car. He disclaimed any and all responsibility by saying he wasn't God and couldn't possibly have known about all the things that were wrong with the "cah." I thought that was rather funny because he knew everything about anything mechanical when we were on the auction grounds, when he was doing the bidding. Anyway, he never said he was sorry or even offered to reimburse us in any way, never even offered to take the car back. What he did say was that he didn't want the car. Naturally! Who but me would?

SO NOW, ENTER: MY HUSBAND (!)

...who had some conversation with Swindalapera whereby he advised him that we would seek compensation another way. But Swindalepera, having had, I'm quite sure, these experiences many times before, remained adamant and noncommittal. He was a cool crook who must have had many years to perfect his act.

Luckily, at the Department of Motor Vehicles, there are dealer complaint forms to be filled out, so we proceeded with this method. After a week of waiting, we were finally interviewed by a State Examiner. He looked at the defective brake rotors and found there to be many discrepancies in Swindalapera's operation. We also reported his operation to the auction house, where they simply said they would "watch him." In the meantime, awaiting the final outcome, I had the car to do with whatever I wished. Quite naturally, that was out of the question, so I began to mentally record a list of options open to me at that time.

My initial thought was to return the car to the auction arena where I had purchased it, with the hope it could be re-auctioned and I could receive at least the price I had paid for it. Since many improvements had been made, I was even hopeful of receiving somewhat more than that. When I spoke to the manager by phone, he instructed me to bring the car to the auction grounds the next day so we could make arrangements to re-auction it. When I appeared with my newly washed and polished car in tow, after a brief conversation the manager did a complete about-face and suddenly decided he did not want to re-auction the car at all. He said he was presently involved in litigation resulting from the sale of a car at auction whereby the buyer had been fatally injured. In this case, the woman buyer had been married to the attorney who was suing the auction house. While I was shocked, I was not surprised at this piece of news, but was very upset at having driven the long distance when he could have told me all of that over the phone. It would have saved me time, energy, frustration, and the gasoline my son and I had used to drive the distance with two cars. One to drop off at the auction, and my son's car to drive me home.

Throughout this whole ordeal, it has been my sad observation and experience that no one involved in the automobile business – new, used, or any other kind – gives too much thought to those of us who simply expect a car we can depend upon. Simple traits I have always felt to be an inherent part of human nature seem to suffer serious voids among people engaged in these occupations.

ENTER: MY NEWSPAPER AD TO SELL A USED CAR!
After discarding the notion of re-auctioning the "cah," I decided to sell it privately, even if I had to take a substantial loss. My phone rang off the hook, and this time I was the one trying to sell a used car.

I tried being honest with the prospective buyers by advising them of the remaining work to be done and explaining how my loss would be their gain. The only person even mildly interested was a disillusioned father having problems with his daughter, who had just returned home from college after an unhappy love affair. After listening to the poor man's tale of unhappiness, his anguish became real to me, and it took great control not to sell him the car then and there at half price. I think it was the 89,000 plus miles that overwhelmed him.

ENTER: THE NEW CAR SALESMAN AND THE TRADE-IN DEAL!

The New Car Salesman is not as good an actor as the used car dealer. Sympathy is hopefully gained immediately as they look at you with slightly watery eyes and tell you, honestly, they can only expect to earn $75.00 on each sale. In fact they *insist* on showing you their records. So the prospective buyer knows right then and there that he is doing business with Diogenes' dream and is supposed to feel more at ease. After looking at one particular compact car that appealed to me, and after enduring some rather intimidating remarks about the '92 Chevy I was driving (remarks made in order to justify a much lower offer as a trade-in)…the salesman offered to let me drive the car I was interested in. The only hitch, as far as I was concerned, was that the condescending salesman would have to accompany me. Nevertheless, I've always believed that, while the wheel may turn slowly, retribution does come to those who wait. In this case, it was a short wait.

About a half-mile down the road, the "new" car began to sputter, slow down, and eventually just died. The now sheepish-looking former super salesman began to make all sorts of pathetic excuses regarding the condition of said "new" car; how this could have happened was a "complete mystery" to him. The car was "brand new, simply left over from last year…never been driven," he profusely exclaimed.

After a quick call to his office, a truck with a booster cable arrived. Even then, it took some doing to get the car started. Needless to say, I had now lost interest in new cars and, upon returning to the car lot, the engine on my vastly improved '92 Chevy, which had been the butt of some rather low-keyed humor on the salesman's part, turned over immediately after switching on the ignition. With a newly acquired sense of triumph, I drove away waving brightly to the salesman, who was left scratching his head. At least my car started!

You may have surmised, as you have read about the various journeys made during my almost impossible quest to find a usable and safe automobile for my young son, that I do not give up easily – especially when it concerns a member of my family. Even when all appears to be lost, I always manage to see the "pot of gold" at the end of the rainbow. Sometimes, after arriving at the "end" and even in a state of complete exhaustion, it doesn't always matter to me if there is no gold. Indeed, there have been times when I couldn't even find the pot! What does matter is the satisfaction and knowledge that I have done my very best for the people I love. That's the important thing to me. However, during this particular period, I had begun to feel that, perhaps, the rainbow, the pot, and certainly the gold had all vanished, but…nevertheless…I had to try…*one more time.*

BACK TO A USED CAR LOT!

At another well-advertised used car lot I again found a very nice compact model car. Unfortunately, this time I ran into an expatriated German salesman who made jokes about the second World War. He said that although the Germans had "lost" twice, still *he* as a good fighter would, most certainly, be on my side to fight with the sales manager in order for me to come to a better financial arrangement than the one originally offered to me on paper. I earnestly implored him not to bring the unhappy events of World War II into the picture, because by that time I was beginning to lose the quality my friends tell me is my main character trait: cheerfulness! The very thought of buying another automobile from that particular salesman suddenly filled me with insane hysteria. His learned technique was so smooth and effortless, it was obvious he had successfully used exactly these same phrases many times before. So it must have come as a shock to him when I quickly said goodby and left. On the way out, I noticed his picture on the wall in the office listing him as *Salesman of the Year!*

ENTER: SON'S FRIEND
AND FRIEND'S DESIRE TO BE RID OF CAR PAYMENTS!

If we can just remember to be patient, sometimes the Fates work for us as well as against us. Right then, and for some time now, I felt They had been weeping for me. In any case, my son called to tell me of a friend who was going into the service and wanted to sell his "new" car with the new owner simply picking up the small monthly payments. The car was already in Pittsburgh.

Quickly, I advertised the '92 Chevy again for a ridiculously low price. I sold it immediately and sent a check out to my son in Pittsburgh, who was sleeping on a couch somewhere…(oh well, by now you understand my motivation).

Some Weeks Later: Enter Husband and Wife Calmly Relaxing Over a Leisurely Breakfast, the Likes of Which They Had Not Been Able To Have for Many Weeks!

My husband and I were enjoying breakfast one morning some weeks later when the until then forbidden subject of the "cah" was carelessly and unintentionally mentioned. What I actually said was that I thought the automobile companies should really hire more women dealers and salespeople to sell cars to their customers. My reasoning was that women would more honestly share information regarding the true state of an automobile, and it might go a long way toward dispelling the anxieties and trepidations people have with the automobile industry in general.

It took a most powerful thump on my husband's back to quiet his sudden fit of coughing. Whereupon, he arose quickly from the table, kissed me on the cheek, and mumbled something about checking his retirement plan. What I really think the poor man needs is a vacation.

Come to think of it, I've always wanted to travel on the Orient Express. Maybe I'll begin checking that out and surprise him!

Note on My Car

Jeffrey Widen

Rain pounded the ground. Droplets ricocheted off the parking lot. I hustled from my office, splashing through puddles in my path. My baseball cap was pulled down over my eyes so the bill would protect my glasses. I could feel drops from the deluge thumping on my raincoat.

I clicked my remote and the car lights and horn answered back. I flung open the door and rolled into the driver's seat, glad to be out of the downpour. As I leaned forward to slip my key into the ignition, I saw a soggy piece of paper tucked under the windshield wiper. It didn't look like a ticket and shouldn't have been one anyway. I grumbled as I climbed out of the car and snatched it, being careful not to tear it. Back inside, I started the motor to warm the engine so I could get the heater going. I flicked on the dashboard lights and looked at the note in my hands. It was written in pencil and was still somewhat legible. I slipped off my droplet-sprinkled glasses and squinted.

The note was direct. "One of your most prized possessions is missing. If you want to retrieve it, meet me at the high school baseball field tomorrow night at 7:00. And bring your glove."

I didn't play baseball. Didn't have a glove. *What prized possession?*

This has to be a mistake. I started to crinkle up the paper as I mentally listed my prized possessions. A voice inside my head made me stop. *Take this seriously!*

I dreamed about baseball gloves and prized possessions all night. The next morning I scoured my house for something valuable that might be "missing." Nothing. I decided to go by a Goodwill Store and pick out a used glove, so I wouldn't look like a rookie. I'd played catcher when I was young, but what I got was an outfielder's mitt with a nicely broken in pocket, one tattered enough to look like I'd owned it for years.

Throughout the day I had trouble concentrating as I visualized one part of my life after another for something I could call my "most prized possession." No deal.

I ate a light lunch and dinner…too excited to eat much anyway. I drove to the deserted baseball field and waited. To kill time I grabbed the glove and pounded the pocket. Memories of my old catcher's mitt fluttered by. It had been one of the old fashioned whoopee cushion types used by catchers for years. I remember stuffing sponges against my palm to soften the pop of a pitcher's fastball.

I was pulled back to the present by a sharp tapping on my driver's side window. Outside stood a stranger. He was well dressed, sporting a dark brown derby on his head and a broad grin. His face flashed a gray-tinged handlebar mustache and muttonchop sideburns. He looked as though he was out of the 1920's.

He signaled me to roll down the window, and I saw no reason not to. "Name's Tris," he said. "Grab your glove and walk with me."

I shrugged, grabbed the mitt, pounded the pocket with my fist, opened the door and climbed out. It'd stopped raining, and the smell of ozone filled the air.

From a tattered bag hanging from his side by a leather strap angled across his chest, he pulled out a glove. It had no leather laces strung between the fingertips. It looked like the gloves players used in the early 1900s. He also pulled out an old baseball, which was well broken in, tattered and greenish from grass stains. He walked about twenty paces away and hollered, "Let's have a catch."

The ball spun through the air, and my left hand instinctively rose to catch it. It snapped into the pocket. It felt so good! I threw it back and heard it thump as it hit his glove. Back and forth the ball flew between us. Each time he hurled it, it spun more tightly and hit my glove with a louder pop.

Tris grinned. "Now you're getting it, son," he hollered through the crisp evening air.

After about ten minutes of whipping the ball back and forth, my arm was getting tired. Clearly, his was not! Curiosity finally took over and I asked, "What's this all about, Tris?"

"Well, Mack, (*How'd he know my name?*) this is how I see it. I've been asked by some folks to talk with ya. Seems like a lot of things that make your world go 'round have been slipping away from your life 'cause they ain't bein' attended to."

"What people? Who?"

"Don't matter, does it? Really?"

"Who are you, Tris?"

"Just an old baseball guy who cares, son."

My confusion was starting to work on me. I was getting frustrated and my arm ached. Tris nodded toward the bleachers, so we strolled over and plunked our butts down on one of the benches.

"Here's the deal, young man," Tris said. "Your life has become boring. Tedious. Way too safe for a thirty-year-old. Put simply, you don't play anymore. You've lost contact with other folks. When's the last time you laughed...or even smiled, for that matter."

I had no answer.

He tipped back his derby, wiped his mustache and focused his blue eyes deeply into mine. "I'd like you to take this ball we've been tossin' and study it every day. It's older than you are, and it carries the secret of your missing most prized possession."

"I don't understand, Tris. What can a old baseball show me?"

"You *are* a tough one. I'm gonna tell ya the word, but the rest of the work is gonna be up to you, Mack. Your most prized possession is your imagination! It's plumb gone and it's time to find it." He reached out and patted my right shoulder reassuringly. Then he slapped his knees with the palms of his hands and rose from the bench. "Gotta go now, son." He winked at me. "By the way, what's a Goodwill Store?" Before I could answer, he strolled off, re-centering his derby and dropping his glove back into his weathered bag.

I sat on the bench, the cool evening air engulfing me. The old "seasoned" baseball lay cradled in my right hand. My eyebrows were knitted in concentration. What had just happened? I realized there was no explanation, and stopped struggling to come up with one.

I pounded the ball into the pocket of my newfound glove. I took a deep breath and felt a smile spread across my face. Then I laughed. Then I laughed a lot. I felt free.

Merry-Go-Round

Caroline Hobson

As far back as 3 years of age,
I can remember going to a cafeteria
in Long Beach, CA, with my parents,
maternal grandmother, and favorite uncle.

We were ushered to a separate room,
glassed in like a sunroom.
We were special but I don't know why.
Did my grandmother own the cafeteria?

After dinner we always went to ride the
merry-go-round on the pier.
Grandmother rode in the chariot like a queen
and my father stood beside my horse as we circled.

I went with a Seniors group to San Francisco
and one of the attractions was
a merry-go-round.
I was impressed with the change in mood to childish glee
that some of my serious friends expressed.

How many years later did I ride with a
5½-month-old great-granddaughter
in a rocking chariot on a carousel?
She stared at the overhead mechanism
and I said to myself, "She's going to be an engineer!"
She clapped hands when we finished our ride.

My sister found nothing merry about a carousel:
She became deathly ill at a moment's notice
and became queasy if anyone
suggested a ride.

The Baseball Park

Sherry Stoneback

As a child, Ian was small for his age, always the short guy, but he had a giant personality, one that centered on humor and, as he grew older, compassion. When he was six, he looked four, a little blonde-haired baseball player that gave his all. I thought he was too little for baseball. I didn't want him to get hurt, or get his feelings hurt because the other boys could play better than he could. I needn't have worried. Ian's size never bothered him, and he has never taken a back seat to anyone because of his stature. He instinctively discovered over the years that character was the measure of a person.

I have a picture of that first morning that reminds me of all these things. It shows him in white polyester pants, into which he's tucked a very long red shirt with a number on it. The pants benefited from tucking the shirt, as they were much too loose at the waist, but this has caused the bottom half of the number to be obscured.

The baseball uniform was the smallest available. The pants were supposed to stop and bunch just under his knees, but his hung down loose around his ankles. The whiteness of the pants were a reflection of the boys' "baseball moms'" expertise in managing the fine art of laundering clothing with grass stains. His shoes looked big, too, with little cleats on the bottom that, though I worried he or someone else might be hurt in a tumble, turned out were mostly good for collecting mud and bringing it into the house. There weren't really many "tumbles" in baseball, anyway.

One required item that surprised me, given the age and size of the six-year-old boys: an athletic cup. I asked Ian if he needed help putting it on, and he said, "Oh, Mom, don't embarrass me." I assumed from that remark that he knew what to do with it. What did I know about six-year-old boys? Surely, the coach had explained it.

The majority of the parents had grown up in the neighborhood, stayed and were raising their kids there. Only slightly incestuous, which can be good, I guess, but hard on those of us army brats who moved into the neighborhood with our kids, wanting to break the cycle, to live there and stay a spell, to feel like we belonged. There was quite a lot of buzzing behind hands and furtive looks at those of us who were "new" in the last decade or so. I didn't care, didn't have time for more friends than I already had, and I didn't want to join their gang anyway. Yeah.

When we arrived at the ballpark for the first game, I saw many parents chatting and getting caught up on what I could only assume were the events of maybe last weekend. I assumed they hung out nearly every day, which was true of the stay-at-home Moms. Ian was assigned to right field, where he could do little damage. Or maybe they just thought his parent, or parents, would be disinclined to object. They were right if that was the reason.

The game started and in no time Ian started to wiggle and jiggle like he had to pee really bad. One of the moms looked at Ian and said, "Oops, looks like we're gonna need a time out early." He was clueless to everything except what was going on in his pants, already a man through and through at six.

I didn't say anything, disappointed they'd gotten a chance to focus on my kid acting silly. He kept wiggling, and then pretty soon, when everyone was looking his way, he bent over, reached into one of his pant legs, extracted the cup, and with no embarrasment whatsoever pulled out the waistband and dropped it back in.

I was ashamed later, but when someone asked, "Whose kid is that?" I didn't claim him.

WHO DO YOU THINK WINS?

Barbara Nuxall Isom

The coach called one of his 9-year-old baseball players aside and asked, "Do you understand what cooperation is? What a team is?"

"Yes, coach," replied the boy.

"Do you understand that what matters is we win or lose as a team?"

The boy nodded yes.

The coach continued, "I'm sure you know when an out is called you shouldn't argue, curse, attack the umpire or call him a peckerhead or asshole. Do you understand all that?"

Again, the boy nodded yes.

"And when I take you out of the game so another boy gets a chance to play, it's not good sportsmanship to call your coach a dumb ass or shit head, is it?"

"No, coach."

"Good," said the coach. "Now go over there and explain all that to your grandmother."

(Author unknown)

In my eye, my youngest grandson, Nick, appears to have the instinct of a natural athlete. He is 11 years young and has been playing ice hockey and scoring many goals for several years now. He projects a nonchalant personality until the competition begins, and then he responds, surprising even his coaches.

He has been desirous of trying a sport besides hockey, and this summer he has been playing baseball. These summer teams are supposed to be composed of four traveler players (regular baseball team members) with the remainder of the team being pickup players. By the time I arrived for a visit and to cheer, his team had lost two of their traveler players (one now had a cast on his arm and another had been hospitalized with a mysterious abscess on his brain). The coach's son, a traveler player, was at shortstop, and B.A. (as he was known), the other traveler player, alternated between catcher and pitcher. Nick had started as a fielder, but because of the loss of two regular players and his aptitude, he had been placed at second base. He was doing an adequate job, but it was clear to my daughter and me that he didn't understand his position.

Firstly, we invested in a new aluminum bat for him, found an unoccupied baseball diamond at a school, and proceeded to work with our number one guy. My daughter had pitched softball in her youth, not overhand baseball, but she took the pitcher position and her 76-year-old mother, me, was the catcher. *Nobody was watching.*

Fortunately, he hit most of the pitches – I was just giving her a target and shagged a few balls. Next, we explained that he needed to take a second to throw, so as to hit the first baseman's mitt. I threw grounders to him, and he picked up and threw to his mother on first base. We got that down and advanced to discussing when the shortstop covered second and how to sweep down "paint the dirt" for a tag when he did.

The next game Nick was directly involved with all three outs in the second inning. My daughter and I "high-fived;" however, he struck out once. We needed to work on that level swing and not trying to kill the ball.

The team had good coaching and, because our two traveler players were so talented and the others contributed surprisingly, we made it to the semi-championship game of the tournament. The opposing team was very talented, and we didn't really expect to win, so we were pretty relaxed and just encouraging. The opposing pitcher had a bad habit of pointing his finger and pulling his thumb as if to shoot a gun when he struck out one of our players. Our team hung in and miraculously tied up the game. Our little first baseman was the runner on first when the opposing team had a huddle on the pitcher mound. The first baseman returned with the baseball hidden in his mitt hoping to catch our runner leading off base. Since our runner didn't lead off, he ultimately had to surrender the ball to the pitcher. This got my attention in a big way. What kind of grown man would encourage 11- and 12-year-boys to cheat? Is it any wonder that grown players think it's okay to cheat?

Now they have doubled our attention, and we care more about the outcome of the game, so the volume of encouragement is increased. They played two extra innings to try to break the tie, and then it was what they call "sudden death." The other team still didn't manage to get a run, and now it was our turn. They placed my Nick as a runner on second base, as he was the last out in the prior inning. One of our traveler players, the coach's son, was up. He tried to connect, but they purposely walked him, which some of the group didn't like, but I said that, unfortunately, it was fair and done in baseball all the time.

The next batter was a little guy who hadn't hit all day. Some fellow on the other side yelled, "Go ahead and pitch to him; he can't hit anything." Now my daughter was fired up and started encouraging our batter. Would you believe, he connected! Popped the ball over the shortstop and it fell in the hole behind him. Nick took off like lightning and slid into home with the coach hollering, "Make sure you have tagged the base," whereupon Nick put his hand on the bag and the catcher cleated his hand. Nick was upset about the cleating because he was sure, upon being questioned, that the catcher had done it on purpose. Nick goes to school with him and considered him a friend.

How did it happen? Suddenly we are competing for the championship! Talk about a "Bad News Bears" team. Alas, the championship game was rained out. By the time it was rescheduled, we had lost our coach and short-stop to a planned vacation. We had to recruit two players to make a complete team. B.A. pitched outstandingly and the team played valiantly, but we lost the championship to a well-trained team.

Following this experience, my daughter enrolled Nick in a basic baseball skills camp for a week. The coach involved there has been practicing for a long time and is known for addressing the boys before the lesson of the day. My daughter decided to eavesdrop the first day. She heard him tell them an old Indian story about the two wolves inside of each of them. He said they are at battle. One wolf is evil, full of anger, jealousy, greed, and resentment; the other wolf is good, full of joy, peace, love, humility, empathy, and truth. He asked, "Do you know which wolf will win?"

Silence. Finally, he answered for them: "The one you feed."

...WOULD BE THE FIRST TO GO

Sabine Ramage

Winter silence
Sometimes broken
By January rain
Ragged steel gray clouds bursting
Giant, heavy raindrops hammering
Rooftops
Windows
Pavement
Collecting in mucky puddles
Gushing noisily along curbs
Flooding ditches
Reverberating noises of
Gleeful laughter
Splashing
Running
Frolicking
Feet stomping
Delighting in play
As darkness falls
The quiet calm returns
Cold, wet feet
Glowing velvety brown eyes
Rosy-cheeked grin
Before stepping inside
Her muddy boots
would be the first to go...

ONE PAIR OF SLIGHTLY USED CHUCK TAYLOR BASKETBALL SHOES

Fred Bridges

Garage and estate sale signs cover the lawns on most sunny days. These are where Americans hope to find that one bargain their once-in-a-lifetime appetite will savor.

I walked by a neighborhood garage sale, and there before my eyes hung a pair of shoes that no one wears today – Chuck Taylor high top basketball shoes. The tag said $1.25. During the depression, I had dreamed of owning a pair of these shoes, but never had the $5.00 to buy them. This pair was still solid with a rubber logo over the ankle bone and few sweat stains over the toes. I thought there must be a story behind these shoes.

I paid the $1.25 and took them to my garage. I wondered how old they were, if they had been worn by some local hero. Computers are real time savers when doing research, and soon before my eyes was a picture of Chuck Taylor in his high top shoes. Chuck was a tall slim man, ideal for basketball in those days. He was posed, ready to shoot a two-handed set shot.

My curiosity was now aroused. I returned to the house where I had made the purchase. I rapped on the door, and a lady peered at me from behind a screen door. I explained that I had purchased the shoes at their garage sale, and heard a male voice say, "All sales are final."

I replied that I was not trying to return them, but was interested in their history – who might have worn them and where?

A tall man emerged, peering at me as if he thought I might want to steal his valuables. "Why would anyone want to know about a pair of tennis shoes?" he asked.

I explained how Chuck Taylor was once the envy of every young boy. His high top shoes cost a fast fin, and Chuck's autograph was on the rubber logo. Those shoes made a young lad feel five inches taller as he dribbled down the basketball court.

The former owner invited me to his patio and said he had once played in those shoes. He related how he had worn them in college. Now you could see his hands touching the ball's grain – cutting, dribbling, placed for the two-handed set shot. The swoosh of the ball through the net echoed across the patio.

His grandchildren listened in awe as he related this tale. When we shook hands and I left, he had a tear in his eye. Two days later, I returned with the shoes, now encased in a shadowbox, and a copy of an old sports page where he had sunk a two-handed set shot to win a close game.

EVENING PRAYER

William Killian

The sun appears to sleep,
yet it brightens the day for others.
It has guided us well today,
and now we rest.
We rest amid unfinished lives,
we blanket our pain and our hopes
in the quieting darkness
as we surrender to the night.
We embrace our dreams,
allowing them to work
from the depths of mysterious wonder.
As our unconsciousness
expands into the universe,
freeing us together as one,
we fall and keep falling
until the sun carries us into morning.
Gratitude will dance us tomorrow,
and our song will be joyous—
it will be the richest day of our lives.
Good night, sweet soul—
you are safe, loved, and whole.
Amen.

Keeping the Sabbath

Anita Curran Guenin

In an episode of Dr. Who,
an electrical being
intakes people
through television sets.
What if it is happening
to watchers now, television
sucking faces off, taking them
to a lost and found where there
is no ticket to retrieve them?

On the sabbath,
people watch football games,
faces captured unaware
while worshipping
the screens; square, oblong.
How does television's
mesmerizing rays
make us buy what we
don't need, eat when we're
not hungry, stay awake when
we're tired?

Is there something within
the waves that drowns reason,
makes the remote too heavy
to pick up, press "off"?

GUM

Willene C. Auslam

He was only six years old and a very active little boy who loved his Texas ranch life. He asked, "Why can't I stay here and ride my horse? Roy'll be here, and he could take care o' me."

"No, this is Sunday, and we're all going to church. Then we're going to Grandma and Grandpa's house for dinner. Wesley will be there and probably Lee. You always like playing with your cousins. Quit stalling and get dressed," his daddy told him.

He obeyed, but pouted all the way to town and church.

Sunday School was okay. Miz Craig always had something for them to cut out or color. And her stories were pretty good, too. But, oh, church was another story. The preacher talked too long about stuff he didn't understand. If he misbehaved, sometimes Mama took him outside and gave him a spanking – not hard, though, and that was better than trying to sit still inside.

This day, when he got too wiggly, Mama just reached over and gave him a little pinch. It didn't hurt – except for his feelings. He stiffened up and slid off the pew. He was quiet and not bothering anybody, so Mama just left him under there.

After a while, though, that got boring too, so he bobbed back up, chewing and announcing loudly, "I got me some gum." People around them tried hard to muffle their laughter, but it was hopeless. Even the preacher got tickled and simply announced the closing hymn.

It's a Boy
Army Hospital, Heidelberg, Germany, 1953

Una Nichols Hynum

Pushing midnight. Soothing
womb water washes down my legs.
Good, I think, the baby's near.

An orderly tells me to lift
myself onto a gurney. Too late.
The grinding labor of birth has begun
with a furious primeval growl
I can't believe is coming from me.

The doctor catches the baby
who's not breathing,
slips a tiny oxygen mask
over his face. Like a wild thing startled
from hiding he whimpers, sampling
the air, the light.

In our room I count fingers, toes,
check penis, nuzzle the nape
of his neck, give in to the urge
to lick this child, to taste this creature,
to mark him as my own.

Birth and Death: Cosmic Balance?

Esther Halvorson-Hill

My nursing career spanned several decades. Starting with nursing in Intensive Care, I quickly progressed to nursing management and ended my career teaching.

When I was a nursing student, I faced my first experience caring for a dying patient. This man had a dissecting aneurism, and there was no hope of his survival. I remember watching with wonder as the life force left his body. The animation was gone, leaving just a body growing colder. There were no flashing lights, no angels singing, no visible spirit ascending. Just a quiet passing.

I was upset and emotionally drained. A caring supervisor sent me for a break to the cafeteria that was on another floor of the hospital. On my way, I passed the nursery and heard a newborn baby crying. All at once something clicked in my brain, and I somehow saw the balance of life. Oh yes, now it made sense – new life coming into the world to replace those lives that were ending.

Many years later, I was teaching a group of nursing students: RNs returning to school in pursuit of baccalaureate degrees. They brought their unique nursing experiences to their learning. Those who had dealt with birth or death as midwives or hospice nurses tended to have qualities in common. I found them to be empathetic, creative, and possessing a spiritual dimension. Two stories come to mind.

The first was related to me by a student who had been a midwife with her own practice in home deliveries. She told of a couple who had mixed feelings about being parents. They were both busy people with active careers, who weren't certain if they wanted to share their time with a new baby.

The pregnancy progressed well, with no apparent problems. On the day of the birth, the labor seemed quite routine. The fetal heart tones were good with no hint of distress. However, when the baby emerged, the cord was wrapped around its neck. The baby was blue and didn't take a first breath.

In the words of the midwife, "I quickly and carefully removed the cord and was preparing to take lifesaving measures when I heard the strong voice of the mother saying, 'Give her to me!' What to do? Time was of the essence. Somehow I knew (divine intervention?) that I should give the babe to its mother. She held the baby in front of her and said, "I want you! I need you! Breathe!" The baby took a deep breath and let out a lusty cry.

The second story was of another student who had a background as a midwife. I sent her out to care for a hospice patient. The purpose of the visit was to give an enema to a lady dying of cancer. As it turned out, the woman had taken a turn for the worse and was much weaker than when the appointment had been made.

As related by this student: "I found this delightful lady who seemed content with death, but who was saddened by being unable to keep doing the things she enjoyed. She told of how she loved working in her garden. Now she was confined to bed. I looked around, and there was no wheelchair or walker. What to do? I found a wheelbarrow in the garage and padded it with blankets. With help from her husband, we got her up and into it. I took her out to her garden and carefully lowered her onto the soft ground. It was a beautiful sunny day. We spent the time weeding, cutting flowers, and throwing snails against the fence. When she tired, I took her back into the house. As I tried to clean the dirt from her hands, she begged me to leave it. She said she loved the smell of the earth. She fell asleep content with a sort of joy radiating from her face."

We heard that she died very peacefully the next day, and the student said, "Oh no, I forgot to give the enema."

I just smiled and said, "You did so much more. You cared for her spirit."

Mother's Day

Margaret Golden

I always knew I would be a mother. I wasn't so sure about getting married, but I was quite sure I would be able to nurture and raise children. I examined myself and decided I would be able to care for an infant, and then return the child to the mother when she was able to care for it. Luckily, I never had to do that!

I was the best babysitter in town. I was on call almost every weekend to care for a child while the parents went out on the town. This was before TV, so I read books to them and sang with them and invented games to play with them.

When we had our first child, life was perfect. My husband had a good job, teaching in an elementary school. We had our beautiful child and thought he should really have a brother or sister to grow up with. So we had four more kids and ended up with three sons and two daughters – ages 1, 3, 5, 7 and 9! And we discovered that parenting is not for those who tire easily!

There are so many things to do when there are children in the house. You have to encourage their maturity and respect their juvenile ideas. At the same time you pray they will grow into self-confident adults. You have to support them when things do not go so well, urge them on when they need to keep going, and comfort them when they need support.

This is when you find yourself going to basketball games and concerts. This is when they learn to drive a car – they are going to the prom – and you stay up all night worrying about them.

These responsibilities never end for mothers and fathers until the time when you need them to help out with the car that won't run, and they come over and fix it in five minutes. Or when they give you directions to the business that has moved to a new location. Or when your computer dies. I don't know how people can survive without children!

THE CHILDREN'S HOUSE

Mary R. Durfee

A small city in upstate New York at the foothills of the Adirondack Mountains was the home of one of America's most successful socialist Utopias, the "Oneida Community." It was based in Oneida, New York, and it lasted from 1848 to 1880. Of great historical importance, it is now on the National Register of Historical Landmarks.

When industrialization overran agriculture, this religious, perfectionist community developed a work ethic so deep it became one of the most impressive manufacturing companies of the 20th century. The production of what was to become known as Oneida Silverware was such a successful venture that it became famous worldwide. The founder of this community was John Humphrey Noyes. He was born in Vermont in 1811. Noyes came from a well-established home, and his mother prayed before his birth that her son would become a devoted minister of the gospel. But while growing up, Noyes was known as a rebel and showed little interest in theology until suddenly he came down with a life-threatening illness. He humbled himself before God, and Noyes was healed miraculously. At this point his theory of Christ dying on the cross for the salvation of sinners was comparable to Noyes' own illness, and he felt he was cleansed of all sin.

He went to Yale Divinity School, and his views on life were labeled as perfectionism. All he wanted was a perfect world, a "utopia," and a "Garden of Eden." He believed in the second coming of Christ, and he wanted to have this "Garden of Eden" ready here on earth to receive His coming. But followers were hard to get. Very few believed in Noyes' doctrine of perfection. Eventually, he was forced to leave Vermont. With a few recruits, he came to New York State, where he purchased land in Oneida and started up his foundation of truth and a communal life style.

The membership grew in Noyes' new "Oneida Community," and they adapted communism by which to live, whereby everything was shared equally. The members built a large communal house and referred to it as the "Mansion House." The men and women lived together as one under the leadership of John Humphrey Noyes. Every woman was married to every man, and every man was married to every woman. Children born were deemed a product of perfection. You just couldn't choose a man to father your child; you had to be matched to each other, and then approved by a third party. The babies born stayed with their mothers until the babies were weaned at 15 months. Then mother and child were separated and transferred to separate quarters.

Noyes had his own views on childrearing practices. He used nature as an example: separate the wheat from the chaff, chicks from the hens, and lambs from the ewes. To abandon one's self was for the good of the whole.

Noyes had a special structure built on the north lawn of the community Mansion House. He called it the "Children's House." Although very little has been written about the Children's House, nevertheless, it existed and played an important part in the community's belief of personal and social perfection by separating the children from their parents. It was bitter, but that was their way of life. The children had to live in the house until they reached 13 and 14 years of age.

The Children's House was designed to incorporate a child's imagination, like the ancient castles of yore with tall towers, a gingerbread-house look, colorful and inviting, surrounded by a large fenced-in playground where they could romp and play in fresh air and sunshine.

The furniture for the house was made by craftsmen proficient in carpentry and built in size to match the growth of the children. The craftsmen built cribs for the babies, small beds for the toddlers, and tables and chairs of different proportions. The ladies sewed blankets and spreads. The walls were decorated with paintings and artwork. Portraits of the elders were placed in prominent spaces.

The Children's House was connected to the three-story mansion by many tunnels and secret passages so the adults could reach the children at a given notice. These "special" entrances served not only as a safety feature for protection but also as a means of supplying daily needs. Emergencies were few; the children were well cared for mostly by their teachers and volunteers, who took turns as scheduled.

Schooling was done on a daily basis. The children were taught music, art, Latin, and Greek. Various skills were taught, such as cooking, sewing, knitting, nursing, and carpentry. The children were told to read as much as they could, and one hour a day was devoted to the study of the Bible. Toys were few and dolls were forbidden. At one time, the girls were lined up with their dolls and marched by a huge open fire pit, where they had to toss their dolls. Why? Any bond to their mothers must be broken.

At ages 5 and 6, children were incorporated into the workforce along with their elders. They were given tasks that their small hands could handle, such as the shelling of peas and beans, the picking of nuts, grapes, and berries; strawberries were their favorite. Tasks thus given were no more than they could handle.

The class of juveniles from 12-17 numbered about twenty. They were put into various jobs where their families also worked. For instance, some worked in the trap shop, some in the shoe shop, and some learned the skill of bag making. Also, there were farm chores, such as cleaning the horse barn, the dairy barn, and various other cleaning jobs. Those more talented were assigned to the carpentry business. Working in the lumber mills was a big responsibility. As trees were cut down, replacements had to be planted. The grounds around the mansion and additional buildings were well groomed with lush lawns and flower beds. All these duties and tasks were always under the strict supervision of experienced personnel.

The young girls ages 10 to 12 were given responsibilities, such as washing dishes, preparing vegetables and fruit, setting up the dining room, and acting as runners between the Mansion and the Children's House to get needed supplies. Most of the supplies were stored in the large basement below the Mansion.

The Children's House had its own set of regulations. Proper guardians were assigned, but they could not be a parent of any of the children. It was their responsibility to oversee their care to the utmost, working and playing with them, attending to all their necessary needs, such as a bruised knee, a cut finger, a drink of water, or to settle a dispute. The smaller tots were picked up, kissed and hugged, although the latter was highly discouraged.

The staff of guardians and volunteers consisted of great-hearted motherly women who loved children but were unable to bear their own. Their job was solely the welfare of all of these children to keep them happy, contented, amused, and mold great habits. In addition the guardians must know where the children were every minute. It was strictly parental care. Other volunteers came in to feed them, dress them, mend their clothes, and do all the chamber work.

Noyes loved the children, and to that end strove to provide the best for them. He took the quote from Christ's "suffer the children to come unto me" and applied it to himself. He was often seen surrounded by children – playing with them, seated on his lap, embracing them, brushing tears from their eyes, wiping dripping noses. At one time it was said that Noyes himself had fathered 30 of the 75 children in the Children's House. What woman wouldn't want her child's father to be the great leader of God's future Eden?

A detailed routine at the Children's House was followed to avoid any confusion in everyone's schedule. The janitor lit the fires and rang the bell at the foot of the stairs at 6:00 a.m. You could hear the thump of the children's feet as they sprang from their beds and came pattering downstairs into a common room, where they dressed. They had their own hook for clothes. A motherly volunteer assisted them in washing and combing their hair. They were allowed 20 minutes to dress, and then were off for a quick run in the garden before the breakfast bell was sounded. After breakfast, they assembled in the parlor for a 15-minute Bible reading. In the meantime, they were given the once-over as to the state of their looks, their clothes, shoes, and general appearance. At this time the children were allowed to talk about any concerns they might have or questions that needed answers – a time similar to going to confession for your bad deeds and asking for forgiveness.

After this session the older children were assigned errands and chores to be performed. The younger children went to playtime. At 8:00 a.m. a bell rang for braiding for 1½ hours. Later, the children were allowed to go to the playground for exercise and games consisting of contests: who could pile the most wood, pick the most butternuts or potatoes or some other suitable job that was beneficial.

After dinner (our lunchtime), the children could do as they pleased – perhaps go to a concert held in the parlor or to a singing session. But at 1:30 the children had another stint at braiding. Afterwards, the children went outdoors for business of one kind or another. At 5 o'clock some of the children were allowed to go to their parents for the rest of the day, but only if they were scheduled beforehand and had permission to do so.

Before supper (evening meal), the children were gathered together again for another assessment as to their appearance after their busy day before they were allowed to eat their evening meal. At 7:00 p.m. the smaller children retired for bed. The older ones were given an hour with their books and pencils, and then they retired by 8:00 p.m. Volunteers came in and relieved the regular house corps. After that, the night watchman visited all of the sleeping rooms once or more during his rounds.

The children had visiting days scheduled with their parents to go out beyond the perimeter of their house. They toured the farms, explored the woods, picked flowers, and romped with their playmates across the fields. The children watched their dads work at their various skilled trades. The children were encouraged to learn as much as they could about their father's trade, as these were skills that could be handed down to future generations.

Sundays were spent with one hour of worship at the chapel, conducted by John Noyes himself. Visitors from the outside were allowed, and sometimes as many as a thousand outsiders attended the yearly strawberry festival. Games were played with the children, adults, and guests. Croquet was a favorite, as prizes were awarded after the tournaments. There were bountiful picnics held throughout the day along with other fun activities. This style of life continued for 30 years, and then in 1879 Noyes was forced by outside pressures to break up his communistic style of life. Noyes left for Canada and his son, Theodore Noyes, took over. The dissolution of the complex marriages followed and couples left this Community House, quickly got married and settled in and around the surrounding communities. The buildings attached to the community were torn down eventually and dismantled. The farms were sold along with all material goods.

The Children's House was sold to a couple who had it moved across the road to a piece of land they owned, facing the front of the original Mansion House. The new owners had the Children's House restored, and it still stands today, a house full of memories to be handed down to future generations; a historical saga of the life and times of a most unusual Utopian community. Three generations of children were part of a labor force that saw the success of a famous manufacturing plant, Oneida Community, LTD, come into being. This communal style of living caused no harm to the future generations born of these descendants. Who can boast of an industry that started out producing animal traps and reached prosperity by the production of silverware worldwide?

Author's Footnote: The last remaining person who was born in the Mansion House and spent her childhood growing up in the "Children's House" recently died on June 20, 2010. She was 97. My great-granddaughter is a descendant of the "Children's House."

It's Written on Your Forehead

Shelly Fletcher

Raising a child is a challenging voyage, and to stay afloat the adults need to develop a bag of tricks to survive in this choppy sea. During the formative years of my life, my maternal grandmother was most responsible for my upbringing.

Mabel North was a God-fearing woman who had lots of experience with children. She had been mothering someone practically her whole life. She lost her own mother when she was a teen and had to take over that role for several of her younger siblings. Through the years, besides single-handedly raising her own two daughters, she often took in some of her nieces and nephews. Grammy had that parenting role pretty much down to a system by the time I came along. No matter who she was mothering, we all were expected to follow the same rules. We were expected to love Jesus, do our best to be helpful to others and, most especially, we all needed to mind our P's and Q's. In our house, Grandma was boss, and her words were never questioned.

Grammy really dug into her bag of tricks to keep us honest. I was repeatedly reminded of the importance of telling the truth. I knew that Jesus would know if I were lying, but according to Grandma, so would she. I was told she'd always know if I were telling a lie because, if I did, it would be written all over my forehead!

What…written on my forehead? That sounded mysterious and magical, like some of the stories I had heard from the Bible. As a mere child, I would never question God's ability to write the word *LIE* on my forehead. In the Bible there was a burning bush, a parting of the Red Sea, and even water that turned into wine. It made sense that God would create humans with a built-in internal truth-or-lie monitoring system. I figured it probably had something to do with the blood vessels in your head rushing to the surface of the skin to spell out "L-I-E" in big red letters any time you lied. Yep, I believed the words in the Bible, and I believed the words of my Grandma.

I basically tried my best to do what was expected, but sometimes temptation came along and tested my character. At times like these, being a kid can be a real challenge. My test came one Saturday morning when I was about five years old. I was excited about going outside to play. I hurriedly dressed, ate my breakfast, and ran to the front door to make my escape. Just as I reached for the door knob, I heard my grandmother's voice.

"Shelly Lynn, your bedroom is a mess. You need to go back in there and clean up that whole room before you go out to play."

Disappointed with this delay, I sulked off to my room, with Grammy's words, "And don't come out until your room is all cleaned up!" resounding in my head.

I opened the door to the devastation that would be my downfall. My bedroom looked like a war zone. There were toys on the bed, and toys scattered on the floor. Clothes were thrown all over the furniture, and even my Tinker Toys had somehow oozed out of their cardboard drum. Hardly an inch of carpet was free of my discarded messes! I wasn't capable of tackling all of this! Crying, I flung myself onto a corner of my bed. I couldn't get through this whole mess in only a day, or even a week. I'd never see the front yard or my little friends ever again. I was doomed!

Then, amidst my grief, an idea hit me. Grandma had said to *clean* my room, but she hadn't specifically detailed *how* I should go about doing it. My bedroom had a large closet and, in my opinion, that closet was my solution. Quickly, I bounded off my bed and started kicking and throwing all of those toys and clothes onto the closet floor. As I worked, I was so proud of my ingenious plan. Within fifteen minutes, the floor was cleared, the bedcover straightened, and the bedroom would pass any inspection. It wasn't easy, but with a big push I was even able to close the door of that jam-packed closet.

Full of self-confidence, I skipped out of my room, down the hallway, and into our living room. I was now free to spend the whole day outside with my friends, and I was raring to get going. Just as I reached for the front door, I heard my Grandma's voice: "Shelly Lynn, are you finished already?" Panic froze me in place. Again, she inquired, "That was mighty fast, young lady. Are you sure you cleaned up your whole room?"

Just like in a "Tom and Jerry" cartoon, I felt like I had a little white tiny angel sitting on one of my shoulders and a tiny red devil propped up on my other shoulder. One moment, that evil little devil was trying to convince me I *had* done as I was asked to do. After all, Grammy never told me I couldn't just throw all of my junk into the closet. So, logically, I deserved to be rewarded. However, I also had that nagging voice of the good little angel whispering in my other ear. Was it technically a *lie* to say that I had cleaned my room, when all I had really done was hide all of my messes? Is this what I thought Grammy *really* wanted me to do when she told me to go clean up my room? If I went outside, would I be guilty of telling a lie?

I was truly torn and had a hard time deciding the right thing to do. Finally, I decided to cover my bases, just in case. Just prior to answering Grammy, I snapped the palm of my right hand hard against my forehead. Holding my hand firmly over my forehead, I distinctly answered, "Yes, Grammy. I cleaned up my whole room!"

As I mentioned before, an adult has to be pretty sharp if they expect to come out ahead when it comes to child rearing. My grandma was a champion at this. It didn't matter that I hid my forehead from her when I answered. Somehow, my grandmother *knew* I wasn't telling her the truth, the *whole* truth, and nothing *but* the truth. She didn't need to see the letters *L-I-E* on my forehead.

Gently, she took my hand and together we walked down the hallway, back to my room. Together, we spent the morning cleaning my room, and it wasn't so bad. As we worked, she told me lots of wonderful Bible stories… stories about forgiveness and love. Hmmmm…what a poignant topic, forgiveness and love. As always, Grammy had successfully pulled another parenting miracle out of her bag of tricks!

THE WHISTLER

Helen Moriarty

The most despicable thing I ever did was in the second grade, when I was seven years old. I whistled.

I had been trying to learn how to whistle for a long time. My sister, Fran, would give me pointers from time to time, but she always ended our practice sessions by saying, "You just get the knack of it all of a sudden." Well, I had finally gotten the knack of it.

It was a Tuesday, a sunny spring day just made for whistling. I whistled at the bus stop, and on the bus, and right up to the school doors. We weren't allowed to whistle in school.

The 48 desks in my second-grade classroom were aligned in neat orderly rows. Sister Julia, our teacher, wouldn't have it any other way. Everything in Sister Julia's world (and we were a big part of her world) had to be neat and orderly and correct. That was why she had been given the plum assignment in the school: the First Communion class. Now that we had reached seven, the supposed "age of reason," we were old enough to go to confession and receive Communion at Mass on Sunday. But only after we had been prepared – by Sister Julia.

Sister Julia was old. Some people said she was in her nineties, but no one knew for sure. My older sisters, Beth and Susan, had her when they were in elementary school, and so had a few of my aunts and uncles. Her vision had deteriorated to the point of near-blindness. She wore glasses with thick Coke-bottle lenses. Even with these, she couldn't see very well. She was always telling us to "write darker, press harder." (I still have a bump on the middle finger of my right hand from pressing the pencil into the paper.) She often accused us, as a class, of writing lightly on purpose just to taunt her. She didn't hear very well either. Sometimes, when she was asking us our spelling words, she'd tell people they were wrong even when they were right. But no one had the nerve to point that out. So the next person would just repeat the same letters, but louder, and they'd be marked correct.

When Sister Julia started swinging her rosary beads, you knew someone was in big trouble. That year, in our class, the someone was almost always Ned Alderucci. Ned was a nice kid – not too bright, full of mischief. He was the class clown and the class troublemaker. If something bad happened, you could bet that Ned was involved.

In the 1950's parochial school classroom, there was no such thing as hyperactivity or a learning disability. Just bad kids. And what bad kids needed was punishment. If they got enough of it, they would (presumably) become good kids. The last thing they needed was special attention.

The only special attention Ned Alderucci got was being sent to the coat closet when he misbehaved. That was the worst thing that could happen to you short of being sent to the principal's office. Ned usually managed to stop just short of behavior that would bring down the ultimate punishment. So he spent a lot of time in the coat closet. Maybe he liked it in there.

The coat closet was at the back of the room. It was where you put your jackets and hats and boots. It was fine for that. But if you were sent to the coat closet for punishment, you had to drag your desk back there, the vinyl accordion door was pulled closed, and you were banished. It was dark in there, of course. And the voice of the teacher must have been muffled. So you sat there alone in the quiet darkness and fell further and further behind in your schoolwork.

On this particular Tuesday morning in the spring, we were working on math. Sister Julia turned to the blackboard to write some problems. And I whistled. Out loud. Loud enough for Sister Julia to hear. I hadn't thought about it or planned it. It just happened.

Sister Julia whirled around in anger. "How dare someone whistle in my class!" she screeched. "Now I know no young lady would ever whistle. So which of you boys did that?" There was silence.

I was squirming in my chair. If she had asked, "Who whistled?" without the boy part, I would have had to confess. But I knew whoever owned up to this was going to be in big trouble. And I had always been a good girl. I didn't want to blemish my reputation and my future prospects by admitting my error. At St. Francis of Assisi School, reputations had been ruined for lesser infractions.

The silence continued. I thought I might get some dirty looks from people around me, but it seemed no one knew who had done it. When it became clear that no one was going to confess, Sister Julia announced that all the boys would stay after school that day until one of them admitted he had done it.

All the girls heaved a sigh of relief – all except me. Should I raise my hand and confess right now? Should I make a clean breast of it and hope for clemency? Should I do the right thing, reputation be damned? No. I just sat there and did my math problems. And I got them all correct.

Sister Julia smiled as she put a gold star on my paper. "Always such good girls, you Moriartys," she said. I swallowed hard and returned to my desk.

The rest of the day passed in a blur. At recess, Patty Bresnan came right up and asked, "Was that you that whistled?"

I looked shocked. "I don't even know how to," I said. "Besides, Sister Julia said it was one of the boys." I was beginning to believe my own lies.

The end of the day finally came. The bell rang. All of the girls, smirking, filed out of the classroom. All of the boys, glum faced, stayed in their seats. I approached Sister Julia's desk. I was going to tell her.

"Yes, dear, what is it?" she asked.

I felt my nerve dissolve. "Oh, nothing," I said.

"Well, then, hurry on out, dear. You don't want to miss your bus."

I didn't find out what had happened until the next morning. All of the boys had sat at their desks, staring at Sister Julia, with Sister Julia staring back, until almost five o'clock. Then Ned Alderucci stood up and confessed.

"I did it," he said. "I whistled behind your back."

"Well, why didn't you admit it earlier?" she asked. "Why didn't you say so this morning, or at three o'clock, or at four o'clock?"

"Well, Sister," he replied, "I was sort of hoping someone else would own up to it."

He was sentenced to detention for a week.

"I'm not surprised," Sister Julia said. "He's such a troublemaker."

I was overcome with guilt when I heard what had happened. Was there any way I could make it up to Ned? What if I went to him and told him I did it and that I was sorry? He'd tell Sister Julia, and then she'd punish him for telling lies about good little girls. What if I went to Sister Julia and confessed? She'd think I was just feeling sorry for Ned and trying to take the blame to spare him. She'd tell me I was very caring, but it wouldn't work.

What could I do? Well, our First Confession was just a couple of weeks away. I'd been wondering how I was going to come up with something to confess. Now I had a doozy. A perfectly legitimate rotten thing I'd done – a bona fide sin.

When I went to confession for the first time, I mentioned disobeying my mother, just to warm up to The Big One. Then I blurted out: "I did something wrong, and I didn't own up to it, and somebody else got punished for it."

I heard what sounded like a little chuckle on the other side of the screen. "It wasn't robbing a bank or anything, was it?" the priest asked.

"No," I said. "I whistled when Sister Julia turned her back, and when she asked who did it, I didn't say anything, and Ned Alderucci finally confessed he'd done it, and he got detention for a week!" For my penance, I got three Hail Marys. The standard. Apparently, there was no extra penalty for such a heinous crime. Had the priest even heard what I'd said?

Just as I was about to leave the confessional, forgiven but not feeling any better about it, the priest said, "About the whistling. I wouldn't worry about it. It's over and done with."

Well, I have worried about it. And it won't be over and done with until I tell Ned Alderucci the truth. At our twentieth high school reunion, someone said they'd kept in touch with Ned. He was married, living in Florida, had three kids and owned a couple of gas stations. I think I need to find his address and write him a note:

> Dear Ned,
>   I know you didn't whistle in Sister Julia's class. I know because I'm the one who did it. Did you ever wonder who you'd taken the blame for? Did you ever think it was a girl who did it? I wish I could go back and do the right thing. But I can't. All I can do is let you know that I think you were a prince to have done what you did. Thank you. And I'm sorry.

A Really Sticky Situation

Helen Jones-Shepherd

While perusing my *Essential Thesaurus* recently, I came across multiple synonyms for "teacher." I was surprised to find the following: schoolteacher, instructor, educator, tutor, coach, trainer, lecturer, professor, pedagogue, guide, mentor and, last but not least, guru. After thinking about this for a few minutes, I realized that at times a teacher becomes one of the many cited above. One particular memory flooded my thoughts about a substitute assignment I had many years ago for the San Bernardino School District.

The assignment was to be for at least a week, if not more, depending on the return to good health of the teacher for whom I was substituting. An unusual assignment this was for me, since I was to be teaching a single class of students ranging in ages from 8 to 21 years. These students had been expelled from their schools numerous times, and this class was an attempt to rehabilitate them, or at least spur them on with a desire to learn. As an English instructor, I was to encourage these students. The Principal in charge of this particular program described them to me as "a real hard-core group." When I accepted the job, I remember thinking what a challenge this would be, very similar to an assignment I had with autistic students. Challenge was the operative word here, believe me.

The classroom itself was a challenge, since we were in a portable trailer to the rear of a middle school and locked in by the Principal himself, who would check on me periodically during the day. I thought this rather odd but intriguing, being the type of person who loves a good mystery.

The room had several large round tables with newspapers spread around, Scrabble boards, books, dictionaries, and other games to keep the students involved in some form of mental stimulation. There were about nine or ten students in the class. As I recall there were around six boys (or men, depending on their ages) and approximately four girls (or young ladies).

First, I'll tell you about one girl in particular, called Sheila, who was sixteen years of age – a pretty child dressed in tight-fitting clothes, her hair dyed a flaming red and heavy makeup applied to her face. One might mistake her for a prostitute. She was withdrawn, and I found it difficult to get her to participate in our present activity, or any other. This youngster was having none of it. I quickly assessed that she had been forced into this program, and she expressed no hesitation in letting me know, with her continuous complaints and use of curse words spewing from her mouth all period long. She definitely was trying to shock me with her string of expletives, but I just went about helping the others, while circulating through the classroom. When it was time for a break, the girls and I, including Sheila, headed into the restroom, which was down the hall from the classroom. As Sheila and I stood in front of the mirror over the sinks (powdering our noses) she continued her filthy language, trying to rile me.

Hmm, this little gal is spoiling for a fight; I can feel it. Suddenly inspired, I said, "Sheila," smiling directly at her, "what a lovely color that blouse is on you. It really brings out the blueness in your eyes."

The sternness in her face faded away and, astonishingly, she cracked a half-smile. Upon resuming our work in class, she came up and asked for a section of the newspaper she wanted to read, and queried, "Would you help me with some of the words?" She read a few items, such as the entertainment page and an article on fashions quite well. I praised her for her excellent articulation and she smiled. This time, I could see she was pleased with herself and her self-confidence grew as she read more. Sheila turned out to be the best reader in the class.

I was now feeling much better about this challenging group, but little did I know what was still to come.

One other student, a tall, maybe 6 ft. 3 in. African American young man, wanted to play Scrabble, and he helped me clear the board of tiles. Several other students who weren't reading joined in. Jeffrey sat next to me and smiled amicably. While waiting for his turn to play, with everyone engrossed in the game, he suddenly reached across and put his hand up my skirt. Shocked and appalled at this behavior, I quickly removed his hand and from somewhere came my reaction and words as if from my Guardian Angel, my protector. I grabbed him by the collar, pulled him toward me, picked up a newly sharpened pencil, placed it at his throat and said in a firm voice, "You do that again, you son of a bitch, and I'll stick you!" He immediately pulled away, walked to the other side of the room and stood there, gazing out of the window.

After that shocking behavior, nothing more was said, but in the ensuing days Jeffrey was my self-appointed helper and keeper of the peace, which included the elimination of dirty language from the rest of the class. Smiling broadly, he brought me donuts one day, which I shared with the class. Surprisingly, Jeffrey and the class presented me with a small hand-picked bouquet of flowers at the end of my assignment, several weeks later.

So, maybe, a teacher is more than a schoolteacher, a coach, or a mentor, as I mentioned earlier. Regardless of what synonym you might use for me on that challenging assignment, with these recalcitrant, difficult, thrown out of every school in the district students…a very, very sticky situation, when handled the right way, had definitely become an extraordinary and wonderful discovery for us all!

What's A Person To Do?

William Goodboy

I was a senior at South Hills High School in 1963 -1964 year, and I had been taking acting classes at the Pittsburgh Playhouse School of the Theatre since '62. Shirley Jones and George Peppard also studied there. I heard that the Playhouse was having an open call for auditions for the musical, *West Side Story*, coming to the Playhouse after its long successful run in New York City. I was a dancer back in the 60's and attending the high school I did, releasing that type of information was not the healthiest situation for a young boy.

Only one person in my high school circle of friends knew about my dance background: Charlee, a female friend in my homeroom. She knew because at that time we were both taking classes from Esther Wills and Jerry Abbott's School of Dance in Dormont, Pennsylvania, a suburb of Pittsburgh, and we had several classes together. We had a made a pact between us not to reveal this to anyone for fear of harassment or worse. I had 10 years experience at three different dancing schools in Tap Dancing, four years in Jazz, four years in Ballet, two years in Acrobatics, and one year in Russian. The one hour of Russian was the toughest of all the other nine hours in my week.

At my next acting class, I thought I would ask Mr. Baker, my drama teacher, about the auditions. I was not much of a singer except in the church choir with the other men, and when the pianist at the audition asked me what key I sang in, I had no idea what he was talking about. Of course, I came to audition as a dancer, never realizing I had to sing as well. I was asked to pick something from the show and not really knowing the music, chose the song "Tonight."

What a disaster! I am not a tenor! I always sang bass in the church choir, but after my rendition of that song, Duncan Noble, the dance instructor at the Playhouse, was kind enough to say we would work on the voice. I guess at that time my dancing background was enough for him to see my talent, since I would be singing with the chorus anyway. I then became Luis, the only blue-eyed member of the Shark Gang.

Once rehearsals began, it became difficult for me to have Mom and Dad's car every night to get there. Occasionally, Mom would take me out and drop me off. I rode the streetcars into town at night, and Mom would pick me up in front of the old post office on Smithfield Street. There were bathrooms under the sidewalk in front of the old post office building. Each one had its own set of steps down into the most horrible smelling bathrooms imaginable. Facing the old post office, to the left of the front steps, were two gigantic green magazine stands. These were always locked by the time I got to town from the Playhouse on the trolley. That was our meeting place.

One night, after exhausting rehearsals, I came to town still dressed for the part I was rehearsing. I was tired. I had long sideburns to the bottom of my ear lobes, long hair slicked back like a punk, and of course was wearing blue jeans and my cousin Bob's black leather motorcycle jacket. I was leaning against the closed magazine stand when a police car came up Fourth Avenue. The cop rolled down his window and said, "Hey buddy! What are you doing there?"

Well, my very truthful answer was, "Waiting for my mother!"

He asked me if I was a smart ass, and they stopped the car. The one on my side got out and approached me. He told me to assume the position! But the only positions I knew at the time were First, Second, Third, Fourth, and Fifth positions (ballet). Of course, after he frisked me I saw my mother's car coming down Smithfield Street. I pointed to my mother's car and said, "See! There she is!" I asked him if I could go, and he released me to get into my mother's 1953 DeSoto for the ride home. The cops were both laughing with their heads down as they walked back to the squad car. I guess now they had seen everything! But I made it home that night without a police record.

So what's a person to do? Always tell the truth and don't dress like a punk!

SHAKY BRIDGE

Judy Ray

Mrs. Watson was snipping brown dead blooms from her rose bushes when she heard a cry, which she thought came from the direction of the river. She straightened her aching back and turned to listen more closely. No, nothing now, except a faint quacking from the ducks downstream. She must have been imagining things. Then an agitated roar rose as two motorcycles raced around the dangerous curve. "Those boys!" she muttered, shaking her head and grasping the pruning secateurs tightly with her gloved hand. She snipped a few more drooping flower heads and was pleased to see yet more buds. That's enough for today, she told herself, mustn't overdo it.

This was Mrs. Watson's first real day of retirement. The children had started school again after their long summer holiday, and for the first time in forty years Mrs. Watson was not with them in the picture-filled room with its pygmy furniture. She would miss it all, of course, her busy responsibility in that circle of bright, stumbling, scrumpled youth. But it was time.

She had gone into town that afternoon by the back road that led past the little Museum with its rusty mill wheel and giant tools, past the swimming pool where a concrete dolphin leaped in a frozen arc. Outside the Public Library a girl wearing her high school uniform was sitting on a bench and reading a textbook, her straight heavy hair flopped over her face. Mrs. Watson didn't recognize the girl, though Ashton was a small enough town for most inhabitants to be familiar by sight. She was struck by the intensity of the girl's concentrated reading and of the brown unfocused eyes that glanced up.

Mrs. Watson spent a long time in the library, yet when she came out the girl was still there. It's good to see a real scholar, the retired teacher thought at first, until the girl looked up and Mrs. Watson saw the full lips tremble, the shy eyes watching a group of giggling teenagers gathered across the street outside the GOBBLE AND GO. The girl was caught unhappily in her role of serious student locked in a book world. She would have liked to join the others. Mrs. Watson hesitated. She wanted to talk to the girl, to encourage her. But remembering that she was no longer a schoolteacher made her self-conscious, a new and unpleasant feeling. She moved on, a small white-haired woman with apple rosy cheeks, leaning sideways from the weight of her basket of books.

At school Mrs. Watson had not thought she was saving the children. She was cultivating, preparing the ground, sowing seeds. But a few years before, the whole town, indeed the whole district, had called her a savior. Newspaper headlines had read: SCHOOL TEACHER SAVES MAN ON ASHTON CLOCK.

Ashton was built at the confluence of two rivers, which had other official names on maps but which were referred to by local residents simply as the Brown and the Green. The Green, broad and impressively swift, turned with a swirling arc just below the town. At its bend, the Brown flowed into it. At least one knew logically that the Brown flowed into the faster Green, but visually it was hard to tell. The brown water moved slowly, spreading wide at the junction, then seemed to turn back on itself, churning a busy pool. The waters, with their separate colors, did not appear to flow together. An artist of the scene could paint green in one direction, brown in another, and would not have to blend the brush strokes.

Across the Brown from the town rose the foothills of a mountain range, which gave a natural dramatic particularity to the site of Ashton. And a quarter century before, the town council had voted to give their municipality an uplift by placing a clock on the mountain.

Ashton had no clock tower, no tall church with a four-faced or even a one-faced clock. The mountain clock surely outdid all such traditions. Its stark white hands and markers, contrasting with the grey and ochre rocks, were so huge that Ashton's mountain time was visible from far beyond the edge of town. No children could sidle home late with the excuse that they "didn't know what time it was."

There had been endless discussions about the project, and exclamations of approval as well as ridicule and criticism were voiced when the clock was erected. But it had seemed to bring unity to the town, as if its people were all one family glancing up to check the time on the living room wall.

Mrs. Watson did not often glance at the clock during the day. But the adventure of the "saving" came about when she caught sight of something shining on the mountain, and a dark movement against the white of the clock markers. She assumed some repair was being made. But by first light next day she still saw movement up there. She called the police to ask if there was a problem, and was told they'd check into it. With concern and curiosity, she decided to investigate further. She set off by the shortest route, which started with crossing Shaky Bridge, a narrow hundred-year-old footpath bridge with weathered crossbeams and metal hawsers, swaying wildly with each step above the river. She was glad the wind was not gusting fiercely down the valley as it sometimes did. Several of the townspeople would no longer step across Shaky Bridge, claiming it to be unsafe, preferring to make a detour by the newer bridge upstream.

After safely crossing, Mrs. Watson climbed up the steep footpath, stepping around bracken and brambles. From close up it was hard to see the clock as a clock. It became a structure of scaffolding and beams attached to rocks. She climbed yet higher, taking a path that wound around the cliff. She heard something crash down the side of the mountain, and a voice yelling. A man had scaled the scaffolding and climbed out on a horizontal beam. He had a canvas backpack, a box beside him, and some rocks within reach.

Mrs. Watson called out, "Hey. That's quite a climb! Can you get back all right?"

"Get back? You get back!" he shouted. As he looked in her direction, Mrs. Watson recognized the young man. Charlie Ross had been in her class years ago, and she might have forgotten the small tufty boy if he had not kept something of that elfish look about him as he grew up, and if he had not stayed in town, working in the Golden Cross Hotel with its convivial public bar.

On Friday and Saturday nights the Golden Cross changed the atmosphere of small-town Ashton. As the patrons, many of whom drove in from farms and valleys around, left after spending hours with their beers and darts and music and more beers, parties and arguments often spilled out into the parking lot. Voices got loud, spoiling for a fight, urging insults to justify the first blow, fortunately of fist fights – no knives or guns. Sometimes a stumbling, drunken soccer game in the road in the middle of the night – loud and wacky – would distract the combatants. Sometimes one of them got dangerously close to the swift river, but no one ever remembered anyone drowning in town.

Years ago people came to these ochre mountains to look for gold. Below the hill adorned by the clock the town council put up a sign that read, "To the gully where the gold prospectors are buried." It was not much visited anymore, but sometimes visitors asked questions, wondering if the prospectors were buried in a mass grave, if they died around the same time from some kind of disease, if they died one by one from accidents, or if any of them ended up rich. When the Golden Cross grew lively at weekends, it seemed as if the old prospectors had managed to return, with the gleam of adventure and dreams in their eyes, fortune and misfortune in their pockets.

"Get back!" the man shouted again from his precarious position on the beam. "I'm going to blow up this clock."

"Charlie Ross!" cried Mrs. Watson, holding on to a stumpy bush for support on the narrow path. "Whatever has got into you!"

The slight young man looked startled at hearing his name. Then he scowled. "Leave me alone, teacher!"

"But Charlie! I want to talk with you. Can you get off the beam this way?"

"Go away, Mrs. Watson. I'm going to blow up this clock. I wish I could blow up the whole town."

"What's happened, Charlie? It's really hard to talk like this, shouting so much. Can you come over here? I don't think I can get on that beam."

"Go away!"

"But if you do anything to the clock, you might fall."

"Of course I'll fall. I'm not on a jungle gym now." Charlie turned away from Mrs. Watson and began to take the backpack straps off his shoulders. He leaned over, looking down and from side to side.

"Charlie Ross! I've been thinking about you. How you've been working hard at the Golden Cross all this time."

"Not any more. I got fired."

Mrs. Watson noticed how high and thin the young man's voice sounded. "Well, now. Tell me what happened." She moved a few steps and sat down on a rock.

"Ever since I worked there, Mr. Older made me start the day cleaning up the doorways. And the passage. And it's disgusting. It's all spewn with vomit most days. And then he says I don't polish the front steps enough. I'm sick of it. And I said I wasn't going to do the cleanup anymore. So he fired me. And I went to Helton's to ask for a job, and they said they couldn't hire me because I'd been fired by Mr. Older. I'm sick of this town."

"Sounds tough. But that's not the whole town. Maybe you could get a job over in Jesselton. You know, Charlie, when you were in school you were a pretty tough kid, hanging in there."

Charlie pushed at his pile of rocks and they rumbled down the cliff, bouncing and scattering. He hung his head down and shook it from side to side. Mrs. Watson got up and brushed off the seat of her pants, but instead of moving back along the path, she stepped closer to the bars that framed the huge clock and looked for a way to pull herself up. Charlie inched back along the beam and jumped off onto the rocky hillside above the teacher.

"Thank you, Charlie. Can you help me get turned around here? It's a bit steep for me. Then I could follow you down."

Now, on this first day of retirement, Mrs. Watson remembered again the adventure of saving the clock, as well as Charlie, as she glanced up to the hill. She realized she was listening again with one ear for the small cry, now repeated, she had heard while snipping roses. It really could be a child. She couldn't ignore the possibility where there were the dangers of rivers. rocks, and who knew what else. She grabbed hold of the first tool at hand, a broom, a life-saving broom, stiff bristles up, held like a staff as she hurried along. Beside the river, she looked across at a white cottage where goats were grazing, watched by a sheepdog. Goats. Kids! That must have been it. She was glad she didn't have to go swaying across Shaky Bridge this late in the day.

THE VIEWING

Louise Larsen

I love being in my new school, Garfield, about six blocks away from my home. My neighbor, Lillian Hack, and I walk to school together each morning. Garfield is for 6th graders only, which makes me feel very grown up. My old school, Lincoln, is for "babies" in grades 1 - 5. Lincoln is behind my house. I just had to cut through a vacant lot and a hollow to get there.

Walking to Garfield each day is an adventure. Along the way, I peek into the hole of a wren house piled with sticks and leaves. At a catalpa tree just off the path, Lillian and I pick off hanging fronds. We put them into our mouths and pretend we're smoking "lady cigars." We run about three blocks, then jump over cracks on the sidewalk in front of the school. We sing "Three Blind Mice" and whistle through our teeth.

We have spelling tests on Friday and carry a paper list home to study. Once a month there's a book report to write, but no other homework. We carry our lunch in a brown bag – no books or backpacks load us down. We are carefree and happy. I love gym class best because we have to go down into the basement to the girls' restrooms to change into blue loose-fitting knee-length bloomers. Then we cross over the vacant lot to Roosevelt Jr. High. Miss Perkins, our long-legged teacher whose hair is bobbed short, blows a whistle and we line up for exercises. We run races, and she times us with a stopwatch. We do broad jumps and vaults. On the mat we jump over crouched classmates. I was champion at this as I could catapult over seven other girls and somersault at the end. We bring our sandwiches from home and drink half-pint cartons of milk that we pay for each week. I like my school day. It just seems to float by with no worries.

The last period is music at 3 p.m., and by then I can't wait to start home. I meet Lillian at the door and we start our Big Adventure. We run four blocks, then stop and catch our breath, walking sedately to the corner of Fifth Street, where we see the big red building, Bauer Funeral Home. We walk up the four steps, then knock, using the heavy brass knocker. A man opens the door and we ask politely for Mr. George. Mr. George comes forward.

We ask in hushed tones if he would take us to do the viewing. He nods. We pass Parlor B, then enter a room with a big floor-length wooden closet. Mr. George turns the closet door key and opens the closet door wide. There hanging from a hook is THE MUMMY!

We stand back and gasp.

The mummy is brown and shriveled – really only a skeleton of bones. His cheekbones are sunken and his eye sockets push forward in his face. His ribs are double-bones down his side and his hip bones hang loosely. His leg bones are elongated with big, bulgy kneecaps.

Lillian and I hold hands and stare at the mummy in silence.

After several minutes, Mr. George nods, closes the closet door and locks it with a key. He leads us to the outside door. We thank him several times and leave Bauer Funeral Home. We walk the last block to Ninth Street, half fearful, half scared – not saying a word, but each with our own awesome thoughts.

The next morning Lillian and I talk incessantly about the mummy. We review piece by piece the story Mr. George told us. The mummy was found ten years earlier at the bottom of the Mississippi River in Alton, Illinois, when the Ace Barge Company was dredging for debris. The *Alton Evening Telegraph* announced the finding of the skeleton of an unknown male about 40 years old, about six feet, two inches. They asked anyone who knew anything of this man to call the newspaper phone number, 22418. The newspaper ran the story for three nights, but no one came forward to identify the skeleton. The Bauer Funeral Home then cleaned the mud off the man and kept him in a locked closet at the Home. The mummy could be viewed upon request every Tuesday and Thursday from 2 to 4 p.m.

Lillian and I feel sad, but we are, of course, fascinated by the story. He feels like our dear friend. We never miss a viewing.

Symbiosis

Claudia Poquoc

Rough, brown lichen covers a lizard-skinned rock
with shades of green and gold fungus hiding below
the older algae.

Like these brown spots on her hands—
and other scaly-skin that surfaces at summer's end along with
parched lips that house a drying tongue

which no longer flows with a torrent of thoughts
to pay homage to her watery word womb—
but instead, like lichen and rock – merges with silence.

BREAKING THE SOUND BARRIER
(an autobiography)

Anne Whitlock

If I speak softly
it's because the air is heavy with incense
and I have known terrible silences.

When I was a child,
the world spoke a different language.
I lost the golden tenor of my father's voice
when I was four.
I spent the first four years of school
sitting on a bench.
Enough was said between my mother and me
to fill a thousand volumes
but not one word was understood.

I learned to hear the voices in books.
Lewis Carroll was my teacher
and George MacDonald.
I fell down a rabbit hole
and escaped on the back of the North Wind.
My only companions lived
in the fairy tale section of the library.

At 17 I thought I had a dialogue with God.
In the quiet convent chapel
as the morning sun filtered through the glass
to the cooing of the doves
I tried to force His voice to speak to me.

At 20 I free fell through space
and screamed in silence in a darkened chapel
to a God who didn't answer
but left me to look in the patterns of my life
like tea leaves in a cup.
I learned that silence
is more than the absence of sound.

For 19 years I taught children
who weren't my own,
but I have sat next to that lonely child
on a school bench
and she has heard my voice.

Who is to say that the absences of our life
are not as valuable as its events?
The past was perfect
and all that matters in the flow of time
is the moment,
the precious moment,
that cannot be measured
not even by analog.

Now I can speak
and I have much to say
before I go into that great silence.

Taking Care of Business

Anita Curran Guenin

Light rain pecks at our faces like curious wild creatures while the manager leads my daughter, grandson, and me to the Cremation Garden on the hillside. Bill is his name, and he carries a rolled up map. Using it to point, he says, "This one holds five urns and has more frontage along the walk." It didn't seem like a hard sell when he added matter of factly, "Only one spot left in this section, and prices are going up every year."

The Cremation Garden is like a condominium of gravesites with crisp-edged grass, shrubs under tight control. My gardener daughter says, "A Japanese maple would fit on the site."

Will she come and trim it, I ask myself. Will anyone come? And for how long into the future? The location is not far from Route One, which meanders along the Rhode Island coast, so not inconvenient for the willing.

Parting company with the manager, we go down the hill to the main cemetery with its spacious rows of gravestones and tombs. Along a dirt path that follows the Pawcatuck River, I find my great grandfather's grave. In 1928 he was buried in "free ground;" his squat granite marker says simply, "Father." As far as I know, he was forgotten by his few descendants until I rediscovered him during genealogical research. James O. Smith married late in life, but his young wife died at age twenty-four, leaving him with two young daughters. One was my grandmother, who was boarded out with a couple. When I'd ask her about her family, she only told me about her birth mother, Nellie. No one else.

Maybe the somber spirit of James, hovering around his stone, would rest better if someone of his flesh were nearby in death, if not in life. I wonder, sometimes, if we are not being led to these places, these decisions, by our lost and neglected ancestors. There are many stories from genealogical research that offer testament to events difficult to explain in logical ways.

I decide to buy the space in the Cremation Garden, hoping to be first to use it. I feel strangely content with the idea that I will return to my beloved

New England soil. It's also a relief to know my family will not have to make any decisions about where I should go when I die. Maybe I will have some company in time.

My young grandson twirls, head back, tongue sticking out to catch raindrops. Maybe he'll visit this place someday, remembering he had a chocolate sundae with Mom and Grandma, his hair still damp from August rain.

Nature's Magic

Terrie Jacks

It's winter.
Melancholy has found me.
It's come for another visit
reminds me you're gone.
I don't need a reminder.
The empty house is enough.
I need a distraction.
I dress warm,
go outside, take a walk,
find an undisturbed path
in the park.

Ahead I see a shelter, a shelter
with two wooden benches
made from cedar logs sawed in half.
The backs and legs are
branches of various thicknesses.
The roof is held up by rough logs,
some still have their shaggy bark.
This wooden retreat reminds me of you.
It's a comforting place to rest.

Slumbering plants surround me,
a bird sings, a squirrel scampers by.
On occasion other people take the path.
One couple seems to be getting acquainted,
they stop, converse with me, then move on.
He takes her hand.

The hush returns. Another couple appears,
walking apart except for conversation.
They travel along the path
checking out the winter sights.
Avoiding the shelter.
A third couple absorbed with each other,
kiss, hold hands and drift away.

I release a long sigh.
I miss you.

The tranquility is soothing.
I sit awhile longer
breathing in the crisp air.
The sun begins to disappear.
It's time to leave.
Heading home I smile, content.
Nature weaved its magic.

EXTRA BLANKETS

Terrie Jacks

I ascend the stairs
to a bed once shared
where extra blankets
are now necessary

a substitute for the warmth
once provided

Separation

Margaret McKerrow

Only one tea bag needed, shall
I make a pot or steep it in a cup?
"I've lost my other half,"
people say. My other half
is not lost but just away.

I wake up early, no one to tend
to, no special purpose for the
day. Where's the freedom that
I yearned for, what is this
unsettled ache?

Chores to do…different now;
can't use the vacuum cleaner
hurts my back, where does
he keep the leaf blower…
Remember to take out the trash.

I'll have quinoa for dinner
healthy salad and yoghurt,
I'll finish my novel and have
tea with my friend
but I'm…

Missing you more than expected,
Independence not number one.
When did *you* become part of *me*?
Equal balance to make the whole sum?
I don't like living alone.

Looking forward to steaks on the
Barbie, crackers and Brie with our
favourite wine, cards by the fire,
tea and chats in the early morn hours,
planning our days one by one.

WAATIMACHI[1]

Andrew J. Hogan

Lucy Martinez was outside scraping away the monsoon-germinated weeds around her little Florence Junction ranchette when her cell phone rang. It was the jail, where she worked.

"Lucy, it's Raquel." Raquel Vega was the chief orderly in the infirmary of the Pinal County Adult Detention Center. "Maria's back in the infirmary in diabetic shock. She's refusing food and intravenous glucose. The captain told me to call you. Maybe you can talk her into eating."

Maria Magdalena Ramirez was an immigration detainee, technically in federal custody, but the Pinal County Adult Detention Center was under contract with the Immigration and Customs Enforcement service to house immigration detainees who were too seriously or chronically ill to hold in the other ICE facilities in Florence. Maria was originally incarcerated at the Florence Detention Center, but her erratic eating behavior, binging on junk food followed by fasting, left her in a coma in her bunk. Lucy and Maria were both Yaqui; not really friends, not relatives by blood or birth, but still somehow connected.

"I'll be there in fifteen minutes," Lucy said.

After crossing the Gila River into Florence, she passed the ICE Service Processing Center, where the Border Patrol assembles the illegals it's captured for deportation back to Mexico and elsewhere. Lucy's grandmother, Asu Rosa, had worked in the kitchens there during World War II, when the center was used as a camp for German and Italian POWs. Asu Rosa left the Yaqui Valley after the Mexican government built the Angostura dam across the Yaqui River and stole the water from the villages. Asu Rosa didn't want to live among the Mexicans, who'd made a slave of Lucy's great grandfather, forcing him to work on the henequén plantations in the Yucatan. Like other Yaquis, Asu Rosa had fled north across the border and settled in Arizona.

---

[1] able to remember [Hiaki Dictionaries]

Working at Camp Florence paid for her little house in the Yaqui town of Guadalupe, near Tempe.

Lucy passed by the Central Arizona Detention Center, a privately run facility that contracted with the ICE to house a thousand immigration detainees. She had considered working there after her suspension as a Pinal county deputy sheriff, but she decided to stay with the Pinal County Jail because she was already vested in the retirement plan, and correctional officers at the jail were unionized.

She checked in at the reception desk and proceeded to the infirmary. Unlike Lucy, Maria was a native Yaqui, born in Torim to a family of tribal activists that left her deeply suspicious of Mexicans, especially those from Sonora. She frequently refused to speak Spanish to her fellow inmates or the guards. One day in the detention center cafeteria, Maria was ranting in Yaqui and Lucy told her "kopalai." Since then, Maria had been calling on Lucy for all kinds of special favors: to intervene for her when she got into trouble, or to get her more access to medical care than was customary.

Lucy found Maria lying in an infirmary bed, sweating and mumbling, probably in Yaqui. She'd been hooked up to an intravenous drip.

"I thought she refused treatment," Lucy said to Raquel.

"She did," Raquel said. "But then she became incoherent, at which point the doctor decided she was incompetent and could be treated because her condition was life threatening. I think he added a little tranquilizer to keep her incompetent until her situation stabilizes. Don't ever tell her about an advance directive, or the next time she will end up dead without treatment."

"So what set her off this time?" Lucy asked.

"I wasn't there, but Jeannine said it was one of the detainees. Elvira, the fat, bitchy one with orange and green spiked hair."

"I know who you mean."

"Well, she was ragging on Maria about being an India. I guess Elvira is from Cuidad Obregón, not far from Maria's home town, and she hates Yaquis. Maria's so pint-sized she couldn't stand up for herself. Of course, nobody else will stand up for her because some of the detainees from Sonora understand enough Yaqui to know Maria is constantly dissing them."

"So let me guess," Lucy said. "She got upset, refused to eat, her blood sugar crashed, and here we are again."

"Right," Raquel said.

Lucy had a hard time turning Maria down. Her story was a modern version of what had happened to her Asu Rosa. The Sonoran State government kept building dams along the Rio Yaqui, siphoning off the water for new irrigated commercial farms and its thirsty capital, Hermosillo, leaving the downstream Yaqui villages with only enough water to irrigate half of their crop lands. To escape this poverty, Maria married too young to an abusive husband who lived in Hermosillo. Fleeing him, Maria crossed the border into Arizona and moved to the High Town settlement in Chandler. After she was pulled over for suspected drunk driving (in reality, low blood sugar) and was arrested for driving without a license, the sheriff's department turned her over to ICE when they suspected she was here illegally. The Florence Project took up her case for humanitarian parole because of her abusive husband; they were obtaining police reports from Hermosillo to document her husband's abusive behavior, and also arguing that, as a Yaqui, she had the right to visit Yaqui territories in the U.S.

Since Maria was currently stable and unconscious, any discussions of her behavior would wait until Lucy's regular shift on Monday.

Lucy left the jail and drove over to the Carestone assisted living facility in Glendale to visit her mother. She'd broken a hip a couple of weeks earlier and was upset about not returning to the little house on Calle Iglesia that she'd inherited from Asu Rosa. Since the surgery, Chepa had been showing signs of dementia. Physically, she was capable of returning home, with assistance, but Lucy and the doctor were stalling to see if the memory problems might improve.

Lucy knocked on her mother's apartment door and went in. Chepa was watching TV. "Who are you?" Chepa said.

"It's Lucy, Maala."

Chepa made a quizzical face.

"Your daughter."

"Oh. Are you here to take me to dinner?"

"Sure, what's on the menu?"

"Chipped beef." All of a sudden Chepa's memory was back. "Your favorite. Are you hungry?"

"You betcha," Lucy said.

Back in the apartment after dinner, Chepa became agitated. "Lucy, when can I go back to my house? The physical therapist says I won't be needing any more sessions after this Thursday."

Lucy had grown up in the house her mother inherited from Asu Rosa, along with a series of uncles who "walked with" her mother over the years. Her father now lived with another Yaqui woman in Pascua village in Tucson. She'd met him several times while visiting Tucson for Easter celebrations, but like most Yaqui fathers he had little to do with any of his children. He'd written a barely legible note congratulating her when she graduated from ASU with her degree in criminal justice. She was the first polisiia in their family's history. Hopefully, her ancestors would realize times had changed, and anyway she wasn't becoming one of the Mexican federales – that would raise their ghosts out of their graves, for sure.

Lucy guessed this was a good time to raise the memory issue. "Dr. Farnsworth is worried you might have had a little stroke during your hip surgery," she said.

"My hip is fine. I just told you that," Chepa said. She leaned back in her chair and smiled. "Maybe you're the one with memory problems?"

"Okay, what about when I came here today and you didn't recognize me?"

"Of course I recognized you. You're my own daughter. That's silly. How could I not recognize you?"

"Haven't you been forgetting things since the surgery? Nurse Tatum told me you got lost getting back to your room from bingo last Tuesday," Lucy said.

"That's nonsense. Who told you that?"

"Nurse Tatum."

"Who's she? I never met her," Chepa said. She gave Lucy the look that says you're an idiot.

"Nurse Tatum is the one who takes you down to the therapy pool. Dirty blonde, taller than me, a little on the heavy side."

"Oh, you mean Agnes. Why didn't you say so?"

"Okay, Agnes said you got lost on your way back to your room after bingo last Tuesday."

"I didn't go to bingo last Tuesday. I had to go see Dr. Farnsworth."

"That was the Tuesday before last," Lucy said. "I took you to see Dr. Farnsworth, remember?"

"Are you sure I didn't go in the van? I remember going somewhere in the van."

"No, I took you to the doctor. You went in the van to get your hair done."

"You know, you're not a police officer anymore. You can't just come into someone's home and start interrogating them."

"I'm not interrogating you. I'm trying to get you to see that you've got memory problems since the surgery."

"I'm not answering any more questions without my lawyer. I know my rights, young lady."

"What's my name," Lucy said.

Her mother crossed her arms and glared at her. After ten minutes of silence, Chepa fell asleep in her chair. When Lucy woke her up, she said, "Are you here to help me get to bed?"

"Yes," Lucy said.

By Monday, when Lucy returned to the Detention Center, Maria was well enough to return to the general population in Pod E200.

"Maria, what happened on Saturday?" Lucy said.

"Oh, my diabetes went crazy. I must've ate something bad," Maria said.

"Don't you know how to avoid foods that are bad for you?"

"Yeah, but sometimes I got to have something, to make myself feel better."

"What about your argument with Elvira Sanchez?" Lucy said.

"Yeah, her whole family's a bunch of Yaqui bigots. According to Elvira, the Yaquis are always blocking the highway, protesting for some handout from the government instead of working."

"You didn't say anything to provoke her?"

"Nothing she could understand," Maria said.

"You think people can't guess that you're dissing them when you scream at them in Yaqui?" Lucy said. "You've got to learn to keep a lid on it in here. Some of these people could hurt you bad if you make them mad enough."

"Hey, I ain't afraid to die. It might be better than this."

"That why you refused the medicine when you went into shock on Saturday – to kill yourself?"

"No, man, I just don't like that bitchy Mexican orderly. I won't take no orders from her." Maria looked up at the clock. "Hey, I got to meet with that gringa lawyer from the Florence Project in ten minutes. I got to get my papers from the cell."

"All right," Lucy said. "Good luck."

Lucy checked her cell phone in her locker. There was a message from Dr. Farnsworth's nurse about her mother. She called the office, and the receptionist passed her through to the nurse.

"Lucy, Medicare wants to discharge your mother from Carestone. They say she's recovered from the hip surgery, and her mental problems are too sporadic to justify continued nursing home care. They agree she probably needs someone around to take care of her, but that's custodial care, and they won't pay for that."

"How soon does she have to leave?" Lucy asked.

"Friday. Thursday is her last physical therapy session."

"I guess I could take some leave and see how she does at home alone. My place is too small for the two of us."

"I'll send you a list of places around Phoenix that might take her, but they will all run a couple of thousand a month, more if she needs help with medications or activities of daily living."

"Thanks. I'll figure something out."

Wednesday morning, Lucy found Maria yelling in Yaqui at some of the other detainees. It was different from previous outbursts. Maria was taunting them, but she was smiling. She sounded happy.

"Ramirez," Lucy called from across the room.

Maria turned around, first frowning, then smiling. She came over to Lucy, almost skipping. "Lucy, I'm getting out of here. The gringa lawyer, she got me humanitarian parole because of my diabetes, and because I can't go back to my twisted husband in Hermosillo, I can get out of here as soon as I got a place to stay."

"That's great, Maria." Lucy gave her a hug, against regulations.

"I just don't want to have to live with a bunch of Mexican bitches in some halfway house, you know?"

Lucy had a really bad idea. "I might know someplace you could stay. I don't suppose you know how to cook?"

"My wakavaki soup is to die for," Maria said.

"Okay, I'll be back tomorrow, hopefully with good news."

Maria went back across the room and started lecturing the 200E Pod detainees again in Yaqui. They were all smiling. Either they were glad to be rid of Maria, or they couldn't help being happy when one of them escaped ICE detention, even if it was an obnoxious India.

"Maala, sit here in your armchair and rest. I'll bring in the rest of your stuff from the nursing home."

By the time Lucy had everything put away, Chepa was asleep in her chair. Lucy made some lunch and woke her mother up to eat it.

"I found somebody to stay with you for a few days, just until you get your full strength back."

"I don't know about having strangers in my house. I'll be all right alone," Chepa said.

"Oh, she's not a stranger. Remember Rogelio Gonzaga from Torim? This is his niece, Maria Magdalena."

Chepa gave Lucy an uncertain look.

"She's supposed to make the best wakavaki soup in the whole pueblo."

"Oh, well, all right, but just for a few days, until I'm stronger."

After lunch, Lucy talked Chepa into taking a nap. She drove out to the detention center, where Maria was waiting for her on the benches in the visitor area.

"Why didn't you wait inside? It's hot today," Lucy said.

"I wanted to be free so bad, I didn't care about the heat," Maria said, wiping the sweat from her forehead with her sleeve. "Can you believe it, that bitch Elvira had one of the guards bring me out a refresco? It was cherry, which I hate, but I drank it anyway."

All the way back home, Lucy kept up the small talk, but in the back of her mind she wondered if she was crazy to expect this to work.

After two weeks, Chepa and Maria had settled into a comfortable relationship, even though Chepa's memory problems worsened. Lucy left work early to take Chepa for a follow-up evaluation with Dr. Farnsworth, but she found Chepa still in her bathrobe, sitting at the kitchen table and sharing a Twinkie with Maria.

"Maala, why aren't you dressed? We have to be at the doctor's in half an hour," Lucy said.

"Who are you?" Chepa said.

Maria stood up, half a Twinkie in her hand, and motioned Lucy aside. "She had a bad night last night. She didn't know my name this morning either."

"Why are you eating Twinkies? What about your diabetes?"

"Haven't you heard? Twinkies are going out of business. I just had to have some before they're all gone." She popped the remaining half Twinkie into her mouth. "Besides, I shared with Chepa, and she seemed a little more alert afterwards."

"Maala, come on. You have to get dressed to go to the doctor."

"I'm not sick," Chepa said. "And I'm not going anywhere with a stranger. My daughter will take me to the doctor, if and when I need to go."

"Maria, get her dressed, please," Lucy said. "We can all go together."

They were a little late getting to the physician's office, but it was all right because Dr. Farnsworth was running late, as usual. Chepa was given a form with her contact and insurance information, but she couldn't manage to sign it.

"You can sign it for your mother, Ms. Martinez," the receptionist said. "Right here on the bottom."

"Don't give that to her," Chepa said. "She's not my daughter." She grabbed the form out of Lucy's hand and gave it to Maria. "Here, you sign for me, Maggie."

"Maggie?" Lucy said.

"She doesn't like the name Maria."

"Since when?"

"Since this morning," Maria said. "She always called me Maria before."

"You don't look so good. You're sweating. Your breath smells funny, like nail polish remover."

"I had to bribe her with Twinkles to get her dressed. She made me share."

"How many?"

"Five."

A nurse opened the door to the waiting room. "Mrs. Martinez, the doctor will see you now."

Chepa didn't seem to recognize her name, so Lucy took her by the elbow, but Chepa shook her off. Lucy let Maria lead Chepa into the exam room. Maria was sweating even more profusely, so Lucy showed her to the patient chair, while she and Chepa stood by.

Dr. Farnsworth came into the exam room. He looked at Maria in the patient chair, and then rechecked the chart. "Mrs. Martinez, how are you?"

"Do I know you?" Chepa said.

"I did the surgery on your hip, Mrs. Martinez."

Just then, Maria slid out of the chair onto the floor.

"My hip is fine," Chepa said. "Please help my daughter, she's very sick."

"I thought you only had one daughter?" Dr. Farnsworth said, looking at Lucy.

"I do, and she's on the floor of your office," Chepa said. "Help her, please."

"She's diabetic," Lucy said. "She ate five Twinkies to persuade my mother to get dressed for this office visit."

"It looks like she's developing ketoacidosis. You're sure she's diabetic?"

"Yes. She was in the infirmary at the jail a number of times for both hyper and hypoglycemia."

"I'd better give her an insulin shot. Then we'll call the ambulance. She's going to need intravenous treatment in the hospital at least overnight."

"She's going to have to stay in the hospital?" Chepa said. "Who's going to take me home?"

"I'll take you home, Maala," Lucy said. "Later we can visit Maggie in the hospital as soon as she's feeling better." Lucy looked at Dr. Farnsworth.

He shrugged. "This is out of my league," he said. "I'll get you a referral for a neurologist. These aren't your usual stroke symptoms."

Maria's condition was grave by the time she was admitted to St. Luke's and placed in intensive care. After a few days, her condition stabilized, and Chepa and Lucy went for a visit.

"Asoa, how are you feeling?" Chepa said.

"Much better, Maala," Maria said. "But I'm not really your daughter."

"Nonsense," Chepa said. "When you get home, I'm putting you on the Yaqui diet for the sugar. I already threw out all those terrible Twinkies."

"No, not my Twinkies! Those were the last ones ever. I could've sold them, like for collectors."

"You probably would've eaten them," Lucy said.

"You put her up to that, didn't you?" Maria said. "Just like in the Detention Center, you were always trying to keep me away from the junk food."

"I'm going to bake you my special Curisi dessert. Your cousin Lucy got me some high protein flour to help keep your sugar down."

"Tell her the rest," Lucy said.

"We're going to be taking the aerobics class at the Guadalupe Senior Center together," Chepa said. "Turns out they let non-seniors with disabilities take the class too, so the sugar got you into my class."

"I hate exercise class. I hate being bossed around," Maria said.

"You've got to do something about the sugar," Chepa said, tears in her eyes. "Cousin Lucy told me of all the times you went to the hospital for the IV treatment. You've got to bury me, not the other way around."

"You'll like the class, Cousin Maggie," Lucy said. "All the instructions are given in Yaqui."

Lucy was outside, scraping away the new weeds sprouted from the recent rains, when she saw the postman pull his truck up to the neighbor's mailbox. In her mailbox, Lucy found a letter from Dr. Lucinda Torrez at Foothills Neurology. Chepa's MRI scan showed evidence of a fornix infarct, which was most likely responsible for the memory problems Chepa had been experiencing. There was number to call for more information. Dr. Torrez was busy with a patient but called back in fifteen minutes.

"Ms. Martinez, this is Doctor Torrez. We met at your mother's neuropsychological evaluation."

"I received your letter, something about a fornix infarct. Is that some kind of stroke?"

"Yes, it's a very rare kind of stroke that affects memory processing. The fornix connects different parts of the brain. If it's damaged, then memories from different parts of the brain can become scrambled. This seems to be the case with your mother – a confabulatory syndrome."

"Is that why she thinks I'm her niece, not her daughter?"

"Probably what happened is that she lost some of her memories of you. When her brain began to heal, it started rebuilding its memories. The person living with your mother became the daughter, and the person visiting became the niece. Her brain is confabulating what memories she has left with her current experience."

"Is this permanent?" Lucy said.

"Let's say it's becoming more permanent. Right after the stroke, there were a lot of gaps that might have gotten refilled correctly if anyone had known your mother had had this rare kind of stroke."

"But now she's filling in the gaps in whatever way makes sense?"

"Right. There's no real medical treatment to restore a patient's missing memories, especially once the confabulated memories become established in the months following the infarct. You could try psychotherapy to help her recognize when she's confabulating her memories. Unfortunately, the process of memory rectification can be stressful because the patient has no other memories with which to replace those confabulated. Sometimes, the patient ends up disoriented." Dr. Torrez told Lucy to call back after she had thought more about her mother's condition, in case she needed more advice.

Lucy went into her pantry for the small bag of brittle bush leaves Yaquis used as incense. She put the dried leaves in the little pottery dish Asu Rosa had given her as a child and placed it in front of the statue of La Virgen de Guadalupe that Asu Rosa had brought with her from Torim.

"Kialem vata hiwemai / chukula hubwa teune teunevu," she chanted five times, as the leaves burned. *First you just look, later you will find, find.* These were the only lines in Yaqui she could remember from the deer dance she had attended at the Pascua Pueblo when she was a teenager.

Lucy dialed her mother's number. "Ne'esa, it's Lucy. I got the report from the neurologist in the mail."

"Why would they send the report to my niece, instead of directly to me?" Chepa said.

"There must have been a mix-up at the office. I'm listed as one of your emergency contacts, in case Maggie is unavailable," Lucy said. "But, overall, good news. It looks like the little stroke you had should resolve itself without further treatment."

"Wonderful," Chepa said. "I am so sick of those doctors treating me like I'm an idiot. Do you want to talk with your cousin? We're leaving to go to our exercise class at the Senior Center in a couple of minutes. She's mad at me because I found her stash of Reese's Peanut Butter Cups and threw them away."

"Does she still sneak off to the snack aisle at the grocery looking for Twinkies?"

"Yes, she always comes back empty-handed. I hope they don't start making those things again," Chepa said.

"Me too."

"You're a wonderful niece, Lucy, looking out for us the way you do," Chepa said. "If your mother were still here with us, she would be very proud of you."

STROKE

Grenith Fisher

They took pictures,
Sliding her body
Into the long, cold tube
That must have frightened her,
But mother couldn't tell us
How she felt; she'd had
A near-fatal stroke.

I never saw those images,
But I know what they look like:
Clots and blocks, broken signals,
Bloody red walls,
Doors to movement and speech
Plastered over, marked forever,
"No Access."
Beyond the barricades,
Where she felt and reasoned,
Expressed herself and
Gave weight to her days,
Her powers rot.

She knows, feels the damage,
The putrefaction
Of her own dying cells.
She has found a crude way
To broadcast her pain:
She throws her head back,
And keens in wild mourning
For the loss of herself.
She howls every day,
Sometimes for hours,
And we can find no way
To comfort her.

All along the disinfected hall
Of the nursing home,

Others hear her audible anguish.
They find her upsetting.
There have been
Complaints.

PUZZLES WITH MISSING PIECES

Kathleen Elliott Gilroy

Every event or simple happening has a back-story. What came before: Where was the baby before it became a baby? Where is the mind before you realize you have one?

This writing will not go into all of my back-story. I myself do not have it all. Yet I have gained more in the past three years than in sixty long years before my long-ago friend and I reconnected. This essay is not even about that friendship that endured, sight unseen and with no other contact of any kind, all those years.

What is important to this writing is what happened to me after I received Electrical Shock Therapy in the first two months of 1953. I want to say here that this treatment (also called ECT: electrical convulsive therapy) is still being used, but the procedure is different now than when it was given to me. There is better monitoring during the process; more safety features are used, primarily because of what has been learned from the past. It is still the first resort for severe depression that may or may not involve attempted suicide, or detachment from reality psychosis. The treatments can still cause convulsions and other side effects, including horrific headaches that blacken the world like an ugly funeral veil, distorting vision and sound and body stability.

There are enough side effects troubling doctors and psychiatrists that many countries have banned this process. Statistics now indicate that it is not uncommon for elderly women, in particular, to still have this treatment when they become stressed while in convalescence facilities.

Further, it is now recognized that brain tissue is destroyed in the treatment. However, it is theorized that this process may restore natural chemical balance that is hyper-connected in brain regions. So it is still a quandary.

I remember this connection I made in understanding Ernest Hemingway: he committed suicide after treatment with ECT. He reportedly said: *suicide was his option because ECT had destroyed his memory and he could no longer write.*

As for my missing pieces, I have read several accounts of people who had similar responses, and who went through their bouts of depression again. They too describe how missing pieces haunt their current lives, partly because there are no connections left to what is half-remembered, what slips in and out of the mind like a nagging sense of foreboding, an unease that there is something they should be aware of but can't grab hold of. An intuitive sensibility, in a way. So, when the reached-for event is brought to light, even briefly, one feels the loss all over again.

Now, here is my own perspective – not going into the process of treatment, but what it has done to me.

I suspect I was two months into being sixteen, because I have invalid memories for accuracy. I do know it was winter in Salt Lake City, snow on the ground, the beginning of a New Year. Major traumatic events had occurred in my life, particularly after my father was killed in an industrial accident in October of 1952. However, even when he was alive, our family had serious issues. My older sister had run away from home at age fifteen and had not been located. Our father was a very strict disciplinarian, and our mother was prone to volatile outbursts.

There were four of us children, and I was the third: a quiet one, a reader, already painting and writing poetry. I liked solitude and church. I belonged to the Cadet Corps of the Salvation Army and played in the band there, too.

All of my birth siblings and both parents have now passed away. Those who gave me safe harbor even briefly, after the events I am referring to, are unsung heroes. Now, too, I add thanks to the significant teenage boy who has grown into the man who helped me with some of my memories after we re-connected as friends, following sixty years of no contact. What has not come back is not meant to be, and I have accepted that now.

Here is how my life was catapulted into the world of a fairly new science for the treatment of bipolar mental illness and suicidal depression. I was not bipolar, but I did seriously attempt suicide, for reasons I will not go into now. The thesis here is what happened because of the treatment I received. This is important to relate, because the treatments I received have still left blank places in my memories, and affected much of my adult life.

The suicide attempt is what initiated the procedures on me. My younger brother and I were home alone, as usual. He was only thirteen. We had been very close, looking out for one another. This made the event even more sad and frightening for him. It also became a justifiable reason to resent what I did because, after the fact, he had no one to sustain him. It changed his life to a great extent, and not for the better, either. Yet he was the one who saved my life.

Now that I have been given a chance to retrieve even some of those memories, it is time to give back, by sharing my experience of the treatments, and to also prove that, even without all the memories, life is given to us for a purpose.

I have succeeded at many endeavors in life and had successful careers, as well as a family. This has required learning to adapt in the way I learn and how guarded I am in how close friends can be, if they become part of my life.

The Electrical Shock Therapy I had has never been shared with extended family and very few friends. I have learned to adapt for what I did not have, including the loss of memories regarding my life before the treatments and after. I have many missing puzzle pieces. I am deeply grateful for some of the memories given back to me through discussions with my long-ago friend. But those, too, are fragmented pieces. Electrical Shock treatments in 1953 left residual impacts…

The night I changed the course of some lives it was already dark outside and bitterly cold, with wind blowing off the mountains. Our neighborhood was dark and silent when I went outside. I was barefoot, prone to pneumonia and severe bronchitis. For a long time after the events, I had brief dreams of me walking in that snow. As parts of the event became clearer, I heard myself telling my brother, "I am ready to die. So I am going to die. Leave me alone out here."

He slammed the door. Later, numbed, and even less cognizant, I went inside and hung myself in the bathroom. My younger brother actually helped save my life, but I can't recall any of that or the actual act of hanging myself. From what I have heard, my brother ran to the nearby fire station just up the street, and they performed CPR.

My mother was located at a tavern she frequented. I know nothing of all that personally. It has never been discussed by anyone either – nor has my stay in the hospital and all that followed. I believe, from what I have learned about when I left the city and from recent discussions with my long-lost friend, I was in that hospital for at least a month or more. My mother had me released after that and put me on a Greyhound Bus, out of her life.

I had a journal to write in. However, I had forgotten many days of my life and certainly had no ability to direct the new course of my life.

The world I walked into after the treatments was like seeing the world through cellophane that encased me physically, separating me from other humans. The treatments left me with excruciating migraine headaches that could drop me to my knees into a fetal position. They would persist for hours. I do remember those, and, even without that, I felt like a voyeur existing in a different place. Other people and I seemed not of the same species. I avoided people as much as possible.

I did have occurrences of a quick dream regarding one visit from the friend who reconnected with me. He had brought me a stuffed toy kitten (I always loved cats). I asked if all that had happened and he said yes. He and some of his friends had visited me, but none knew why I was there.

I had frequent quick dreams of being wheeled from the room while strapped onto a bed. Wheeled out of the corridor and into a room. I had straps over my head, too, and a brace of some kind by my neck. These have been fleeting images. They have occurred over many years, just a glimpse, and then they're gone.

I was being treated for attempted suicide, but instead of death happening, I lost most of my memories of prior years, and still have minimal recall of the neighborhood I lived in when all this occurred. Ever since, I have periodically had episodes of "seeing through a veil" and not being part of what is happening in the world around me.

Sometimes, over the years, I dreamed I stood before an audience in a large auditorium, playing an instrument. I could not see the instrument, nor hear it, but there was a sense of it niggling me to recall… to let the dream finish. A silent auditorium until the friend of long ago reminded me of this: "What happened to your bagpipes? Remember when you played them in front of the whole auditorium at Granger High School? And at the Salvation Army Church?"

Those words! That recognition, however brief, and I ran to gather a packet my older brother's wife had sent to me when he died six years earlier! I remembered reading some of the notes, seeing my mother's beautiful handwriting, and the words on one note she wrote as she was dying and could not speak: "Kath's things. In a suitcase or trunk. At Bill's house. All this time. Send it. Her bagpipes. Her sketches."

I felt cold air whoosh through me… Who was playing the bagpipes now? Why had I not processed that information six years ago? But now I knew it had been me on that stage, at the school, at church, and I was given the memory of the old man visiting from Scotland who had smiled with pleasure when he said, "You talk and sing with a lilt of a brogue as if you came fresh from the boats." Those few connected memories were a mighty gift! I also knew those items were long gone to a different place. But it was enough. The bagpipes and all else were part of my previous life.

I cannot describe this aspect: many people, even immediate family, often say, "Why are you so weird? You talk to yourself a lot, in a whisper, or walk around singing."

I talk in my sleep a lot and sing too – not loudly, they say, but they know it is happening. I like being alone, working in quiet with no radio or television to disturb me. I avoid phone conversations and pace while I speak. Yet I have functioned among many who graduated college. I have my own way of learning what is necessary. I have earned my own living and bought a home for my family. I rescue animals. I still write or paint or draw once in a great while. I still sew. I have not re-learned how to knit. The needles and yarn seem odd puzzles to me. I stare at them and set them aside. I function very well, over all.

Despite this, I did not allow mirrors tn my home for most of my life, and I still don't use one, but have allowed one in the bathroom within the last ten years or so. I avoid it and know how to brush my hair without it. Makeup is not something I need. I have never felt as if I am the person I see in a mirror or photo or shop window. Dissociative symptoms, perhaps. But I do not see "me" when I see an image of what others see as me.

I married when I was seventeen, still going through residual side-effects from treatments. I had been living with my older brother and his good wife when I met the man I married. He followed me when I tried to avoid him and was already a dominant person regarding me. The best I can say is that my children from that marriage helped me want to be better mentally and physically. It was not a good marriage. How much any of this has to do with the treatments and all that preceded them is a moot issue now. He has passed away, but I left him before he died, and I did take care of him through his illness. It was a volatile marriage that has kept me single, content to fill my life with select writing friends, animals, family members.

Due to all this history that came after the treatments and through many other events, I do not feel comfortable interacting too much with others. It makes me uneasy and brings back negative feelings. When alone, I often have a need to pace the floor or go out of the house to find peace by walking in the yard, even at night. I confess here: I also work in the yard a lot, and see me as someone separate from myself, one whom I can outwardly observe and protect in some way.

Now then, this I have learned by research to better understand myself and accept me. In the nineteen fifties, Electro-shock Therapy (EST) was harsher. The dosage was much stronger and more treatments were given. In some cases lobotomies were performed on suicidal patients even younger than I was. So I am blessed in not having had that done.

I am not the only survivor who has lost chunks of memories. I am fortunate not to have been kept there longer than I was. I surmise I did receive current to both regions of the brain simultaneously, and probably did have seizures afterwards, because it was a common happening then. And I have brief, fleeting moments of things attached to both sides of my head. I was also fortunate not to have been sent to a psychiatric hospital/facility. I also know that was often a dead-end journey worse than death.

I also know now that, on my discharge, because of my mother's request or demand to have me released, I should have been on medication. This never happened. I like to think it would have made a difference in all that followed after the release, but I will never know for sure.

Have I had relapses of despair or other issues? Yes. But here I am: persevering even through major illnesses, like cancer, and surviving it. I am blessed with fine children, all adults now, grandchildren, and a great grandson. I have thoughts of having missed connections with my re-found sister, with my younger brother, who found me shortly before he died, with many old friends. But it is the moving on that has given me better coping skills and helped me know there is an upside as well as a downside to most of life's happenings. And I learned to love my mother again and to forgive others.

OH, THESE WITHERED ARMS!

Sandra Shaw Homer

Oh, these withered arms!
How they held my sister's child
Against my aching breast,
How reined in the racing horse,
Chest and hooves pounding a single beat;
Or clutched the old rope swing
Soaring under the maple tree;
How hugged the muscled back
Of the lover thrusting into me;
And pulled my body through the salty sea,
Trusting, as I always have,
In these strong arms to save me…
And now, how they betray me!

Hands

Billie Steele

Hands,
once vibrantly busy,
now old and gnarled,
lie uselessly
in my lap.

THE HAWK

Grenith Fisher

Hawk in a high wind,
Holding on, stiff winged,
Against a bitter winter sky,
The bird seems hostage to the air.
Bound and pushed by frigid hands
That slide along its wing tips,
Dissembling its feathers,
And disrupting all its plans.

Hawk in a downdraft,
Looking for a warm push
To help it stay aloft.
Turning, tipping, flapping, veering,
Using what it finds to use,
The bird persists against the gale,
And trusts the nature of the thing:
The wind is always what it is.
It will stop.

A gentle breeze will barely move
The tree that keeps its nest in place.
The bird will screech and soar and glide,
A feathered dart aimed straight for home,
Where undisturbed by fickle winds,
It will eat and mate and rest,
And scan its universe for prey.
The hawk is always what it is.
It endures.

Banana Bread

Olga Humphreys

We were poor. We had just moved to San Antonio from Wisconsin. My parents bought a tiny home with a huge yard on the outskirts of town. We were surrounded by neighbors who worked really hard for a living – painters, construction workers, plumbers, and of course my parents – all trying to make a living.

You could tell what type of work people did by the items on their trucks. The painters all had brushes, spattered gallons of paint, and ladders. The plumbers had brushes, tubes, old gallon containers, and old towels. The carpenters had stacks of different colored wood, saws, ladders, and tables of different sizes.

One of our neighbors was a "frutero." He sold fruit in all the neighborhoods. He had a large truck with homemade wooden rails. He carried his fruit and vegetables in wooden crates: onions, tomatoes, corn, zucchini, jalapenos, apples, oranges, and of course bananas. I would let my mama know when he was driving by, but she always shook her head "no." I really did not understand why she would not buy fruit and vegetables.

Mama always knew how to stretch her meals. We ate rice and beans with almost every meal. She made it taste like a piece of steak. We always had hot, homemade meals, but never second helpings or snacks. Now I realize how healthy and economical this practice was for our family. But I always thought there had to be a reason we did not have Cokes, cookies, or chips like other children at lunch time.

Mama was strict and serious, so we never asked questions. We were very respectful of our parents. We spent summers playing in the large back yard. We had no store-bought toys, but we became resourceful children. My brothers fixed up bikes that were given to us. I learned to jump rope. My sister and I had daily tea parties with saltine crackers and Kool-Aid. We used our imaginations!

One very hot summer day, the frutero brought a large bag of ripe bananas to our home. They were very ripe, almost black. *Yuk*, I thought, *these are rotten.*

Mama was so happy, and she thanked the frutero. She said, "Let's get to work."

"What are we going to do with them?" I asked.

She proceeded to have us peel and mash the bananas. Mama always had eggs, milk, sugar, and flour. So she folded the mashed bananas into the dough. She then poured the batter into loaf pans, round pans, and cake pans. I watched intently and wondered what it would all taste like. Mama told us she used to be a helper in a German family's home when she was fifteen years old. She said she was taught to bake banana bread and banana pudding.

We baked all afternoon. If you have ever smelled banana bread baking, you can imagine what scents came out of our tiny kitchen. All four children were so excited when we got our first slice with a cold glass of milk. My daddy came home and had a huge slice of banana bread and smiled. He did not smile very often.

To this day, everyone in our family loves this bread! I bake it all the time. My children love it, and I have taught them to bake it also.

I have often wondered what ever happened to the frutero, our considerate neighbor who did not ask any questions, but knew we would appreciate his large bag of fruit. I wondered why we did not send him a loaf of the bread we baked, why we did not send a thank you note, why we did not go visit, and why didn't we know his name. We just knew him as "el frutero."

I hope I get to thank him one day for sharing the fruits of his labor, and of course for the banana bread.

GIVING THANKS FOR APPLES

Joan T. Doran

Summer vanished yesterday on wings of dragonflies
with my unripe peaches left behind.
Here on my counter, no blush
warms their woody cheeks.
By themselves, abandoned, stilled
they'll only shrivel in the waning light,
fragrant more of paltriness than summer sun.

What feast-filled table I had planned!—
A meld of peach with tender bird
round and roasted ripe perfection
I'd present you on a platter,
watching pleasure in your face, and thankfulness
for what full-handed nature's gift
could become through human hands – and human pride.

I know, pride doesn't get you anywhere—
and standing here with flushing cheeks
hopes shriveled by presumption and delay
I must remember it's not clever hands that turn
earth's axis; human plans don't ripen anything
for nature always turns the tables.
In this waning light, let's now give thanks for apples.

The Gloves

Shirley Shatsky

My friend handed me the elegant gloves
"You have small hands."

A creation out of a French workroom,
the black kidskin is embroidered on the back
with minute silk stitches
blooming into delicate flowers.

Her young, beautiful mother had filled them
with memories of special moments she would
recount to her only child when life had slowed.

She spoke of afternoon teas on delicate china,
luncheons with lady friends who wore hats
and fur scarves,
an evening party with her handsome husband,
dancing until the small hours of morning.

Now, my friend can no longer share any memories
of long ago, or hours earlier, and though
elegant gloves are not part of my wardrobe,
I cherish her gift that is bound so closely
with the many happy moments of
her beloved mother.

I keep them safe for the once joyful, talented friend
I hold dear
for whom life has dimmed.

GRITS ANYONE?

Carole Kaliher

Recently friends were discussing food choices from our childhood. Since I was born in Louisiana, one of those common choices was grits. It's ground corn, similar in texture to cream of wheat, only a little coarser. In the south, it's served for breakfast instead of hash browns, usually with butter or white gravy. I was the only one in our group who liked the *idea* of grits, or tasted the dish.

This discussion of childhood food choices led me to examine the way I grew up in a rural area in the 1950's. My family would have been considered poor or, at the very least, of a lower middle class. Funny thing about that is we didn't know we were poor because our friends and neighbors were in the same boat. We were never hungry, but we didn't have the most beautifully furnished house or the best apparel.

At that time, people didn't have credit cards to buy things they couldn't afford. They saved their money until they could pay for it with cash. We had used furniture that we didn't change until it was dead – not just mortally wounded. Of course, these days, our furniture would be considered "antique" or "previously owned," just fancy descriptions meaning old.

Growing up in So. San Gabriel as a child, I didn't know that paste came in a jar for art projects. Paste to us was a mixture of flour and water. I was in first grade when I discovered the wonder of a jar filled with creamy paste. The same holds true of envelopes and stamps that had lost their glue; we used egg white to restore their adherence to paper. The egg white residue inside the shell worked the best!

Mom and Dad lived through The Great Depression, so they knew the difference between wants, needs, or what was merely convenient. We didn't dine out, but on Sundays we'd have a pastrami sandwich, which we ate in our car before going to a movie. That was our tradition: church, lunch, and a movie. It stayed that way for years until we started attending church in San Gabriel instead of Los Angeles. After that, the pastrami sandwiches were gone as well, because we had lunch at home, and then went to the movies.

Mom always had some part-time money-making job. She raised chickens and turkeys, sold the eggs, and then sold fryers only when eggs weren't plentiful. She dressed the fryers and turkeys for customer orders during the holidays. ("Dressed" not meaning clothing, but pulling out the feathers. It's the proper way of describing what she did. I helped with the pin feathers.)

Mom loved to gamble. I grew up listening to the race results on the half hour. At twelve I could tell you where the thoroughbreds were running at any given time of the year. For years, the routine continued.

After I was married, Mom stopped raising poultry for extra money because it was too tiring for her. A friend of a friend suggested she act as an intermediary for a bookie. She took calls from the bettors, they gave a code name, and the bookie called them back. After a few months she was busted and taken to the Temple City Sheriffs' Station. My mom went with them wearing her hat, gloves, and carrying a matching purse. Can you imagine what the officers made of her proper appearance?

The bookie had assured her that, if anything went wrong, he would take care of it and he did. She was released, and the charges were dropped when she couldn't assist the officers in locating the bookie. Their transactions had been accomplished anonymously, so she couldn't help in the police investigation. The situation went away as well as the fifty dollars cash a week she had received. To give some perspective on why she took a chance dealing with a bookie, in 1960 our apartment rented for sixty-five dollars a month, so two hundred dollars extra money was quite a sum.

Dad told me what happened, or Mom may have never mentioned a thing to me. Her mantra to keep my sister and me on the straight and narrow was, "What will the neighbors think?" I hope that police car was unmarked, or the neighbors would have had a lot to think about.

Mom wanted her daughters to be ladylike and proper, and that's the way we grew up. I admired my mom's survival instincts. She had to use those instincts because she was an orphan at ten, an assistant to a housekeeper at twelve, a factory worker at thirteen (hiding from inspectors because she was too young), married at sixteen, and a mother at seventeen. And I always thought I had an unusual childhood!

When people ask me what are the most vivid memories of my childhood, I answer, "The deep love and admiration I felt for my mom, and…oh yes…gambling and grits."

Homemade

Irene Thomas

Her name was Louisa, and if it were up to me, she would be called Queen Louisa. I would make a golden crown for her to wear, and around the base would be printed the words:

Eat It Up

Get Used To It

Do Without

Make It Do

and Wear It Out!

Those were the theme words of The Great Depression, and she used them justifiably. Her good nature and laughter made her a joy to be around. Once I asked her, "Mom, why do you laugh all the time?" Her answer: "If I didn't laugh, I'd cry!"

Friday was her baking day, and by the time I was out of bed, the kichen surfaces were filled with bread mixtures rising before being baked. There were always loaves of bread, pans of biscuits, coffeecakes, and anything else she could think of to make her family happy. After baking, items were wrapped in used commercial bread-from-the-store covers or wax paper. By the time Thursday came around, bakery items were scarce again. I was happy about this, for then we had to buy nickel day old coffeecakes, and the baker made vanilla frosting with peanuts in it that I relished.

Monday was laundry day, with rows and rows of clean clothes hung outside to dry. I still maintain that nothing can rival sinking between sheets and pillowslips that have been dried in sunshine.

Tuesday, of course, was ironing day. All day long the hot irons were lifted from the stove to make our worn clothing look a little better and more acceptable.

Wednesday and Thursday were used for any chores that needed doing. I especially hated socks made from old underwear. Ugh!

When summer's heat arrived and I got out of school early, I could smell the fruit cooking in our back yard. My father would borrow a great big kettle and fire logs placed under it to cook bushels of fruit at a time. We had grape juice, grape jelly to be eaten in winter with peanut butter, and oh…the joy of opening a jar of sunny-gold peaches. Apple butter took a long time cooking, and even though I tried to help by stirring with the long, long paddle, I didn't last very long. That fire just reached out to my legs, and I gave up.

It wasn't only fruit that was cooked out in the back yard. The aroma of tomato catsup with its tangy, spicy frangrance stayed with you even after you left the yard. There was also pickle relish. If anything growing was edible, it had to be prepared for use during the harsh winter months.

I guess one of the things Mom did on Wednesday and Thursday was mend our clothing. She cut cardboard to fit in our shoes that had the holes in the soles, so we didn't get holes in our socks. Until I started making my own dresses, she made all our clothing, took care of the celluloid collars my father wore when he got dressed up, and did any mending needed.

She passed on to us her faith. I remember one winter when starvation was staring the family in the face, she told us that God takes care of the flowers and the birds, and He will take care of us also. I wondered at such a strong faith when food was really scarce.

My father finally got a job with the WPA, and when it came time to wrap up his lunch, he told my mother to just give any meat to the girls and put jelly on his bread. His job was to break up rocks to build a fence around a city building. I was doing some nightly baby-sitting at the time and made twenty-five cents an evening, fifty cents if they returned after midnight, so I didn't eat at home. I just ate the leftovers on the table after the lady finished her dinner before she walked a long way to assist her husband in his tavern.

We lived twenty blocks from the church. My father took the girls to Sunday School in the morning, while Mom stayed home to prepare the Sunday meal. Then, in the evening after everything was cleaned up, she would walk the twenty blocks with me as her partner.

It was she who created our homemade school. On the clean side of the butcher paper she taught me the alphabet, how to draw plants and flowers, how to read…in fact, her life was one spent giving of self and love.

I am very proud to say she was my mother. Queen of the homemade… she made our house a home!

Chesapeake Bay

Phylis Warady

I t's the height of the Great Depression. Mom's off on her monthly shopping trip in nearby Baltimore. She leaves us kids in the care of my step-dad. Lunch is tunafish sandwiches made in advance by Mom.

Afterward, we take a walk. End up on a narrow stretch of beach sand edging Chesapeake Bay. Mind you, my step-dad isn't much of a talker. However, I do sense his deep love of the sea in all its facets. Still, I'm a kid. And tend to get restless if standing too long in one place. As for Jackie, he's even worse at standing still and fidgets as if he's got an army of red ants in his pants.

Suddenly I begin to run. I head straight toward the bay where, fully clothed, I plunge into the cool water and start plowing forward. Jackie plunges in right after me.

My step-dad emerges from his reverie and yells STOP!

But we don't. We're too busy plowing through bay water. Even though I can't swim a stroke – I keep on going, my goal the thick-braided rope that divides relative safety from beyond, where the water's over my head. Jackie follows my lead, despite already having trouble keeping his nose above the waterline.

As for my step-dad, he quits yelling STOP and jumps in after us. Plows through the water to first rescue Jackie, then me, before we drown. True to his nature, he says nothing to either of us as he drags us back to beach sand. Then, carrying Jackie in his arms, he makes sure to keep a firm grip of my hand as he heads for home.

Once there, he strips off our sopping wet clothes, dries us off, dresses us in dry ones, puts Jackie down for his nap. Then he focuses on all three pairs of brand new leather shoes that each cost $5. Enough to buy three carloads of groceries at the commissary.

I watch him carry those shoes over to the kitchen's cast-iron sink. Watch him prime its pump to wash away the bay water. Watch him transfer all three pairs to the roof over the kitchen's attached porch, where I guess he hopes they'll dry before Mom gets home.

Once she does arrive and sees those shoes, she's too stunned to speak. After all, who wouldn't be rendered speechless after viewing the end result of pumping spring water into already soaked shoes? Especially if, afterward, your clueless mate sets all three pairs upon the porch's roof shingles to bake several hours in the sun on a day when the temperature's 110 in the shade. Causing their toes to curl to such a radical degree they resemble shoes pictured in storybooks featuring tales first told in either Greek or Turkish fables.

Indeed, my most vivid memory of that long ago afternoon is of Mom seated in the wicker rocker, rocking back and forth, back and forth, with her head cradled in her hands.

Insomnia

Marilyn L. Kish Mason

Two hands converge
at the top of the clock,
tossing and turning begins.
Wall-to-wall worries
muddle the mind,
eyelids refuse to meet.
Synapses leap like spastic frogs,
in a pond of half dreams,
half promises of sleep.
Downy white pillows
at the head of the bed
have too many secrets to keep.

Parched desert tongue
tries to cry out,
immobilized by fear
of self-made monsters
crouched in dark corners,
their victim unable to hear
mother's soft lullaby
long faded away.
Alone, defenseless,
comes desperate hope
of praying night into day.

The Alchemist's potion
works its magic.
Panic and pain subsides.
Slumber seeps into
darkened spaces,
where danger and fear reside.
Dawn spreads sunlight
through uneven shadows,
the new day begins,
all appears to be right.

The Gill

Marie T. Gass

I woke up this morning thinking of missing my gill, angry at the doctor who'd eliminated it without my permission during a nearby surgery. "Oh, by the way…" he'd said as they wheeled me out of the recovery room, "I closed your gill for you."

"Closed my gill?" I couldn't imagine the right side of my head without that little slit in front of my ear, right before the ear rounds off into the rest of the ocean.

As children we would sometimes hold our legs together, feet out to the side, pretending to be mermaids. We'd wrap each other's legs in shimmering green from the fabric stack, look in the mirror and smile, fingers in our hair and beet juice on our cheeks and lips. I'd envy my sister Lola's dark skin and beautiful black hair; she was the lucky one from our generation, like Auntie Kay and my youngest daughter. We both were mermaids, but only I had a gill.

Every time I had to see a new doctor, they'd say, "You know you have a gill here. It's called a _____. Left over from the transition from the fishes. Did you know that?"

"Yes," I'd say, fingering the tiny hole.

"Where does it go?" I'd asked once.

The doctor had shrugged. "No place," he'd said, peering at it with a lighted magnifier. "It's just there through the layers of skin."

On the way home that day it struck me that I ought to be able to swim then, since a had a gill. But for two childhood summers my sister and I had sat at the edge of the pool, watching others learn to swim, adamantly declining to wet more than our toes. We were terrified of drowning.

As a young adult, the year I came back from college, my sister's husband, Paul, who was a swimming instructor using his parents' back yard pool, said to me, "I can teach you how to swim," though so far he hadn't taught my sister. "There's nothing to be afraid of – it's a private heated pool, and no one will be there except you and me. Just do what I say."

I pulled my bathing cap over the gill and gulped. I would do this if I drowned. Who knew – it might work. I was on the edge of being the only person I knew who couldn't swim.

In the pool I was great with the warmup exercises: face under water, squatting until the water lapped at my chin. I began to hope just a little bit. Maybe I'd been wrong and swimming was a possibility for me. I took a deep breath and smiled at Paul. He was going to be my savior from all the future ridicule: "You can't swim? Everybody can swim! My little kids can swim. I'll show you sometime."

I could see myself watching them do laps and tricks and it helped me not one whit.

"Okay, this is it," said Paul then. "You're going to float."

At that time I was skinny as a rail, skipping desserts to fit into my wedding dress. All systems were GO. It couldn't have been a better time in my life to learn to swim. I had confidence. Even if I drowned – but I wouldn't for sure, because everybody could swim, nobody drowned learning to float. And Paul was there. No jeering onlookers. I could screw up until I learned.

I actually believed I would go home that day a swimmer. The first attempt at floating felt wonderful, lying flat on the warm water, looking up at the blue sky, Paul's hands under my back for safety. I was still looking up at a cloud when he slipped his hands away and I sank like a stone, tumbling and gasping as I tried to find "up."

Paul toned his laughter down to a smile just as I came out of the water. "It's okay," he said. "It's okay. You must have changed position."

I became suspicious. I hadn't even wiggled.

"Yes, you must have," said Paul, "or you'd be floating by now."

Always my fault, even when I hadn't a clue what I was doing wrong. All the little childhood incidents where I'd been unfairly blamed marched through my brain, one by one, until I cut them off. "No negatives," I told myself sternly. If this is ever going to work, this would be the time. I must maintain optimum conditions.

"You can't quit now," said Paul. "That's only one try."

I thought of how far I'd gotten in earlier tries in my history – namely, holding my nose and dunking. This was my chance. So I swiped the water from my eyes and stood up in the pool. "I'm ready," I called.

On the second attempt I made an effort to look placid as Paul steadied me, reviewing what I should be doing with my feet and arms. Again like a stone. This time, Paul had to do some convincing. When I rose up out of the water the third and last time, there were two men laughing. Paul was bent over holding his stomach, and the man I'd met only recently, the man I was to marry, laughed with him. By the time they'd both finished wiping their eyes, I was gone.

"C'mon back," called Paul. "We can do it!"

"What am I, stupid?" I muttered walking home, my terry wrap getting heavier from the soaking wet suit. "Never again! I mean it!" I told myself. So much for the luck of the gill. So why did I want there to be other ways of being special, unique?

But the idea of even a god/doctor's closing it up without asking first rankled me. It was a different era. When I'd said to him, "But I liked the gill. I wanted it," he'd shrugged and said, "Oh well, too late now," and I'd kept my mouth shut like a proper patient.

This year a new friend from Ireland told me that people with heavy bones do sink like stone. 'They can't help it," he said. I was gratified.

What reminded me of the gill this morning, 46 years after the swimming lesson? I don't know. Paul is gone now, and so is my sister. My husband snores in the next room, his time zones awry since his brain injury. I'm not planning to go swimming ever again, though I did investigate water aerobics for arthritic seniors and was ready to attend until an emergency major surgery interrupted my plans.

"You are a special little girl," I whisper sometimes to my first grandchild during a goodbye hug. Haley has no gill. She is skilled at everything, but doesn't need any of them to be special. I am special, too. But I still miss my gill.

A Question of Race

Billie M. Steele

To which race do you belong? That question seems to be very important in the United States. Even the 2010 census asked us to designate our race: white, African/American, Hispanic, or Other. That is the question. This question has held even more significance in our nation's past. In fact, let's just go back seventy or eighty years to the era of the Great Depression.

On a rundown farm in the distant hills of central Oklahoma, there lived a man and his wife. Well past middle-age, they had already raised a son and were in the process of raising a lovely young daughter. They were now expecting a third child.

Like thousands of others, this couple was struggling to survive. This was nothing new to them. Each had been born in Indian Territory, and each had been raised in a large family by a widowed mother. They had lived through World War I and experienced a brief time of prosperity during the 1920s, but when the Depression hit, the aging husband had been unable to find adequate work to support his family. So they had retreated to the family farm. Money was short, but here they eked out enough from the vegetable garden to put some food on the table.

"If only," the woman mumbled to herself, "if I could only have a bologna sandwich, I would be satisfied." But there was not enough money to buy the healthy food they all needed. There was certainly not enough money to pay a doctor to come out to advise the woman during her pregnancy and, due to her age, she was not doing well at all.

Finally, a doctor was convinced to make the trip to attend the woman during her travail, but he arrived after the birth of the new baby girl. He looked at the mother and her new daughter, decided they both were okay, and he left.

Back in his office in town, the doctor realized he didn't have enough information to fill out the birth certificate for the newborn child. He didn't remember my father's name, and he didn't know what I had been named. He remembered my mother's name and that she'd had two prior births before mine.

He thought my father was a white man, but to what race did my mother belong? Lying on her bed after a long, hard labor, my mother seemed to be dark-complected. Was she white? Could she be Indian? Maybe she was Black. Well, the doctor decided, my father was definitely probably Caucasian. As to my mother's race, the doctor recorded on my birth certificate that she was definitely "human."

So now, when it comes time on some form to indicate to which race I belong, I don't check White or Black or Hispanic or Asian. I check the block that says "Other," and I write in the word "human." I tell people who ask that I am one-half human, and I can prove it with my birth certificate.

So what's the big deal about which race we belong to? We all belong to the "human" race. We are all made in the image of our Creator. Let us join our resources and strive to improve conditions for members of the "human" race all over the world.

Morning Constitutional

Tilya Gallay Helfield

At exactly 11:00 a.m. every weekday morning, Helen Ferguson left the servants to their allotted tasks and set out on the road to town. It was the only concession she ever made to the climate – shopping for groceries daily instead of once a week, as she had in Montreal. Food spoiled so quickly in the tropics! However, Mrs. Ferguson believed in making lemons into lemonade and referred to this activity as her morning constitutional. But she would not be going into town today.

She walked briskly, white platform shoes clicking on the tarmac. Despite the heat she wore white cotton gloves, a straw hat, and matching tote. Her cotton dress, pale blue like her eyes, was beginning to pucker in damp creases around her waist.

Her friends had hooted when she'd told them about the move to Jamaica. "Helen's so active and systematic," they said. "The laissez-faire life down there will drive her mad!" But Mrs. Ferguson dutifully left her beautiful home, influential family, and childhood friends and reorganized her household into a fair approximation of the one she'd just left. Doreen brought morning tea to her bedroom promptly at eight o'clock. At nine, she served breakfast – orange juice, a single poached egg and one piece of lightly buttered toast, marmalade and tea – on the oak dining room table she'd shipped from Montreal, set with the sterling silver flatware and Crown Derby Mrs. Ferguson's grandmother had brought from England as a bride. Doreen had once brought a strange fruit to the table that smelled faintly of sugared pears, but Mrs. Ferguson had sent it away with a firm rebuke, and after that their fresh orange juice appeared with unfailing regularity every morning.

"Not that it's anything like the juice we had at home," she told John. "Everything here has such a wild, saccharine taste."

The wives of the other bank executives served breakfast on vibrantly coloured island pottery with gaily appliquéd mats and napkins embroidered by native girls. Once, John had even suggested that they dine on the veranda!

Mrs. Ferguson soon set him straight. "Really, my dear, we're not savages. It's just a step from native dishes and napery to native food and dress, and thence to native behaviour. One might as well eat in the garden!" The garden was a deep disappointment, resisting all her attempts to curb its wild growth, to grow roses, phlox, and petunias from seeds brought from her orderly garden in Montreal.

As she walked along the road, Mrs. Ferguson passed barefoot schoolgirls in straw boaters and neat blue uniforms carrying their books and shoes; a donkey ridden stiff-legged by a tall bearded man, toes pointed skyward to keep his feet from touching the ground; a boy leading five goats on a leash. Statuesque loose-limbed women strutted, holding scarlet and saffron umbrellas against the noonday sun, hips swinging under bright cotton shifts, pelvises pushed forward. Great gold rings glinted in their ears, and their turbaned heads supported straw baskets filled with mangoes, pawpaws, guavas, tamarinds, and scarlet bananas no bigger than her finger.

All the girls moved in that insinuating way. Even fat Ernestine, who stood over the laundry tubs every morning, her huge hips undulating rhythmically with every pass of the scrub brush. And Doreen...Mrs. Ferguson didn't want to think about Doreen, who never quite met her eyes and smiled secret smiles when she thought she was unobserved. Mrs. Ferguson would have fired her in a minute, as she had her predecessor, if only she'd dared.

During the five years the Fergusons had lived in Jamaica, many of their acquaintances had succumbed to the Island way of life. Donald McConnell laced his breakfast coffee liberally with rum; his wife Iris walked to town in a cotton shift, like a native. On Saturday nights Ian Henderson, wearing shorts and an open-necked shirt, could be seen strolling down E Street with a black girl on his arm.

Because the Fergusons were the most senior members of the expatriate community, they had a duty to hold the line. Mrs. Ferguson had always insisted that John dress appropriately, although she suspected that, once he was safely in his office, he removed his jacket, rolled up his shirt sleeves and loosened his tie like the younger executives did.

No one knew John had left the family firm in disgrace. Her father had arranged for this job with the bank in Montego Bay with the understanding that he would go to jail if he ever returned to Montreal. Things had gone pretty well since then. There was a bad moment when funds went missing at the club and another over that idiot Dorothy Henderson, but she'd replaced the money, had a little chat with Dorothy and sorted it out. Of course, John drank too much, but everyone did in the Islands.

The day was hotter than usual. The road skirted the northern perimeter of the island, winding through orchards of banana, pineapple, and avocado trees, then fields of sugar cane twice as tall as a tall man before plunging towards the white ribbons of sand that hugged the turquoise sea and the sky. But Mrs. Ferguson wasn't going to the beach either.

As she began the steep incline that led into the mountains, the road darkened and cooled, became choked with bamboo, akee, and woman's tongue. Giant cottons laced with lianas arched overhead like cavernous cathedrals, and the damp salt sea spray carried the scent of freshly picked tobacco leaves strung to dry above smoldering charcoal fires. In a clearing great curved-horned cattle grazed in the shade, white egrets perched on their backs. Above them, nimble goats bleated from their rocky perch.

She'd found Cora, Doreen's predecessor, bawling in the kitchen one day. Mrs. Ferguson had made the man responsible give the girl money and had sent Cora home to her family to have the child. But after her confinement, she refused to take her back. "She's a good little worker, but easily replaced. One can't give the impression that one approves of this sort of behaviour."

She'd hired Doreen, only to be faced once again with the same problem! No, not exactly the same problem. Doreen required stronger measures.

It was hotter than ever, despite the altitude. Above her, the damp air oozed with heavy fumes of hibiscus and frangipani, making her feel faint. A stray sunbeam pierced the gloom, glinting on corrugated tin-roofed shacks in whose open doorways silent men smoked and stared with insolent eyes. Her heart fluttered with sudden fear, but she pressed on.

She passed two half-naked boys tormenting a dirty yellow dog in a courtyard littered with tires where black pigs rooted and hens scratched in the red earth. A door opened before her, then closed behind her with terrible finality. A toothless crone, swathed despite the heat in a heavy dark robe, sat at a wooden table under a smoking hurricane lamp.

"You got the money, Mistress?"

Mrs.Ferguson fumbled in her bag and brought out a delicate amethyst brooch. The Crone snatched it from her and held it to the light.

"It was my grandmother's," Mrs. Ferguson said. "It's worth sixty pounds."

"What you want?" the crone asked. "Spell? Potion? Somet'ing to make your man young again?"

Mrs. Ferguson fought down the hot bile that rose in her throat. "There's a girl...she's to have a child...my husband's..." She couldn't continue, but there was no need. The crone nodded, reached into the folds of her robe and poked a small paper packet across the table with a dirty talon.

"Give to her in coffee, Mistress. It come sweet, lak sugah."

"No one must ever know!" Mrs. Ferguson warned, as she slipped the packet into her purse.

"Don't anxious yo'self. She be right till she go home at night. Next day, she be too sick to work. After t'ree days, she doan botha you an' yo' man, no mo', nevah!"

Mrs. Ferguson stepped outside the shack and took a deep breath. The air seemed cooler now, and she made her way to the road with quickening steps. She felt strangely light-bodied, as though her feet were floating above the ground past the silent smoking men and the boys with the dirty dog. She began the steep descent down the rutted path.

She paused to straighten her hat as she came to the road leading to town. She'd invite some people in for drinks and dinner tonight. Not Ian Henderson, of course, but perhaps the McConnells, and some of the young executives from John's office and their wives. She opened her bag, took out her gold-rimmed reading glasses, a small note pad and a fountain pen, and began to write a shopping list – a ham, a veg, perhaps green beans, ingredients for a salad, and canapés, of course, always a good choice with drinks on a hot Island night. For dessert, she'd have Doreen do custard tarts. She'd gone to great pains to teach the girl to make them from the recipe Mrs. Ferguson's grandmother had brought from England.

She put her glasses, notebook and pen back into her purse. Her eye caught sight of the paper packet the crone had given her.

And coffee, of course. She mustn't forget to buy coffee.

Pigeon Morning

Holiday Inn – Bethesda

Ruth Moon Kempher

looking
from my tenth floor window
down to about floor eight—

three pigeons (I thought)
on a parapet, arranged themselves
as lookouts, looking in three different directions:

the center pigeon surveyed
the Thai restaurant across the street, hoping
perhaps, for litchi beans or rice—

the one on my right
was watching as traffic turned left
beyond prim beds of tulip and yellow pansies

the one on my left
preened himself, egotistical or
looking for lice, and then

the fourth pigeon
(I hadn't noticed) was self-betrayed.
A movement of pink feet

lifted into existence
wing ribs, spreading, fanning
from what had seemed a shadow on concrete.

THE SEAGULL

Maggi Roark

Walking alone along a deserted pier in the early morning mist I heard
a frenzy of wings and screeching. Near the top of a lamp post a seagull
hung, upside down, thirty feet in the air. One yellow foot was tangled in
a fragment of fishing line left behind among the plastic bags and bait and
stale French fries. Desperate to pull away he crashed and slammed against
the iron pole. Shrill cries, frantic pounding, while beneath him I stood
frozen in a shower of feathers. I remembered my phone and dialed for
help, a recorded voice asked me to wait and offered me Musak. Looking
up I whispered *Hold on. Help's coming,* and watched his movements slow.
His weary neck hung loose, defeated wings fell open. Silence thickened the
damp morning air.

Two Footnotes to WWII Photo History

Richard Lampl

Personal accounts of notable events of World War II are fading away with the passing of the veterans of that war. The conflict ended more than 70 years ago. Both verbal and written history recorders have a strange way of altering facts to fit some personal objective. Half-truths become full-blown truths. Stories of big events become distorted. Often, two or more witnesses of the same event come away with two or more versions of the same story. Which version is correct? The unvarnished truth is often lost in the retelling. The facts are changed slightly to make a better story or to make someone more of a hero or heroine than they deserve to be.

Undaunted by this practice, I have personal, first-hand information about two WWII wartime stories concerning two famous photos whose subject and facts have been the center of controversy since they happened in 1945. The first photo is the raising of the flag on Iwo Jima, taken by Associated Press photographer Joe Rosenthal. The second is General Douglas MacArthur's return to the Philippines as immortalized by *Life* magazine photographer, Carl Mydans. I may be clearing up some questionable facts or (I hope not) may be adding to the controversy. Certainly, my first story about the famous flag raising photo leaves a lot of room for doubt, but the second story about General MacArthur can certainly be added as one more piece of honest information about the incident.

First, my personal attachment to the flag-raising photo during the battle of Iwo Jima and the Rosenthal photo. This famous photo was used as a model for the Marine memorial statue in our nation's capitol. My cousin, Harold Weinberger, claimed to have some personal knowledge on the subject. On a visit to his home in Los Angles just before he died in his nineties, he told me he was leader of one of several Marine photographic groups on Iwo Jima at the same time as Rosenthal. Cousin Harold told me his photographers also took pictures of the flag-raising on Mt. Surabachi. Rosenthal, he said, endured many of the same hardships on Iwo Jima as the fighting Marines with one difference: Rosenthal had the option of returning to a beached landing ship, probably an LST or LSM, to sleep in comfort at night, while Cousin Harold and his Marine photographers had to stay on shore in the open.

There are many conflicting stories about the flag-raising. History gives the nod to Rosenthal. There is no question he took the best flag-raising picture, but he did not have to share the hardship of sleeping on the ground like the Marine photographers who took similar flag-raising pictures.

The rest of the Rosenthal photo story is well known. In brief, Rosenthal missed the first flag-raising ceremony and posed a picture of Marines standing in front of the previously hoisted flag. He was descending from Mt. Suribachi when he learned a second, larger flag was on its way up to replace the original. The Stars and Stripes of the first flag could be seen by troops from a large part of the island, but not all of it. Those in command believed a second, larger flag would be seen by all Marines on battle-scarred Iwo Jima and would increase the morale of all. Rosenthal hurried back up the mountain to replace the posed picture with an actual action shot that would become famous.

Rosenthal was quoted in an interview: "Out of the corner of my eye, I had seen the men start the flag up. I swung my camera and shot the scene." Now, recorded history being what it is in the retelling, this led to two subsequent, but different versions. In one, Rosenthal raised his camera to his eye and shot. In another, he just pointed the camera in the general direction without aiming. In either case, he did not know what he had captured on film, and only saw the final product after it had been printed across the country in all AP newspapers.

I am satisfied with the extra piece of knowledge supplied by Cousin Harold. Historians please take note: Rosenthal slept on board a ship at night, while Marine photographic units had to endure the hardship of the battle for Iwo Jima both day and night.

My second footnote concerns *Life* photographer Carl Mydans' equally famous photo of MacArthur walking ankle deep through water on his dramatic return to the Philippine Islands.

Three years earlier MacArthur had been rescued from the Philippines just before it was captured by Japanese forces. He had been deemed too valuable a military leader to be left behind for imprisonment by the Japanese. He vowed, "I shall return," which he did when the Philippines were reconquered with MacArthur as leader in 1945.

MacArthur was a known publicity hound with a strong ego. It is believable he would want the photograph of his symbolic return to the Philippines to be as memorable as possible. Walking in a dramatic fashion through water, surrounded by soldiers and with landing craft in the background, was just the kind of picture an egocentric person would like to have taken in honor of the event. Critics of MacArthur said he asked the photographers to take many pictures of the landing until he was satisfied the right photo was taken to augment his "I have returned" statement. They said they saw him go back to his landing craft and repeat his walk through water many times until he was sure the best picture had been taken.

Did MacArthur repeat his walk time and time again or was this just the tale told by many reporters who were irritated by MacArthur's self-promotion? Or did Carl Mydans take the right picture one time, the right time? My solution to the conflict surrounding this story is undeniably more logical and authentic. Was the photo posed by MacArthur? Was it rehearsed? This was long before today's sophisticated cameras and digital technology. Photographers took one picture at a time, often with only one opportunity to get a good shot.

The man who told me the real story, Dr. Roger Egeberg, undeniably had his facts right. He is in the picture on MacArthur's left. He was General MacArthur's doctor in the Pacific campaign from Australia to Tokyo. Doctor Egeberg and I shared membership in a writing club for many years before he died in 1997. According to Doc Egeberg, MacArthur made several landings in several different places that day, while being followed by photographers. It was thus incorrectly assumed that he staged his ultra-moment in the limelight. The story of many rehearsed walks through water before MacArthur was satisfied has been told and retold many times. As a bolster to Doc Egeberg's story, Carl Mydans to his dying day insisted he took only one shot, the one that appeared in *Life* magazine.

Historians please take note: other photos of other MacArthur landings on the Philippine shores were also taken that day. This naturally led to the mistaken conclusion by the media that the photoshoot was rehearsed.

More details about the human side of MacArthur are found in Dr. Egeberg's book, *The General: MacArthur and the Man He Called Doc*. The Mydans photo with Doc in it is on the book jacket. I hope my small contribution to the re-telling of the stories behind these two famous photographs adds a little knowledge to these events.

1939 – 1945

Mary D. R. Norman

Unless you experience first-hand the diminishments and obscenities of war
you cannot come to know and understand the graciousness of peace.

When your Daddy comes home every evening from work
and you eat dinner together, and talk,
you do not dream that suddenly, one day, he will be gone
your country and the Army have called him to danger overseas
and sporadic airletters will become your only frail hope.

If you are an over-protected 8-year-old child,
sent away overnight from your home and family,
put on a ship with suitcase and gas mask,
along with hundreds of other confused and frightened children,
then literally sent down the River Thames to an undisclosed destination,
what do you understand of that big word, "War"?
How do you learn to cope in this new hostile environment?
Slowly and painfully, toughened by deep hurt and homesickness,
You will develop survival skills which will sustain you for a lifetime.

When food is abundant you overindulge and sometimes you throw it away
but with shortages and rationing you learn resourcefulness and thrift
for hunger is a strict, demanding teacher.

And it is not until the blackout is enforced to mislead
the bombers in the night sky
that you come to appreciate the luxury of unrestricted light.

Until you have run for your life, night after night, through falling shrapnel
and have crouched, shivering, in a shelter with bombs screaming down,
hearing neighbors' houses blown apart,
smelling burning and wondering who is left alive,
you will not know the innate hatred born of gut fear.

And if, at age 9, you see killing first-hand in the sky above your home,
as a Spitfire pilot is machine-gunned to death on his parachute,
you will know immediately that you are a child no longer,

for you are aware of your own capability of revenge, even murder.
And with that goes the adult responsibility of learning
forgiveness and acceptance
of people and events far beyond your control.

When victory and peace finally come—
to the world, to embattled England and to the reunited families
after six years of endurance, you join in the celebrations.
For you are a survivor, seasoned by war
and already strong beyond your years,
entrusted by life with memories too awful to lead you anywhere
except with certainty along the paths towards
Peace.

Veterans Day Salute

Maggi Roark

Near an intersection outside the Recruit Depot a young man sits alone, at ease, leaning into his thoughts. His buzz cut and clean fatigues announce *new recruit.* At the signal light an older man with faded hair and worn camos paces the median between the surge and stall of traffic.

The streets are lined with flags to honor the young and the fallen with colors that snap in the holiday's fitful winds. Waves of cars ripple between the signal lights, most with drivers hunched into late afternoon going-home positions, eyes on the road. A few slow to salute the seated soldier with a wave and a tap on the horn—looking through the man with his cardboard words:

> *homeless vet*
> *anything helps*

THE DAY WORLD WAR II REALLY ENDED

Suse Marsh

The dramatic and unforgettable days and months of World War II were supposed to be officially over in May 1945. The time that followed was the time of the "Occupation" of Germany, and our family happened to live in the demographic area occupied by the French army. These first few months were worse than the time of war. Anyone who had a large home was told to leave so the French officers could move in. Whatever food we had stored was taken from us, and no woman was safe from being raped by the French soldiers and their allies, the Moroccans. We found a place to live with our neighbors who were missionaries and had Swiss citizenship. During the day my mother planted a garden with the help of us children, but at night we never stayed at our own house; it was not safe.

My father was missing in action; we had not heard from him in over six months. In June of 1945 a comrade of my father's stopped by and brought some of his personal belongings. He told us that my Dad never came back from one of his messenger trips; he had to ride his motorcycle at night without lights. My father was stationed in France, but the Germans had retreated slowly as the war came to an end.

Gradually, some order returned to the country. It was summertime. We had fruit and vegetables to eat. We also kept chickens for eggs and rabbits for meat. We had no dairy products, no flour, no sugar, and no fat.

It was a quiet Sunday afternoon. My sister and I had just returned from visiting a great aunt who lived nearby. We showed my mother the gifts we had received, made from porcelain: mine was an elephant family and my sister's a dog family. Suddenly, a neighbor came running to the door, screaming, "Frau Klaiber, Frau Klaiber, your husband is at the bottom of the hill, take your wagon, he can't walk anymore."

I can't remember what went through my mind or how we ran down the path to the bottom of the hill. There was a soldier dressed in a German uniform, sitting by the hiking path with crutches by his side. And yes, it was

MY DAD! We had not seen him in over a year and had no idea he was alive! I don't recall the date of that Sunday afternoon in summer of 1945, but that was...

The day World War II really ended!

We later found out that my father had a severe accident when he collided with a Jeep while riding his motorcycle on a mission at night. He was in a military hospital when the war ended, and he became a prisoner of the English army, because that part of Germany was in the English occupation zone. After several months of healing, he was released and discharged by the British. He hitchhiked on an English army truck to Pforzheim, which is eight miles from were we lived.

He could barely walk on his crutches and was stopped by a citizen of Pforzheim. The woman asked him were he was going. and then told him he could not go there because that was the French zone. He would be taken prisoner right away, wearing a German uniform.

My dad knew a path along the river, and the kind woman got her wagon and pulled him out of the main thoroughfare to this path. He made it safely to the bottom of our hill, where he collapsed.

A few weeks later all men from our town that had not been discharged by the French army had to show up at city hall. My father did not go, since he was unable to walk. His accident and injuries were a blessing from God, for the men who heeded that call were loaded onto a truck and shipped to a prison in France.

Dad was 42, Mom 39, Suse 10, Ursula 8, and Hans-Martin 5 years old at that time.

The Worst Kiss

Carole Marlowe

We are out of time, out of options. We tried everything and still
we are here at the dreaded place of leaving.

Trapped in the tangle of Viet Nam, an obscenity we knew was
insane from the start, and yet here we are. You have to go.

Draft board number thirteen obliterated any escape.

Just you and I alone in this airport surrounded by uncaring
glances, our college friends left behind long ago as they fret
about new furniture. All the family goodbyes done, finished.

Bone thin, both of us. Worn raw by duress. Your starched
uniform wrinkled by my clutches.

I want this last kiss to be memorable, sustainable, somehow a
kiss that will keep you safe, carry you above the carnage. But it
is a blur of trembling kisses and hugs boxed within crushing fear
and sadness. Our hands are the last to separate.

This is really happening. I am watching you walk across the
tarmac into the certainty of harm's way. How can I bear this?
How can I move from this spot and walk alone to my car?

A Gun Waits

Anita Curran Guenin

In America, guns wait
in shoeboxes, under mattresses,
on high shelves within
the Christmas boxes.

Mine was made by
the Charter Arms Company.
Sounds like an hotel,
but it's a home for bullets.

"Saturday Night Special"
is its name,
chamber for five rounds,
snub barrel fits in pocket or purse.

The NRA instructor says
32 calibers don't have
stopping power,
flashes his manly Glock.

Our class sees a film.
A man climbs through
an unlocked window,
attacks lone women with no gun.

Adrenaline rises,
flight or fight.
My gun calls to me,
"Shoot him!"

At the range, cardboard
effigies in the gloom.
Noisily, I kill several and
pass my final exam.

The Real Thing

Lollie Butler

If every showered person pooled their soap remnants,
we'd be clean.

If every sandwich shop saved bread crusts,
we'd be fed aplenty—
       and the birds as well.

If every politician spoke the truth on Wednesdays,
the world would wake up honest
on a day in the middle of the week.

It only takes a whistle to call a hungry dog.
It only takes one leaf to launch a season.

We sat at the segregated lunch counters,
marched with those willing to die for freedom
       —the real thing—
fasted in prisons, refused to throw the first stone,
carried banners, sat resolute on the bus,
took up posters that read, "NO BLOOD FOR OIL!"
read rosters, inscribed names,
saluted gravestones and put the folded flags away—
only to raise them again.

Let the mouth that cries, Peace in our Time!
look to his own supper table, his wife's bruises,
his children's sunken eyes and the gun under his pillow.

In his own garden, let him get down on his knees
and plant a rose named Peace
that in his lifetime, he may see it bloom.

Kissing a Cow

John W. Barbee

Sunday afternoons were always fun when I was young. After church, most of my father's family would gather to have a meal and visit. There were aunts, uncles, and cousins by the dozen. Sometimes we had stewed chicken and dumplings, but most of the time the meals were fried chicken with mashed potatoes and gravy, fresh or canned vegetables, and homemade bread. And then there was dessert. Puddings, cakes, and pies were great, but best of all was homemade ice cream. Gallons and gallons of homemade ice cream with fresh sliced peaches, strawberries, and black walnuts for toppings.

After the meal we would split up. The women would clean up, and then visit the parlor to do needlework or quilting. The men gathered on the porch to talk crops, weather, and baseball. After a time one, then another, would catch a short nap. All of the kids were free to run, play, and raise a little hell.

We were a generation of boys. Out of about forty cousins there were only three girls. The mix of kids varied from week to week. Sometimes my Aunt Nina's boys, Sheldon, Ivan, and Dana, were there. Aunt Irene's boys, Kenny and JR, plus their sister, Bonnie May, added to the mix, and Uncle Keith's son, Billy Dale, often got to tag along. There were others: Jim, Larry, and their sister, Iris, plus many more. Best of all were Uncle Jack's boys, Bill and Bob. They were my favorites. Bob was two years older than me, and Bill was four years older. During the week, the three of us would explore hills, rivers, ponds, the dump, and old mines whenever we got the chance. Bill was boss of our gang of three and, by age and personality, he was the leader on Sundays of cousins galore.

The fateful "Sunday of the Cow" we were at Uncle Fred's farm. Memories of the meal are long gone, except for dessert, which was homemade ice cream. We all ate until it hurt to move. Evening came, time to milk the cows, so Uncle Fred sent his border collie, Old Shep, to bring the cows in from pasture. That dog was something special. Without pointing or gesturing, simply telling him to get the cows for milking, he was off to the right pasture. Quickly, he was running down to whichever field they were in, then he would herd them back to the barn for milking. Old Shep was a joy to watch work, so we all walked down and climbed on the fence leading to the barn to observe.

It's a known fact that dogs are smart and horses are dumb, but for real stupidity cows are the winners. The male cousins perched on the fence, discussing what pitiful animals cows were, while the three girl cousins gathered off to one side. At this point I must say a little about the three girls. Jean could throw a rock or spear a frog as good as any of us boys, and Bonnie could be counted on to swipe some Zigzag paper and a bag of Bull Durham tobacco from her dad to share with us.

They were tomboys, but Iris was different. Beautiful, with fair skin, curly hair, always wearing a nice dress, she was a young lady. Polite and proper, she was the cousin that was different. I once heard one of my uncles say that his brother must have brought the wrong baby girl home from the hospital. "She didn't act like a Barbee, Bond, or Brandt."

This was the crew gathered at the fence, talking about how dumb cows were. At this point cousin Bill took over, saying that in addition to being dumb, they were ugly. Calling attention to how they slobbered and drooled, he said he would "Buy a soda pop for anyone who would kiss one on its snotty nose."

A dare from Bill was something I couldn't resist. Jumping from the fence, I grabbed the next cow that came by and, holding her head, gave her a big kiss right on her slobbery nose. For a moment there was silence. Then there was cheering, laughter, and hooting. I was a hero, honored as the cow-kissing cousin by all but Iris, who turned away and quietly threw up. She got some on her new shoes and tarnished her perfect reputation a little.

My father became known as the brother whose idiot son kissed a cow. This title only lasted a few months until another cousin did something even worse. Iris unbent a little, I matured a little, and we were all great friends for the rest of our lives.

So if you ever want to know how to kiss a cow, just ask me, and I'll tell you how...*Don't!*

Saturday Bath on the Farm

Tom Leech

Out on the farm on a Saturday night,
We kids hauled water to the house from the well down the path.
With a bucketful balanced on each side,
This was the night we took the mandatory weekly bath.

No easy task, heisting those heavy pails
Up on the wood-burning stove and into a warming pot.
On the floor nearby, the round metal tub,
With a washrag, bar of soap, and stiff brush – the whole darned lot.

Mom and grandma were the matrons-in charge,
Getting the next kid into the tub filled with warm water.
Off went our duds and into the tub we went,
Made no difference whether uncle, cousin, son, or daughter.

There we sat in that old tub on the floor,
Mom soaping your ears and giving your back a scrub and scratch.
When Grandma dipped hot water from the pot,
That warmth on your skin was a feeling no shower can match.

Finally, scrubbed clean now, your turn was over.
Out you came, then grabbed a towel to use before you got cold.
Standing on the floor, naked as a bird,
Modesty's no big problem, not when you're just six years old.

But no hanging around, your turn was done.
On went your clothes, and then the next candidate drifted in.
And you headed out to the family room,
To the pot-bellied stove, where kinfolk played Old Maid or Gin.

Was there an order to the weekly bath?
Seemed no plan but there was wisdom in getting there early.
The first ones in got the freshest water,
And then – yeaa – you didn't have to follow Uncle Curly.

Ah, that felt so good to be freshly scrubbed,
Wolfing down that popcorn, scratching the old Irish Setter.
Then singing some tunes round the piano.
What spa – none that we knew – could have done it any better?

Inside Out

Kathleen O'Brien

Outside: white-washed December skies;
 in living room, a tabby lies
on wooden window ledge and spies
 plastic feeder with sparrow prize.

At lifted paw, two brown birds rise;
 silent "Sophie," in plotting wise,
waits patiently with agate eyes.
 To get beyond clear glass, she tries.

She dreams of wearing feathered guise,
 of shrinking to a mini size,
of leaving heavy earthly ties,
 of headlines reading: "House Cat Flies."

A Haunted Booth With Promise

Gilda A. Herrera

When I started noticing that the door, which was always locked at night, hung open every morning, I knew something odd was up.

Late Saturday night, I sneaked into the front office of my grandpa's gas station and hunkered down with a pillow and blanket. If something crazy was happening, I intended to witness it. Nothing had ever been stolen or left behind. Maybe it was some homeless guy or some runaway kid. Or possibly ghosts? What showed itself turned out to be odder than any ten-year-old boy like me could have imagined.

I leaned back on Grandpa's recliner, not a bit sleepy since I'd prepared by taking a long Saturday afternoon nap. I thought back on what had led me to this action.

My grandpa, Billy Simpson, had worked as an auto mechanic most of his life, but he was also one superior carpenter. Grandpa loves old stuff from his personal past, which goes back quite a ways since he's pretty old. No one was surprised when he decided to build a telephone booth to sit outside in front of our gas station, located on a triangular island of asphalt and concrete. Three streets surround our business. We live in an attached house Grandpa built behind the station a long time ago.

Grandpa called the phone booth "the convergence of the best of the top-of-the-line American phone booths."

Dad said, "Pop, no one uses phone booths anymore, not with everyone carrying a cell phone."

Grandpa responded, "Sure, cell phones offer convenience, immediacy, but what do they lack?"

Dad got quiet. But the smarty-pants kid in the room, being me, had been watching Grandpa build his phone booth, so I knew the answer. "Privacy!" I yelled out.

Grandpa nodded. "Right, Jacoby. My phone booth will have a pay phone in it, a comfortable seat, be roomy, have nice windows to look out of, and be soundproof."

He built the old-fashioned but new phone booth out of mahogany. It had folding doors, an overhead light one could turn off or on, room to stand or take advantage of the padded stool, and the coolest, black shiny old pay phone. Grandpa refused to say where he got the pay phone. I think he'd had it for years in that auto bay where he hoarded the old stuff he accumulated.

Folks loved it! They paid a quarter just to sit in it and talk on their cell phones because no one, even standing right outside the booth, could hear a word. People without cell phones used the pay phone – more of them than one would have guessed. Grandpa charged a quarter for each ten minutes of usage. We often had a queue of folks waiting to use it. The quarters went into my college fund. Grandpa and I were the only ones allowed to use the phone booth and not pay.

Two weeks later, an old pal of Grandpa's came by. He told us he had an age-less phone booth from London, England, and did Billy want it? "It could balance things off in front of the station with your other one," he said. "Only problem with it is the door squeaks loudly."

So we got a second phone booth, a bright red one. Grandpa sound-proofed that one too.

His old friend had chosen what he called "the perfect symmetry spot for the London booth to sit on." I thought that was just him being persnickety. He and my grandpa were both stickler adults about getting everything just right – which meant their way.

The day the London booth was delivered, the old codger whispered in my ear, "That red phone booth may be haunted. Keep on open eye on it." He winked at me, so I figured he liked to tease youngsters, but his words and actions made me suspicious. So when the door to that London phone booth, which Grandpa locked every night, kept hanging open in the mornings, I decided to investigate by keeping watch over it one Saturday night.

Staying awake all night wasn't easy, even if I had taken a long nap, but that loud squeaking door jolted me back to consciousness. In my stocking feet I quietly zipped to the office front window. I was so surprised, I couldn't even gasp. A man stepped out of the red booth. He wore an evening suit that looked like those 1890s photos my younger sister collects. (Yeah, she's really weird, but aren't most sisters?) The man wore a top hat, a coat with tails hanging out, a tweed vest, and carried a cane. He shot out of that red phone booth running hard. He went lickety-split down the street, a British bobby wearing a dark blue police uniform chasing after him.

The outside grew eerily quiet. Suddenly, the red booth's door squeaked again, and someone else came out of it. A young girl about my age, with long-flowing red hair and wearing a long, soft white dress, walked slowly with her head down. She was writing on a writing pad with some sort of feathery pen. She went to the corner and sat down on the bus bench.

I decided to go outside and talk to her, so I hurriedly slipped on my sneakers. I mean, it really had more to do with finding out if she was a ghost than me hoping she would talk to me. My grandpa would say I was instantly sweet on her. Luckily, I was wearing jeans and a tee-shirt, not one of my usual nighttime superhero pajamas.

"Hey," I said as I approached the bus bench.

She looked up and smiled at me, so I sat down.

"Busses don't usually run this late," I said, trying to be helpful.

She nodded and continued writing.

"What are you writing?" I asked, feeling confident she wouldn't mind and really wanted me to talk with her.

"A poem. It's a poem about a phone booth."

I furrowed my brow. "Funny thing to write a poem about."

"I agree, but it's my last memory of my life."

I felt sick to my stomach. She was a ghost. I wasn't scared, though. More like really sorry she wasn't real anymore.

"Don't feel bad for me," she said, in her soft voice as she lifted her head. "I had a wonderful life. Not like those two."

I followed her gaze. The man in the olden-times suit and the English policeman were running back towards us. They rushed back into the red phone booth.

"Who are they?" I asked.

She sighed. "The man, I fear, is Jack the Ripper. That policeman has been chasing after him for decades." She looked toward the office. "I didn't mean to snoop, but I saw you have bikes inside your garage. I always wanted to learn to ride a bike, but never got the chance."

"I could teach you now, if you'd like. You can borrow my sister's bike. I'm Jacoby Simpson."

"I'm Emily," she said, smiling. "I'd love that, Jacoby."

So I ran inside and retrieved the bikes, hoping she wouldn't disappear while I was gone. Emily set down her quill pen and notepad and waited for me.

She got the hang of balancing on a bike right away. Before you could stomp on a bug, we were riding up and down and around the parking lot. We laughed and rode as if there were no phone booth waiting for her. Emily looked so happy. I felt like a wish I'd never made had come true. Who would have known that riding bikes under dim street lights could be so great?

When I walked her back to the red phone booth, I asked, "Will you come back here?"

"I'm not sure. If I do, I promise to bring you a poem. I'll write about you and me riding bikes, Jacoby." She stepped into the red phone booth, closed the door, and soon all I could see was a thick fog swallowing her.

A couple of weeks later, Grandpa's old codger friend came by. "See any ghosts lately?" he asked me.

The red phone booth's door hadn't been found open since that Saturday night.

"Only once," I said truthfully.

"Sometimes they only come by once. But one never knows when they might come by again." He patted my shoulder and went to talk to Grandpa.

I didn't say anything more to him. I felt lucky I'd gotten to meet and talk with Emily one time.

It didn't seem right for ghosts to be coming and going near our gas station and home. Yet that didn't stop me from going to the bus stop every morning and checking to see if a poem had been left there for me. I think someday there will be one. Emily seemed like a dependable person who kept her promises.

THE LAST HAIKU

Neal Wilgus

robots have spoken
cyber messages only
away with words…

CONTRIBUTOR'S NOTES

NANCY ALAUZEN resides in Bridgeville, Pennsylvania. She works full-time for a non-profit in Pittsburgh. Desiring to help jobseekers, she published a self-help booklet titled "66 Power Tips To Help You Land The Job You Want" and articles on Workforce Development. Recycling is Nancy's passion! She has also published articles on recycling. Nancy's article, "You Don't Have to Look Too Far," was published in *OASIS Journal 2014*. A short story on Nancy's life is included in a book titled *My Dirty Little Secret Before Success*, 2013, by James Tudor. [177]

BILL ALEWYN lives in Arizona with his wife and cats. Over the years his essays and short fiction have appeared in several publications. His play, "An American Execution," was awarded first place in the 2012 Beverly Hills Guild/Julie Harris competition. In 2013 his short play, "The Faulkner/Hemingway Letters," was featured at the WIT Kauai Shorts festival and, in 2014, was awarded first place in the League for Innovation national competition. [1, 111]

WILLENE CHRISTOPHER AUSLAM has enjoyed creative writing since fourth grade, when she and three friends formed their own writers' club, each trying to outdo the others with their own poems and stories. Writing interest is continuing throughout life, and she has had published works in former issues of *OASIS Journal*, *The Fort Worth Star Telegram*, *Snippets*, and *Good Old Days* and *Reminisce Magazines*. She remains a Texan at heart, but now resides in Happy Valley, Oregon. [229]

MARY MARGARET BAKER, better known to family and friends as Margie, was born 81 years ago in Pittsburgh, Pennsyvania, the second youngest in a family of seven chidren. She has enjoyed writing and making art since the age of fourteen. She has taken classes in painting and writing. Margie's paintings and those of her niece, Jan, were displayed at an art show at the local library. She enjoys various activities and eating out with friends and family. Her stories have appeared in local bulletins and in OASIS Journal 2012 and 2014. "Left Behind" was a scary experience that happened to her. [65]

BOBBIE JEAN BISHOP is grateful for her connection to poetry, grateful how she appreciates other poets and their inspiring work. Her poems have appeared in small journals since 1973. [10]

BERNADETTE BLUE, born near Lake Erie in Ohio, currently resides with her husband in the southwestern desert in Marana, Arizona. She fell in love with the music and magic of words at an early age, while listening to her grandfather's old family stories. While her published work has been in poetry, today she is taking the leap and organizing her journals into an autobiographical novel. She is happy to be included in this year's *OASIS Journal*. It is her sixth time in the publication, and still a thrill. [24, 39]

PETER BRADLEY lives peacefully in New Hampshire with his wife, Janice, and their female German shepherd, Zoe the Wonder Dog. His work has appeared in *Rattle, Penny Ante Feud, OVS Poetry Journal, Naugatuck River Review, The Poet's Touchstone, Calliope, Still Crazy Poetry Journal, The Outrider Review, Nerve Cowboy, Blue Collar Review, The Barefoot Review*, and soon in *Hypertrophic Literary* and *The Cape Rock*. [114, 188]

FRED BRIDGES' education includes a BS from Utah State and an ED from the University of Oregon. He is retired from the military, having served in both the Navy and Army. During his civilian career, he taught math, science, and PE. Writing was not in his resume until he discovered that the point of writing was to tell a story in your own words and style. When he realized this, writing became fun. [225]

LOLLIE BUTLER is a graduate of the University of Arizona's MFA Program and has taught Creative Writing to women in the state prison system. Currently she manages a mentoring program for the National Alliance for Mental Illness of Southern Arizona. Her writing credits include an award from the Robert Frost Foundation, the Bush Presidential Library, and her work is published in various periodicals. Recently her book of poems, *The One Thing that Saves Me*, was published by Finishing Line Press and is available on Amazon. [148, 323]

JACK CAMPBELL: I held services for my Underwood typewriter the day I got my first computer, leading to a fun retirement with spellcheck and printout at my beck and call. Memoirs, fiction, and poetry have been spewing from a bottomless well to the delight of family and friends, who now know where I come from, but, more importantly, where they came from. That computer is now my wife's only rival. I have published a book of my Army/Navy service for family and friends, and a book of 70 short stories. At 87, the end is not yet in sight. [105, 160]

LAWRENCE CARLETON is 68 years old. He started writing about three years ago when his Parkinson's disease made it too difficult to keep playing his trumpet in jazz bands. He has had a few stories published in *The Guilded Pen* (San Diego Writers/Editors Guild annual anthology) and *A Year In Ink* (San Diego Writers Ink annual anthology). His short story writing is, in the main, an attempt to prompt interest in unfamiliar points of view, but sometimes he just likes to tell a good story. [133]

TERESA CIVELLO's work has appeared in OASIS Journal 2010, 2011, and 2014, as well as in the SouthWest Writers SAGE. Two of her stories placed 2nd and 3rd in the 2015 New Mexico Press Women's Communications Contest. She acknowledges both Maralie BeLonge, Program Supervisor of the Albuquerque Osher Lifelong Learning Institute for creating an extraordinary writing program, and Grace Labatt for taking time from her editorial work to provide insightful critique. [197]

ARIS DENIGRIS: "Adventures with a Used Car Salesman" was written about 25 years ago. I was surprised that my young son kept it all these years. He has become the musician he wanted to be and has performed in Carnegie Hall, Lincoln Center, traveled all over the world with a jazz group, been profiled in *Guitar Player* magazine, and was recently listed as one of the greatest jazz guitarists in the country in a book by Scott Yarnow. He lives and composes music in southern California. My three sons tell me I'm a late bloomer in my 85th year. [203]

BUCK DOPP is a freelance writer for *Today's News-Herald* in Lake Havasu City, Arizona. His short stories have appeared in *OASIS Journal* (2010, 2011, 2012 and 2014) and in *A Long Story Short* e-zine. Buck retired from a 27-year career in business management in 2009 to devote himself to writing. His first novel, *Kingpin and Eli*, published in 2013, is available on Amazon.com and Kindle.com. Buck is the past president of the Lake Havasu City Writers Group, which has published his stories in its anthology, *Offerings from the Oasis*. Visit the author's website at www.buckdopp.com. [157]

JOAN T. DORAN chairs the Literary Arts Guild of the Center for the Arts, Lake Sunapee, New Hampshire Region. Her published book of poetry is *Herding Mice at Three A.M.* [35, 70, 293]

ELISA DRACHENBERG: For more than a decade I have been submitting my stories to various magazines and have been lucky enough to get them published. And even though I'd still rather clean the entire house – in my eyes a dreadful activity – once I do start writing, there is no stopping. While choosing and deciding continuously which words fit best, I invent characters, create their lives, focus on their stories and arrange their fate. They, of course, need me to give them life. And, frankly, I need them to live a more thoughtful existence. [41]

MARY ROSE DURFEE: This is my eighth year with IMAGO Press and it finds me well and healthy at 99 years of age. Indeed, what an honor to still be able to write and have my story accepted for publication in *OASIS Journal*. In searching genealogy records, it was a surprise when I discovered my great granddaughter, Bianka Gebhardt, is a descendant of John Humphrey Noyes, who founded the Oneida Community "Utopian Society." It prompted me to write the "Childrens' House" submission, which goes back three generations on her father's side. [235]

GRENITH FISHER is a retired caseworker in geriatrics living near Pittsburgh, Pennsylvania. As a child there, she learned to love the vivid power of stories, rhymes, and the wonderful dramas of 1940's radio. She developed a voracious reading habit, but did not try creative writing until she became a college student at age 45. In 1988, West Virginia University granted her a BS degree and a Waitmam Barbe Creative Writing Award for her poetry. She has continued to write in this form as a personal diary – for pleasure and, as the saying goes, to find out what she really thinks. [280, 290]

ALEANE FITZ-CARTER, 86, is fourth generation removed from slavery. She has degrees in Education and Music from University of Nebraska, Omaha. She taught black history and black music at University of Nebraska, Omaha. She later moved to Los Angeles, California, where she taught music appreciation for Los Angeles Unified School District, from which she retired in 2009. She's a pianist, singer, storyteller, actor, member of Screen Actors Guild. She was invited by the Kwa Natal Zulu churches of South Africa to perform at Bishop Desmond Tutu St. George Cathedral in Cape Town for the Nelson Mandela Freedom from Apartheid celebration. [123]

MARK FLETCHER makes his home in a quiet retirement community in Southern California with his wife, Shelly. He has been published twice in previous years of the *OASIS Journal*. Writing for personal interest is something that came to him after retirement and has enhanced his later life. As well as attending a weekly writer's group, Mark has been instrumental in assisting others to move their books through the self-publishing process. [37]

SHELLY FLETCHER makes her home in a quiet retirement community in Southern California with her husband, Mark. As a middle school teacher, she often entertained her students with stories of her childhood memories.

She has been published previously in *OASIS Journal*. Writing her childhood memories is a common topic that she now takes to her weekly writers group. [240]

ANTOINETTE V. FRANKLIN: poet, author, educator, actress, born in San Antonio, Texas to Nathaniel and Ruth Ella Lara Franklin and parent of Alexis Franklin. Published 15 books of poetry, short stories, and essays. Books may be purchased at Amazon.com and at Barnes and Noble Book Sellers. [122]

MARIE T. GASS is an Oregon writer who has always enjoyed the stories and poems in *OASIS Journal*. Retired from teaching, she is trying to revive the visual arts and musical facets of her life as well. So many exciting things to do, so little time. [7, 302]

CELIA GLASGOW: When I was introduced to Dick, Jane, and Sally my first day of school, I fell in love with reading. After earning my Masters Degree in mid-life, I had a wonderful time teaching English as a Second Language to foreign military and government personnel at the Defense Language Institute at Lackland AFB. After retirement I enrolled in various OASIS writing classes to explore writing, the flipside of reading. San Antonio OASIS tutoring program director, Gloria Jennings, sponsors a writing group at our local OASIS location; we read each other's work and offer suggestions and encouragement. [101]

MARGARET GOLDEN lives in the Pacific Northwest. For much of her life, she raised her five children while teaching ballet, tap, and jazz dancing in her hometown. Later, she became a United Methodist Minister in the Oregon-Idaho Conference. Margaret is now retired and enjoys attending concerts with Cecil, her husband of 58 years; working jigsaw puzzles; and seeing her seven grandchildren. [233]

BILL GOODBOY was born and raised in Pittsburgh, Pennsylvania, and was always creative in Dance, Puppetry, Art, and Writing. His creative writing career began with crayons on the wall. He studied Journalism and Communication in college, wrote seasonal articles published in the Hornepipe newsletter for the former Joseph Horne's Co. Department Store, and wrote a monthly column, "Cycle of Life," for the Western Pennsylvania Genealogical Society. He taught a "Writing Family Stories" course for Senior Citizens in the Pittsburgh area at Community College of Allegheny County. Now he's a senior in his own "Cycle of Life," writing for Joan Zekus's Scribes. [250]

DIANA GRIGGS was born and raised in England, has lived in San Diego for fifty-five years. She has been published in *OASIS Journal, Magee Park Anthology,* and *San Diego Poetry Annual.* She thanks Mary Harker, her OASIS poetry teacher and class, and her Bluestocking poetry critique group for all their encouragement. [20, 36]

ANITA CURRAN GUENIN was born and raised in Rhode Island, and now lives in San Diego. She has received prizes for poetry in *OASIS Journal* as well as for haibun and haiku from The Haiku Society of America. She is grateful to her classmates for their thoughtful criticism and to teachers Mary Harker and Naia for sharing their valuable knowledge. [18, 228, 262, 322]

ESTHER HALVORSON-HILL is a retired Associate Professor of Nursing. During her long career as a nurse she held positions of staff nurse, Senior Clinical Nurse, Charge Nurse, Floor Manager, Inservice Director, and Director of Nursing. After retirement she became a professional musician, both vocal and flute. Esther graduated from Stanford University in 1963 and received graduate degrees from Oregon Health Sciences University and Portland State University. Now exploring skills she had in her youth, she has begun writing again. She has written articles for the *Lake Oswego Review* and is currently a member of the Jottings Group in Lake Oswego. [231]

TILYA GALLAY HELFIELD was born in Ottawa, lived in Montreal, where she wrote a weekly humorous column for *The Sunday Express* and *The Suburban,* and now resides in Toronto. Her short stories and essays have appeared in *TV Guide, The Fiddlehead, Viewpoints, Monday Morning* and online - "*Stars*" (www.carte-blanche.org 2009) was re-printed by Nelson Education Ltd. in *Canadian Content, 7e* and *Maple Collection* 2011. Six of her short stories have appeared in *OASIS Journal*; two won awards. Her collection of short stories, *Metaphors for Love,* was published by Imago Press, 2015 and is available at www.amazon.com and www.barnesandnoble.com. [307]

GILDA A. HERRERA, former print journalist, now writes fiction in various genres including science fiction, mystery, fantasy, romance for all ages. Her young-adult, science-fiction novel *Dinary Thumb and the Purple Danger* was released in 2013 by Alban Lake Pub. A fantasy novel for youngsters, *Being Eight, Asleep and Awake,* is scheduled for release November 2015. Her short fiction and poetry has appeared in on-line and print magazines such as *Frostfire Worlds, Stories for Children Magazine, Stories that Lift, Orion's Child, Beyond Centauri,* and anthologies. [130, 329]

MAURICE HIRSCH has four poetry collections: *Taking Stock, Stares to Other Places, Roots and Paths,* and *Rails and Ties.* His work is in *Switched-on Gutenberg, Lake City Lights, OASIS Journal 2014, 2013, 2012, 2011,* and *2010, Winter Harvest: Jewish Writing in St. Louis, 2006-11, New Harvest: Jewish Writing in St. Louis, 1990-2005. Rebound* reflects on my years with a non profit arts organization. As a lifelong photographer, much of what I write is tied inexorably to what I see. My visit to the old Missouri State Penitentiary is a good example of my linking photography and poems. [104, 110, 128, 196]

CAROLINE HOBSON: I was always a writer. In elementary school I kept a list and brief review of all the books I read. I wrote sketches and skits for my class. Years later, on a business transfer to the East Coast, I wrote every Christmas to 125 people we'd left behind in California. I've written reviews for all the trips I've taken and distributed them to friends and family (some who've kept them all). I write my children e-mails every day, my extended family every week and joined a Creative Writing group. I can't think of a reason to stop writing. [218]

ANDREW HOGAN received his doctorate from the University of Wisconsin-Madison. Before retirement, he taught at SUNY-Stony Brook, the University of Michigan, and Michigan State University. He has published 46 works of fiction in *OASIS Journal, Hobo Pancakes, Subtopian Magazine, Twisted Dreams, Thick Jam, Midnight Circus, Grim Corps, Long Story Short, Defenestration, Foliate Oak Literary Magazine, The Blue Guitar Magazine, Flash, Stockholm Review of Literature, The Beechwood Review, Short Break Fiction, Cyclamens and Swords, Pear Drop, Festival Writer, Lowestoft Chronicle, Fabula Argentea, Mobius, Thrice, The Lorelei Signal, Fiction on the Web, Sandscript,* and the *Copperfield Review.* [268]

SANDRA SHAW HOMER has lived in Costa Rica for 25 years, where she has taught languages and worked as a translator and environmental activist. For several years she wrote a regular column, "Local Color," for the English-language weekly, The Tico Times. Her writing has appeared in Oasis Journal 2014 and on a few blogs, notably Allyson Latta: Memoir Writing and More, Off the Beaten Track, and her own blog, Writing from the Heart. Her first travel memoir, Letters from the Pacific, is available in paperback as an e-book. She is working on a memoir of her life in Costa Rica, Evelio's Garden, an excerpt of which can be found at Miss Move Abroad. [288]

OLGA HUMPHREYS is a wife, mother, and grandmother. A graduate of the University of the Incarnate Word in San Antonio, Texas. Retired Health

Professional after thirty-five years in the work force. Enjoying retired life by caring for a young granddaughter, volunteer activities as a Reading Tutor with the OASIS Program. Also volunteer with the Mission Group at St. Matthews Catholic Church and Refugee Support Ministry. Published her mother's recipes in a book titled *At Her Table* in 2012. [291]

UNA NICHOLS HYNUM: graduate of girls's school in Connecticut and San Diego State University. Long time member of Live Oaks Poetry Circle and OASIS Workshop with Mary Harker. Also member of Haiku Society San Diego. Nominated for the Pushcart award 2015. [69, 88, 176, 230]

BARBARA NUXALL ISOM: I was so excited to receive word of my acceptance for the third successive year I nearly jumped up to click my heels together, but questioned my landing position. I am a native Oregonian, but have been fortunate after raising my family to become somewhat of a world traveler. I also enjoy quilting, Tai Chi, reading, and my writing classes. Your dedication and support is so much appreciated that I am inclined to submit a proposal to our Senior Center suggesting we add a writing class to our agenda; it is such good therapy. [25, 221]

TERRIE JACKS has lived in several different states and spent several years in England. She has taught school, substituted, worked at Wal-Mart, and currently volunteers as an OASIS tutor. Besides volunteering, Terrie has been compiling credits with her writing. She has been published in various Missouri Baptist University chapbooks and their literary magazine *Cantos* since 2012. The online journal *cattails* has published some of her haiku, senyru, and a tanka that was selected as an editor's choice. Her poems have appeared in *OASIS Journal 2012, 2014*, and *2015*. In 2014 she began to ilustrate folktales published in the *Korean-American Journal.* [117, 191, 264, 266]

HELEN JONES-SHEPHERD, born in New York, received her B.A. and M.A. in English Composition/Literature in California, where she has taught English Composition, Literature, and Children's Literature for over 28 years. She has enjoyed teaching as an Adjunct Professor at Cal State University, San Bernardino, Riverside Community College, San Bernardino Valley College, and Chaffey College through 2013. At present, she is writing her memoirs, short stories, poetry, intriguing travel experiences, and hopes to publish a book of them. Several of her stories and poems have been published in other publications, as well as past editions of *OASIS Journal.* [247]

CAROLE ALIHER, born in New Orleans, Louisiana, the fifth of six children, always loved to read and write. Transplanted to California in 1946, she worked for Pacific Bell Telephone until marrying Jim Kaliher, in 1959. While rearing six sons, attended college classes and currently enjoys her fourteen grand-children and one great-grandchild. After becoming a widow in 1997, followed her husband's advice: "Get back to your writing." Previously published in local papers, magazines, and *Oasis Journal,* she facilitates a writing class in California, where she receives inspiration, support, and friendship from her fellow writers. [295]

YASUE AOKI KIDD was born and raised in Japan. Now living in California, she finds creative outlet in writing, both in Japanese and English. Since 1995, she has been a publishing member of a Tanka group in Japan. (Tanka is the oldest form of poetry in Japan, predating even haiku.) She enjoys writing tanka, and also contributes essays and critiques to the tanka magazine. She is writing a memoir in English for her children and grandchildren. The submitted nonfiction is an excerpt from a memoir. [83]

WILLIAM KILLIAN has had three books published by Imago Press, and he is currently working on a new book of poetry, *Some Just Walk Away.* Bill is a union actor, SAG-AFTRA, AEA, and his websites, one for his acting and the other for his basketball coaching, are www.williamkillian.com and www.freethrowdoc.com. Known as "the Free Throw Doc," he recently made 199 out of 200 free throws at a contest in Nogales, Arizona. A CD of his songs, "Family Crisis," is available. Bill is the lyricist; musicians include the Gila Bend Band, Lisa Otey, and Larry Dean. His author's page is www.amazon.com/author/killian. [145, 227]

LINDA KLEIN: "An Elephant Advocacy" is my second poem published in *OASIS Journal.* I have also had a poem published by the National Library of Poetry. "Advocacy" was prompted by an OASIS workshop assignment to show, through the voice of an animal, how as a creature of God it is valuable and worthy of preservation. I chose an elephant, recalling my 2005 visit to a baby elephant rescue camp in South Africa, where I had an opportunity to interact with and learn about elephants. I gained an appreciation for their remarkable memories, gentleness, and loyalty. [102]

FLORENCE KORZIN: My life with poetry began at age 70 when I took an Emily Dickinson poetry class. The teacher, Deborah Clayton, said that if anyone wanted to write a poem she would read it and comment. I never thought I could write a poem. About a month later, Deborah gave us a prompt: "Write a poem about a dream." I thought about the dream I had about a blade of grass, which became the subject of my first poem. The door to poetry opened for me, and I stayed in the class for 18 years and wrote many poems. [22]

This is RICHARD LAMPL's seventh successful submission to *OASIS Journal*. He keeps his writing skills at a peak 12 years after retiring from a career of aviation and aerospace writing. He shares his writing time with volunteer work as a docent at the National Air and Space Museum, a host at Strathmore, his local community music center, and divides additional volunteering time for servicemen and veterans at the USO between Walter Reed National Military Medical Center and Ronald Reagan National Airport. His No-Name Monday Night writing group welcomes new members from the Washington-Bethesda-Rockville area. E-mail: marich10@netzero.com [313]

ROY LAOS was born in Tucson, Arizona on August 5, 1953, a fifth generation Tucsonan. He has owned businesses in real estate sales, mortgage lending, and private consulting. In 1977, Roy was elected to City Council for Ward 5 and served in this capacity until 1990. In 1982, he unsuccessfully ran for Congress in Southern Arizona. He currently runs and operates his family's retail store, "Roy's Corner," located at 647 S. 6th Ave. Roy has always loved poetry and began writing in 2007. [143]

LOUISE LARSEN, a 1939 graduate of Washington University and native of Alton, Illinois, has lived most of her adult life in St. Louis, Missouri. She has been involved with OASIS for 20 years or more – attending classes and lectures, sharing her stories, and serving as a volunteer classroom tutor for over 10 years. She was an "Opinion Shaper" for the former St. Louis *Suburban Journals*, and has had her fiction, non-fiction, and poetry published in the *Webster-Kirkwood Times, Reminisce, Good Old Days, The Storyteller*, and Missouri Baptist University's *Chapbook: The Write World.* [170, 257]

TOM LEECH is the author of books covering a variety of topics. *The Curious Adventures of Santa's Wayward Elves* is a children's illustrated book with co-author and wife, Leslie. Early travel experiences led to *On the Road in '68: A year of turmoil, a journey of friendship.* Tom's years as Forum Editor for San Diego Magazine Online led to *Outdoors San Diego: Hiking, Biking & Camping.* From his primary career as a presentations coach came *How To Prepare, Stage & Deliver Winning Presentations*, 3rd Edition (AMACOM) and *Say It Like Shakespeare: The Bard's Timeless Tips for Successful Communication.* [326]

MARLENE C. LITTLE, a member of ASPS, resides in Arizona. Her first poem, "Little," was published in a 1960 National Anthology. Subsequent works were published in newsletters, newspapers, websites, *OASIS Journals 2013 & 2014*, and several seasons of the *Avocet* journal. Two of her poems were featured in *Arizona 100 Years, 100 Poems, 100 Poets* in 2012, celebrating Arizona's

Centennial. She's currently retired from some 20 years of Federal Service and also served as a business education instructor for many years. She enjoys reading, quilting, and genealogy. Recently she finished her first book of a planned trilogy on early Arizona. [115, 192]

CAROLE MARLOWE is recently retired from serving as a Tucson Unified School District Fine Arts resource teacher. She has been a teacher of English, drama, and dance; served as lead teacher for at-risk students in an alternative high school; and has been a trainer of teachers in classroom management, gender equity, and personal boundaries in the classroom. The national awards she has won defending the First Amendment include the Penn/ Newman's Own First Amendment Award. She is the author of *Finding Safety*, a book for teenagers about abuse. [321]

SUSE MARSH was born, raised, and educated in Germany in the beautiful Black Forest Region. She is currently working on her memoirs for her children and grandchildren, letting them know how life was growing up in Germany during World War II and afterwards. Excerpts from her writing were published in *OASIS Journal 2004, 2010* and *2012*. The Pittsburgh Scribes group is a great inspiration with Joan Zekas as our faithful moderator. [319]

MARILYN L. KISH MASON: I am a retired accountant. After dealing with the reality of numbers during my career, I am now thankful to indulge myself in the fantasy of poetry. I do draw from life experience, but love to veer off onto The Road Not Taken. *OASIS Journal* has published several of my poems in past editions. My poems also appear in other publications. I signed up for the fall semester of Mary Harker's OASIS poetry class and look forward to joining my fellow poets in learning new techniques, adding my voice to a group of talented poets. [301]

MARGARET S. McKERROW: Having lived in Southern California for most of my life, now retired and family grown, I have time to appreciate every change of season whether in family dynamics or our fickle California climate. I am grateful to be able to share my meanderings on paper and would like to thank Imago Press and look forward to reading the 2015 edition of *OASIS Journal*.   [17, 267]

HELEN MORIARTY was educated at Trinity College, Washington, DC; Oxford University, Oxford, England; and George Mason University, Fairfax, Virginia. She began writing a story about her childhood as a means of sharing her history with her young son, Scott. The project took on a life of its own and now comprises 12 stories; she has several new works in progress. She would like to thank the members of the Washington Expatriates Writers Group for their kind words and gentle support over the years. Helen recently relocated to Seattle to be near her son. [243]

ELEANOR WHITNEY NELSON spent her professional career as an exploration geologist working around the world with her geologist husband, often in remote, primitive areas. Today, retired and living in Arizona, she spends her time writing. Her short stories, memoirs, poems, and mysteries can be read in anthologies such as: *Chicken Soup for the Soul* (*Dog Lover's*; *Loving Our Dogs*), *The Story Teller*, *A Way with Murder*, and *OASIS Journal*. This year's entry describes coping with adversities appearing later in life. Less dramatic than situations encountered in earlier years, these new ones are more challenging than any in the past. [29]

MARY NORMAN was born and raised in Southern England. After working for Her Majesty's Foreign Office in Luxembourg for two years she came to the U.S. in 1954. She has lived in Arizona since 1965, including six years in Patagonia, Arizona. There she was a member of the Patagonia Poets, who published two books of poetry. In Tucson, Mary is an active member of OLLI, attending literature and poetry classes. Having an extensive family on both sides of the Atlantic, Mary travels frequently to England. "Whether I am flying East or West across 'the pond', I am always flying home!" [316]

JUDITH O'NEILL, a former Peace Corps Volunteer (Dominican Republic 1963-65), presently a retired technical writer and teacher living in Falls Church, Virginia, has published short stories in *Ellery Queen's* and *Alfred Hitchcock's Mystery Magazines* and in numerous short story anthologies. One of her stories was nominated for an *Edgar Allan Poe Award* by the Mystery Writers of America and appeared in *Best Mystery and Suspense Stories, 1989*. Born in St. Joseph, Missouri, she grew up along the Missouri-Kansas border, an area that has provided settings often reflected in her writing. [8, 59]

BARBARA OSTREM: Thrilling encouragement to be selected again for publication in *OASIS Journal 2015*. I've been active in creative writing class for ten years and have made many new friends. Soon to be 81 and a widow for seven years, I am blessed to have a supportive family of two daughters, their husbands, five grandchildren, and two great-grands. Portland, Oregon is my home, where my friends and I share mutual interests like book club, gardening, lunching out, and going to movies. [21]

ONNIE PAPENFUSS moved from Minnesota to Arizona in 2004 to bask in the pleasures of retirement with her husband. For three years she has enjoyed writing monthly book reviews for the Green Valley, Arizona newspaper. Bonnie has written short stories and poetry about nature and aging. A member of the Society of Southwestern Authors, Bonnie has had poems and/or short stories published in Stuart Watkins book, *Arizona: 100 Years, 100 Poems, 100 Poets* and *OASIS Journal 2013* and *2014*. Her poetry has also appeared in two chapbooks composed by Stacy Savage and published to benefit charitable organizations. [54, 166]

CLAUDIA POQUOC began her formal study of poetry at Writers Haven in San Diego in 1987. She hosts the *Bluestocking* women's poetry revision group and teaches poetry to elementary school children in Southern California. Her first song and poetry book, *Becomes Her Vision*, includes a CD. Her latest book, *Keeper of the Fields*, was published in September of 2014. Her poems appear in *San Diego Poetry Annual*, *San Diego Writers Ink*, Magee Park anthologies, and other publications. [202, 259]

ROBERT J. POURIEA: I started writing three years ago. I am overwhelmed by having something published three years in a row. With only a High School Education, I served 20 years in the Navy, married. We had two girls. I lost Ruth after 52 years. I'm now 85 years old. Now under the guiding of Pat Arnold, I am learning so much and enjoying writing so much. I'm proud to be part of *OASIS Journal*. [64, 119, 155]

SABINE RAMAGE lives in the Portland, Oregon area, where she pursues adventures in cooking, traveling, gardening, studying foreign languages, reading and photography. She is thrilled to have her writing selected by the OASIS Journal for the second consecutive year.She writes about her various feats and exploits on her blog at www.incahootswithmuddyboots.com. [224]

DAVID RAY is author of 23 books, including *Hemingway: A Desperate Life*, of which a reviewer in *Poet Lore* writes, "David Ray condenses scenes from Ernest Hemingway's jagged biography into hard nuggets of poetic truth." Other titles include *After Tagore: Poems Inspired by Rabindranath Tagore*, *Sam's Book*, *The Death of Sardanapalus*, and *When*. *Music of Time: Selected & New Poems* offers selections from fifteen previous volumes. *The Endless Search* is a memoir. An emeritus professor of University of Missouri-Kansas City's English department, where he also edited *New Letters*, David now lives and writes in Tucson, Arizona. [200]

JUDY RAY's latest book is *From Place to Place: Personal Essays* (Whirlybird Press, 2015), about which Tucson poet Richard Shelton writes, "A brilliantly crafted and beautifully written series of essays," and author Barton Sutter writes, "Judy Ray has the spirit of an explorer, the conscience of a Quaker, and the descriptive power of a poet." Previous books include *To Fly Without Wings: Poems, Pigeons in the Chandeliers*, and chapbooks *Fishing in Green Waters* and *Judy Ray: Greatest Hits 1974 – 2008.* [252]

NANCY SANDWEISS is a retired medical social worker who began writing poetry in Mary Harker's San Diego OASIS class some ten years ago. Her poems have appeared in *OASIS Journal, San Diego Poetry Annual, A Year In Ink*, and *McGee Poets' Anthology*. She recently published a collection of her poems titled *Love Remains* and thanks Bluestockings Poets and her fellow OASIS classmates for their ongoing support and helpful critiques. [32, 100, 109]

MURIEL SANDY is a student of creative writing at OASIS San Diego. Her articles have appeared in numerous American and foreign newspapers, and magazines. "Two Eggs, an Orange, and Six Black Olives," appeared in *OASIS Journal 2014.* Once again, she is honored to have her work accepted for publication in *OASIS Journal 2015.* Her first unpublished travel book, *When West Meets East: A Year in Asia on Our Own* was nominated a finalist in the San Diego Book Award competition, 2015. Muriel is associated with two writer's workshops. [171]

BARBARA SCHEIBER: At age 93, I'm grateful to the writing group that supports and inspires my creative efforts. Their insights were bedrock for me as I wrote my novel-in-stories, *We'll Go to Coney Island* (published by Sowilo Press in 2014), and prize-winning fiction published in *OASIS Journal, Antietam Review, Whetstone*, and literary anthologies. I began writing fiction and poetry after a career as a journalist and radio script writer, later an advocate for people with disabilities, spurred by my fourth child's genetic condition, Williams syndrome (www.barbarascheiber.com). My cheers and gratitude to Leila Joiner for her gift of continuing *OASIS Journal!* [68]

PHYLLIS SELTZER: My writing, drawing and painting is a gift, an amazing release of emotions. Since losing my husband, David, three years ago, artistic expressions are my therapy. My poetry was chosen as the "Editor's Choice Award" by the National Library of Poetry. Another poem was a semi-finalist in a Poetry Guild contest, several articles appeared in newspapers, and I am finalizing a book of personal essays, poetry and art. I credit this to just "putting one foot in front of the other." This is my fifth appearance in *OASIS Journal.* [151]

SHIRLEY SHATSKY: Deborah Clayton's Tuesday morning poetry workshop at the West Los Angeles OASIS has been an inspiring experience for over 15 years. Through her guidance and our in-depth discussions, all of us have grown as poets. Also, as a volunteer working with sick children and their parents in one of our large teaching hospitals, I've been thrilled to be part of this extraordinary healing world. I'm a lucky woman. I've had a number of poems published over the years. [150, 294]

BILLIE STEELE, widow, was born in the back hills of Oklahoma, traveled a lot, attended seventeen grade schools and five high schools, earned Masters plus Degree in Education. Taught at Navajo Boarding School in Tuba City, Arizona, Frink-Chamber and Wynona, Oklahoma; taught seventeen years as special education teacher for the Mentally Handicapped, Learning Disabled, and the Severely Emotionally Disturbed at Central Oklahoma Treatment Center in Tecumseh; has five children, four step-children (one deceased), two foster children who are included with her 21 grandchildren on earth (one in heaven), over 30 great-grandchildren, and *three* great-greats. [27, 289, 305]

SHERRY STONEBACK is from Oregon, having settled there in her teens. She is a member of Pat Arnold's Creative Writing Class, and is semi-retired from 30 years' nursing. Her piece, "The Garden," was published in *OASIS Journal 2014*. She has written several guides (technical writing for meeting standards) for Home Health agencies, Hospices, and In-Home agencies. Her favorite thing to do is spend time with her grandsons. [86, 219]

ERIN GILROY THOMAS has spent many years writing personal journals as well as travel journals. In this same time, she has also dabbled off and on in writing poetry. She won her first publication of a poem written for a Junior High school competition for creative writing. Throughout these years of writing, most of Erin's words were meant for personal growth and/or sat-isfaction, so were rarely shared with others. It is only with encouragement from family that she now willing allows some of these secret thoughts their own opportunity to be passed on to others. [175]

IRENE THOMAS: Such a pleasure to see something I wrote in print! Had I chosen a time in which to be born, I would have asked for just these 92 years. So amazing to have spent the greater part of it with my husband, three sons, and the following progeny. Now the memories are precious, even the sad times that made me appreciate the good ones all the more. To the many who have supplied the prose and poems in *OASIS Journal*...my hat is off to you! Many, many thanks. Especially to Leila Joiner, whose efforts make this all possible. [144, 297]

SUSAN C. THOMPSON began her teaching career in a Massachusetts sixth grade. Following four years in the classroom and a year of graduate school, her focus became Special Education. Later, she served as an Education Specialist, coordinating programs for special needs students in foster care. After retirement Susan volunteered in a local elementary school helping with reading instruction. Since then she has devoted all her available energies to volunteering for Community Hospice in a variety of ways. Her leisure time activities include reading, opera, theater, writing, and exercising daily. Many of her writings are inspired by her many European vacations. [164]

PHYLIS WARADY: This past January a shortened version of her award-winning essay, "Road," along with a shapshot depicting a rutted road nowadays seldom traveled, appeared in the anthology, *Passing Through*. In March her short story, "A Girl's Best Friend," was published for the 2nd time by *Metonym Literary Journal*. Then in June her memoir piece appeared in *Well Versed*, published by The Columbia Chapter of the Missouri Writers' Guild. Finally, to round out the year, in November, Imago Press plans to publish her essay, "Chesapeake Bay," in *OASIS Journal 2015*. [299]

MO WEATHERS spent his childhood roaming through the forests and plains of Oregon. Following a hitch in the Navy, he attended the University of Oregon, graduated with a degree in Mathematics, then served 22 years in the Air Force, retiring in 1987. Mo and his wife, Lois, whom he met on a blind date, live happily ever after in Milwaukie, Oregon's Rose Villa retirement community. They have a son who's helping XCOR Aerospace build a spaceship and a daughter who's a Lutheran pastor and has started a new, alternative church in Bellingham, Washington. [97]

JUNE WEIBLE: I was born in Rhode Island and moved to the midwest as a toddler. I have called Missouri my home for nearly 70 plus years. My career was spent in sales and marketing; I am currently a restaurant hostess. As a busy mother and grandmother, I do set aside time for my writing. Most are stories about our collective families and an ongoing genealogy study. Some of my work is pure whimsy. These will be my legacy. Sharing these in a writing class and listening to other contributors is always enjoyable. [81]

ANNE WHITLOCK is thrilled to be once more included in OASIS Journal. She is grateful to Leila Joiner for providing this venue, to Mary Harker for her poetry class at San Diego OASIS, and for the encouragement and example of fellow writers. She remembers sitting at her aunt's kitchen table at the age of six or seven with a pad and pencil, announcing that she was writing her autobiography. Seventy years have gone by, and she is just now getting started. Her story, "Kid's Day," is a tribute to a neighbor's struggle with Alzheimer's. [57, 130, 260]

JEFFREY WIDEN was raised in Los Angeles. He was a sports medicine doctor in Ashland, Oregon for 40 years. He wrote a newspaper column on sports injuries and has written prose and poetry in many writing classes. He has journaled for over 35 years. He's been published anonymously in the national magazine of AA (*The Grapevine*) and in other periodicals. He lives in Portland, Oregon with his wife, Lois, who edits most of his work. He enjoys bicycling events and getting positive letters from publishers. He gets inspiration for writing from observing unique people, places, and things around him. [215]

NEAL WILGUS has published over a thousand poems over the past sixty years, as well as a scattering of short stories, two of which won the *OASIS Journal* Fiction award. He's also author of *The Illuminoids* (1978) and a long string of LEAK News Service satires – and was a book reviewer for *Science Fiction Review* and *Small Press Review*. Some of his poems and satires are collectd in several chapbooks. He publishes more often these days in the UK and elsewhere. Neal lives and writes in Corrales, New Mexico. [94, 333]

ILA WINSLOW: Four straight years you've published a part of me. Thanks go to Creative Writing Instructor Pat Arnold and you, Leila, for continuing the *OASIS Journal*. It's nice to be published. Yea!! Yea!! I'm 78 X glad to be a part of this writing group. [154]

JOAN ZEKAS: Hearty congratulations to Leila Joiner for perservering and publishing yet another OASIS Journal! It contains such a wonderful variety of stories. I continue to moderate our Pittsburgh Scribes writing group. We will have our Book Celebration again (in April 2016), when we will read our stories and exchange door prizes related to our stories. This is my 8th appearance in OASIS Journal. My short stories have been published in various magazines, including Reminisce, Grit, Lithuanian Heritage, and others. [183]

ORDER INFORMATION

Copies of *OASIS Journal 2008* through *2015* are available for $14 at:

www.amazon.com
www.barnesandnoble.com

Copies of *OASIS Journal* from previous years (2002-2007) may be ordered at a discount from the publisher at the address below as availability allows. Please enclose $10.00 for each book ordered, plus an additional $3.00 shipping and handling for the total order to be sent to one address.

Please make checks payable to Imago Press. Arizona residents add $0.81 sales tax for each book ordered.

Proceeds from the sale of this book go toward the production of next year's *OASIS Journal*. Your purchase will help us further the creative efforts of older adults. Thank you for your support.

To view submission forms, information about *OASIS Journal*, and winning selections from the current anthology, go to: www.oasisjournal.org

Imago Press
3710 East Edison
Tucson AZ 85716

CPSIA information can be obtained at www.ICGtesting.com
Printed in the USA
LVOW06s1324181015

458742LV00001B/321/P